Some Readers' Comments on *A Ton of Gold*

From the git-go, this story grabs your attention and hangs on to it through to the very end. I love books that I can't put down, and A Ton of Gold is that kind of book! Callan weaves a mystery from the past into an exciting present day story, complete with intriguing and feisty characters. Don't miss this great book!

— S. Sehon

I0541265

Overcoming obstacles is a theme about which many authors write. Callan has perfected that art in this riveting tale of deceit and disappointment. Throw in a legend and the reader is hooked. A fast, entertaining read. I highly recommend it.

— Book Editor

A Ton of Gold is well-written, has a compelling storyline and believable characters. Highly recommended reading for adventure readers.

— Elaine Faber

A Ton of Gold captivates the reader and doesn't let go. Great plot, great characters, great dialogue. I would recommend it to anyone.

— Paul Paris

"A Ton of Gold" by James R. Callan hooked me on the first page of the Prologue and kept me eagerly turning the pages through the last word of the Epilogue. The plot was beyond intriguing and the characters were so well developed that I felt as if I knew them by the time I finished reading the book. Without giving away the story because you'll want to experience it for yourself, I will only say that it was a great read and I highly recommend it.

— Patricia Gilgor

James R. Callan has blended science and legend and come up with a fast-paced mystery that keeps one guessing until the end. A good read.

— B. Norris

I had read "Cleansed By Fire" and thought Mr. Callan couldn't write a better book. I was wrong! "A Ton of Gold" is one of those books that keep your attention from Prologue to Epilogue

—sunnyreader

A Ton of Gold

A Crystal Moore Suspense, Book 1

A Contemporary Suspense

By

James R. Callan

Pennant Publishing

Publisher's Note:
This is a work of fiction. All names, characters, places, businesses, and events are the work of the author's imagination. Any resemblance to real persons, places, businesses or events is coincidental.

Copyright: © 2015 by James R. Callan

ISBN: 978-0-692-54370-2

Pennant Publishing

This book is dedicated to Jamie, Kelly, Kristi, and Diane.
Could a parent be any luckier?

Prologue

The Year: 1834

RIP Johnson wrapped his large hands around the metal cup, capturing some of the heat from the steaming coffee. The first slender fingers of sunlight were beginning to poke through the tall pines, turning dust particles into floating bits of silver. A wispy fog drifted up from the small lake. Rip had just started toward the cliff for a better view of the lake below, when the sound of hoof beats stopped him. They were coming fast. Probably Billy hurrying back for some hot coffee. Rip had sent him out at first light to check the trail behind them.

Billy Watkins raced his horse into the clearing, reining in his mount a short distance from Rip. The youngster slid off the sorrel gelding and ran the few feet to stand in front of his boss.

"Injuns." He paused to catch his breath. "Couple of miles back. Coming this way. Looking for us."

"How many?"

"More 'n forty." Another deep breath. "In war paint."

"Armed?"

"I seen lots of rifles. They was definitely following our tracks. They're coming after us." Worry covered the rider's face as thickly as the dust did.

For a few seconds, Rip stared down at the grass, just beginning to emerge from its winter slumber. Forty well-armed Indians were more than a match for his eight men. He looked to his left and his gaze fell on his son, pulling on his small boots.

"You're sure of the number?"

"Yes sir. Counted thirty-eight. And there was more. But I decided to get the hell out of there 'fore they saw me."

Better to ride, and fight another day. Rip shifted his focus to the wagon. Too heavily loaded to move fast. He looked past it only a second and made his decision. He wouldn't leave it for the Indians. Half turning, he located his foreman.

"Hank, lots of injuns coming. Get your men and push that wagon off the cliff, into the lake. Then mount up."

Hank cocked his head to one side, a frown on his face. "In the lake?"

"Fast as you can. Then brush out the tracks. And I want us moving out in three minutes." He pivoted in the other direction. "Cookie, put out that fire and load your stuff. Move it."

By now, his son was standing beside him. "What's happening, Pa?"

Rip laid his hand on the eight-year-old's shoulder. "Injuns headed this way. I'll saddle Blaze for you. Then I want you to ride north as fast as you can. Don't wait for me; I'll catch up with you."

"I'm hungry, Pa."

"Grab some jerky from Cookie. Get your slicker. Leave everything else." Confusion creased the young boy's face. "Move it, James Joseph."

In less than a minute, Rip had the small sorrel mare saddled. He picked up his son and put him astride the horse. "Don't stop, unless you hear gun shots close. If you do, get off Blaze and find a hiding place for yourself. And don't come out until I call you."

"But, Pa, how will you find me?"

"I will." Rip slapped the mare on its hindquarters and it galloped out of the clearing.

The men were struggling with the wagon, its large wheels barely moving. "Come on, Cookie. Let's give 'em a hand." The cook, well over two hundred fifty pounds, and Rip added their muscle to the task. Now, with all eight men straining, the wagon wheels turned a bit faster. It reached the point where the ground began to slope toward the cliff and the wagon began to move on its own, slowly picking up speed. The men gave a last push, then straightened up to watch the wagon tumble off the cliff. It splashed into the water, sending a ripple

2

all the way across the narrow lake. In only seconds, the wagon and its heavy cargo sank out of sight.

"Hank, brush out those tracks. Cookie, kick some dirt over those coals. Let's saddle up and get out of here. The injuns can't be far away."

It took only a minute for the men to gather bedding and saddle horses.

"Keep a sharp eye. We're outnumbered. We'll come back later for the wagon. Let's move."

With that, Rip spurred his horse and headed north, seven men close behind. They had not covered half a mile when Cookie caught the first bullet. His weight shifted left and his horse cut to the right, sending Cookie tumbling to the ground.

Rip turned in time to see the cook hit the ground, blood spurting from a hole in his chest. Rip knew nothing could be done for the jovial man who sang while he cooked.

Sounds of rifle shots overpowered the pounding of hooves. Each man bent forward, chin almost touching the horse's mane, trying to provide the smallest target possible. Periodically, one would turn halfway and fire a pistol shot in the direction of the Indians, not with any hope of hitting one, but perhaps causing them to slow down a bit, lose a little ground.

A bullet shattered the left knee of Hank's buckskin mare. The horse went down and Hank flew over its head, landing hard on the ground, breaking his shoulder, leaving him an easy target.

Within five minutes, only Rip and Billy were left. When no lead whizzed by for several minutes, Rip allowed himself to believe they had outrun the Indians. Even as the thought rested in his brain, a rifle slug tore through his heart. Rip was dead before he hit the ground.

Billy panicked. He turned in the saddle, firing wildly at the pursuing Indians. Within a quarter mile, the eighteen year old son of a preacher lay dead on the dusty, east Texas trail.

The Indians rounded up the white-man's horses. As they started to leave, their leader noticed one of the horses was a small, sorrel mare. He slid off his mount and began to walk around the area. He stopped beside a low growing cedar bush and pulled back some branches.

James Joseph crouched there, a hunting knife in his hand. In a single quick motion, the Indian snatched the knife away with one hand, and grabbed James Joseph with the other. The small boy struggled, but it was wasted effort. The Indian placed James Joseph on the horse, took the reins, and jumped onto his own mount. He set off to the south, pulling the small sorrel mare and its young rider behind him.

Chapter 1

The Year: 2012

CRYSTAL Moore stood in her stocking feet, glaring at the row of shoes in her closet. Her raven hair, flipped up just below her ear lobes, looked like it had received three strokes with a brush. Dark circles under her eyes belied eight hours sleep.

"Terrific, I'm late and can't find a single shoe to wear," she grumbled.

"One won't do any good. Need a pair." Brandi Brewer, a mug of hot chocolate in her hand, lounged against the door to Crystal's bedroom. "What kind you looking for?"

Hands on hips, Crystal surveyed the jumble of shoes. "Something that'll match my outfit."

Brandi appraised her housemate's attire and shrugged. "Which part?"

Crystal's frown only deepened.

"How 'bout those by the foot of the bed." Brandi pointed the mug at a pair of charcoal slings.

Crystal turned her head and focused on the shoes. "They'll do." She padded over and stepped into the Guccis.

"Coffee?"

"Don't have time. Didn't sleep well last night, and can't seem to get going." She rummaged in her purse, found a tube of lipstick and bent down to look in the mirror over the dressing table.

"Guess not. I got up to go to the bathroom in the middle of the night. No news flash there. When I passed your door, you were really thrashing around. Thought you had a man under the covers."

Brandi giggled. "Who's Dr. Coup?"

Crystal's hand jerked, sending a slash of bright coral from lip to nose. Slowly, her shoulders sagged, like a balloon losing some of its air. Her eyes glazed over and she stood motionless, barely breathing.

Dr. Krupe. The brilliant Dr. Krupe. Why couldn't she purge his memory from her brain?

She forced her mind back to the present, straightened her back, focused her eyes. "I don't know any Dr. Coup."

"Well, he was on your mind last night. Heard it going and coming back."

"I don't know anybody by that name." She snatched a pale pink tissue from a box on the dresser and tried to repair the damage. "And why were you eavesdropping?"

"Eavesdropping? You were talking in your sleep, for God's sake. And I have to pass by your door to get to the bathroom." The short, auburn-haired woman turned and sauntered into the living room.

Crystal examined the image in the mirror. Her upper lip retained an orange glow on the right side. She glanced at the clock, shook her head and tossed the tissue at the wastebasket. She dropped the lipstick in her purse and hurried into the living room.

Brandi sat on the couch, feet curled under her, thumbing through a magazine.

"Sorry I snapped at you," Crystal said as she stopped to gather papers off the coffee table. "I had a lousy night and so far this morning, things aren't improving. But that's no excuse to lash out at you. Sorry."

"Forgotten."

"See you tonight. I promise to be in a better mood." Crystal dashed out of the apartment.

* * *

Crystal pulled open the heavy glass door to the offices of Intelligent Retrieval Systems. Pam Ragley, the receptionist, looked up. "Hi, Crystal. Dr. O'Malley wants to see you the minute you get in."

Crystal arched her eyebrows. "What's up?"

"I don't know. But all hell's broken loose. All I can tell you is, he's on the warpath."

"Thanks for the warning."

Crystal paused at the open door and tapped lightly. "You wanted to see me?"

Dr. Mark O'Malley, the thirty-five-year-old president and principal owner of IRS, Inc., motioned her in with his left hand while he continued to write on a pale green pad of paper. She settled down in one of the dark blue leather chairs opposite his desk and waited.

Crystal didn't mind waiting. It gave her time to study Mark. She knew he was her boss and she shouldn't mix business and pleasure, but just watching him caused a little flutter in her stomach.

He dropped the pencil and glanced at the small, digital clock on the corner of his desk.

"Sorry I'm late," Crystal said.

"Hasn't been a good morning. Give me an update on your project. Where does it stand?"

Crystal felt a slight blush rise up her cheeks. "It's still behind schedule, but I think we're catching up. We should be ready to load data in a week. Ten days at the outside."

Mark's sapphire eyes bored into hers but he said nothing. She looked away, repositioned herself in the chair and slipped her fingers under her thighs. The silence seemed to stretch on forever. "We might be able to load data this week, maybe Friday, if all goes well," she said, although her voice lacked any conviction.

A jumble of thoughts milled around in her head. *This is not at all like Mark.*

He let out a long sigh. "It seems like everything is falling behind." He ran his fingers through his hair in frustration. "Rooney's unhappy." Rooney Associates provided the venture capital that was helping Intelligent Retrieval Systems grow. "They've got a new consultant. He went over our last report, and apparently, he didn't like it. So, he's stirring them up. They're coming to look over our shoulders and see what we're doing and why we're not doing it faster."

Now, Crystal's face mirrored the concern of her boss. She knew Sally's project had bogged down recently. Phil's group had just started a new project and would have nothing to show. And her project wasn't ready to show investors.

"At any rate," Mark continued, his voice losing some of the sharpness, "we need to put on a good dog-and-pony show when this guy gets here. The next round of funding is due in a couple of months. Not a good time to make them unhappy. Or cause them to have second thoughts."

"They can't—"

"Oh yes they can. The bulk of that inch-thick agreement insures they can do almost anything. And while I *think* Rooney is fair, I *know* he's hard-nosed. He'll do what he thinks is best for Rooney. See if you can push—"

Pam's voice came over the intercom. "Sorry to break in, Dr. O'Malley, but Crystal's grandmother is on line one and sounds like she really needs to talk to Crystal—right now. What should I tell her?"

Mark frowned at the intercom, then at Crystal. "Transfer it to Crystal's office. At least one of us should be working."

Crystal felt like she had been reprimanded. She left without a word and trudged the fifty feet to her office. She collapsed in her chair and reached for the phone. *Probably nothing more than Nana finding some new guy she wants to match me up with.*

She forced a smile on her face and tried to sound as bright as possible. "Hi, Nana. What's up?"

"Somebody tried to kill me."

Chapter 2

CRYSTAL Moore's eyes shot wide open and she sat bolt upright. Disconnected pictures, all bleak, flashed in Crystal's mind, as a chill descended over her. "Tried to kill you!" Her voice almost failed her. Her chest felt like something was crushing it. She could feel her blood pulsing in her veins. "Are you Okay?"

"I'm fine."

"Where are you?"

"Home. Where else would I be?"

In the hospital. "What happened?"

"Some fool tried to run me off the road."

Crystal's back relaxed slightly. "Nana, I don't think he was trying to kill you."

"Were you here?"

Crystal reminded herself that this was her grandmother, her only living relative. "Okay. Tell me what happened."

"Well, I was going to town. And some redneck tried to run me off the road. Clear as could be. Meant to kill me!"

Crystal rolled her eyes toward the ceiling. She worried about her grandmother driving, or living alone, for that matter. At seventy-six, reactions slowed. Maybe her grandmother shouldn't be driving at all.

"Every week somebody tries to run me off the road while I'm driving to work. He just wasn't paying attention, that's all."

"That dog won't hunt. *I* was paying attention. I saw him. He looked right at me, then pulled over in my lane. I could see it in his eyes. He intended to run me right off the road—or hit me head-on. He cotton-pickin' meant to kill me."

"Did you call the police?"

"What for? They'd give me the same routine you are."

Crystal took a deep breath and let it out slowly. "What do you want me to do, Nana?"

"Nothing. Nothing you can do."

Crystal struggled to keep her voice as neutral as possible. She dearly loved her grandmother but Nana could be difficult sometimes. She saw the world very clearly, with seldom a doubt on how to interpret it. "Then why did you call me? Just to worry me?"

"No." Crystal detected a trace of hurt feelings in her grandmother's voice. "Because I wanted you to know somebody's trying to kill me. And if I die under questionable circumstances, I want you to tell the police it was *murder*. And make sure they *do* something. You know how old Billy Goat is. If you don't stick his nose in it, he can't find—"

"Nana!" Crystal cut her off. "Bill Glothe's been the sheriff for ten years—and your friend a lot longer than that."

"Ugly truck. One of those, ah, what-cha-ma-callits. Ah, four-by-fours. Big as a dump truck. Puce."

"Puce? They don't make puce-colored cars."

"Well, maybe he painted it, I don't know. Looked puce to me."

"Are you Okay? Is there anything I can do for you?"

"Yes and no. I'm fine and there's nothing you can do. Just remember what I told you. Anything happens, get Billy Goat on it."

"I will," Crystal promised. "I love you, Nana."

Crystal swiveled her chair around and gazed out the window. Already, the sun was baking the shops and restaurants in the trendy West End Historic District. An area of old warehouses, next to the schoolbook depository of Lee Harvey Oswald fame, had been transformed into a modern, attractive area popular with tourists and locals alike.

Her thoughts gravitated back to her grandmother. *Maybe I ought to go get her and bring her to live in Dallas.* The corners of Crystal's mouth curled up slightly. *That'll be the day.*

Eula Moore was a maverick. A five feet two inch, gray-haired dynamo, she lived in the middle of three hundred twenty acres in East Texas. Her nearest neighbor's house stood nearly a mile away as the crow flies and two miles by the pot-holed road. A trip to the store in the closest town covered twenty-four miles roundtrip.

When Crystal's granddad died five years ago, she felt certain her grandmother would sell the place and move into town. But Eula steadfastly refused even to consider such a thing. She loved "The Park," as she and her husband had named it fifty years before. Why would she want to move?

Crystal understood. After her parents died in an auto accident when she had just turned seven, her grandparents took her to raise. At first, she was so angry at the world she hated everything. But month-by-month, the pain eased and The Park helped in the healing process. The beauty made it difficult to stay bitter, and the tranquility slowly dried her tears. She pictured one of her favorite spots, a hill that fell off sharply to the water, across the lake from the house. Her seven-year-old eyes had seen it as a sheer cliff overlooking the ocean, promising adventure.

"Pam said your grandmother sounded a little distraught. Is there a problem?" Mark stood in the doorway.

Crystal swung her chair around. "I don't think so."

Mark cocked his head to one side and scrutinized her. "Did you do something to your mouth? The right side looks discolored, or something."

Crystal touched her face where the lipstick had smeared. "Oh, no. No. I was, ah, just rubbing it and it got red, I guess." By now, her cheeks had a pink glow.

Mark nodded a couple of times. "Remember, you promised to take me to see your grandmother's place. And try the fishing."

"Next time I go, I'll invite you."

"Don't forget." Mark started to leave, then turned back. "Oh, I'll be out of the office tomorrow. Hot prospect down in Waco. But I'll be back Wednesday for our lunch meeting. Looking forward to your presentation." He paused a moment, as if checking a mental to-do list. "We'll put together such a great demonstration the venture capitalists will throw money at us." He winked, gave her an encouraging smile and left.

Crystal leaned back in her chair, relief spreading from head to toe. That was more like the Mark she knew.

She recalled the first time she met Mark. And the events leading up to it. She had been writing her dissertation in information retrieval at Stanford University, but a misunderstanding with her advisor had effectively killed that. Crystal had felt discouraged and worthless. After a week of sitting in her room crying, she left school and returned to Texas.

Sally Pampson appeared in the doorway. "There's to be no smiling here today. Rooney's coming." She plodded over and slid into a chair. "What's caused such a contented look on such a hectic day?"

"Oh, I was just thinking about my first interview with Mark."

"Wasn't much to mine. Whatever he said, I just repeated my mantra, 'I can do that.' Finally, he asked me what I *couldn't* do. I looked him square in the eye and said, 'Work for a low salary.'" Sally leaned her head back and roared. "He hired me. Can you believe that?"

"Well, my interview certainly didn't go that way. I was really down at the time, wasn't sure I could do anything. When he said he needed a project leader, I wanted to run out of the room, but was too scared to get up and leave. I remember thinking, 'This will be over soon; it's almost lunchtime.' Would you believe he ordered in sandwiches and we kept going? I'm not sure I answered any of his questions. I was so nervous, I went to the restroom four times."

"You could have just kept going out the front door."

"Didn't have the nerve. Then about 4:00, he offered me the job. I was terrified. I couldn't believe he really wanted me. What if I couldn't do it? What if I didn't have the brains for this work?"

Crystal's smile faded as she remembered her apprehension. What if she were humiliated again? She might never regain any confidence, any self-respect.

"Well, Mark made a good decision. And so did you," Sally declared.

"He wasn't too happy with me this morning."

"He's not happy about anything today. Mark is completely confident about his abilities and IRS, but he's not so confident about the good judgment of the venture capitalists. And he doesn't know who they've hired as a consultant." Sally pushed herself up out of the chair. "I guess that's my cue to get back to work."

For a minute, Crystal sat there thinking about her first weeks at IRS and how Mark had helped her regain some self-confidence.

Mentally, she shook herself. *Now, he needs me to produce.* If they were to load data this week, she and her group would have to really push. She picked up the phone and punched a button. "Hi. Get the team together in the conference room in, ah, ten minutes. Thanks."

Chapter 3

BRANDI Brewer finished washing the last of the dinner dishes, dried her hands with a bright, floral dishtowel and turned to face her housemate. "All right. What's going on?"

Crystal put away a skillet, keeping her back to Brandi. "What do you mean?"

"I mean, something's going on with you right now and you're clamming up. You couldn't get it together this morning. You wore mismatched clothes. And no earrings. Not like you at all. And to top it off, I fix my specialty for dinner and you can't string five words together."

"Lemon chicken is the *only* thing you fix that doesn't come out of a box." Crystal gave a half-hearted laugh, but her eyes remained cloudy.

"That's what makes it my specialty. Now, what happened at work today?"

"Nothing much."

"You know I don't give up. Might as well tell me now and save us both a lot of energy."

Crystal shrugged, walked into the living room and slumped into an overstuffed chair. "Mark was on a tear today, that's all."

"That gorgeous hunk? Hard to imagine those deep blue eyes angry."

"The venture capitalists are unhappy. They're going to send in somebody to pick at our work."

"Big deal."

"It's never good to have the 'bean counters' checking on research. They're too shortsighted. Only concerned with what you've done for them this week. Never look at the long range good you might be accomplishing."

Brandi settled back on the couch and put her feet on the coffee table. "Okay. I'll buy that. What about Dr. Coup?"

Crystal glanced up for an instant, then refocused on the marble top of the table. She didn't want to think about Dr. Krupe, much less talk about him.

In a singsong voice, Brandi asked, "What's the scoop on Dr. Coup?"

"Krupe," Crystal said without looking up. "Has an 'R' in it."

"Okay, Krupe. Was this an affair gone bad?"

"We had a misunderstanding. It was a long time ago. Not important now."

Brandi snorted. "Not important? You were sure worked up about it in the middle of the night. Not the first time, either. And did you look at yourself this morning? It's a little early for Halloween. He dumped you, right?"

"No. He did not dump me."

"I've been the dumper and the dumpee. When I did the dumping, I forgot it. When the guy walked, it bothered me. Maybe a lot. Maybe a long time."

"It wasn't an affair. He was my dissertation advisor at Stanford."

"Well, I'm not very smart, but I've been to street U., and I can tell you this from experience. If you don't deal with it, talk about it, scream and holler, you're going to keep having nightmares and bad mornings. Been there, done that. Let's get rid of that devil."

Crystal squirmed in her chair. She studied the picture of a Spanish mission on the opposite wall as her eyes became moist.

Brandi's voice softened. "Come on. Tell Mother Brewer what happened."

Crystal didn't want to talk about it. But Brandi was right about one thing: the nightmares weren't going away. They were getting worse. Right now, she struggled to hold back tears. Why did he still have the power to destroy her self-confidence, her self-esteem? To make her uncertain of everything she did?

Contrary to her intentions, words began to tumble out of her mouth. "He asked me to come by his house to talk about my research. He'd never done that before, and it was a nasty night, but of course I went. He was the Great Dr. Krupe, the high priest of information retrieval. You couldn't say no.

"We discussed a few points, he made a couple of suggestions and in ten minutes, the meeting was over. I got up to leave. It was . . ." Her voice began to falter and it was several moments before she could continue. "The rain was really coming down. He offered to help me with my jacket, so I handed it to him and turned around."

Her throat began to close, as if to prevent more words from coming out. She shut her eyes. She didn't want to continue, but the words had been bottled up for a long time and now they escaped. "I felt his breath on my neck first, and he was saying it was too nasty to go home right now. I should stay until the rain stopped." A slight tremor rippled through her body. "And then his hands were up under my sweater and he was groping my breasts, pulling me back against him and kissing my neck." She ducked her head down, blinking her eyes, trying not to cry.

After a minute, Brandi leaned forward and whispered, "What happened?"

"I managed to push his hands away and turn around. He was looking at me like I was a … a ripe peach. I felt … ." She shuddered. "I picked my jacket up off the floor and said I wasn't about to go to bed with him." Crystal looked at the ceiling, then back at the Spanish Mission, all the while blinking rapidly.

"And?"

"As I put on my jacket, he puffed up and said I had misinterpreted. He was just helping me with my coat and suggesting I might want to wait until the rain eased up a bit. If I had misread it, that was my lack of experience."

Crystal swallowed and there was a catch in her voice as she continued. "He said I often had trouble interpreting things correctly. And perhaps we'd better talk about my paper in his office the next afternoon."

She was quiet for a while, her eyes closed, her head bowed. Finally, Brandi said, "Well, that's not so bad. Let me count the times. There was Fast Freddie. And Sleazy Sam. And Fat Tony, and—"

Crystal's voice rose an octave and the despair came from down deep. "He was my *advisor*."

"Fat Tony was my boss."

"Did he fire you?"

"I quit. How come it's never anybody I like? Oh, well. What did old Poop do?"

Now, the tears refused to be held back. Crystal's body shook and she hid her face in her hands. Brandi went over, sat on the edge of the chair and wrapped her arms around Crystal.

After several minutes, Crystal went on without raising her head. "The next day, I arrived at his office, expecting him to apologize for his behavior the night before. Without so much as a hello, he started in on my dissertation. He told me it was worthless. There was no originality, no merit to it. I should trash it. I could start over, if I wished. But I would have to come up with another proposal and try to get it approved by my committee." She swallowed. "And get another advisor, which he thought might prove to be difficult."

A low moan escaped from Crystal. "He said, to be perfectly frank, he didn't think I had the ability to make it. I should consider whether I was wasting my time in school. I certainly was wasting his time." Her body shook with silent sobs for a minute before she could finish. "So I quit. Left. Gave up my Ph.D. I was so close." Her voice became a whisper. "So close."

"That bastard." Brandi had her arms around Crystal, and fire in her eyes. "Dr. Creep didn't get your body, so he raped your mind."

For a long time, neither woman spoke, muffled sobs the only sound. The tears finally subsided and Crystal got up and trudged into the bathroom to wash her face. When she returned she apologized for her loss of control.

"Don't apologize. Get mad. And if you get the chance, get even." Brandi jumped to her feet and looked down at her housemate. "And don't call it a misunderstanding. When Dr. Creep couldn't entice you into bed, he drummed you out of school. That's not a misunderstanding, that's an assault." For a moment, fire blazed in Brandi's eyes. Then, a grin crossed her face. "I was wrong when I called him Dr. Creep. He's Dr. Crap."

The tiniest hint of a smile made its way onto Crystal's face. "I like it. Dr. Crap. Dr. Lester Crap."

"Lester? Lester the lecher."

Crystal actually laughed. "Dr. Lecher Crap. Describes him perfectly."

"Dr. Crap don't know jack."

"Dr. Crap is a big fat sap."

"And you don't give a damn what he thinks."

"And I don't give . . . a . . ." Crystal's voice trailed off as the smile evaporated from her face.

Chapter 4

CRYSTAL drew diagrams on the white board while Phil Wilson and Sally Pampson, the other two project leaders at Intelligent Retrieval Systems, loaded their plates with food. Mark was already at the table, a sandwich, chips and several strawberries adorning his plate.

The lunch was not a social event. They all knew that in their profession, you either kept up with new research, or quickly fell behind. So, each Wednesday, one person reviewed a current technical paper. The responsibility rotated through the group.

This week, the task fell to Crystal. She finished the diagrams, turned around and began her talk. A navy and white, knee-length linen dress emphasized her model-thin figure. Her hair, black and shiny as obsidian, provided the perfect frame for a heart-shaped face. Her almond eyes reminded one of aged bronze. A tanned and flawless complexion made most makeup unnecessary. Today, a dainty, silver hummingbird hung from each ear.

Twenty-five minutes later, she finished describing the material in the paper and began her conclusions.

"What they found is that there is no statistical difference in these three methods." Sally raised a forefinger as if to object, so Crystal quickly added, "*When* applied to the specific problem of transcripts of spoken language."

"Okay. If you limit it to people talking, I won't object," Sally said.

The telephone rang, but nobody paid any attention.

"Maybe you should still object," said Phil.

The phone rang again. Mark frowned at the offending piece of plastic. Pam knew they did not like to be interrupted during these sessions. "Why do you say that, Phil?"

On the third irritating ring, Mark grabbed the phone, listened, then pointed the receiver toward Crystal.

With the discussion suspended, Sally and Phil replenished their plates. Talk shifted to food and the weather, no one wishing to continue analyzing the research without Crystal's input.

Crystal listened intently while twisting the phone cord around her hand. She replaced the phone in its cradle. "Mark." Her voice quavered. "I've got to go. That was the sheriff from Wooden Nickel. Nana's been in a car accident."

"Is she hurt?"

"The sheriff doesn't think so, but she refuses to go to the hospital. So he really doesn't know. I've got to go."

"Can you call her?"

"He said she wasn't answering the phone, the door, or questions."

Chapter 5

NORMALLY, Crystal enjoyed the drive into East Texas. Today, her mind grappled with the little information she had. Nana had been in an accident; Bill Glothe didn't think she was hurt; he didn't know. And Bill was right. She wasn't answering the phone.

Nana's stubborn streak stretched from the crown of her head to the ball of her foot. She might be seriously injured and refuse to see a doctor. Nana's call about someone trying to run her off the road replayed itself in Crystal's mind, and as much as she tried to lock out the thought, she couldn't forget her parent's death. An auto accident ended their lives. Unshed tears clouded her vision. *Please, dear God, not Nana, too.*

An hour later, she turned off the county road into The Park and almost instantly felt the transformation begin. She had been gripping the steering wheel so tightly her back and shoulders ached. Now, her muscles began to relax and her breathing slowed to fit the more relaxed pace of life in the country. For the first time since Glothe's phone call, she allowed herself to take a more optimistic view.

The trees thinned slightly and the drive leveled off. The lake shimmered off to the right. Up ahead, the house rested under a canopy of tall pines. From this angle, it appeared rather unassuming. Cedar shakes, weathered to the same color as the trunks of the trees, covered the exterior. One could drive almost up to the house without being aware of it.

A car Crystal did not recognize was parked under the shed. It jolted her back to the reality that this was not a pleasure trip. Worry quickly replaced Crystal's momentary feeling of tranquility. She slammed her mind shut to the image trying to resurface: her parents' auto crash.

She parked and rushed in the back door. "Nana," she called.

"On the veranda."

Crystal hurried through the bright living room with its high ceiling and glass wall overlooking the lake. As she stepped out onto the huge covered porch, her eyes immediately focused on the bandage. Trying not to let her voice show the level of her concern, she asked, "Nana, what happened to your head?"

"Where're your manners, girl? You remember Melva, don't you?"

Crystal looked chagrined. "I'm sorry, Mrs. Larson. How are you? I haven't seen you...in a year, I guess."

"I'm doing just fine, Crystal, and no need to apologize. You're concerned about your grandmother, as you should be. So am I. She thinks she's made of rock. Mostly her head, I reckon. She'd rather see her casket coming than admit she was hurt or sick." Melva, at seventy-four two years younger than Eula, eased herself up out of the high-backed rocker. "I've heard all about the accident. Didn't find it all that interesting the first time, so I think I'll mosey on before you get the details."

"If you stay, maybe I won't have to tell her about it." Eula sounded like a kid who had just broken a window at school.

"Not a chance, Nana."

Eula turned her head and spoke to Melva, who was already entering the house. "We're still set for the weekend?"

"I'm not the one with a banged-up noggin. Let's see how you feel in a day or two."

"I'm fine. Get packed."

"Already am. Good to see you again, Crystal. See if you can get ol' rock head to rest a bit." The last was spoken over her shoulder as Melva plodded through the living room and left.

"Okay, Nana. What happened?"

"Nothing much."

"I didn't drive all the way from Dallas for 'nothing much.' Let's have the details."

"Well, like I told you, somebody's trying to kill me. I got in my car to go down to Nickel this morning. You know how the county road has that steep hill running straight down to the highway, and the lake on the other side? Well, I guess the Good Lord was keeping an eye on me. Just as I started down the hill, a squirrel ran across the road. He started, then stopped, then went back. You know how squirrels are. Anyways, I hit the brakes. Well, my foot went right down to the floor. No brakes at all. I pumped 'em a few times. Nothing."

Eula shifted in the chair, getting into her story. "Now, you know I've always thought those people in movies were pretty dumb. When that happens to them, no matter how steep or curvy the road or what might be ahead, they always try to steer down the road.

"Well, I said to myself, I don't want to plow out onto that highway—or into the lake, and I'm only going faster all the time. So, I hit the emergency brake and steered off the road for the softest spot I could find. Ran into a cedar tree."

Crystal grimaced. "And your head?"

"Well, I hit the tree a little too hard and banged my head on the steering wheel." Her look turned more defiant than defensive. "No, I didn't have my seat belt on."

"I wasn't going to ask."

"Yeah."

"No. I knew you didn't. Nana, you really should set a better example for me."

"If I race back and forth to Dallas, I'll be sure to wear one. They irritate my bosoms."

"That's just an excuse. What did the doctor say about your head?"

"Doctor?" She jerked her hand in disgust. "I bumped my head; I didn't break a leg. If I went to the doctor for every bump and scrape, I wouldn't have a place to live. Doctor'd own it. And would've retired long ago. Probably on my Park."

Eula was too young to have been a pioneer, but Crystal knew her grandmother was clearly from independent, pioneer stock. "What did the sheriff say?"

"Why, he pitched a fit. Threatened to give me a ticket. I said no ol' Billy Goat's gonna give me a ticket 'less I hit some*body*. Did the cedar tree file a complaint?"

Crystal shook her head. "It's a wonder he didn't take you to jail. What else did he say?"

"That I didn't have any brake fluid and that's why my brakes didn't work. Shows what he knows."

Sometimes Nana seems to be going through her teenage years again, Crystal thought. But she said, "Did he check the brake fluid?"

"Yes."

"And?"

"There wasn't any. And that's my point. There should 'a been. You know I check those things all the time. It was full last time I checked. And I don't have a leak. I never have to add fluid."

"But there wasn't any fluid in it today?"

"No. But don't you see? Remember what I told you a couple of days ago. Someone's trying to kill me. Someone tampered with 'em. Leaked it all out. Didn't work when they tried to run me off the road, so they tried messing with my brakes. That didn't work either."

Crystal sighed. Her grandmother truly believed someone was trying to kill her. Was this a sign or symptom of a serious problem? *But usually, Nana's mind seems so clear.*

For a long time they rocked quietly, enjoying the day. The sun slid behind a stand of tall pines until the entire porch rested in shade. A light breeze drifted up through the trees from the lake, carrying a slight hint of honeysuckle. Crystal knew it would be blistering hot in Dallas. But here, with the water and the trees it was just pleasantly warm.

Her mind flooded with happy memories of summers long past—sitting in the porch swing, listening to the woodpeckers, or watching the big, arrogant crows prancing around like they owned the place.

Today, half a dozen squirrels were playing tag at the edge of the grass. Brilliant cardinals shared a feeding platform with a goldfinch. A brown-headed nuthatch was sampling sunflower seeds at another feeder. And darting here and there, hovering and squeaking, were the hummingbirds. They flitted about too fast for Crystal to count.

Nana was right. Why would she want to leave The Park?

* * *

Over dinner, Crystal asked, "Why do you think someone is trying to kill you? Has anyone made any threats or said anything about killing you?"

"No. Person'd be a fool to come right out and say it."

"Has anyone *hinted* at it? Or acted hostile toward you? Do

you have someone in mind?"

"No. Who'd want to kill an old lady like me?"

"Then, why do you keep saying someone is?"

"'Cause they are." She looked at her granddaughter and shook her head. "Seems pretty obvious to me. First, a bum tries to run me off the road. Now, some skunk messes with my brakes. What would you call it?"

"A reckless driver and a leak in the brake fluid line. Where's your car now?"

"Billy Goat had it towed to the Possum Stop in Nickel. You can run me down to get it in the morning."

"Could we get it now? I hadn't planned to spend the night." Crystal saw the disappointment in her grandmother's eyes and quickly added, "Unless you were really hurt."

"Can't. Possum closed at six. Tubs'll open it up at seven in the morning."

Crystal's mind pictured the mechanic, slender as asparagus. "Nana, why do they call him Tubs? I've never seen an extra ounce on that man."

Eula giggled. "Ain't that the truth? Hardly casts a shadow. But when he was in grade school, he was a real porker. Everybody started calling him Tubby, then Tubs. Time he got out of high school, he'd grown a foot taller and just stretched the same pounds a lot farther. But everybody'd called him Tubs for so long, it just stuck." She paused to drink some tea. "We can go early in the morning. You're just going to have to spend the night with your grandmother. What's happening with you and Dud?"

"Doug."

"Doug, Dud. What's happening?"

Crystal got up and began stacking dishes. She did not want to talk about her "boyfriends", as Eula liked to call them. "Oh, we go out occasionally. Nothing too serious."

"Wasting your time there. Not going anywhere. Got anybody else on the string?"

Crystal resisted the impulse to agree, deciding it best not to answer at all.

"Thought not. I'm thinking maybe 'cause you lost your father when you was just seven, then your grandfather checks out, you might just think the men in your life will disappear on you."

Crystal continued clearing the table and said nothing.

"'Course, I also think something happened at Stanford. Don't know what. And you sure ain't telling." Eula gathered up the glasses. "But something did. I could tell soon as you got back. You were different. Not as sure of yourself."

Crystal almost dropped the stack of dishes she was loading into the dishwasher. She had never mentioned the problem at Stanford to Nana. Never hinted at it. In fact, she'd never talked about it with anybody before Brandi pried it out of her the other night. Was she sorry she'd talked about it with Brandi?

Chapter 6

THE next morning, Crystal and her grandmother pulled into the Possum Stop at 7:20.

"Couldn't find no problem with the brakes, 'cept they was dry. No leaks, no holes, no loose fittings. Just no fluid. I filled 'er up and it's ready to go."

Tubs had worked on Eula's cars for years and Crystal had always felt he did a competent job.

"What would cause that?" Crystal asked.

"Well," Tubs scratched his ear. "A real slow leak that I mightn't find, that could take a long time to run low." He sucked on his teeth. "That's about it."

"Or somebody lettin' it out." Eula said it half under her breath, but the tone was clear.

Tubs looked sheepishly at Eula. "Yes ma'am. That'd do it."

"Did you see any evidence of tampering with the system?" Crystal asked.

"No, ma'am. But that might be purty hard. Eula run over a lot of brush and stuff. So if'n somebody messed with it, not likely I'd know. 'Course, I wasn't lookin' for that. And now, well, there'd be *my* workin' on it."

Crystal decided to be direct. "Let's assume for a minute that someone did tamper with the brakes. Can you think of anyone who would want to cause Nana to have an accident?"

Tubs studied his grease-covered boots for several seconds. When he looked up, he said, "Well, Eula does talk purty blunt to folks sometimes. But I can't rightly say I know anybody what don't like her."

* * *

Crystal followed her grandmother back to The Park, gave her a long hug good-bye, and started the drive to Dallas. Her thoughts turned to the events of the last three days. Perhaps the first incident could be dismissed. A lot of drivers had their minds on other things, and it took only a moment of lost concentration to wander across the center stripe. Maybe the guy was dialing his cell phone. Or texting.

But this brake business bothered her. *Nana really is good about taking care of her car. Always has been. Of course, brake failures can come on without warning. But then, Tubs didn't find any evidence of a sudden failure. Or anybody tampering with it.*

Crystal became aware that she was grinding her teeth. She took several deep breaths and rolled her shoulders to ease the tension. *Nana lives in the middle of her Park,* she told herself. *She doesn't see that many people often enough to make an enemy. Had to be a leak.*

Chapter 7

AT Intelligent Retrieval Systems, Mark replaced the phone in its cradle and looked up to see Crystal standing in the doorway. "You look a little more relaxed today," he said, motioning her in. "Everything Okay?"

Crystal filled him in on the accident, Eula's reaction to it, the sheriff's opinion, and Tubs' comments.

"So, what do you think?" he asked when she finished.

"Spoiled food, not poison."

Mark raised his eyebrows. "Spoiled food?"

"What I mean is, the incidents were carelessness, not an overt act to kill Nana. Why would anyone want to kill my grandmother?"

"I can't imagine. But she doesn't sound like the paranoid type to me." Mark shifted in his chair, indicating a change of subjects. "You'll be glad to know your new RAID system came in yesterday. In fact, I think Bobby Don already has it on your LAN."

Crystal had been anxiously awaiting the RAID, or Redundant Array of Inexpensive Disks, for several weeks. This particular RAID could store twenty trillion characters of data, roughly the equivalent of more than twenty million novels.

"Terrific. I think we'll be ready to load and test the full Department of Public Safety database starting Monday." She looked a little sheepish and her enthusiasm turned to embarrassment. "We're not going to make this week."

Sally Pampson stuck her head in the doorway. "Hi. You wanted to see me?"

"Yeah, come on in." Mark turned back to Crystal. "Glad your grandmother wasn't hurt. Better stay in touch, though. See how her paranoia goes. Let me know how the new RAID works. And when the data is loaded."

* * *

Mark got up and closed the door after Crystal left, then turned to Sally. "Just wanted to know how JT was working out." JT Gonzales had come to work for IRS only five months ago. Sally had supervised her the entire time. "You're still behind your projection for the history/folklore project. Is that you, JT, or someone else on your team? Or some mix of those?"

Sally, thirty-seven and slightly overweight, relaxed in one of the easy chairs in the conference area of Mark's office. Her brown hair was short and permed so that she could, as she put it, just run her fingers through it in the morning and it was combed. "Actually, maybe a mix of JT and the project. Everything was sailing along until we got into the testing phase. Then she slowed to a crawl. I don't know whether it was because our methods were new to her or what. She was really zipping along before. But a couple of weeks ago, POW. Like she hit a brick wall. Progress just stopped.

"Good news is, she's moving again. Maybe something was going on in her personal life. I don't know. She doesn't talk much—like I do. But for a week, she snailed along at about quarter speed."

"How's the testing going now?"

"Great. With Rod's handy-dandy book reader, we've scanned in over eighty-thousand pages and we've spot-checked a good bit of that already. 'Course, there've been a few glitches we've had to iron out. We're getting there. In fact, we're ready to scan in the rest of the material."

Mark nodded a few times. "And Rod's machine has helped?"

"Oh, yeah."

Rod Tucker was Mark's best friend and a top-notch mechanical engineer. A product of Texas A & M, Rod could convert almost any idea into hardware. While he didn't work for IRS, Rod believed helping a friend was the most important thing a person could do. In this case, he had made a device that automated the scanning of books into a computer. Load twenty to thirty books into the machine and it would process them with no further human intervention.

That was only part of the solution. Intelligent Retrieval Systems' software did the hard part - making all that information easily and quickly accessible. Sally's project would allow people to research Texas history and folklore thousands of times faster than they could without this new program.

"So, the project's back up to speed, if running a bit behind." Mark made it a statement, but Sally recognized it for the question it was.

"Yeah." Her hazel eyes twinkled. "Speedy Gonzales and Pampson on the move. We'll be ready for the big hoedown. I've got some examples I think will wow them."

"Great. The deep pockets will appreciate that. So will I."

"Guess I'd better get hopping before anything else slows us down."

Chapter 8

OVER dinner with Brandi, Crystal had recounted her visit with Eula. Now they relaxed in the living room. "The thing is, Nana has always kept her cars in good shape. As far back as I can remember, she would check everything: oil, radiator, transmission fluid, and . . ." She paused and raised a finger. "Brake fluid. It's Nana, not some service station man, who tells me I need to replace a fan belt or something." She shook her head. "It's hard to imagine her car slowly losing its brake fluid and her not noticing it."

"How easily can you imagine someone trying to kill your grandmother?"

Crystal tilted her head to one side. "I can't. That's what makes this so puzzling."

"Is there a third choice?"

"Third choice?" Crystal frowned. "What do you mean?"

"You've said either it was a total accident, or someone is trying to kill her. Any other choices?"

The frown persisted. "I certainly can't think of any. Can you?"

"No. But then, I'm not too smart. I thought—"

The phone interrupted Brandi, and she answered it. After a moment she said, "Oh, hi, Doug. How's it going?"

Immediately, Crystal began waving her hands in front of her roommate's face. When Brandi looked up, Crystal was shaking her head and mouthing "no".

"Ah, she's not here right now, Doug." She listened for a few seconds. "No. I have no idea where she went, or when she'll be back. But I'll tell her you called."

She hung up the phone. "What was that all about?"

"I can't deal with Doug right now."

"Just tell him what's going on. He's a nice guy, and he really likes you."

"He'll want to know all the details, and then he'll tell me they were just accidents and I'm being silly to worry."

"Which is sort of what you're saying."

Crystal took a deep breath and let it out slowly. "Yeah. And I'd like to have someone reinforce my feelings in that direction."

"But not Doug?"

Crystal shrugged.

"Want me to ask Tom?" Brandi was dating Tom Hawkins, a detective in the Dallas Police Department. "Or ask him yourself. You know how easy he is to talk to."

"I don't know."

"How about Mark? You think he's pretty levelheaded. Discuss it with him. After work. When he can concentrate on you. I mean, your problem." Brandi raised her eyebrows and wiggled her head.

Even Crystal had to smile at Brandi's suggestive look.

Chapter 9

"**PUT** in a landing and a ninety-degree turn in the stairs," Mark said.

"It just isn't necessary. A flight of stairs is not dangerous, except perhaps to the elderly. And it *is* my house, after all."

Rod Tucker was standing in the den of Mark O'Malley's sprawling ranch house. Located about thirty minutes south of his downtown Dallas office, the house seemed an extension of Mark himself: the unlikely combination of Texas country and high tech. It sat in the middle of twenty acres, had a pickup parked prominently on the circle drive, and had four Merced-based computers that controlled just about everything.

"You're wrong. Stairs *are* dangerous," Mark said. "Why are the English so stubborn?"

Rod lived about three miles away. Last week, he had finished a deck outside his study and now was planning some stairs down to the back yard, about eight feet below. Mark was concerned that Rod's young son might fall down the stairs.

"We're not stubborn, just firm in our beliefs," Rod said. "But, I'm an experimentalist. Let's just test this theory."

Without another word, he walked over to a door and opened it. On the other side, stairs led down to the garage under the den. He turned and looked at Mark as if to say, "I have to prove everything to you." Pivoting back, he let his knees buckle and tumbled down the stairs.

Mark ran to the door, afraid of what he might see. Rod lay in a crumpled heap at the foot of the stairs. The back of his head was on the concrete floor and his right arm was folded under his back. His legs sprawled at strange angles, and he was not moving.

Mark took the steps two at a time, fearful of what might have happened to his friend. As Mark descended the stairs, Rod's left hand began to move. It came up and adjusted his glasses, still hooked behind his ears, if somewhat askew. Then, with the suddenness of a five-year-old, he bounced up and faced a slightly pale Mark. "See, they aren't dangerous. You can fall down a flight of stairs without sustaining injury."

Mark was too stunned to say anything.

He knew Rod was tough as rawhide and strong as a new well rope. And he realized Rod believed most things wouldn't hurt him. Apparently, he applied this to his son as well. Mark just shook his head and followed his friend up the stairs.

"I don't expect Ethan to fall on the stairs," Rod said. "But if he does take a tumble, he'll simply roll down—and the grass will be softer than your garage floor."

"Ethan doesn't have as hard a head as you do. And he may not understand the dangers any more than his father does." Mark went to the small refrigerator in the den and took out a Dr Pepper. "You're out of your mind. I will talk to Joan this week. Your wife has always had more common sense than you."

"But, I just showed—"

"I'm not discussing this topic with you anymore. I'll talk with Joan and she'll straighten you out."

Rod gave his small laugh. "Please remember, it *is* my house."

"And Joan's. And Ethan is my Godson."

Just then, a rather feminine voice said, "Mark?"

"Yes?"

"You have a visitor coming. Crystal Moore."

A grin spread across Rod's face. "I see you've added some improvements since we hooked up Shannon's camera."

Only a month ago, Rod had helped Mark install a digital camera and sensors near the gate on his drive. Rod had concealed the camera in a fake log that could elude close scrutiny. The area around the gate was bathed in a soft light, unnoticed by visitors, but sufficient for the camera to record all arrivals. Information from the camera was relayed to one of the computers in the house. Mark had given that particular computer the name "Shannon." After analyzing the data, Shannon's synthesized voice passed the message to Mark.

"I liked knowing someone was arriving," Mark said. "But I

decided knowing *who,* would be even better. So, I have the computer scan the license plate and check the results against a list of likely visitors. If Shannon finds a match, it tells me who it is. Otherwise, it simply says I have a visitor and displays a picture on the monitor."

"What does it do about me?" Rod rarely drove a car, unless he was going somewhere with Joan and Ethan.

"It knows that you are about the only person who would ride a bicycle to my house. So, it expects it to be you. But, if the rider didn't have some of your characteristics, it would not identify the visitor as you."

Rod gave his self-conscious laugh. "What kind of characteristics?"

"It tries to decide if the rider is the kind of person who would deliberately throw himself down a flight of stairs," Mark deadpanned.

"So, Crystal's coming over on a Friday night." Rod went on the offensive. "What happened to Gloria?"

"Nothing's happened to Gloria. In fact, we're going out tomorrow night." Mark felt a bit defensive. "Crystal's coming to talk about her grandmother."

"Her *grandmother*? Does Crystal often come over at night to talk about her grandmother?" Bits and pieces of a snicker escaped Rod's tightly closed lips.

"She's never been here before. But several things have happened—"

Just then, the doorbell rang. Mark threw up his hands, abandoning his defense, and went to answer the door.

When he and Crystal returned, Rod was gathering a few items into a backpack.

"Hi, Rod," Crystal greeted him brightly. "Your book-reading machine is working as smooth as custard."

"Thank you. Mark said it seemed to be holding together."

"There's an understatement. Without it, we wouldn't be making nearly as much progress. I think you should charge IRS a royalty, or maybe a reading fee."

"I might just do that." Rod picked up his backpack. "Up for a few sets tomorrow?" he asked Mark.

"Sounds good. Eight-thirty?"

"See you there. Don't let him work you too hard, Crystal," Rod said as he left the room.

* * *

"Before we start on why I called and wanted to come over to talk to you, I've got a question." Crystal was standing by the fireplace. She had on well-fitted jeans and a crisp cotton shirt with an intricate design embroidered on the front. She wore just a touch of blush to complement her coral lipstick, applied more skillfully than it had been Monday morning.

"Fire away. Would you like something to drink?"

She cocked her head to one side as if debating with herself. "How about a Coors?"

"You've got it."

"May I look around in here?"

"Sure."

When Mark returned, Crystal was checking out the CD rack. "Looks like a pretty eclectic collection."

"I enjoy all music——well, almost all. I love the Meyerson," he said, naming the famous Dallas symphony hall. "At the same time, I also enjoy going to Jimmy Joe's New Honky-Tonk. I know. Weird. That's what my mother says." He handed her the beer, with a napkin wrapped around the bottom half of the bottle.

"Is this your father?" Crystal pointed to a picture of Mark, clad in dusty jeans and denim jacket, with his arm around an older man. Mark nodded. "And this is your sister?" Crystal indicated a picture of a beautiful blonde woman.

"No. Just a friend." His face suddenly felt warm.

Crystal studied the picture of the woman a minute longer, a slight frown on her face.

This close to Crystal, Mark was aware, not of perfume, but a fresh, outdoor scent. "So, what was your question?"

"What is this plaque? The one with the bull on it."

Mark looked at the plaque, then took a drink before answering. "That's a story from another life."

"Come on, Mark. You said you'd answer."

"Actually, I said 'Fire away'. I did not say I would answer." He walked over and settled onto the couch.

"Okay. Technically, you didn't say you would answer. But

37

you know how curious I am. Why not just tell me?"

Mark contemplated his Dr Pepper for a moment. "On one condition: it's between you and me. It does not go to the office."

"Deal."

Mark hesitated, deciding just how much he wanted to divulge. "I grew up in Mesquite. When college time came, there wasn't enough money. So I rode in rodeos to help pay for college. I'd ridden all my life and thought I was pretty good. I found there was more money to be made riding bulls, so that's what I did. I paid for most of my college as a bull rider."

Crystal threw her head back and laughed. "That's terrific. I'll bet you were the only member of MIT's graduate school that rode bulls."

"I rode bulls to pay my way through Texas. When I went to MIT, I had a fellowship. No more being thrown in the dirt—or up in the air. No more hoping the bull didn't step on you. Some of those bulls weigh a ton or more, and their hooves can be sharp. They can do a lot of damage if they step on you."

"Did you ever get gored?" A mischievous smile crept across her face. "I know that's a little, um, gory, but did you?"

"No. No goring, no broken bones."

"Did you get that scar riding bulls?"

Mark fingered the scar that traced his left cheekbone. "Yeah. A big red bull up in Elk City rubbed me the wrong way and when I went off I hit the fence."

Crystal grimaced. "Sounds terrible."

"Actually, I did my eight and won some money to boot. That took some of the pain out of it."

"Did your eight?"

"You're supposed to stay on the bull for eight seconds. Only use one hand. Have some sort of style. And hope for a bull that makes you look good."

"Is that all? Just eight seconds?"

"Believe me, it seems a lot longer."

"And just how does the bull make you look good?"

Mark grinned. He hadn't thought about bull riding in a long time. "You need a bull that looks like the meanest critter in the world, that is very active in the ring, a bull the judges can't believe anybody could stay on for the full eight, but in fact isn't that tough to ride."

"Did you get those very often?"

"No. Maybe one a year, if I was lucky."

Crystal pointed to the plaque. "And this was for . . .?"

"That was for being too dumb to know when to quit."

Crystal stared at Mark, and the corners of her mouth turned down. She shook her head no.

"Actually, it was for rookie of the year. Best newcomer to the circuit—in bull riding. Of course, it was the last plaque I ever got. But I paid for college and that's what counted."

"Why didn't you get a scholarship to Texas?"

She asked the question with such innocence that Mark ignored its impropriety and simply answered it. "My grades in high school weren't good enough."

Crystal raised an eyebrow, but said nothing to the surprising statement.

"I was smart enough. My SAT's were high. But I hadn't been concerned about grades. You know the bit: it's not the grades, but what you learn, that counts. I learned a lot, more than most kids in my classes. I just wasn't worried about grades. Result: no scholarship." He paused for a moment to take a drink. "So I rode bulls. *And*, I got more concerned with grades."

"Did you enjoy it? Bull riding, I mean."

"Yeah. Mostly, I enjoyed the people, the other riders and ropers. Quite a bunch. Straightforward. Friendly. Say what's on their minds. And they *do* like to have fun."

Mark looked out the window, a faraway smile on his face. He had forgotten what good times those were. He remembered the smell of rodeos, the hot animals, his own sweat, the leather. He could almost feel the rope, tight around his right hand, and two thousand pounds of raw power restless under him, waiting to explode. The surge of adrenaline when the gate opened. The thrill of a successful ride.

Saturday had been ample compensation for a sore Sunday.

The clock on the bookshelf chimed and jolted Mark back to the present. "But, that's not why you wanted to come over. What's on your mind?"

She took a drink of her beer before answering. "I've been thinking about what you said yesterday afternoon. About Nana not sounding like the paranoid type. You're right. She isn't. I can't remember her ever sounding paranoid. Generally, she's the reverse. If people around her are worried about something, she just dismisses it."

"That could be the theory of opposites working."

Crystal looked puzzled. "Theory of opposites?"

"Goes something like this: if two people are facing a problem, the angrier one gets, the more subdued the other becomes. Person A gets a little madder; person B gets a little more subdued. They may even change sides. If person B begins to get mad about it, then person A will become calmer. In the past, when others worried, your grandmother was calm. Now, nobody is concerned about these incidents, so she is."

Crystal studied Mark for a minute. "Did you just switch sides? Or is that the theory of opposites working in our discussion?"

"Could be. But I prefer to think of it as considering all sides. Maybe she's making more of it than it deserves. Then again, maybe someone is out to injure her."

Mark saw worry and tension work their way down Crystal's face. Her eyes, normally so shiny and alive, now looked dull and brooding. No doubt she had considered the possibility that someone wanted to injure her grandmother, but this was probably the first time an outsider had said it. Mark knew that one asked for an independent opinion, hoping it would reinforce what she wanted to hear, not what she feared.

Crystal frowned at the bottle in her hand and abruptly set it on the mantle, as if it had suddenly become colder. She stared at the floor and wrapped her arms around herself.

"Crystal, I'm not saying there's someone out there. I'm saying you have to consider it." For a moment, Mark just watched her. Her expression didn't change. "What do I tell you to do when you start a new project at IRS?"

Crystal looked up and gave a half laugh. "Finish it on schedule."

Mark chuckled. "True. And my other generic instruction?"

She thought for a minute. "Consider at least three different ways to approach the problem. Don't just grab the first thing that comes to mind and run with it. Even if it turns out to be the way you eventually solve the problem, you'll have more insight from having considered alternatives."

"Consider alternatives." His eyes turned toward the large window opposite the fireplace. Outside lights accented a bright-pink Mimosa tree. *Why would someone want to injure an old lady?* "Has anyone tried to buy your grandmother's land?"

"No. Nana would never sell her Park."

"That's my point. She wouldn't sell. If someone wanted it badly enough, they might try to scare her off."

"She won't scare. But I see what you mean. She hasn't mentioned anything like that."

"Would she?"

"What? Tell me if someone offered to buy it? I don't know. I mean, she would if it came up. But she might just dismiss it, not think to say anything about it."

"You might ask her, casually. It's worth checking. Has she had any boundary disputes? Does anyone share mineral rights on the land?"

Crystal shrugged. "I don't know. I never heard any discussion about that sort of thing. She and my granddad bought the land over fifty years ago. I can't imagine any boundary dispute coming up now."

"Understand, I'm not suggesting there is one. I'm just saying you have to consider all possibilities. You think of your grandmother as a sweet old lady whom no one would ever try to hurt. If she's right, then there *is* someone who would do her harm. You've said she's strong willed. Strong-willed people can rub others the wrong way. Someone may see her as unreasonable, arbitrary."

For a minute, neither said anything. Mark broke the silence. "At IRS, when a project comes along, there are two possibilities for you. It might go to someone else, in which case, you're mildly interested in it. The second possibility is it becomes your project. Then you must look at it from all angles, consider all facets."

Crystal nodded several times. "Okay. This project is clearly mine. I'll consider all possibilities. It's too late to call Nana tonight. I will tomorrow."

* * *

Mark watched Crystal drive off. He glanced at his watch. It was nearly ten, but he knew Josh Kinsolving would be up, if he was home.

On the fifth ring, Josh answered.

"Hey, how are things going?"

"Terrific, Mark. What's on your mind?"

Josh was never one to waste much time. A long time employee of Schlumberger Wire Line, he understood efficiency. Josh managed one of the oil well service company's offices in East Texas.

"I'm not looking for any proprietary information. But is there new interest in the Wooden Nickel area?"

"You mean any drilling? Not that I know of."

"I really had in mind land acquisition, or leasing of mineral rights."

There was silence on the other end of the phone. Mark wondered if Josh was considering the ethical aspects of answering or just trying to remember anything. Finally, he said, "I'm not aware of any activity in that area. What's your interest?"

Mark chuckled lightly. "It may be nothing at all. But one of my employees has a grandmother who lives alone out there. Has half a section. A couple of things have happened in the last week, and she, the grandmother, thinks somebody is trying to kill her. I doubt there's anything to it. The police don't think so. Anyway, I'm just looking for anything that might be a motive."

"Sorry. Don't know a thing. You think somebody really is trying to kill her?"

"Probably not. On the other hand, she doesn't sound like the kind easily spooked. If you hear anything . . ."

"I'll call you. And, Mark." Josh paused just a second. "Don't dismiss it too quickly. Wouldn't be the first time someone got killed over an oil lease. Or timber."

Chapter 10

MONDAY afternoon, Mark called a meeting with his project leaders. Crystal was the last to arrive in the conference room. "Sorry," she said as she slipped into a seat, a half-finished donut in one hand.

"We only beat you by thirty seconds," Mark said. "Okay, guys, we've got the date for the Rooney visit. They'll be here two weeks from today. It's not clear yet what happens on that Monday. But Tuesday, they're expecting demonstrations and status reports." He hesitated a beat. "We need to shine. They're putting a good bit of money into IRS and it's up to us to convince them it was, and still is, a wise thing to do." Mark looked at each of his three leaders. "I know you don't like to think of outsiders controlling things, but let's face reality. We're almost there. Almost. But right now, we need them. At least for another year."

Crystal, Phil and Sally all nodded agreement.

"How come they're bringing a consultant?" asked Sally.

"Actually, on a first deal like this was for me, it's pro-forma to have a consultant. The unusual thing is that they didn't do it at the beginning. That's why I was surprised. And why I'm a little concerned. Not over them hiring one, but the timing. Right before the second round of funding is due."

"What about trade secrets?" Phil asked.

"Oh, I'm certain Rooney has had him—"; Mark looked at Crystal and Sally. "—or her, sign a non-disclosure agreement. But I'll confirm that with Rooney."

After a few more questions, Mark turned to the main business of the meeting. "Okay. Let's start with you, Crystal. Where is the IPPI project and what will we be able to do—with certainty of success—in two weeks?"

"We hope to start loading data tomorrow. If all goes well, we should finish that phase by Wednesday. We'll test for the next week, then take two days to develop a 'show and tell.' I think we can give an impressive demonstration," she concluded.

Mark nodded. "Are you cutting it a little close? You've only allowed two days to develop and perfect the demo. That leaves little room for error. See if you can tighten things a bit and allow a little leeway on the demo. You don't want it to crash." He turned to Sally. "How about you?"

Sally was leaning back in her chair. Crystal thought for an instant Sally might have been asleep. She leaned forward, suddenly animated. "We're really rolling now. Barring any unforeseen problems, we'll give y'all a demo next week. We won't be completely finished for a while, but I think we can knock their socks off with what we have. We're going to impress even you, Mark."

"I'm not the important one to impress. But that's a good place to start. When should I schedule your demo?"

"How about next Wednesday?"

"Good. We'll all be there." Mark glanced at Phil, then looked at the other two. "You all know Phil's group has just started on their help-desk project. So, they're not going to have much to show. Mostly, it will be the plans and projections, and possibly a toy system to give them a feel for it. I believe that will be sufficient. They understand our timetable. They won't expect a completed system.

"But, Phil has come up with an idea that I will present to the VC guys to show that we're looking ahead, even as we are handling today's projects."

Crystal pushed the last of the donut into her mouth and glanced at Phil, who averted his eyes immediately. She guessed Phil's age at about fifty-five. He was tall, with gray eyes and mostly gray hair, which constantly looked like he had just emerged from the barbershop. Phil regularly wore a coat and tie, the only person in the office who did. He always exuded confidence and spoke with authority.

"Do you want to explain it, Phil?" Mark asked.

Without looking up, Phil said, "Ah, why don't, ah, maybe it ought to wait until after Rooney's visit."

"I think it's a terrific idea and we certainly want to put it before Rooney." Mark looked at Crystal and Sally. "Phil has suggested that we could apply some of the new IR techniques to monitor medical costs." For several minutes, Mark explained what might be done and how that could be commercially successful.

Crystal's mouth dropped open and she turned toward Phil with wide eyes. She had described exactly such a project to Phil only a few weeks ago. They had talked about it over lunch one day. He had been enthusiastic about its possibilities.

But, it had been *her* idea. Not Phil's.

She didn't understand what was going on. She stole another glance at Phil, who was looking at his hands, folded in his lap, and squirming slightly in his seat. Was he waiting for Mark to credit her?

Mark finished. "Any questions?"

No one spoke. Crystal started to, but didn't. *Am I being petty? No. That's my idea.* Still, she hated to make a big scene in front of everybody.

"Okay. Let's get after it. Make your people understand the importance of the next two weeks. Remind them that Rooney Associates is paying their salaries. And if I can help speed things along, don't walk, *run* to my office and ask."

He looked at each of his leaders, and gave a thumbs-up. Sally got up and left immediately, but Phil didn't move.

Maybe he's going to tell Mark it was my idea, Crystal thought. *If I sit here, it will be more difficult for him.* She got up and left without saying a word. But her mind was racing, bouncing between confusion, disbelief, and anger.

* * *

Twenty minutes later, Crystal burst into Mark's office, her face ashen. Her eyes looked as if they were holding back tears. Her steps were uncertain.

"Mark. The sheriff just called. Nana's house is on fire. Her car ... ." Her voice faltered. "Her car's there, but ... they can't find ... ." Her lower lip began to tremble, and she put her hand up to cover it. Her other hand grabbed the back of the chair to steady herself.

Chapter 11

"**HAVE** they ... ." He stopped and for several moments, just looked at Crystal, sharp lines creasing his forehead. "Let's take my truck and go check it out ourselves. Meet me in the parking lot in three minutes."

She took a deep breath, slowly regaining some control over her voice. "You don't have to go with me. I can drive myself." And then quickly, "But if you can, I'd ... ." Her voice trailed off.

"Three minutes. In the parking lot."

She turned and ran to her office.

* * *

Most of the trip was made in silence. For a while, they listened to a classical station. But when the reception began to flicker, Mark turned the radio off. Occasionally, he asked her about some landmark, or a community they passed through.

They sped east on Interstate 20. The countryside slowly began to shed its parched look. Around Dallas, what didn't get watered by man was yellow and brown by this time of the year. Go seventy miles East and the fields were green and growing.

To a Yankee this would present a real paradox. True to the image of Texas, there were large herds of cattle in the fields, although not many longhorns. But rather than the sagebrush and tumbleweed cliché, this part of Texas was downright lush. Perhaps all the movies about Texas were made in the western half of the state.

When they turned off I-20, they were in the pine forests and rolling hills of East Texas. "It isn't much farther, now," Crystal said. She gave directions when necessary but otherwise said nothing.

"The next road on the left is Nana's drive."

Mark slowed and turned between two pine trees that must have been over ninety feet tall. He rolled down his window to enjoy the crisp, fresh scent of the pine forest.

The driveway, a mixture of iron ore and sand, curved around to a bridge built out of railroad ties. The cutout of a roadrunner, his feet churning in the breeze, marked one edge of the bridge. On the other side, chasing in full stride, was Wile E. Coyote.

"Somebody out here has a delightful sense of humor," he said.

The road turned and began to climb. Mark glanced over at Crystal. "This place is absolutely beautiful."

"You can see why Nana won't move," she said, but today's circumstances stripped all enthusiasm from her voice.

They started a long, winding climb and now the acrid smell of burned wood began to invade the car and a gray haze permeated the woods in front of them. A low moan seeped from Crystal's rigid form.

Up ahead, pickups were scattered among the trees, hastily parked anywhere that would not be in the way. A little closer in, a sheriff's cruiser guarded the scene.

Two fire trucks stood a safe distance from the smoldering house, gently vibrating as the pumps worked to fill their tanks. A long hose from each truck snaked several hundred feet down the hill, disappearing into the lake. With no fire hydrants within miles, firemen would draw water from any available stream or lake. This time they were fortunate to have an ample supply within reach of their hoses.

The fire appeared to be out, but the closer they got, the worse the house looked. The trees seemed to be untouched by the fire, except for two which were singed around their bases.

Small spirals of smoke drifted up from holes in the roof. While the house had not burned to the ground, what remained was a structure, no longer a home. From this distance it appeared that the center of the building had been destroyed, while the two ends escaped the worst of the fire.

Mark stopped the truck a short distance from the police cruiser. Crystal had both hands on her face, covering her mouth. Her eyes were wet. Her entire body appeared as tight as a banjo string. A faint gasp escaped her drawn lips. Several seconds passed before she could move a hand to open the door.

The sheriff walked over to meet them.

"I'm so sorry, Crystal." He put an arm around her shoulders and held her.

The officer appeared to be in his mid-sixties, a short, stocky man with a weather-beaten face and a nose that had obviously been broken a few times. His hair was a bit longer than generally found on a law officer, but not long enough to hide large ears. A wide belt with a huge silver buckle cinched in most of an ample stomach, the rest bulging out like a squeezed balloon. His brown, western-cut shirt and brown jeans looked much newer and cleaner than his boots, which clearly had ridden many a dusty trail. He wore an old, but clean, buckskin Stetson.

After a minute, Crystal stepped back. She blinked excessively and the light in her eyes had faded to darkness. Stress lines formed across her brow. She swallowed and in a voice edged with fear said, "Sheriff Glothe, this is Mark O'Malley. I work for him."

The sheriff stuck out a hand that seemed a size too large for his height. "Howdy. Pleased to meet you." He had a slow Texan drawl that seemed so contrived in movies, yet was absolutely natural from him.

"Hello," Mark replied. "Was anybody in the house?"

The question had been lodged in Crystal's mind, but she could not ask it.

The sheriff looked a little surprised, perhaps that the question came from Mark. He stared at Mark for a moment, then turned his attention to Crystal. "They had a hard time getting the house under control, and then it was too hot to enter for a while. So, we don't know too much yet." He paused. "But there is a body in there."

Crystal gasped. She turned toward the house but her feet didn't move. Instead, she sank to her knees and began to sob quietly. "Not Nana. Not Nana, too."

It was barely a whisper, but it screamed in Crystal's head. Her parents, her grandfather, and now her only remaining family.

Mark knelt beside her and put his arm around her, pulling her to him. She folded in like a rag doll, limp against his shoulder, the soft sobs continuing.

Mark looked up at the sheriff and said quietly, "I saw a car near the house."

The sheriff's look was sufficient to answer Mark's implied question. After a minute, Gloths said almost in a whisper "It's Eula's." He stood there, thumbs hooked in his belt, watching Crystal, unable to offer any comfort to the young woman he had known all her life.

Finally, he spoke to Mark. "I'm going on back to see how the picture taking's coming along. If I can do anything, holler." He turned and plodded toward the house.

For a long time, Crystal wept for her grandmother. Mark simply held her. After a while, she pulled back a little and without looking at Mark, said, "I think I'll go sit by the lake for a bit."

"Would you like me to come with you, or would you rather be alone?"

"Alone, I think." And she started down the hill toward the lake.

* * *

It tore at Mark's heart to watch the energetic Crystal he knew, transformed by sorrow, shoulders slumped, head drooping, feet dragging. Grief had devoured her spirit. He hadn't known Eula Moore, but Crystal's sorrow was so consuming he felt depressed that he would never have that opportunity.

Mark's grandparents had all died before he was old enough to know them. But he vividly remembered his father's death. Mark had finished his Ph.D. and was working in Minnesota. He could still hear the words: your father has suffered a heart attack; he's in intensive care—the doctor doesn't think he'll survive.

Mark had been lucky enough to get a plane to Dallas in less than three hours and a fast taxi got him to the hospital in record time. One look at his mother told him he was too late. Too late to say good-bye. Too late to say I love you. Too late to hold his father's hand one last time.

First, grief had overwhelmed Mark. Then guilt. He hadn't talked to his father in three weeks. He hadn't visited him in seven months. He loved his father and they shared a good relationship. But Mark let his emerging career get in the way.

He didn't have time . . . and then, there was no time.

At that moment, he had decided to move back near his mother. Whatever the situation, Mark hated to make the same mistake twice.

So he understood some of the feelings flooding Crystal's mind and overwhelming her heart right now: grief, guilt, despair, so many things she would like to have said, an empty spot that wouldn't be filled; and already, loneliness.

He started toward the house, watching one of the firemen take something from a fire truck and head back to the charred house.

Mark walked over to talk with Glothe. "How did the fire department get notified?"

"We got a lucky break. Well, not so lucky, seeing as how Eula's dead. But Jimmy over there," he nodded at one of the firemen, "he was driving down the oil road and saw the smoke. Said he knew right away it was a house. 'Course all the volunteers have radios with them. So, he radioed in the call and came right on up. Said he tried to get in to see if there was anybody in there. But it was too hot and smoky, and he didn't have his bunker gear till the first truck got here."

"Did I see one of them taking a body bag in?"

"Yeah." Bill Glothe turned to spit into the dirt. "Body's burned pretty bad. Don't want Crystal to see it."

"The medical examiner's already been here?"

"No ME's in the county. Willa Waltherson, she's the Justice of the Peace, she handles it. She's come and gone. Accidental death in a fire. Slim's finished taking his pictures."

"Have they determined how the fire started?"

The sheriff shook his head. "Off hand, they think it started in the kitchen. Makes sense. Either that or an electrical short."

For a few minutes, neither man said anything. Glothe watched the men working. Mark looked down toward the lake. A lonely figure huddled on the small dock, arms around knees, looking out over the water. She was too far away for Mark to hear any sounds of grief, but from time to time, a shudder ran through the slender back.

Mark considered going down to the lake, then decided it would intrude on Crystal's grief. This was a good-bye better said in private.

He turned back to the sheriff. "Is it all right if I go in and look around?"

"Real mess in there—water and everything burned. And some of it's still smoldering. But if you want to, go ahead. Don't touch anything, though. We'd like to find out exactly how it started."

"Thanks. I'll keep my hands in my pockets."

"Suppose I ought to go in myself and check on the bagging of the body. Guess I've been avoiding it. I've known Eula for . . ." Glothe cocked his head to one side. ". . . I guess forty years. Thirty-five years ago, the wife and I started going camping with Eula and Dan, that was her husband, Crystal's grandfather. Did 'til he died five or six years ago. Eula was quite a gal. Kind as could be, but tough. Nobody ever whipped their shoes on her. Dan used to say nobody ever broke her, never even got a bridle on her. 'Course, he managed her pretty well." He let out a long breath. "Anyway, we had a lot of good times together. I'm going to miss her. Everybody in Nickel will."

Chapter 12

MARK heard the car before he saw it through the trees. An old, faded blue Chevy, in need of a new muffler, rumbled to a stop next to the sheriff's car. A tattered bumper sticker proclaimed, "Truth is all we've got."

"Here comes the fourth estate," said Glothe. "That's what Sam calls himself. Never said what the other three was."

"Actually, the term goes back a couple of hundred years to the British parliament. It had three estates: peers, bishops and commons. Someone thought the newspapers were about as powerful, and referred to them as the fourth estate."

"Oh." Glothe looked like he was sorry he had mentioned it.

Sam Teeter walked with a slight limp. He was a short man, with light brown hair just beginning to let his scalp show through on top. He wore beige slacks and shirt, and was carrying a small notebook and tape recorder. *Somehow*, Mark thought, *he looks more like a large tumbleweed than the fourth estate.*

"We heard you coming, Sam," Bill greeted him.

"The old blue goose does announce my arrival. I can't afford a trumpet. Long time no see."

Glothe turned to Mark. "This is Sam Teeter, editor of the Wooden Nickel Gazette. Also the paper's comedian. We ate breakfast together a few hours ago. Sam, Mark O'Malley, Crystal's boss."

Sam nodded. "Glad to meet you. Sorry it had to be under these circumstances. Where's Cris?"

Glothe answered. "Down at the lake."

Sam turned his head and gazed toward the lake. "What happened?"

"Well, we don't know yet. Looks like the fire started in the kitchen. Eula was on the floor in the kitchen. At this point, we don't know whether she fell and hit her head, got overcome by smoke and passed out, or what. Body was burned pretty bad. If it wasn't her house and her car outside, we wouldn't know for sure who it was."

"Who called it in?"

Glothe filled him in with the information available. "They did a good job containing it. It didn't even get to the car shed."

"Timing being what it is, we'll just get it in this week's paper. Everybody knew Eula. It's page one." He looked back toward the lake. "I guess I'll go offer my condolences to Cris."

Mark looked at the tape recorder. He wasn't surprised the editor of the local paper wanted to talk to the grieving granddaughter but it didn't seem like a fair thing to do at this time. "Let me go down first and tell her you're here. See if she's ready."

Sam Teeter locked Mark's eyes with a penetrating gaze. "Mr. O'Malley, I've known Cris a lot longer than you have. I probably understand her and her feelings better, too. I said I was going to offer my sympathy, and I'm quite capable of doing that on my own. If you're concerned that I might interview her and ask her questions that will make her feel worse, that's because you're not from around here. You can rest easy. And you can stay here." Then, abruptly, he turned and started down the hill.

Glothe laid a hand lightly on Mark's shoulder. "It's okay. He thinks of Crystal as the daughter he never had. He won't do anything to make matters worse."

Mark watched Sam negotiate the hill, the limp more pronounced as the slope got steeper. As he neared the bottom, Crystal raised her head and saw Sam. Slowly, she got to her feet, put her arms around him and laid her head on his shoulder.

By now, several of the volunteer firemen were putting their equipment away and taking off their heavy protective clothing. The sheriff had gone back inside and was talking with the fire chief.

Mark surveyed the area. He still had trouble with yellow fire trucks. Everybody knew fire engines were red. And while he had to admit the yellow really did stand out, somehow, it just seemed to destroy yet another childhood memory. He shook his head, and walked over to join the sheriff.

"I think everything will be fine," Glothe was saying. "Not likely anybody would come up here."

The fire chief, whom Glothe had called Buddy Wright, stood with his hands on his hips and his square jaw thrust out. Mark judged him to be in his mid forties, and not one who laughed much, even when he wasn't around a fatal fire. "Well, we're going to wind up pretty quick now. Jimmy'll take the body to the funeral home. Willa's signed off on it?"

Glothe nodded.

"I'll be back tomorrow to do some more checking. Still don't really know how or where it started. But nothing reaches out and grabs me that this is anything but an accidental fire. Eula was just in the wrong pen at the wrong auction."

"Your men did a fine job, Buddy. Don't think there was any more they could have done. And from what Jimmy told me, Eula was probably dead by the time he got here."

"Thanks. Sorry as we are over the way things turned out, don't think there was anything we could've done about it. Call you tomorrow when I'm ready to wrap this up."

Buddy plodded out the door, his powerful shoulders drooping, his muscular arms hanging at his sides. Mark suspected the weariness was not so much from the physical work, as from the emotional toll taken today.

"Is there anything Crystal needs to do here?" Mark asked the sheriff.

"Not's far as I'm concerned. Only one funeral home in town. She's gonna need to make some arrangements with them tonight or tomorrow. Tomorrow oughta be soon enough, unless she's planning on moving the body someplace else."

"I can't imagine she would."

"I figure she'll be 'round here for a few days, if anything comes up. But I don't reckon I'll need her."

Crystal trudged in the door. For a moment, the sun reflected off a shiny, cloisonné earring, sending a jolt through Mark. Not foreseeing today's events, Crystal had chosen bright, laughing clowns to adorn her ears.

"Crystal, I was just telling Mark the boys are taking Eula to the funeral home. You might want to drop in and talk to them tomorrow. You probably know your grandmother used Travis Logger as her lawyer. You're staying in the area tonight?"

"Yes." She looked at Mark. "If you need to get back, I can rent a car." Her voice was a lifeless monotone.

Without thinking, Mark glanced out the back door toward the shed.

"No. No. I couldn't drive Nana's car. Not for a while, anyway."

"I don't need to hurry back," Mark said. "I'll stay over."

"Thanks." She looked at Glothe, her eyes dark with pain. "I guess we'll be at the Good Night, if they have any space."

"They'll have rooms. If it isn't Founders' Weekend or Ancestors' Day, they're mostly empty." He looked around the room. "I think everything'll be okay. But you might want to take a look today or tomorrow to see if there's anything of value you want to get. You know your grandmother never would have a gate on the place. Now, I've never known that to be a problem. But with no one living here, well, you might want to think on putting a chain across the road, or something. Just to keep the curious out."

Crystal's shoulders sagged and her arms hung like dead weight at her side. Her whole body looked unstable, as if it might topple over at any moment. Her eyes, bloodshot from crying, seemed to sink deeper into her face. This had happened too suddenly. She had had no time to prepare, to think about things like gates or chains or lawyers or funeral homes. *Like my father's heart attack*, Mark thought.

She didn't respond. Mark put a hand on her shoulder. "We'll be here a few days, Sheriff. And we'll talk with you before we leave."

"Much obliged. Oh, one other thing. Sam closes the paper around ten tomorrow morning. Everybody hereabouts liked Eula. Be nice if Sam put when and where the funeral was going to be in the obituary. Lot of people will come."

"I'll try to get it settled before then," Crystal said, her voice almost mechanical.

Bill touched the brim of his hat, and walked out the door.

Crystal surveyed the room for a moment. "Mark, I can't deal with this today. Let's go in and get rooms. Mostly I just want to be by myself so I can cry in private. I promise I'll be better tomorrow."

"No promise necessary."

* * *

At the Good Night Inn Crystal declined dinner and went straight to her room. Mark read last week's Gazette while he ate catfish in the Inn's restaurant. Both were surprisingly good, he thought.

Back in his room he congratulated himself for grabbing a stack of notes on the way out of the office. He sat down at the small desk, powered up his portable computer and began to work. His investors were coming and the death of a relative wouldn't delay them. Intelligent Retrieval Systems had two weeks to look its very best.

Somehow, he would have to talk to Crystal tomorrow about her Identification from Partial Plate Information project. From what he had witnessed today, he doubted she would be able to lead her group for a while. He wondered how much progress her team could make without her. IPPI could be a major factor in determining the second round of funding. And the fate of IRS.

* * *

Next door, Crystal fell into a fitful sleep. Her troubled mind flashed pictures behind her closed eyes, pictures of her Nana dodging cars and careening down hills in a car with no brakes. Part of the time, Crystal was sitting on the dock, looking out over the lake, completely ignoring Nana's calls to her. Then, suddenly, she leaped up and raced after her grandmother's car, which was now out of sight. Dr. Krupe stood at the top of the hill. Crystal tried to go around him, but he reached out with a giant hand. The fingers were snakes that wrapped around her, preventing her from saving her grandmother. She looked around, desperately searching for someone to help. Then, she saw her grandmother come back and go into the house. For an instant, she felt relieved, but quick as a sneeze she plunged into deep panic. Near the door, Phil was talking to Mark. She called to them, but neither even noticed. She saw flames serge through the roof. She looked back at the house. No one was there. She clawed and scratched at Krupe and finally broke away, falling to the ground.

Crystal's eyes popped open as she hit the floor. The sheet was so tangled around her she couldn't move. She could taste panic creeping up her throat. She rolled over, yanking at the sheet, fighting her fear, struggling to free her body. Finally, she managed to break out of the tangled sheet.

She lay there, shaking and wet with sweat. Dr. Krupe had told her she was worthless. Now, all her family had left her. Her mother, her father, her grandfather and now her Nana. All gone. She was cold. And utterly alone.

After several minutes, she stood up, slipped the light blanket off the bed, wrapped it around herself and sat in a chair. She read the clock that sat on the bedside table. 10:35. The night had barely begun.

Chapter 13

IT was mid-afternoon before Mark and Crystal headed back to The Park. They had eaten breakfast at the Nickel Diner, then walked a short block to the funeral home to make funeral arrangements. For a while, Crystal had kept her emotions under control, making the necessary decisions in a business-like fashion. Only when she had to select a casket did the tears come. But she managed to complete the arrangements. The funeral would be Thursday morning at the Wooden Nickel Baptist Church.

Next, they had gone to the Wooden Nickel Gazette where she talked to Sam Teeter. Mark was impressed with the way Sam handled things. He looked like a gnarled, tough old reporter, but he was as gentle with Crystal as a person could be under the circumstances. He managed to ask her questions about Eula that actually brought smiles to Crystal's face. Once or twice, Mark thought she might lose her composure. Each time, Sam would turn a corner and bring the conversation to a less painful aspect.

After lunch, Crystal and Mark stopped by the law office of Travis Logger. The lawyer assured Crystal there would be no problems, probably not even probate. Everything was in good order and everything went to Crystal. They could go over the details of what had to be done after the funeral. Crystal walked out of the office, but Mark stepped back in and asked Logger about mineral rights. The lawyer looked surprised, mumbled something about covering that with Crystal later, and ushered Mark out.

When they got back to the car, Mark said, "You know, Crystal, you don't have to go through the house today if you don't feel up to it."

"It has to be done."

Crystal looked straight ahead as Mark started the car and

pointed it toward The Park. Several minutes passed before she broke the silence. "Nana was such an important part of my life. Even before my parents were killed, I spent summers here. Nana taught me about birds and flowers and bugs and trees. After my parents were killed, she and Granddad were all I had. Then he died. Nana *was* my family. She had a strong will, but she was the sweetest person you'd ever meet. I will miss her. I already do."

Mark glanced over at Crystal. Her eyes were moist but she was smiling at the memory of her grandmother.

* * *

Eula's home was what Mark thought of as a walkout ranch. A general living area occupied the middle, with bedrooms on either end. The center section had a large kitchen, open above a counter into the dining area. The living and dining rooms combined into a room fifty feet long. A large fieldstone fireplace dominated one end.

The ceiling slanted from a normal height on the north side to eighteen feet high over the porch. The south wall consisted almost entirely of glass, overlooking a large porch that faced the lake several hundred feet down a gentle, grassy slope dotted with stately pines.

From the looks of things, Mark decided the fire had started in the kitchen. Ceiling, walls, cabinets and counters were severely damaged. It looked like the fire had escaped from the kitchen through the opening above the counter into the dining room, destroying the wall over the pass-through and parts of the ceiling. Mark saw blue sky through gaping holes in the roof. One large, plate glass panel in the dining room had shattered, most likely from the heat.

Walls and ceilings of the bedrooms on the east end were charred. Much of the damage on the west end came from smoke and water.

Mark felt it best to let Crystal explore alone. There was a time to share grief and there was a time to grieve alone. Her pain showed so clearly, like an open gash through her flesh, all the way to her soul. Mark was embarrassed even to witness it. Every once in a while, he would hear a sob from another room, as Crystal discovered another item that evoked particularly painful memories. She moved like a zombie, no life in her eyes or her actions. Mark felt himself sinking into the sorrow that saturated the air like the strong scent of wisteria.

At one point in their separate journeys through the wreckage, Crystal walked into the dining room and gently placed a half-burned doll on the charred table, beside other things she had salvaged. "Nana gave it to me before I started to school," she said, a catch in her voice. Without ever looking at Mark, she left the room.

He wandered out the front of the house and onto the veranda to inspect the damage there. In the distance he heard a car approaching. *Probably the fire marshal. Or Bill Glothe.*

Mark liked Glothe. In their brief meetings yesterday and today, Bill came across as a straight shooter, not claiming more than he could deliver, not trying to make things look better than they were.

Mark's thoughts turned back to the fire. He tried to picture the path of the flames that would create the burn patterns in the kitchen. And what was Eula Moore doing that she got trapped by the fire? Did she come in to find the fire raging? Or was she in the kitchen when it started? What——

"Hell's bells!"

The voice didn't belong to either Glothe or Buddy Wright. Mark turned and started across the veranda. Through the broken window, he saw Crystal come into the living room and head toward the back of the house. She jolted to a stop, as if hitting a wall, and clasped her hands to her face. A small gasp escaped through her fingers and all color drained from her face. Her eyes rolled back in their sockets, all of her muscles seemed to relax at once, and in slow motion, she crumpled to the floor.

Chapter 14

THE woman couldn't have known who the man was coming in from the veranda, but clearly she was accustomed to giving orders to friends and strangers alike. "Run cold water on a hand towel and bring it here. Squeeze it out first."

Mark was not in an order-taking mood. He could see Crystal, lying on the floor, apparently unconscious, and he intended to check on her.

"You deaf or something? Get me a wet towel!"

The last was delivered with such authority that he at once changed directions and headed for the bathroom to follow orders. When he returned, the woman was sitting on the floor, cradling Crystal's head in her lap, fanning her face and speaking softly to her. The woman took the towel from Mark without comment and gently wiped Crystal's face and neck, then folded the towel and placed it on Crystal's forehead. The harsh tone used with Mark had given way to a velvet-soft voice.

Another woman, whom Mark had not noticed before, was also sitting on the floor, holding Crystal's feet in her lap.

Generally, Mark took charge of a situation, dictated what needed to be done. Now, he stood and watched the two women worry over Crystal. He could not think of anything he would do differently.

Crystal's eyelids fluttered for a moment, then opened. She stared at the woman holding her head. "Nana? Is that really you?"

"And who else might it be?" the woman asked.

Crystal smiled and tears flowed freely down her cheeks as she pulled the woman's head down and held it next to hers. Through sobs, she said, "I thought you were dead."

"Now, why would you think that?" Eula kept her arms around her granddaughter, rocking gently.

Suddenly, Crystal let go of her grandmother and moved her head back a little to look at her. "They found a woman's body here, burned in the fire. Your car was outside."

Eula's arms went slack and a look of anguish descended over her face. "Oh, my God."

Melva Larson frowned. "Bessie!"

Neither woman said another word. Melva closed her eyes, and slowly shook her head. Eula stared out the window. Her very spirit seemed to wilt.

Finally, Eula broke the silence. "Bessie Longson wanted to spend some time here. Buried her last relative and didn't want to go back to her place just yet. We were going camping down by Gun Barrel and asked her to go with us, but she declined. Never did like to camp. So I gave her my car and said to come and go as she pleased." She rocked a little and tightened her grip on Crystal. "Oh, Bessie. Bessie. Why didn't you go with us? I'm so sorry."

Silence again shrouded the group. Mark felt awkward but didn't want to disturb the private thoughts of the three women, even by walking away. Eula took a deep breath and patted Crystal's hand. "What happened?"

Crystal sat up. "Bill and Buddy think it was an accident. Maybe some grease caught on fire while ... ." Crystal stopped, and tried to swallow the lump in her throat. ". . . while Bessie was cooking. She might have dropped the pan when the grease flared. They don't know whether she fell and hit her head, or was overcome by smoke."

"The Justice of the Peace declared it an accident," Mark interjected. "The body was badly burned. At this point, they don't really know what happened."

Eula shook her head. "Old Billy Goat's been thrown again."

Mark didn't know what was going through her mind. But from her tone and demeanor, he had the feeling that whatever it was, she was right.

"Nana, don't start picking on Bill. You weren't here. You don't know what happened."

"You're right, Crystal. I wasn't here and I don't know what happened. But I know what *didn't* happen. Bessie didn't start a fire while she was cooking. Only thing Bessie's cooked for the last few years was popcorn—and she nuked that."

Crystal looked at her grandmother with disbelief. "She couldn't live on just popcorn."

"Pert' near," said Melva. "That, chocolate, granola bars, and an occasional can of Ensure."

"I can tell you this, Mrs. Moore," said Mark. "The fire didn't start in the microwave or the refrigerator."

"Call me Eula. And I been meaning to ask, who are you?"

"I'm sorry, Nana," said Crystal. "This is Mark O'Malley, my boss."

Eula surveyed Mark from head to toe. "O'Malley." She furrowed her brows, tilted her head over, and just studied him. Mark shifted his weight from one foot to the other, uncomfortable under the appraisal.

Finally, she smiled and asked, "Might you be Bull O'Malley?"

Crystal's mouth fell open.

Mark grinned sheepishly. "Yes, ma'am, I just might be."

"You know Mark?" Crystal asked in disbelief.

"I don't reckon it's fair to say I know him, but I've seen him a few times. A so-so roper, but one of the best bull riders I ever saw. Why'd you quit?"

"I went off to graduate school at MIT. It didn't leave me much time for riding."

"Shame. I wondered if it was that old Beutler Brothers bull that tossed you up in the air." She laughed down deep in her throat. "I still got that picture of you and the moon." Eula glanced around at the house and sighed. "Well, I used to."

Crystal looked even more puzzled. "What are you two talking about?"

Mark waved his hand. "Nothing. It was a long time ago."

"Oh, it was something, all right. Bull—never heard him called Mark back then—finishes his ride, and the bull is looking at the clown. So Mark turns and starts walking to the gate. Well, the bull forgets the clown, lowers his head, and comes after Bull, ah, Mark. He gets his horns under the seat of Bull's pants and then flips his head up. Well, Bull goes flying." Eula giggled. "Now, this photographer is in the ring taking a picture of the clown. He's down low, don't you see. So he turns and shoots up to get this picture of

Mark."

Eula put her hands in front of her face like she was holding a camera and demonstrated. "Makes the front page of every paper 'round here. There's Mark up in the air, with the moon in the background lookin' like it's *under* him." She giggled again. "'Course you know what the headline was: 'And the Bull jumped over the moon.'"

"Oh my gosh. Were you hurt?" Crystal asked Mark.

"My pride was crushed and I was sore for a week. But nothing broken. I was lucky. Never turned my back on a bull again."

Crystal turned to her grandmother. "Where was I?"

"If you recall, you didn't like rodeos. Whenever your granddad and me went rodeoing, you took off for a dance or movie or something."

"While I was in high school?"

"High school, middle school. I don't know."

"I hate to be a wet blanket," said Melva. "But what do we need to do about Bessie?"

The happy mood vanished at the single word "Bessie," and once again everyone was somber.

Eula looked at Crystal. "I'm guessing Sam was here. What's going to be in the Gazette tomorrow?" She looked at her watch. "Too late to change it; reckon it's printed by now."

"It's going to say you were killed in the fire, Nana. And your funeral's day after tomorrow."

Eula stared out the window without saying anything for several moments. Long shadows reached far down the hill. Already, crickets were chirping.

"Bessie's got no next of kin to notify. And we're her main friends. Guess we could get Sam to print up a flyer saying I'm alive and kicking, and Bessie's the one that's gone to meet her maker."

"Mrs. Moore," Mark began.

"Eula."

"Eula, I'm really the outsider here, but may I toss out an idea for you to consider, if you don't mind?"

"Toss away."

"Let the paper come out as written. Let the funeral go on as planned."

All three women stared at him with the same look of disbelief. Eula recovered first and blurted out, "Why?"

Mark hadn't thought this through completely. Withholding the truth might cause some undesired consequences. But it would be too late to consider alternatives once they called the newspaper. He plunged in. "I feel strongly this fire was not an accident. And I agree with you one hundred percent. Someone is trying to kill you."

Crystal and Melva gaped in silence. Eula's eyebrows shot up and her eyes blinked several times. "Well. 'Bout time somebody else sees the obvious." She looked at Crystal. "Just cause I'm old don't mean I can't tell when someone's trying to kill me." She turned to Mark. "Young man, you toss ideas a heckova lot better'n you did ropes."

Chapter 15

THIRTY minutes later, the four had a plan. Crystal called Bill Glothe and asked him to come out. Glothe said he was short-handed; could they handle this on the telephone? Crystal insisted he come.

When the sheriff arrived, Eula headed for a back room. "Crystal, you need to break the news. If I just pop out, old Billy Goat might have a heart attack or something."

Crystal told Glothe it was probably Bessie Longson who died in the fire and for a moment, Bill just looked puzzled. "Nana's alive, Bill."

The sheriff flinched and his jaw dropped. He found his voice and asked where she was.

"I'm right here, Bill, and I'm fine," Eula said as she walked into the room. She went over and wrapped her arms around Glothe. Crystal had to smile. These two acted tough as rawhide, but in fact were tender as slow cooked barbeque.

After a few minutes the three women went to Eula's bedroom to see what clothes they could salvage. Mark and Bill stood in the kitchen. Glothe took his hat off and wiped his forehead on his shirtsleeve. "So, why couldn't a dropped pan of burning grease have done that?"

"I'm not an arson investigator. And I hope you can get one out here as soon as possible. But, three things struck me about the burn pattern. First, look at the alligator effect here. That's the kind of pattern you get when an accelerant is used on wood. See how it looks all wrinkled, like alligator skin?"

Glothe put his hat back on, pursed his lips and shook his head. "How do you know that?"

"Grew up next door to a fireman. Second, if the accelerant were grease from a pan, it would be more localized and more circular. See the deeper burns here, almost in a straight line? Not much to the sides.

"The third thing, and most important, I believe, it appears to be heaviest away from the stove and gets thinner toward the stove." He pointed to the area he was describing. "If she picked up the skillet ... . He demonstrated. "... heading for the sink and dropped the pan, it would seem to me that the most concentration would be nearer the stove. These show deeper burning away from the stove and it gets thinner toward the stove."

"She didn't cook, boys." Eula walked into the room. "Figure all you want. Bessie didn't start the fire."

"Now, Eula, you know I got to check facts and not just opinions." Glothe sounded like he was apologizing to her.

"And the fact is, Bessie didn't cook. That's the only *fact* you got. Burn patterns and accelerants is guessing. But I'll just get my glass of water and leave y'all to it."

Glothe ignored Eula's remark. "State Fire Marshall has an office in Tyler. They'll send someone out if we request it."

"You haven't asked for my opinion," Mark said. "But that hasn't stopped me from giving it. I think you ought to put in a request today."

Bill nodded.

"What did the JP say about how she died?"

Eula muttered "Humph" as she left the room.

"Willa said she died in the fire. Burned." Glothe pressed his lips together. "I did ask Doc Simms to have a look. He's a pathologist over at the hospital. He'd be the first to tell you he ain't no forensic man. But he says she was likely dead before she got burned. Skull was cracked. Probably from hitting the counter when she fell. It's got—well, it had—a pretty sharp edge."

"I think Eula's right. Bessie didn't start the fire. Could you get a forensic pathologist to look at the body? Do an autopsy?"

Glothe cracked the knuckles of his left hand. "We do that sometimes. Pretty good guy in Tyler, Doc Haas. Course, usually Willa suggests it and calls him."

Mark didn't say anything.

"Guess I could get Doc Simms to call. Maybe make him think it was his idea."

"Good. How about not letting it out that Eula is alive?"

"That's a bigger stump." The sheriff shook his head and drew his mouth into a straight line. "Sam's printed a story that she's dead. And all the people at the funeral—they oughta know."

Mark knew Bill was right. Nonetheless, he took a deep breath and waded in. "You told Sam what you believed was the truth. And he can't print anything different for a week. In fact, what a great headline for next week's Gazette: Eula lives!" He tried smiling, but Bill was looking deadly serious. Mark's smile faded. "I don't know what to say about the people at the funeral. Just act as if Eula hadn't come back from her camping trip until after the funeral."

Mark could see that Glothe was still unconvinced. "The most important thing is to keep Eula safe. If she's right, and I believe she is, the guy has tried three times. And, he killed someone he thought was Eula." He looked away, then refocused on Glothe's eyes, holding their gaze for several moments before continuing. "If he knows Eula's alive, he'll try again. And he's getting closer, more deadly, every time."

Mark had made his case. Glothe had to decide what to do. Mark heard a noise and turned to see Crystal passing the door. He hoped she had not heard his last statement.

* * *

After Sheriff Glothe left, Mark wandered out onto the deck, partly to get away from the disheartening smell of burnt wood, and partly to let the beauty of The Park blot out the senseless destruction inside. Five minutes later, Crystal came out the door, her demeanor much improved. "We're going over to Melva's for the night, Mark. I think I'd like to stay for a day or two. Why don't you go on back to Dallas and prepare for the VC."

"I could use some time in the office," Mark agreed.

"Check on the data loading for the IPPI. They know what to do, but there is one tricky spot you might check on." Crystal outlined the potential trouble area, what should be looked for and how to handle it. "I've talked about it with Carol and Donald, so they'll probably be Okay. But if you have time, I'd feel better if you looked in on them. I should be back on Friday to oversee the testing."

* * *

Crystal felt drained, but happy. With the venture capitalists coming in ten days, she should be worrying about her project. She wasn't. Her relief at finding Nana alive and well brought into focus what she had known all along, but had been forgetting: family was more important than job.

She turned and started back in the house. The burned kitchen brought Mark's words screaming back in her mind. "If he knows Eula's alive, he'll try again. And he's getting closer, more deadly every time."

Chapter 16

THE funeral took place at the Wooden Nickel Baptist Church. With considerable misgivings, Glothe had agreed to let the funeral go on as if Eula had been the victim in the fire. Her safety, he rationalized, warranted bending the rules.

"Hope I don't get disbarred over this," he told Eula. Crystal refrained from mentioning that he wasn't a lawyer.

Crystal and Melva attended the funeral together, the grieving granddaughter and the best friend. A sad and depressed appearance came naturally for Crystal; she understood the killer would try again as soon as he found out Eula was alive.

A lady from the church spoke first. Melva, the logical choice, had begged off, saying she was so emotionally wrought she wouldn't even try to speak at the funeral. Travis Logger, Eula's lawyer, gave the eulogy.

Eula had been unhappy when she heard he was speaking. "He's just going to be trying for more customers, if I know Travis. 'Course, he'll have to say some nice stuff about me, and he'll probably say it better than most. Can't get new clients by bad-mouthing someone at her own funeral."

Crystal decided Eula had been right. Logger's choice of words could not be faulted, but his manner and delivery made him sound like a politician running for reelection. He looked the part, too. Most of the men were dressed in conservative black or gray suits. Logger wore a powder blue, three-piece suit with a power-red tie and highly polished wing-tip shoes. What caught Crystal's eye, though, was a heavy gold watch chain. She couldn't remember when she'd last seen someone with a watch chain draped across his vest.

Sam Teeter spoke at the graveside. For ten minutes he talked of the woman he had known for fifty years. Half the town had come to the funeral, and few eyes remained dry. Sam's soft eloquence revealed feelings so deep that Crystal found herself wiping her eyes more than once. Sam ended by saying, "Eula Moore was as tough as a two-dollar steak, and as soft as a mother's kiss. Those who didn't love her were those who didn't know her."

* * *

Crystal had firmly refused to have any sort of a visitation, and told no one she was staying with Melva. After the funeral, Bill Glothe drove them to Melva's house, where Eula was hiding.

"Well, how was my funeral?" asked Eula, as soon as the three got in the door.

"It was beautiful, Nana, particularly since you aren't dead."

"Too sad," said Melva. "Needed more music. And food."

Eula chuckled. "Well, since it was really Bessie's funeral, it's appropriate that nobody cooked."

"Sounds like Travis is planning to run for office soon," said Glothe.

"That man talks so much I don't see how he breathes. What did Sam have to say about me?"

"Let me put it this way, Nana. I knew you were alive and healthy, and Sam's eulogy still brought tears to my eyes."

"And everybody else's," added Glothe.

"Bill, did you see anybody suspicious? Or any strangers?" Melva asked.

The sheriff reached up and scratched his large, right ear. "Nope. And I scoped the crowd pretty good."

"Course not. They believe I'm dead and what's a closed coffin gonna tell 'em? They've already been back to The Park, messing around."

Everybody stared at Eula.

"What are you saying, Nana?"

"I'm saying I went out there to look around during the funeral. Figured nobody'd see me."

Glothe shook his head. "Thought we agreed you'd stay out of sight, Eula. Some curious folks might have been out there, and seen you."

"Anybody interested enough to go look should've been at the

funeral. Anyway, I was about to tell you before I got interrupted. Somebody's been there, yesterday or last night."

"How do you know that, Nana?"

"Anything missing from the house?" Bill asked.

"Nothing missing. But the boat's been moved. Not much. Like maybe they tried to put it back where it was, but missed by a mite."

"Now Eula," Bill began, both hands up with palms facing her. "Don't get your back up, but how can you be sure? The house has been burned and you haven't been in the boat in a while."

"Suddenly I look senile or something? Crystal and I went over the house pretty good Wednesday. They might've been in the house but they didn't move anything. But they moved the boat between yesterday morning and today."

Her chin was set and no one challenged her.

Bill chose his words carefully. "You think of any reason somebody'd move the boat? Some kids wanting to fish, maybe?"

"Can't think of any reason. It's rarer 'n hen's teeth for kids to sneak in and fish without asking me first. And then it's off the bank or the dock. I've never known 'em to use the boat. Not in forty years."

"Well, I'll run by and check on it." Bill got up to leave.

"Don't you want to stay and eat dinner?" Eula asked. "Got chicken 'n' dumplings on the stove."

"I'm ready," said Crystal.

"Mighty tempting. But I'd better get back to work. See y'all. Nice funeral, Eula."

* * *

With the midday meal finished and the dishes washed and put away, Eula and Melva sat on the back porch shelling purple hull peas. Crystal changed from her funeral attire to comfortable jeans and a blouse and settled down in a big easy chair in the living room, eyes closed, her mind looking for answers. She didn't doubt for a moment that the boat had been moved. But why? What did burning the house have to do with moving the boat? Unless someone wanted to get rid of Eula so they could check out the lake. For what? Certainly not fish.

She had already made it clear she had to go back to Dallas

today because of the upcoming visit by the investors. She would take Nana's car and arrange to get it back over the weekend. Eula was in hiding and wouldn't need it. Besides, she could use Melva's car if she got desperate.

Crystal decided she would swing by The Park on her way to Dallas. She went back to talk with her grandmother.

"Guess I ought to be heading back to Dallas, Nana."

"So soon? I haven't even had a chance to talk with you about Mark. He looks like grade A."

"Yes. He's nice to work for. Is your car———"

"When I called you the other night, I talked with your roommate."

"Housemate. Is your car okay to drive to Dallas? "

"Of course. She didn't sound like what I expected."

"What do you mean?"

"Not as educated as you."

"Well, she's really nice. And funny. We get along great." Crystal thought about Brandi's assessment of Dr. Krupe. "Besides, she's very smart. Smarter than I am about a lot of things."

"That was Friday night. She said you were over at Mark's. Anything I ought 'o know? Or'd like to hear?"

"No." It came out sounding defensive. "I needed to ask him something about work." *That sounded weak*, Crystal thought.

"On a Friday night?"

"Strictly business, Nana. Got to go. I'll call you tomorrow." She gave her grandmother a hug, said good-bye to Melva and left.

* * *

She parked the car under the carport behind the house and made her way down to the lake. The cobalt blue water made the trees appear even greener. Once more, the lake cast a sense of tranquility over Crystal. Easily her favorite part of The Park, it might have been her favorite spot in the world.

Why would anybody want to search the lake? Probably nobody does; just a dumb idea on my part, she thought. Nonetheless, she tried to imagine possibilities, even wild and silly ideas: a Loch Ness monster, a twenty foot bass, sunken treasure, the body of a famous mobster, the underwater entrance to a cave which had prehistoric drawings on its walls, the gun that killed Lincoln. None seemed even remotely possible.

The ten-foot rowboat was beached a short distance from a floating dock. As Crystal untied the boat from a small tree, something on the ground caught her eye. She reached down to pick up a short, dark brown cylinder. The brand name was lost, but it was one of the cigarillos gaining popularity in Dallas. Not the kind of tobacco sold in Wooden Nickel. And it was relatively fresh. Crystal guessed it had been there no more than a day or two. Would she have noticed it when she was here Monday? Maybe; maybe not. Didn't matter. This butt didn't look like it had been here that long. She dropped it back on the sand, launched the boat and hopped in.

For thirty minutes, Crystal paddled around, looking for any signs of activity, anything unusual. Across the lake from the dock, she checked an inlet where the tranquil reed-covered shallows and a marshy bank gave way to the steep, pine-covered slope. It offered no insight into the mystery. Near the east end of the lake, a small stream trickled in. Today, it was barely running, but the bed and banks gave testament to the greater volume of water it sometimes carried.

Generally, the shoreline was dotted with bushes and small trees, in keeping with the manicured appearance maintained around the house and lake. Occasionally, there was a brushy area to contrast the predominantly tidy landscaping.

Floating near the steep bank, Crystal's mind drifted back to lazy summer days, sitting in the boat, her granddad teaching her how to bait a hook, cast the line under the shade of a cypress tree, and how to set the hook when a fish rose to the bait. She grinned, hearing in her mind her granddad saying, "If you want to catch a fish, you gotta get your line wet." Crystal loved catching the big catfish, but always threw them back into the lake. Once she'd caught an eight-pounder not far from where she sat right now.

She was smiling at that memory when the bullet ripped into her.

Chapter 17

CRYSTAL heard the shot and saw her blood on the side of the boat at about the same instant. Without thinking or looking around, she grabbed the side of the boat and rolled into the water just as another bullet ripped into the boat. Splinters showered her head as she went under the surface of the water.

She'd hardly had time to get a good breath, but her dive was shallow and she quickly returned to the surface. The boat drifted between her and the shooter, rocking lazily from her sudden departure. Her arm throbbed, but her mind ignored it, focusing rather on staying alive.

She eased along the boat until she could just peek under the bow. A man stood near the dock scanning the area around the boat. He held a rifle, clearly ready to fire again, looking for a target. Looking for Crystal.

Another man came into view. He was armed with a handgun of some sort. From this distance, Crystal could not tell much about the weapons.

Slowly she raised a finger and wiped water from her eyes. She had a rather poor view of the two men, but as far as she could tell, she couldn't remember seeing either before. The shooter wore a camouflage tee shirt and cap. Crystal guessed he might be five feet eight inches tall. The other man, a little taller—maybe six feet or so, looked to be older, but at this distance, she couldn't be sure.

Now, past the initial terror and adrenaline surge, her mind acknowledged the pain in her left arm. She wiggled her fingers, then moved her forearm, and finally flexed the entire arm. It seemed to work okay. She paddled back near the middle of the boat, then pulled her left arm out of the water. Blood dripped from a gouge about two inches long that ran across the outside of her biceps. The bullet had missed the bone. And her heart, she noted. She reached in her pocket, pulled out a soggy tissue. It came out a wet glob and she started to drop it in the water. Instead, she pressed it on the bleeding wound and held it there. *That's a waste of effort*, she thought. But it did seem to slow the bleeding.

Careful not to rock the boat, she floated back to the bow of the boat. The taller man now had the rifle and still stood near the dock, but the shorter man was gone. Where? Crystal inspected the hillside but found no sign of him. Cautious not to touch the boat, she moved to the stern and looked around.

He's coming around the lake to look for me, Crystal thought, as she picked out the shooter moving east along the bank. *I can't stay here. I can't stay under water very long. I can't crawl out on the bank. He'd either see me or find my tracks.* She peeked again at the stubby man trudging along the shoreline. *He's got a gun, he's already shot me once, and now he's coming to finish the job. And I'm waiting here like a fish in a rain barrel.*

A picture of Nana's burned house materialized in her mind. She remembered Mark's feeling that Bessie was murdered. *They aren't trying to scare me off.* A shudder ran through her body as her mind spelled out what, down deep, she already knew, but had refused to face. *They mean to kill me.*

Her mind raced through various options, searching for some way to hide from these killers. *He'll have to go around that inlet, still ... .*

Crystal slipped under the surface and began swimming for the eastern inlet, where reeds poked up several feet above the water. If she could get there, they might provide enough cover. Her lungs began to burn and she struggled to keep from inhaling water. She eased her head up, barely exposing her mouth and nose, took a deep breath, checked her directions, then sank below the surface again.

The next time she came up for air, she was at the edge of the inlet. The gunman was only three hundred yards away. Crystal submerged and carefully worked her way in among the reeds. She was crawling on the bottom by the time she felt the cover sufficient. With great care, she turned over and sat on the bottom, her eyes and nose barely above water. She scooped some mud off the bottom and slowly rubbed it on her forehead, cheeks and nose. *My first mudpack.*

She started to smile at that, then the smile vanished. *Maybe my last.*

The murky water provided excellent camouflage for the blue and green plaid shirt she wore. Her legs, encased in blue jeans, were virtually invisible stretched along the bottom silt.

Crystal listened to the gunman crashing through the underbrush surrounding the inlet. It sounded like he was less than a hundred feet away when the noise stopped.

The sudden silence became more frightening to Crystal than the noise of the gunman trashing toward her. Why had he stopped? Was he at this instant taking aim on the back of her head? Her mind raced through various scenarios, all terrifying.

Careful not to move her head at all, Crystal cut her eyes to the left as far as possible, trying to locate her predator. Not fifteen feet away, studying her, lurked a cottonmouth. The black snake raised its triangular head above the water and folded its jaws back, revealing the white lining of its mouth and its needle sharp fangs. Crystal recognized the snake's primordial warning. This was its territory and Crystal was intruding. Sweat formed on Crystal's forehead. A knot formed in her stomach. She knew cottonmouths were deadly poisonous. Worse yet, they were very aggressive.

Slowly, the snake began floating toward Crystal.

Chapter 18

CONFLICTING thoughts flooded her mind, only to be shoved aside by sheer panic. Her eyes were so fixed on the snake, her attention so riveted, she could not manage a clear thought. Its slow movement hypnotized her

The water was shallow. But if she got up and ran to escape the poisonous predator, she would face an even more deadly killer. If she stayed still, she would be bitten. And she would not even be able to rush to a hospital for antivenin.

A slight tremor ran through her body and fear seemed to permeate the interior of her mouth. She wanted to cry, to scream "This isn't fair. I can't deal with two threats at the same time." But any sound she made could be fatal. Her stomach twisted, threatening to expel its contents.

The sound was deafening. The bullet slashed through the water right above Crystal's outstretched legs, sending droplets into her eyes. Then another blast. Weak, trembling and terrified, she sank beneath the surface of the water.

Even as the water covered her, a ray of hope brightened her thoughts. Both shots were way off the mark—*if* he were shooting at her. If he was shooting at the snake, he probably had not seen her.

Crystal had little air when she sank into the water. She had to come up. But she knew the shooter might be looking to see if he had hit the snake, maybe even wading in, hoping to take home a trophy.

Her lungs burned and threatened to suck in something, even if it was water. She pulled her hair over her face, leaned back until she was almost horizontal, then eased up until her nose barely broke the surface.

"See her?" the man across the lake yelled.

Crystal could hear the shooter breaking through the thick

brush.

"Naw. Just a goddamn moccasin."

She took a quick breath and sank back down.

He hadn't seen her. *Thank you Lord. The guy had to be looking in my direction.*

With a jolt, she remembered the snake. Where had it gone? She inched up until her bronze eyes were above the water line and peeped between strands of wet, black hair, searching for the snake. The cottonmouth was nowhere in her field of vision. With infinite care, she swiveled her head to look in a wider arc. Still, she saw no cottonmouth. Far to her right, the shooter was moving away. She said a quick prayer that the snake kept moving away also.

For several minutes Crystal could see the man thrashing through the brush, occasionally slipping on the steep slope and letting out a string of curses. Then she lost sight of him, but could still hear him yelling to his partner. "Think I got her. Blood on the boat, some in the water by it. Don't see no body. Can't see no place she climbed out on the bank."

"Get the boat."

"Naw. Get all wet. Don't need it. Coming back."

"I said, get the boat. Leave it there, stupid, someone's gonna start looking around and find the body. Bring it back. Now."

The chubby man began splashing out in the water, cursing all the way. Then, Crystal decided he must be swimming, since the complaining stopped. After a while, she heard him paddling the boat across the lake. Slowly, she eased up on her knees and turned her head to watch. He had reached the far bank. She shifted to get a better view. The two men beached the boat, turned their backs to Crystal and started up the hill.

After she heard a car start and drive down Eula's road, Crystal washed the mud off her face and waded out of the water, all the while keeping a close watch for the cottonmouth. She plodded around the lake, feeling weak, her arm aching, still bleeding slightly, and water squishing out of her shoes with every step. She desperately wanted several aspirin and a hot shower.

* * *

Bill Glothe took one look at Crystal and shook his head. "You look like you been rode hard and put up wet."

"Thanks. All compliments accepted," Crystal said. She was sitting in the emergency room of the Wooden Nickel Community Hospital. As soon as she had reached Eula's house, Crystal had called the sheriff and asked him to meet her at the hospital. She had located a towel and dried herself. In the closet of her old room she found some jeans and a shirt that smelled of smoke but were dry. She was thankful for that.

The doctor was stitching her wound when Bill arrived.

"If you had any doubts, forget them," Crystal said. "Those men meant to kill me. Not scare me off. Not warn me. Kill me. And if the one guy had been a better shot, or a little faster, I'd be dead right now."

"Sounds like you're luckier'n a three-legged chicken. You get a good look-see?"

"I think I could pick one of them out of a line-up. I only saw the other one from across the lake." Crystal twitched a little.

"Sorry," said the young doctor sewing up the wound. "That should be the worst one."

"What kinda car were they driving?"

"I didn't see it."

"Well, give me a description of the man you saw." Glothe took a pad and pen from his pocket.

Crystal described him as best she could, aided by some prompting from the sheriff. Maybe five feet eight inches, dark hair, potato nose, right-handed, fatigue pants, boots, camouflage tee shirt and a cap. Without a doubt, she could give a better description of the snake. Its image was burned into her brain. But she didn't think Bill would appreciate it.

"Anything else?"

"Only that they also had some sort of handgun. Had a long barrel. I don't know much about guns." Crystal thought for a minute. "There was some writing on the cap. Can't remember what it said. Something about a bar, I think." She shrugged. "That's about it. Oh, maybe one of them smokes cigarillos. Maybe."

"And that's about it for me," the doctor said. "You need to have your regular doctor check it in a couple of days, make sure no infection sets in. Other than that, keep it clean, don't use this arm too much. If the pain bothers you, any over-the-counter pain reliever will do. I don't think you'll have any problems with it. But do have your doctor look at it."

"Thanks. Looks like a neat sewing job." Crystal didn't have the heart to tell him she didn't have a regular doctor—hadn't seen a doctor since moving to Dallas. She slid off the table and followed Glothe into the hallway.

"Called your grandmother yet?"

"No. I'm not going to. And you aren't to call her either. She's had enough. What can she do if she knows, except worry?"

"Don't wanta be around when she finds out we didn't tell her."

"I'll handle her. On the ...," Crystal searched for a word. "... thugs. What can you do, Bill?"

"Truth is, not much. We'll keep a lookout for the guy you described. But it's a pretty general description. Don't know what kind of a car to look for. We can swing by Eula's once or twice a day." He sighed. "Just don't have the manpower to put someone out there. Could be days or weeks 'fore they come back. Course, could put a chain 'cross the drive."

Crystal shook her head. "That'd only slow them down and make them wary, not keep them out. Better to let them in, then catch them." She looked at the sheriff and her eyes were suddenly moist. "Bill, these criminals tried to kill Nana and they'll try again."

"I know. Wish you'd gotten a look at the car. While I'm wishing, wish you'd got the license plate number." The sheriff put his arm around Crystal's shoulder. "Hell, we'll get by there more often, but I just can't promise too much. There's always something pulling us in some other direction."

Crystal stopped at a vending machine, purchased two items, said good-bye to Glothe and headed for Dallas. Glothe was right, Crystal knew. There was no telling when the gunmen would be back. The Park needed continuous surveillance, long-term, and not subject to gun shot wounds.

She had just crossed into Dallas County when she decided what to do.

Chapter 19

SUNDAY afternoon, Crystal drove Eula's car from Dallas to Wooden Nickel. Mark and Rod followed in Mark's truck. When they got to Melva's house, Crystal and Eula got in the truck with the two men and drove to The Park.

Bill Glothe met them there. "Place is clean. I'll just wait here 'til you folks finish."

Mark drove up the drive and stopped near the bridge.

"This will be perfect," said Rod. "But why is there a light pole out here?"

"Some fool drove off the bridge one night," Eula answered. "I said good 'nough for him. But Dan, Crystal's grandfather, put the light in anyway. Said it's okay to make the road easier—for the other fellow."

"Well, it certainly makes my job easier."

With Mark's help, Rod installed their surveillance system. Near the road, he placed a weathered log, a wire extending from a hole in the bottom. With a small pick, he scraped a shallow ditch about ten feet long to a bush. He laid the wire in the ditch and covered it with dirt, then scattered pine needles over that. When he had finished, the area looked undisturbed. "You're sure your phone is still hooked up?" Rod asked as he started climbing the pole.

Eula craned her neck to look up at him. "Sure as you can be when you're dealing with the phone company."

"It was working Thursday," Crystal said and then almost bit her tongue, forgetting Eula didn't know Crystal had been out to The Park. Fortunately, her grandmother did not pick up on the statement. Crystal's blouse, with a three-quarter-length sleeve, hid the bandage on her arm.

When Rod climbed down, he brought two wires, which he

carefully fixed to the side of the pole opposite the drive.

In the meantime, Mark hid a small wooden box under the bush. He stacked rocks around its sides, then gathered another small pile of branches and rocks a few feet away.

"How's it gonna do whatever it's gonna do?" Eula asked Crystal.

"Well, see that knothole in the log?" Crystal pointed. "Actually, that's the lens to a small digital camera. It's focused on the drive. When it sees a car come by, it'll send the picture to the computer in that box Mark put over there. The computer will analyze the picture, pick out the license plate number, and call my computer with the information."

"How's it know when to take pictures?"

"There's a motion sensor in there."

"How's it going to call your computer?"

"Rod has hooked the computer up to your phone line. So the computer can dial out just like you would. Except it will call my computer at the office, and also Mark's computer at his house."

"This the kind of stuff you do at work?"

Crystal laughed. "Not exactly. But we do some pretty amazing things."

Rod and Mark puttered around in the box a few minutes, then completely covered the box with branches.

"That ought to do it," Rod announced.

"Near's I can tell, Rod looks like he ought to be the boss," Eula said. "You think this contraption'll work?"

Rod grinned. "Well, ma'am, we're going to try it out in just a minute."

Mark and Rod checked the area, making sure the computer and camera would not be detected. When they were satisfied, Mark said, "Let's test it."

They all got in the truck, drove past the area covered by the camera, then turned around and drove back down to the county road, where Bill Glothe sat waiting. Mark pulled up next to Glothe's car.

"It's all in, Bill," Mark said. "Let's see if it works."

Mark punched in a number on his cell phone. After one ring, a voice said, "Yes?"

"This is Mark. Any messages from Cam two?"

There was a moment's hesitation. "One. 14:46, today. License IRS INC2. It belongs to . . ." Another hesitation. ". . . You, Mark. Full picture available."

"Good-bye." Mark ended the call. "It identified us, our license number, and sent a picture to my computer."

"How do you know that?" Eula asked.

"The number I called is to one of my computers at home. When I asked that computer if it had gotten any messages from the computer we just put in by your bridge, it said yes and told me it had seen our license go by at 2:46 today."

"Humph."

"Well, hope this does the job," the sheriff said. "Call me whenever you hear anything. Got one quick chore to do, then I'll head over to Melva's." He started the patrol car, gave a short wave and drove south on the county road.

"Lot of wildlife here. Is it gonna call you two every time a deer prances by?" Eula asked, sounding skeptical.

"No, Nana. The computer can tell the difference between deer or other animals and a car or truck."

"Or van?"

"Or van. And if a person walks down the drive, it will send us a picture of the person," Crystal answered.

Eula was looking for something wrong with the system. "Will it tell you if the truck is puce?"

Mark looked puzzled.

"Nana thinks the truck was painted puce," Crystal explained.

"The computer won't tell us it's puce," Mark said. A big grin broke out on Eula's face. "But it will display a full color picture. And since I don't know what color puce is, I'll show it to you and let you decide."

"Humph."

* * *

The front door to Melva Larsen's home opened directly into a large area that served as both living room and dining room. To the left was a comfortable area with a camel back sofa, a love seat (that did not match the sofa), two overstuffed chairs and a coffee table. To the right was a dining table, white with periwinkles painted at each corner, and six matching chairs. Crystal, Eula, Mark and Rod settled in to wait for Bill Glothe to arrive.

Melva came through the door to the kitchen carrying a large pitcher of lemonade and an array of glasses on a tray. She set the tray on the coffee table and began filling the glasses.

Eula took one of the tall, cool glasses and tasted the drink. "Good job, Melva." Then, she turned her attention to Mark. "I don't understand any of this stuff, but I'm sure having a computer keep an eye on The Park is a great idea. 'Preciate it," she said, her skepticism finally relenting.

"I do too. It was Crystal's idea," he answered.

"Well, she never said she thought it up. You know, before she went out to California, 'mong them West Coast people, she was different."

"Nana, don't bore Mark and Rod talking about your granddaughter." Crystal was wary of the direction the conversation was taking.

"She would have said to me, 'Isn't this a good idea I came up with?' She was confident, maybe a little cocky. When she got back, she sure wasn't cocky. Maybe why she didn't finish her Ph.D. or whatever."

"I just sort of burned out, Nana. Now, let's move on to some other topic, please."

"Never did buy that burnout thing," Eula said.

"I certainly know one thing," Mark said. "She's smart enough. If she weren't here listening, I'd tell you she's brilliant at times."

Crystal got up to leave the room. *No*, she thought. *That won't stop this conversation. I've simply got to change the topic. Get someone else on the hot seat.* She smirked. "Nana, you said Mark was a so-so roper. Why so-so?"

Mark almost choked on his drink. "Let's not get into that."

"It's a fair question. I did say that." Eula stared at the ceiling and cocked her head to one side, then the other and back again, all the while pursing her lips. The conversation stopped and all eyes focused on Eula. "Well, to be a good roper, you need three things: rhythm, good timing, and an eye for distance. It's been a long time since I watched him, but my recollection is, Bull was a little shy on the rhythm side."

Rod leaned back and roared with laughter. "That's him; Mr. No Rhythm."

Mark scowled at Rod. "That's 'he.' Not 'him.' Didn't they teach English at A&M?"

"Him. He. Makes no difference. It's you, old buddy."

Just then, the doorbell rang and Melva went to let Bill in. Rod was still laughing.

"I miss a good joke or something?" Bill asked.

Mark jumped in. "Didn't miss a thing. Grab a lemonade and let's decide how we're going to tell Sam it was Bessie and not Eula."

Bill picked up one of the chairs at the dining table, brought it over and sat in it. Melva handed him a glass. The sheriff took a long drink of the lemonade, looked at the group and said, "Well, how're we going to handle this?"

Eula had the first suggestion. "I could just call him up and say 'Hi, I'm back.'"

"Nana! That'd be like dropping a cold egg into boiling water. I veto that one."

"Then suggest something else."

"Write him a thank you note for his eulogy," suggested Melva.

"Too slow," said Eula. "Now, if he was on that whatever net thing, Crystal could send him a net-mail or something from me."

Crystal turned to Bill. "I hate to do this to you, especially since you were against not telling him in the first place, but I think you ought to be the one."

Glothe took a toothpick out of his shirt pocket and stuck it in the corner of his mouth. "I 'spose you've figured out how to go about it, too."

"I have a suggestion," said Crystal.

"Well, let's hear it."

"You just got the written report on Bessie from Dr. Haas. You can start by giving him that to read. That will sort of ease him into the fact that Eula was not the victim."

"And when he asks how long I've known?"

"The truth. And the truth is, you knew only *after* the Gazette was printed. He couldn't change it. Tell him the reasons." Crystal hunched her shoulders. "It's the best we can do."

After another five minutes of discussion, Bill called Teeter and asked him to come over to Melva Larson's house. Eula and Crystal made more lemonade for everyone except Mark, who opted for a Dr Pepper.

Mark suggested they go over what they would say to Sam, and how. "No." Bill shook his head. "If you gotta practice to make it sound sincere, it won't. I'm in deep enough as it is."

Chapter 20

EULA hid in the kitchen when Sam Teeter drove up.

After the pleasantries, Sam settled into an overstuffed chair, raised his eyebrows and looked from Melva to Glothe.

Bill got right to the point. "Afraid I haven't been completely honest with you, Sam, and for that I apologize. Hope my reasons for it will satisfy you a mite. First off, let me tell you that I got a report back from Wilcox. He's an arson investigator with the State Fire Marshall's office in Tyler. He confirmed what Crystal and Mark thought: the fire was deliberately set. Used diesel to start it."

"Can I see the report?"

"I'll get you a copy today. Now, here's a report I got yesterday from Dr. Haas, down in Tyler. Says what I suspected. We got a murder on our hands." He handed a copy of the report to Sam and waited.

Sam read the report.

Autopsy Report on Bessie Mae Longson

The victim suffered a depressed skull fracture, caused by a hard, cylindrical instrument, approximately 1/2" to 5/8" in diameter——possibly an iron pipe or the barrel of a gun. The length of the impact area was approximately 2 and 3/4" long, starting from the hairline above the left eye continuing toward the back of the head. This resulted in skull-bone fragments cutting the dura membrane and brain tissue, and lacerating an artery. CSF leaked. Death was the result of an acute subdural hematoma. The victim was dead before being burned.

When he finished, he fixed a level stare on Bill. "Bessie? What about Eula? You told me Eula was killed in the fire."

Bill swallowed but maintained eye contact with Sam. "When I told you that, I believed it was the truth. We all did. By the time I found out different, the paper was printed and on the stands."

"Then, where is Eula?"

"Right here," Eula said as she came out of the kitchen.

No one said anything. No one moved. Eula just stood in the doorway looking at Sam. Crystal thought the tough newspaperman was on the verge of tears. Slowly, he got up and walked over to Eula, his limp more pronounced than when he had entered the house. He put his arms around her and whispered something to her.

After a few moments, Teeter turned to Bill, still keeping one arm close around Eula. "The funeral? Everybody thought it was Eula's. What's going on?" His voice sounded weak.

"Now, Sam," Eula said quietly. "Don't set your plow too deep. They finally came around to what I've been telling 'em. Somebody's trying to kill me. Maybe if they think I'm dead, they'll quit trying."

"It was my idea," said Mark. "I convinced them to let everybody continue to think Eula was dead. I believe someone has tried to kill her three times in the last two weeks. And the only reason they didn't succeed this last time is because Eula went camping. They killed someone they thought was Eula. I didn't want them to keep trying. They're getting closer every time."

Sam sank into a chair and gazed at the floor. His great relief at seeing Eula alive was tempered by the feeling he had let his readers down. He'd been in the newspaper business for more than forty years. He'd never printed a gross inaccuracy before. Sometimes a small mistake got in, or a misinterpretation. But never an out-and-out, absolutely wrong story. He thought of his bumper sticker: "Truth is all we've got." Maybe he should rip it off. Maybe it was time to throw in the towel.

Eula knelt beside his chair. "I should have called and told you. I'm truly sorry I didn't. Wasn't thinking straight. But I've already got one person killed because some bums were trying to get me. Better to let 'em think they did."

"I gave my readers the wrong information."

"You gave them the best you had. You *did* the best you could." Eula patted his arm. "And if you do the best you can, you *are* the best."

Eula's voice was as soothing as if she were comforting an injured child.

"Who else knew?" asked Sam.

"Just us." Eula swept her arm around, indicating all those in the room. "Except Rod. Crystal and Mark were there when Melva and I got back from camping. We called Bill."

"Why are you telling me now? You still haven't caught the killers. Or have you?" His voice had regained some of its usual strength, but was tinged with an odd mixture of relief and dissatisfaction.

Bill shook his head. "No. But we all agreed that you had to be able to correct the story this week. Last week's paper was already printed by the time we knew. Couldn't change that. But we can get it straight this week. And we can't keep Eula hid out forever. So, we wanted you to break the story. We don't want anyone to know until your paper comes out. That gives us a few more days to try and find the killers before they find Eula. And now we know for certain it wasn't an accident. It was murder."

Sam regarded his feet, as if he were wondering where they came from. At length, he patted Eula's hand, then pulled his tape recorder out of his pocket and said to Bill, "Will you give me everything you have by my deadline?"

Bill nodded.

Sam looked at Eula.

"Exclusively," she said.

Sam's voice was firm and commanding again. "Let's start with the first attempt on your life," he said, pushing the "Record" button.

Chapter 21

THE rest of the weekend passed with no calls from Cam 2.

Monday, Crystal was in the office when her computer signaled that Cam 2 had registered a car entering The Park. She dialed Mark's extension. "We've got a hit; I'm downloading the picture now. Want to come see it?"

By the time her computer had received the picture, Mark was there. "Open it up. Let's see what we've captured."

Crystal pressed a few keys on her computer and a car materialized on the screen.

"Well, it worked." Crystal sounded positive.

"Yeah. Worked perfectly." There on the monitor was a perfect picture of Bill Glothe's police cruiser. "Guess I'd better program it to ignore the sheriff's car. I don't want to get all excited every time the sheriff or his deputy goes out to check." Mark started to leave, then sat down instead. "How's the project going?"

"Good, in spite of the interruptions last week. Actually, they got a lot done while I was gone." Crystal cocked her head to one side. "I still don't know why Rooney's people are coming. Don't they keep up with what we're doing?"

"They do. They have seats on the board, so they get an update each quarter. Rooney had some tough questions at the last meeting. I guess he didn't like my answers."

Crystal scrunched up her nose. "What kind of questions?"

"Wanted to know why projects got behind. He wanted strict timetables. I tried to tell him this was a research outfit." Mark grinned. "I reminded him of the sign in my office. 'Research is what I'm doing when I don't know what I'm doing.' He was not amused. I said, when we know all the outcomes, we're doing engineering, not research." Mark chuckled softly. "I think he wants more engineering and less research."

"Can he just refuse to ante up the next round?"

"You bet he can. There are several ways he can go. He could bring in another VC firm. That's a mixed bag. He spreads out the risk, but he loses some control. If we do well, he doesn't want to be the big dog, he wants to be the *only* dog." Mark picked up a pencil and began playing with it. "He could convince the board to sell the company. That's risky for Rooney, and for me. But he could do it."

"Don't you still have controlling interest in IRS?"

"Yes, I do. But I don't control the board."

"Then you could get a new board. You have the votes."

"It's not that easy. First, it could happen before I could replace the board. Second, you can't dump the board just because you don't like the way they vote."

"Of course you can."

Mark laughed. "Well, I can't get Rooney's two seats. And he does wield a lot of influence. At any rate, I don't see that as an option."

Crystal furrowed her brows and closed her eyes for a few seconds. "Could you go out and get other money?"

Mark nodded several times. "That is an option. Not a good one, in my opinion. I would give up more of the company and then, Rooney and the new investors would have a controlling interest." He paused and pursed his lips. "But I'd do that before I'd let it go under. Of course, here again, Rooney could exert a lot of influence. Any new investor would contact Rooney first."

"It wouldn't be good for Rooney to just let it fold."

"Not the way you and I, and most people, look at things. We don't think like these investment guys do. I'm told that sometimes losing money is good." He shrugged. "I'm thirsty. Shall we walk down to the coffee room and get a soda?"

"Sure." As they walked down the hall, Crystal asked, "How'd Rooney get two seats on the board?" She turned her head to the side and wiggled it, shaking her earrings in front of Mark. Today, her earrings were large question marks. She smiled demurely. "You know how curious I am."

"Part of the dowry. Getting a venture capitalist is a courtship. Only in this courtship, one person, the entrepreneur, really *needs*—

but doesn't want—the other, the venture capitalist. The venture capitalist really *wants*—but doesn't need—the entrepreneur."

"Not all that different from many other courtships, I'd say."

Mark laughed. "Probably true." He put two coins in the machine and punched a button. A Dr Pepper popped out. "What would you like?"

"Same."

Mark handed her the drink and dropped in coins for another. "So the two, the entrepreneur and the venture capitalist, court one another. The entrepreneur is the bashful young maiden and the VC is the suitor. The maiden flirts a little and when the VC shows some interest, she gives him a little peak into the closed, mysterious secrets of her ... business plan." They took the drinks and started back to Crystal's office. "When the suitor begins to talk about a relationship, the maiden reveals more of her plans."

"Sounds sexy."

"It can be exhilarating. The maiden knows that if she still entertains others, it may help keep her suitor's interest high, perhaps keep his expectations for the dowry a bit lower. But at some point, she must pledge her love. Now, if she does this too soon, she'll lose her advantage. She'll give too much dowry and get too few guarantees. If she waits too long, she may lose all the suitors."

"Ah, the plight of the innocent maiden," Crystal sighed, quickly checking her computer as they reentered her office. No news.

Mark settled in the chair facing her desk. "Eventually, a dowry is offered, and often that involves a good bit of bargaining. The suitor may begin by promising to take care of the maiden and protect her from outside forces. If the other interested parties bow out, then quickly, the suitor sees he has no competition and demands more dowry. The maiden now sees the suitor as her only hope and begs her father for more dowry."

"Is that what happened with IRS?"

"Well, let's just say the suitor was very experienced and the maiden was a little naive."

"Are you really worried about this visit?"

"You bet I am. We still need Rooney. And I don't know who this consultant is. I don't know what prompted Rooney to bring him in. I don't know how much Rooney will depend on his judgment. But

Rooney doesn't pay people just to take up space." Mark shook his head. "A damning report from the consultant, maybe even a lukewarm one, could jeopardize our funding."

A thought occurred to Mark. "I wonder if Rooney went looking for a consultant, an expert, to come check us out, or ..."

"Or the consultant found Rooney?"

"Wouldn't be the first time."

"I don't see—"

Crystal was interrupted by a lion's roar coming from her computer, its signal that it had contact from The Park. Both Crystal and Mark turned their attention to the monitor. This time, it wasn't a police car.

Chapter 22

"**WHAT'VE** you got?" Glothe asked when Crystal reached him at his office.

"A blue, ninety-four Chevy half-ton entered The Park at 10:38 this morning." Crystal read off the license plate number. "Can someone check on it?"

"I'll check on it myself. Let you know what I find."

Crystal repeated Bill's comments to Mark. "The only problem is, it'll take Bill at least fifteen minutes to get there."

"Whoever it is isn't likely to get in and out in fifteen minutes. They're looking for something and can't find it. They might not stay too long for fear of being caught, but I'm willing to bet they'll still be around when Bill gets there."

* * *

Twenty minutes later, Glothe called. "If I hadn't been the sheriff, I'd have given myself a ticket for speeding." The line went silent.

"Was the car still there?"

"Yeah. And the driver. Oh, hold for a minute."

Crystal felt her pulse quicken. Bill sounded calm, but Crystal was as excited as if she'd just taken a perfect soufflé out of the oven.

After a couple of minutes, Bill came back on the line. "'Pologize for the interruption. Turns out the car was Smoky Roberts—one of the volunteer firemen. Buddy asked him to come out and check something to do with the accelerant. Anyway, false alarm. But seems like your gadget's doing its thing."

* * *

At 1:26, a truck entered The Park. It was a rust-colored four-by-four. The picture was clear enough, but the license plate wasn't. Mud covered part of its left side; the right side was bent so badly that the camera didn't show the first character. However, the computer had identified the four remaining characters.

Crystal called Glothe's office. The dispatcher told her the sheriff wasn't in, but promised she would try to reach him.

Ten minutes later, the phone rang. "Bill?"

"No, Ma'am. This is his office. We are unable to reach him. We will keep trying. Usually, it's only a matter of ten or fifteen minutes, and then he'll call us. I mean, if he knows that he's been out of contact, he generally checks in."

Crystal hung up disappointed. She considered driving out there herself. But that would take over an hour. Besides, she remembered her last visit to The Park. She didn't want to dodge any more bullets. Or water moccasins. Glothe would call in plenty of time, she told herself.

A few minutes later, Mark appeared at her office door. "You want to try IPPI on it? Is it ready?"

"Ready as fresh-baked bread."

"That food thing again, huh?"

Crystal's cheeks colored slightly. "That's just what came to mind."

Mark laughed. "Just teasing. Have you finished loading the DPS file yet?"

"About an hour ago. Nothing like a real test. With the model, color, and make of the truck, plus more than half the license plate, there's a good chance the IPPI program can determine the owner."

Crystal started the program on her computer, entered the information they had, and waited. In less than three minutes, the program reported that it had over a thousand possible matches in the state. Crystal instructed the program to report only those vehicles registered within thirty miles of Wooden Nickel. In five seconds, the screen was filled with the particulars on the four vehicles that matched the criteria.

Crystal stared at the screen, her eyes wide and her mouth open.

"You look as if you're surprised," Mark said. "Didn't you expect it to work this well?"

She put her finger on the third entry on the computer screen: Randal Kenderson. "I got a call from Randal Kenderson last night.

He wanted to know if I would sell him the timber off The Park. Said it probably would bring more than enough to have the house rebuilt. He was really pushy."

Mark nodded.

"No, Mark, you don't understand. He's been trying to buy Nana's timber for years. And here's his name, puce truck and all."

"Wanting to buy timber isn't a bad thing. Did they get along okay?"

"Like sour pickles and ice cream."

Mark laughed. "I take it that means they didn't get along."

"That's an understatement.

"Did your grandmother have insurance on the house?"

"Insurance? Nana?" She shook her head. "No way. She didn't like insurance. Granddad used to say he didn't spend money where the only way you got any good out of it was if something bad happened. They carried liability on the car only because they couldn't get it registered without it."

"Humm. Well, let's look at what else the IPPI can do."

An hour slipped by before Glothe called. Mark was still playing with the Identification from Partial Plate Information program on Crystal's computer, so she put Glothe's call on the speakerphone.

"Sorry didn't get back to you sooner. Believe it or not, I've been in the middle of a drug bust. Wouldn't think we'd have that problem out here, would you? Anyway, what've ya got?"

Crystal filled him in and explained the IPPI program. "We've got four cars in your area that are possibles." She read the information to Glothe.

"Well, you can forget about Graham. Known him for a long time. Besides, he's too sick to bother anybody right now. We'll get on the other three right away."

"Remember, Bill," Mark interjected. "We don't have a complete match. So it may not be any of these. And we only checked vehicles registered within a thirty-mile radius."

"It's something to start on. We'll be as careful as a hen tip-toeing past a sleeping fox. I'll get someone out to The Park right away. And we'll check these trucks and let you know the skinny."

"One other thing," Crystal said. "Randal Kenderson called me last night trying to buy the timber."

"Mighty interesting. Wonder how he tracked you down? 'Course, that's not so bad. Sometimes, when someone dies, loggers just go in and steal the timber. At least he called."

Mark made a slight sound of disbelief. "Steal it? Wouldn't somebody notice?"

"Logging's going on all the time. Most people are honest. So they see a logging operation and assume it's legal. Time someone figures out it ain't, loggers are gone, and so's the timber. Eula's place is too big. They couldn't get it all. But a lot. Well, let me see what I can find."

* * *

Glothe called again in the late afternoon. "Well, we've checked the trucks you gave me. 'Course, I told you about Graham. The one registered to Wilkins is in the junkyard, and has been for a month. Arnold is on vacation—in that truck. According to the neighbors, he's been gone a week and is not expected back for another week.

"Then, there's Kenderson. The name sounded familiar, but it took me a few minutes to get a picture of him in my mind. I know him. You're right. He buys the right to timber land. Timber's high right now. He's paying good money. But I've seen his work. Really leaves a mess when he's through. Any rate, he's wanted to timber The Park for a long time. You can imagine how Eula responds to that. Like waving a red flag in front of a bull. He keeps trying; she keeps saying no. Anyway, I didn't get to talk to him. Couldn't find him and nobody seems to know where he is. We'll stay on it and let you know when we talk to him."

There wasn't much to tell but Crystal called Mark and reported what Glothe said.

"I'd like to call your grandmother," Mark asked. "Think she'd mind?"

Crystal assured him Eula wouldn't mind and gave him Melva's phone number.

Chapter 23

"**EULA,** this is Mark O'Malley. How are you?"

"Doing Fine. Can you tell me in twenty-five words or less just what Intelligent Retrieval Systems does?"

The question took Mark by surprise. "Surely Crystal has told you what we do."

"I dearly love Crystal, but she can't tell me anything in twenty-five words or less. She gets started on what y'all do and for thirty minutes it all goes over my head. Can you do any better?"

Mark smiled. "Twenty-five words or less? I never have. If I made it sound that simple for a client, we wouldn't be able to charge them as much money as we do."

"I'm not buying."

" Okay. Let's see." He thought for a moment. "We produce computer systems that allow companies to sift through their gigantic haystack of information and find the exact needle they want, quickly, easily, cheaply. That's twenty-five."

"Thank you. What's on your mind?"

Once again, her abrupt change caught him off guard. Before he recovered, she said, "I know you didn't call about my health or state of mind. I know it has to do with the goings on at The Park. I 'preciate your interest and know you're a busy man. So, let's get down to business."

"Do you know a man named Kenderson?"

"No."

Mark frowned with disappointment.

"I know a jackass."

"I beg your pardon?" Mark was confused.

"I know a jackass who calls himself Kenderson. Always trying to timber my land. Can you understand me when I say no? Do

I mispronounce it or something?"

"Sounds pretty clear to me." Mark was smiling again.

"Well, old jackass Kenderson can't understand. I have told him 'no' ever since Dan died. No, I am not going to let him timber my land. No. But he keeps on. Lately, he's gotten abusive. Tells me I'm a stupid old woman. Don't I know that trees grow back? He'll cut only some of the trees, leave plenty. And then new ones will grow back." She paused just long enough to get her breath. "You've never seen the way he leaves a place he timbers. Looks like a tornado's been through. And I'll be dead long before it grows back. I don't need his money. And I'm not letting him in The Park." By the time she finished, she was spitting out the words.

"When was the last time he contacted you?"

"Two, three weeks ago. Could have been four. Why?"

"He owns a puce truck."

"Wouldn't surprise me. Guess I ought to apologize to the jackasses. They're smarter than Kenderson."

Mark shook his head as he put the phone down. Eula was something else. The tragedy of the fire and Bessie's death had introduced him to three interesting and unusual people, people he hoped to be able to call friends: Eula, Bill Glothe and Sam Teeter.

* * *

Crystal was standing in the hall when Mark came dashing out of his office, tennis bag in hand. He glanced at his watch and stopped. "Got a moment to educate me?"

"Sure. Any particular topic, or just general education?"

Mark grinned. "Today the topic is timber. My friend Josh Kinsolving made a remark the other night that just popped into my mind. He said 'Wouldn't be the first time someone was killed for timber.' I ignored that at the time, but now that Kenderson is on the scene, it may be worth considering. I know people get killed for a few dollars sometimes. But this was planned out. My question is this: how much is timber worth?"

Tension lines crossed Crystal's face as soon as she understood the topic had to do with the attacks on her grandmother. "I don't really know. I remember once a friend of Nana's went on vacation. When she got back, she found someone had cut most of the trees on her land. I remember Nana saying they probably stole forty, fifty thousand dollars worth."

Mark nodded.

"And the friend only had—well, I don't know—but I'm guessing maybe sixty or eighty acres."

"So, you're telling me Eula's timber could be worth $250,000?" His voice carried a tone somewhere between disbelief and amazement.

Crystal tilted her head to one side and rubbed her forehead with her left hand. "Hmmm." She looked down at nothing. When she looked up, she was shaking her head. "Hard to say. I know The Park hasn't been timbered in at least thirty years. And I'll bet it's more like fifty. There're a lot of really good trees there. If they took both hardwoods and the pines, it could be more."

"More than $250,000?"

"Yeah. Maybe more."

Mark whistled softly. "I'd dismissed Josh's comment about timber being a motive. Maybe I should reexamine it. Even disregarding the 'maybe more' you added, a quarter of a million dollars provides incentive enough for many criminals."

"Of course, I'm just guessing. Nana would never sell it, so I'm sure she's never had it appraised. To really know, you'd have to ask a timber man."

"Like Kenderson?"

"Like Kenderson. But don't. Nana would boil over."

"I won't. Just curious. Looking for motives." Mark looked at his watch again. "Sorry, but I've got to run. Late for a tennis match."

"Tennis? Must seem pretty tame after bull-riding."

"Exactly. I've never had a tennis opponent step on me." He grinned. "Talk to you tomorrow."

Mark started to leave, but stopped and turned back to Crystal. "Oh, talked to Rooney's office this afternoon. Got a little more information. Their two top dogs are coming along with the consultant. And I found out the consultant's name. Dr. Lester Krupe. Wasn't he your dissertation advisor?"

Crystal felt like someone had slammed her in the stomach with a sledgehammer and a chill raced through her body. She could hardly get the breath to speak. She managed a weak yes.

"Maybe that'll help us some." He turned to go. "See you

tomorrow," he called over his shoulder. "You can fill me in on Krupe then."

Crystal's legs felt rubbery. She leaned against the wall and closed her eyes, the professor's face forcing its way into her mind. She could see him sneering, telling her she was worthless, incapable of doing graduate work, devoid of original thought. Her dissertation? Trash.

Slowly, her back slid down the wall until she was sitting on the floor. Her head sank down to rest on her knees. Her entire body slumped as if she had no bones. For a few moments, she thought she might throw up.

Krupe was coming back to make sure she was recognized as a fraud, a failure. He had destroyed her quest for a Ph.D. Now, he would ruin her career, take away her job and what self-esteem she had managed to regain since she left Stanford.

Why? Why had he done that to her? Why was he coming back now? To make sure she had no part in the scientific community?

The conversation with Mark came back to her. *Maybe the consultant sought out the venture capitalists.* Maybe Dr. Krupe sought out the company funding IRS so he could deal with Crystal, so he could destroy her again.

From a remote corner of her mind, a tiny voice whispered a question. Why do you let him affect your confidence? You are doing excellent work. You are doing original work. Other than Mark, you do the best work in the company. Why do you care what Dr. Krupe thinks about you?

Because he is a recognized authority in the field, she answered herself. *Because his opinion is respected. When he says a work is excellent, people listen. And,* she reminded herself bitterly, *when he says work is insignificant, people believe him.*

I believed him.

She tried to force her mind to other topics, any topic, as long as it was not Dr. Krupe.

It was several minutes before she mustered the strength to pull herself up and stumble back to her desk. Dr. Lester Krupe followed her.

Chapter 24

OUT of habit, Bill Glothe looked at the people in the cars passing by. Generally, he couldn't tell anything about them. But sometimes he caught a snapshot of the person: the young girl checking her hair in the mirror, probably going to see her boyfriend; the businessman, arms straight and stiff as a corpse, worrying over some problem at work—or at home; the elderly gentleman straining to see the road; the young man, so sleepy his head kept bobbing; the mother, trying to scold her young child while she drove; the teenager, keeping time to the music with her head, or texting while she drove.

Sometimes, he recognized the driver. This was one of those times.

That's Kenderson, all right. And if I want to talk to him, I'd better catch him now.

When the traffic cleared, Bill whipped the police car in a sharp U-turn and sped up to catch the rust-colored truck. He flashed his headlights a couple of times, but Kenderson either didn't see or didn't care. After half a mile, Bill turned on his flashing lights. It took another quarter of a mile before Kenderson finally acknowledged the lights, pulled off to the shoulder and stopped.

Bill pulled to a stop behind the truck, got out and walked up to the driver's window.

"What's going on?" Kenderson demanded.

"Just need to talk to you for a few minutes. We can do it back in my car, or we can go to my office. Your choice." Glothe worked at sounding non-confrontational. He knew he couldn't force the issue.

"What about?"

"Come on back, Randal. Won't take long." He smiled and tilted his head toward his car.

Kenderson glared at the sheriff. "Better not. I got to meet a man on some business."

"If you'd rather stop by my office later on today, we can do it then."

"Hell, no. Ain't got time for that. Let's get it over with. But this better not take long."

As Bill walked back to his police cruiser, he made mental note that Kenderson's truck was freshly washed. No mud on the license plate, which was indeed bent. But whether or not it would obscure a number would depend on the angle of the camera. No help there, he thought.

* * *

Bill pulled out a pad and pencil. "You called Crystal Moore last night?"

"Something wrong with that?"

"Well, no. Nothin' wrong. But Eula had told you she wouldn't sell you her timber."

"She's dead; ain't got no say in it now. Stupid old woman. Never could understand trees grow back. Hell, we could have timbered that area three times since she's owned it. Expect her granddaughter'll have more sense."

Bill made a few notes on the yellow pad to mask his anger. He couldn't imagine anyone speaking so ill of the recently deceased. "Randal, that's no way to talk about Eula. 'Pert near everybody around here liked her."

"Not everybody. World's better off without her."

Glothe struggled to keep his temper in check. His tone turned coldly serious. "Where were you last Monday afternoon?"

"I was—." Randal Kenderson stopped, half turned and leaned back against the door, his manner changing from aggressive to cautious. He squinted his eyes. "Why do you want to know?"

The patrol car swayed slightly as an eighteen-wheeler roared past.

"Coroner's report said fire wasn't the cause of death. A sharp blow to the head was."

"So?"

"So, a truck like yours was seen over near Eula's place. Where were you last Monday?"

Kenderson aimed a scorching look at the sheriff. A muscle in his jaw twitched. Barely opening his mouth, he said through clenched teeth, "This truck was in Hahnstout's shop all day." He reached over, opened the door and got out.

"But where were you?"

"We're finished. Don't bother me again 'lessun you got a warrant or something." He stormed off, leaving the door open.

Bill sighed and leaned over trying to reach the door, but it was open too far. He got out and started around the front of his car just as Kenderson pulled out, spinning his wheels and throwing gravel and dirt back on the sheriff.

I didn't handle that too good, Bill admonished himself. *Made him madder'n a wet hen. Even if his truck was in the shop the day of the fire, he still could have been at The Park in a different car. And his truck could have been the one at The Park yesterday.* Bill slammed the door closed. *Didn't find out a damn thing. Except he's mad enough to kill somebody.*

Chapter 25

"HE'S going to be here next week." This time, Crystal did not wait for the probing questions—or the nightmares. She told her housemate about Dr. Krupe's impending visit as they sat in the living room.

For the past hour, ever since Mark had told her who the consultant was, panic had been building. It grasped her heart so strongly she had felt unsafe driving. She shivered, the cold despair overcoming the warm autumn evening.

"So?"

"So, I'm going to have to face him. I can't hide."

"He's not your advisor anymore." Brandi sipped a Lone Star longneck.

"No. But he's a consultant to the venture capitalists who fund IRS. Don't you see? He still gets to approve or disapprove of my work." Crystal reached for her drink and knocked it over. She just sat there and watched the amber liquid spread over the coffee table.

Without a word, Brandi retrieved a towel from the kitchen and cleaned up the mess. Crystal murmured thanks but didn't look up.

Brandi flopped down, took another pull on the Lone Star and studied her friend. "Actually, this is a good thing." The statement brought Crystal's head up. "See, you're still letting this thing bug you. It's baggage. And you're not dealing with it head-on. So, it isn't getting resolved. His coming will force you to face him and once and for all get rid of these devils."

Crystal sighed. "All well and good to say."

"Crystal, I'm not very smart, like you are. I don't know a bigabyte—"

"Gigabyte."

"Gigabyte from a love bite, or a freckle on my behind. But I do know this. If you lay down on the floor, people are going to wipe their feet on you. You've got to stand up to this Dr. Crap, look him in the eye. *Don't back down.* You're better than he is. Remember that. Better."

The last was said with such intensity that it came out as a command. Brandi's hands formed small fists and every muscle in her body was tense. She drew in a deep breath. "He was the creep who tried to get in your pants. And not just any old creep. Your advisor. He's one unethical SOB."

"But nobody knows that."

"Wrong. You know it. And he knows it. Look him in the eye and let him understand you know what an unethical bastard he is. Make him worry you'll tell his boss. Stanford wouldn't put up with that kind of crap."

"I couldn't do that. He knows I couldn't."

"Show him you're stronger now. Make him uncertain. You can do that. You can worry his ass off."

Crystal's head drooped down and she shook it slowly.

Brandi put her hand under Crystal's head and lifted it up until they were looking at each other. "Look him straight in the eye. Say something about remembering what a nice house he had. Then, just the hint of a smile. Keep looking in his eyes with this secret weapon hidden behind your smile. And say to yourself over and over, 'I'm going to the president of the school. I'm going to tell just what a sleazebag you are.' If you keep this little, knowing smile, and keep thinking those thoughts, he'll get the message."

Brandi nodded several times. "He'll hear it loud and clear, like you were shouting in his ears. He'll start sweating. And he'll have more respect for you. Not that you care. But the important thing is, he'll worry. Because *he* knows he's a bastard and knows you can tell the world he is. And if you say it out loud, maybe others will take up the chorus. He's going to be afraid."

* * *

Crystal suffered through another fitful night, tossing and turning, her sleep plagued by nightmares. In one dream, Dr. Krupe was trying to kill Nana. At five o'clock, after lying awake for an hour, she dragged herself out of bed and stood under the shower for thirty minutes. Realizing she wouldn't get any meaningful work done this morning, she decided to drive to Wooden Nickel and visit her grandmother. Maybe that would reset her emotions and allow her to continue life. Nana could always soothe her. The Park was Crystal's safe haven. She called IRS and left a message on the answering machine that she would be in after lunch.

* * *

Eula and Melva stepped off the porch and started across the yard as Crystal pulled her Lucerne into the drive and parked.

"Hi, Mrs. Larson. Hi, Nana. What are you doing out here in the front? Didn't Bill tell you to stay out of sight?"

"I don't give two hoots and a holler what he said. Do I look like I take orders from an old Billy Goat?"

"Glad you're here," said Melva. "Maybe you can talk some sense into old rock head."

Crystal's smile evaporated. "What's going on, Nana?"

"We're going over to The Park. I need to get something." Eula thrust her chin out, making it clear she was ready for a fight.

Melva shook her head. "I've argued till I'm blue in the face. I offered to go get whatever it was she thinks she wants. I'm going to leave her to you, Crystal, and good luck." Melva turned and headed for the house.

The discussion between Crystal and her grandmother lasted only a minute and before she knew it, Crystal was driving toward The Park. "You're supposed to be dead, Nana. The whole point in this was not to let anybody find out you're alive."

"Gonna find out day after tomorrow anyway. What's the big deal?"

Crystal didn't respond. She admitted she had lost; she usually did to her grandmother. Perhaps the best approach was simply to watch over her until this thing was resolved. Whenever that might be. They had so little to go on: a puce truck that probably belonged to a man who had disappeared. Maybe the surveillance—

"Stop the car!"

Eula's loud command jarred Crystal out of her thoughts. She slammed on the brakes and pulled to the side of the road. Her heart rate shot up. "What is it?"

"Look. There he is." Eula was almost shouting. "There's that

108

puce truck. And if my eyes aren't lying to me, that's old jackass Kenderson in it. What's he doing out by The Park?"

Crystal looked down the road. A rust-colored GMC truck was parked across the entrance to The Park. The driver was staring into The Park, as if he were searching for something. He held a tablet in his hand, and periodically, it looked like he scribbled notes on it.

"Let's go," Eula thundered.

"Where?"

Eula looked at her granddaughter like she had just asked where Texas was. "On up to The Park, of course. I want to have a few words with the donkey."

Crystal didn't move.

"Go on. I want to get there before he leaves."

With a sigh and a shake of her head, Crystal took her foot off the brake and eased the car back on to the road, feeling more than a little uneasy.

"Pull up right beside his ugly truck. I'll talk to him through the window."

Only twenty feet separated the vehicles when Kenderson's gaze left The Park and switched to the approaching car. Crystal could tell the instant he focused on Eula. The blank expression was jolted off his face, replaced by one of disbelief. Crystal eased her car to a stop so that Eula's window was directly opposite the driver of the big Sierra truck.

Eula rolled down her window. "I see they still let dumb animals wander around without a leash."

Kenderson's mouth hung open and his eyes were like saucers. His big, beefy face twisted as he tried to justify what he was seeing with what he knew to be fact. "You're dead. They had your funeral. I read about it in the Gazette."

"I'm alive as a sunrise, and a good thing, too. You're out here sizing up my trees again. Well, forget it. You ain't cuttin' a one."

"They buried you." His conviction was faltering and his voice took on the tone of a person trying to convince himself he was right. "I talked to Buddy. He was there. He took your body to the funeral home." He blinked his eyes as if trying to clear away an apparition. "You were dead."

Eula had a smug look on her wrinkled face. "Then you know

I came back from the dead—for the sole purpose of protecting my trees."

For a long minute, Kenderson just stared at Eula. Slowly, the bewilderment began to fade. He glanced at Crystal, then focused again on the feisty old woman. "If you had a near-death experience, then maybe you got smarter. Maybe you know now that timbering your land won't hurt it."

Eula's eyes narrowed and the look she gave him was a blast of winter from the north pole. "Randal, you don't timber land. You rape it. And I'll not have you raping my land, even if 'it don't hurt,' as you say. I don't want you on my land. Move on."

"I don't think you own the county road."

"You're on my land, not the county's. Git."

"Well, pardon me. I did get my wheels off the road and on your land. If your driver'd get her car out of the way, I'd move over five feet."

"Don't bother with five feet. Just keep going." Eula motioned for Crystal to pull forward. Crystal tore her gaze away from the double gun rack in the back of Kenderson's truck and eased past him.

Kenderson spun his tires and jerked out onto the asphalt, then slammed on his brakes and skidded to a stop. He stuck his head out the window and looked back at the two women. "Damn shame you wasn't killed in the fire. Do the area a lot of good. Maybe next time."

The truck's tires screamed as he jammed his foot on the gas pedal. In thirty seconds, the big 4x4 crested the hill and vanished from sight.

* * *

Wrung out by the encounter, Crystal could not enjoy the drive through The Park. While it was fun to see Kenderson's confusion and disbelief, his anger frightened her. When he said it was a shame Nana wasn't killed in the fire, his voice resonated with conviction. The final three words reverberated in her head and sent a chill down her spine. *Maybe next time.* She shook her head, trying to clear her mind. Rehashing that scene would only tie her stomach in knots.

Later, sitting on the veranda, Crystal broached the subject of her grandmother moving into Dallas. "Nana. I worry about you. And today's scene didn't help."

"Oh, Kenderson ain't got the brains to be dangerous. He's

just an unhappy old man. He'd complain if they hung him with a brand new rope."

"He still worries me."

"If you got time to worry, you ain't doing enough."

Crystal opened her mouth to object, but didn't know what to say. Before she recovered, Eula was talking again.

"Maybe that's why you haven't turned Mark's eye yet."

Crystal glared at her grandmother. "Nana! Mark is my boss, not a prospective husband."

"Husband? I didn't mention husband. Did I say husband?" Her expression was one of complete innocence. "But I guess it's been in the back of your mind."

"It certainly has not."

"Why?"

Crystal just stared at Eula. "He's not my type."

Eula cackled.

"Besides, he doesn't consider me that way. I'm just an employee. A good one and he appreciates that. But ... he wouldn't ask me out on a date."

Eula rocked slowly for several minutes and a contented expression descended over her face. "Did you know I worked for your grandfather? When I got out of high school, I started working at his store. I'd been there six months, maybe, when he called me in and said I was fired. Well, I stood up a little straighter and said 'Just why is that?'" Eula pressed her lips together and grinned. "He said, 'So I can ask you out.' I told him he didn't have to fire me to take me out, but he said his father, who really owned the store, had a policy against any dating between people working at the store."

"What'd you do?"

"I said never mind. I quit. I'd get another job somewhere else. And I didn't have a date for the boot scoot Saturday night. He bowed slightly and said, formal as could be, 'Eula Jaymeson, could I escort you to the town dance this coming Saturday?'" Eula gazed out through the trees and smiled. Her eyes sparkled, even as they misted over. "The rest, as you kids would say, is history."

* * *

Crystal drove Eula back to Melva's house. As Crystal kissed her grandmother good-bye, the older woman's arms wrapped around her granddaughter and held her tightly. "Thank you for a wonderful morning. I'm so glad you came."

Crystal got in the car and was backing out when Eula yelled to her. "He really does like you——as a woman. Grandmothers can tell."

* * *

Crystal was signaling to change lanes on the Woodall Rogers Freeway when she saw it——the second vehicle behind her. A big, brownish-red truck. It was as if someone hung a big sign in front of her: the puce truck! Her eyes locked onto the image of the vehicle, looming ever larger in the mirror.

The loud blast of a horn jarred her gaze off the mirror. She gasped as she realized that, at fifty-five miles per hour, she was one inch from a pale yellow Cadillac on her left. The driver was yelling and shaking his fist at her. She straightened up in her lane, then took a quick look in the mirror. The truck was still there.

Her hands were trembling. *Pull yourself together, Crystal. It's just a truck.* She moved into the right lane as she passed Pearl Street, took the next exit, and stopped for the red light at Field Street. When she looked in the mirror, it was filled with the brownish-red hood of a truck. Her pulse began to race.

Suddenly, she felt the truck hit her bumper. Not hard. Just a tap. An involuntary scream escaped her lips. Without looking in either direction, she jammed the gas pedal to the floor and shot across the intersection. Brakes screamed and horns honked, but she ignored them.

The puce truck followed. She twisted her head to one side and then the other, desperately searching for a policeman, but found none. She could feel terror coursing through her veins. She raced ahead. It was only a few more blocks to the office, but she felt as if she were making no progress. The more gas she gave her car, the slower it seemed to go.

At last she reached the parking lot and whipped in, nearly running over the attendant. She found a parking space, shut off the engine and buried her face in her hands. She pressed her arms against the steering wheel, trying to stop the shaking.

Suddenly someone was pounding on her window.

Chapter 26

CRYSTAL jerked her head up, bile rising in her throat. The shaking intensified. She forced herself to look to her left, through the window.

Bent over and staring at her was the young lot attendant, lightly tapping on the glass with the parking ticket. "You forgot to get a ticket, ma'am. You don't have one, we got to charge you the maximum amount."

Feeling rather foolish, Crystal rolled down the window and took the ticket, muttering a brief apology.

Her shaking began to subside. She looked around. The puce truck was nowhere in sight. Gradually, she composed herself. *There are lots of brownish-red trucks in Dallas.* She took several deep breaths. *Just a coincidence.* She got out, her legs rubbery, and checked around in a full circle. Nothing. She locked the car and started across the street to her office.

Why did he follow me off the freeway? she asked herself. *And then on down to the West End?* Crystal tried to order her frenzied thoughts. *He was right behind me at the light. He bumped me. That happens sometimes, a person just gets too close or doesn't realize his truck is rolling a little. He could have pushed me out in front of the cross traffic, but he didn't. I don't even know if it was a man driving, do I?*

All the way from the parking lot to the building that housed IRS she continued to lecture herself on her foolishness. Was it even a GMC? In her panic, she hadn't noticed. Did she even know if it was really puce or not? No. And so what if it was? But she took special care to look at every truck in sight.

By the time Crystal got into the office, she had calmed down. She stopped in the coffee room, got a soda and headed to her office.

She would check her messages, and then tell Mark about Randal Kenderson. She decided not to mention her encounter with the puce truck.

* * *

It was after four when Mark stuck his head in her office. "How's the testing going?"

"Good, I think. No real problems sticking their ugly heads up yet."

"Great. Sally wanted to know if she could get a demonstration. What do you think? Ready to show it?"

"Sure. We might turn up some problems, but ... yeah. Tell her to come on in."

Mark thought it over for a few seconds. "Let's ask Phil, too."

"Fine. The more the merrier."

He looked around. "Let's do it in my office—more room. How about fifteen minutes?"

* * *

Precisely fifteen minutes later, Sally, JT, Phil and Pam followed Crystal into Mark's office.

Sally spoke up. "I brought JT to see the demo. Is that okay?"

"Sure," said Crystal. "I invited Pam to join us."

"It's your show, Crystal," Mark said.

"First, let me fill you in on what it's supposed to do. IPPI stands for Identification from Partial Plate Information, as I'm sure you all know. Right now, if the police have the correct license plate number, obviously they can find who owns the vehicle. But often, a witness gets only part of the number. Or they're not sure about part of it. With IPPI, you input whatever information you have, it scans the DPS database and finds the most likely matches."

Pam stuck a finger up. "What's DPS?"

"That's the Texas Department of Public Safety. DPS in Austin maintains the records of all registered vehicles. So you can put in partial license plate numbers, you can put in make, model, color of the car, whatever information you have. And you can give probabilities to each."

Pam looked puzzled. "That may be clear to everybody else, but I need an example."

" Okay. An eyewitness could say he thinks the first character was either an 8 or a B. We check both, each with a 50% probability. Or they think the car was a dark color, but not black. We might give black a 10% probability, dark blue 30%, dark brown 30% and dark green 30%."

JT looked skeptical. "There are an awful lot of dark cars."

"True. But we also have part of the license plate number."

Sally said, "So if you had six of the numbers on the license plate, then there would be thirty-seven possible plates—since you didn't know what the seventh number or letter was. Then, the color or make of car would limit it even further. And of course, some of those thirty-seven possibilities might not even be plates that have been issued. Right?"

"Correct. *If* you knew that the missing character was in a specific position. If you didn't know which position, you'd have two hundred fifty-three possibilities. And with two missing numbers, it jumps to over sixty-four thousand."

"Wow," said Pam.

"So, any other information you can add really helps. Knowing it was a green Ford truck might cut it to only three hundred actually issued plates. And of those, maybe only thirty are registered in the part of the state where the sighting occurred."

"Then the program uses these probabilities to rank them?" JT asked.

"That's right. The program ranks all possible matches, using the percentages to say which matches are most likely," Crystal replied.

"In a nutshell, Crystal's program makes it possible to find a car without a complete license number," said Mark.

While Crystal was explaining the program, Mark had started IPPI on his computer and typed in the information on the puce truck.

"The case Mark just ran is on a vehicle that entered Nana's Park yesterday. I'm sure you all know by now that a woman was killed there last week when my grandmother's house burned. The program found three possible matches within the area we selected to search." She turned to Mark. "You used the thirty mile radius again?"

Mark nodded. "But there were four matches."

"Right, four. That's a reasonable number for the police to

check. Whereas the thousand it found in the entire state would be rather daunting, if not impossible, to check."

"And suppose none of those turns out to be the suspect?" asked Phil.

"We change the search criteria. We can search by any distance from any base point. We can search by counties, zip codes, whatever. And it's very easy to change the parameters."

Crystal thought of the puce truck following her on the freeway. "Mark, show how easy it is to shift the range of the search—to check, say, Dallas County."

He turned back to the keyboard and typed 'Restrict to Dallas County.' In a few seconds, the display listed ten possible matches and displayed their rankings.

"You can see the ranks, addresses, information on vehicles, etc.," Crystal said. "This search was a little more trouble because the color that the witness gave us was not a pure color. So we had to consider various combinations of red and brown. If it had been pure white, for instance, the list could have been smaller." She looked up at the ceiling for a moment. "Well, maybe not for white. Still, it's far and away better than what the DPS has now."

The group crowded around the monitor to see the information displayed.

"Look at that." Pam pointed to the first entry on the screen.

"What about it?" asked Phil.

"That's JT's address. Isn't it, JT?"

Everyone turned around to look.

JT was gone.

Chapter 27

MARK spoke first. "Pam, go see if you can find her. And tell her to come see me in my office, please." He turned to Phil. "Maybe you'd better help look for her also. Might mean nothing," Mark said as Pam and Phil headed for the door. "So, don't spook her. Be casual, but firm. And walk her back with you."

Crystal and Sally started out. "Pam and Phil will find her. Let's wait for them here."

Crystal sank into a chair, a thousand thoughts whirling through her mind, none of them slowing down enough to be studied.

Mark spoke softly. "Crystal, when we find her, do you mind if I handle this, ask her questions and all? You're so emotionally involved, I think ... well, what do *you* think?"

She nodded several times. "That's fine. That's fine."

"Why don't I go check the ladies room?" Sally asked."

"No, I want to talk with you. Pam will check there, I'm sure," Mark said. "You've worked closely with JT for several months. Tell me about her——not what's on her application. I know she's not married; has one—what, five-year-old boy? What about boyfriends?"

"A live-in."

"Know anything about him? What's his name?"

"Not really. Eddie Ray is all I've ever heard her call him. She seems to really like him."

"Let's hope so, if he's living with her," Crystal said.

"Well, I mean ... I don't know what I mean. I know he drinks a lot, goes to some seedy bars that JT won't go to. He doesn't get abusive drunk, just drinks a lot of beer, from what she says."

"What's he look like?" Crystal was thinking about the guy with the rifle. "He ever come by the office? Did JT ever describe him?"

"Nope. I asked her once and she laughed and said he wasn't very handsome, that's all."

"What kind of car does JT drive?" Mark asked. "Or truck? What about the guy? What's he drive?"

"No idea on either. I know JT has talked a little about buying a new car, but she hasn't bought it yet. At least she hasn't said she has. Mostly, the only thing she talks about other than work is her son, Luis."

Crystal tapped the monitor. "It says the truck is registered to Edward R. Dollar. That's got to be JT's Eddie Ray."

"Right." Mark drummed a steady rhythm on the desk. "You said her work slowed to a crawl a few weeks ago. Ever find out what caused that?"

Sally lowered her head and thought for a moment. "No. Like I said, she seemed to be working hard, just didn't seem to be accomplishing anything." She stopped. "Actually, now that I think about it, she did ask me about one of our other databases, the topological one."

"Why? Crystal asked, looking from Mark to Sally. "She hasn't done any work on that, has she?"

"Shouldn't have," Mark answered. "That was Phil's project. JT's never been assigned to any of Phil's work."

"Best I can remember, she wanted to know about compatibility; could info from the folklore and history base link into the topological base."

Silence again filled the room while questions raced around in Crystal's mind. Could JT be involved? They didn't have a complete license plate number. Still, the program gave that truck its top ranking. Could it be a coincidence? Crystal believed in algorithms, not coincidences.

"What do we get with a hundred and fifty mile radius of The Park?" Crystal asked.

Mark turned to his computer and typed in the request. The computer took fifteen seconds to find sixty-seven in the area, with the truck at JT's address still holding the top spot. Kenderson's was fifth.

It could still be wrong, Crystal thought. *If we had the rest of the license number, or even one more character, it might eliminate*

JT's altogether. And IPPI is still in testing. Maybe a glitch in the program? Back to the coincidence thing?

"Mark?"

Pam, Phil and JT stood in his doorway. Mark glanced at Crystal and said softly, "You're okay with my questioning her?"

Crystal nodded.

"Probably nothing to it anyway." He raised his voice a little. "JT. Come in. Have a seat."

JT shuffled in, head down, spirit deflated. She selected the chair farthest from Sally. Crystal perched on the edge of her chair.

"If you don't need us," said Phil, "we'll get back to work."

"That's fine. Would you please close the door?"

For a minute, no one spoke. Crystal and Sally looked at Mark. Mark looked at JT. JT looked at her hands, clinched in her lap.

"JT, I wanted to talk with you."

JT looked up at Mark, then glanced quickly at Crystal and Sally.

"I've asked Crystal and Sally to stay. Sally, because she's your direct supervisor. And Crystal, because what I want to talk to you about concerns her. Eula Moore is Crystal's grandmother."

JT head popped up and she cut her eyes in Crystal's direction. Just as quickly, her focus returned to the rug.

"As you have probably heard, some strange things have been going on at Eula's place. Last week, things escalated. Her house was burned and a woman was killed. Then somebody shot at Crystal while she was out there."

Crystal's head jerked as her gaze snapped from JT to Mark. *How did he find out about that? Has Nana found out?*

Sally looked at Crystal with a mixture of shock and disbelief.

Mark kept his attention on JT. "Yesterday, we got a picture of a truck entering Eula's property. It matched the description Crystal's grandmother had given us of the truck that tried to run her off the road. When we ran it through the IPPI program...well, you saw the results. The top possibility is registered at your address to an Edward R. Dollar. We didn't get the complete license plate number. But it is a strange coincidence." Mark paused.

The tension in the office was oppressive. JT's breathing quickened as she chewed her lower lip and studied the rug. Crystal could feel her own heart beating.

"JT, I'm not accusing you of anything. But Crystal's grandmother was almost killed, and a friend of hers *was*. And Crystal came within a few inches of being killed. Can you shed any light at all on this? Please."

The tears started. JT looked at Crystal's hands, but her gaze never ventured higher. "I didn't know." Now, she was sobbing. "I didn't know it was your grandmother's place. I didn't know anybody would get hurt."

For a bit, the only sound in the room was JT's crying. Finally, Mark offered her some water. She nodded, and Sally left to get it.

Emotion so saturated the air, Crystal felt she was suffocating, and wished she had asked Sally to bring her some water also. When Sally returned, JT had fished some tissues from her purse and was drying her eyes and blowing her nose. She drank most of the water without stopping.

Crystal, Mark and Sally sat in silence, giving JT time to compose herself. She knew something about the mysterious happenings at The Park and it appeared she would tell them. They did not want to do anything to destroy that willingness.

Finally, her head still bowed, JT began talking. "It was a little over three weeks ago. We had started testing on the folklore project. I ran across a story, a legend, I guess, about a small band of men bringing a wagonload of gold up through East Texas. They had camped on a low hill overlooking a small lake. The next morning, one of their scouts came racing in. He had sighted a band of Indians coming their way."

JT pressed a tissue to her eyes, then went on with her story. "They didn't have enough men to stand and fight and the wagon was loaded with a ton of gold, so there was no way they could pull the wagon and outrun the Indians. The leader ordered his men to push the wagon off the cliff and into the lake. Then, they made a run for it." JT stopped, blew her nose, then continued. "But the Indians caught them and killed everybody, except a small boy. The Indians took him with them. It was years before he escaped and by then, he had no idea where the gold had been hidden, only that it was in a lake in East Texas."

She stopped, drank the rest of the water and dabbed at her

nose. She closed her eyes and said nothing.

Crystal shifted back off the edge of her chair, wondering how this related to her grandmother and wishing JT would get on with the story. After a while, Mark said, almost in a whisper, "What happened next?"

JT took a sharp intake of breath and let it out through her lips. "I didn't believe it, of course. But I told Eddie Ray." She glanced at Mark. "That's my boyfriend, Eddie Ray Dollar; he lives with me and my son, Luis. I just thought it was a fun thing to talk about. But Eddie Ray's eyes got big as silver dollars. He's really sweet, and really loves Luis. But he's not much for working. He started asking me all sorts of questions about it.

"I told him to forget it. He got mad and left and didn't come back for a couple of days. When he did, he started pressuring me to find out more about it. He threatened to leave for good if I wouldn't do this for him. If I lov--." She stopped, and Crystal thought JT blushed a little. "If I wanted him to stay, I'd do it for him."

She looked up at Mark. "Luis thinks Eddie Ray's the greatest, follows him everywhere. I just ... ."

After a moment, JT continued. "By then, we'd loaded most of the data. So I searched and searched and found several other references to a lost wagonload of gold. They were different, but some parts were similar and Eddie Ray got all excited and said it proved it was true. I told him in all these years it had probably been found. So he kept after me to look for anything about it being found. I couldn't find even a hint about a wagonload of gold being found, or even a bunch of gold. That convinced Eddie Ray the gold was there, waiting for him."

Once more, she looked up, her expression pleading for understanding. "Dr. O'Malley, I tried to discourage him—told him East Texas is thousands of square miles—but he said it was in a lake with a cliff beside it. And since I always told him IRS could find anything, why couldn't I find that lake for him. Why wouldn't I do that for him? Then he threatened to leave again, this time in front of Luis."

She paused and swiped at her nose, her tears starting again. "Luis went all to pieces, crying and begging me not to let Eddie Ray leave. So I promised I'd try to find the lake. I knew it was silly and the few descriptions of the lake weren't enough to find it. But I tried."

"That's when you asked me about the topological database," said Sally.

JT nodded. "I took every bit of information from all the stories about the gold. I got an idea of what part of Texas they were in. And then I used the topological base to check every lake that fit the details. I found one in the right part of Texas that fit the information I had, better than all the others."

Mark raised his eyebrows. "One?"

"Yes. It was not a big lake, but it wasn't a pond either. It had a hill on one side. It ran East and West. Then--."

Mark held up his hand. "I'd like to hear all the details, JT. But right now I want to know——did you tell Eddie Ray?"

"Yes." She glanced at Mark, then Crystal. "But you have to know Eddie Ray. He wouldn't hurt a fly. He acts tough and has these tattoos all over his arms and walks like he's stomping on somebody. But it's all show."

Crystal's voice was almost a snarl. "He tried to run Nana off the road. And probably tampered with her brakes."

"And somebody is dead, JT," Mark added. "The thought of gold can make people do things they wouldn't ordinarily do."

JT looked down at her hands, which had shredded the tissues she was holding.

"I think we'd better go talk to Eddie Ray," Mark said. "Do you know where he is?"

She closed her eyes and swayed ever so slightly. She didn't speak.

"JT? Will you help us?" Mark's tone was soft and gentle.

"He should be at home with Luis." She looked up. "I could call and check."

Mark shook his head. "I don't think we should call. He might run." He turned to Crystal. "May be best if JT and I go alone. Might get more out of him if there aren't too many people there. JT, let's go together in my truck."

Crystal sat there, stunned. This was crazy. These attacks on Nana were all because some fool believed a folk tale? Her Nana might have been killed because someone believed a buried treasure story? Bessie *was* killed. Suddenly, she jumped up, ran to her office and grabbed her purse. *They're damn well not going without me.*

She caught them in the parking lot. "I'm going with you."

Mark looked at Crystal but before he could say anything, she continued. "Won't do any good to argue. I'm going—with you or in my own car. Which?"

Chapter 28

MARK, Crystal and JT sat in the front seat of Mark's Ram truck, JT in the middle. Mark asked a few questions: how long had she known Eddie Ray, how did she meet him, where was he from, what did he do, had she met any of his family. JT answered in as few words as possible, most frequently, "I don't know."

Crystal sat in stony silence, staring straight ahead, her mind rehashing the news of the last hour. While the IPPI program gave possibilities, led them in a direction, JT confirmed they were on the right track. Her boyfriend had gold fever and probably was the one snooping in Nana's lake. The Park wasn't a place he might accidentally pass by on the way to the store. *Eddie Ray has been at Nana's, tried to run her off the road, and probably tried to kill her*, Crystal seethed. *Mark should have fired JT on the spot. Or after we find Eddie Ray.* That small thought of vengeance placated Crystal just enough so she quit grinding her teeth. But her hands were still clenched in tight balls. When she opened her right hand, she saw dots of blood where her fingernails had dug into her palms.

She listened as Mark tried a less threatening conversation with JT: what school did her son attend, did he like it, was she enjoying her job, did she like to cook. Each question got a polite, one-word answer. Most of the way, she seemed on the verge of tears. She looked straight out the windshield, both hands gripping her purse.

When they got near JT's house, Mark asked her for directions. Again, she provided the information with great economy of words.

Her house was in a neat, middle-class neighborhood. Kids played soccer in the street; two women visited across a flower garden, and near the middle of the block a tough-looking character with tattoos up and down both arms was playing catch with a young boy. Crystal didn't need to ask which house was JT's.

The grass was trimmed, if not very green. Perhaps it only needed more water. A mimosa tree, with long horizontal limbs, shaded much of the yard. Impatiens filled a flower bed that stretched across the front of the brick house, forming a wave of color from white at the corners of the house, through pale pink, to brighter pink, to shocking pink by the time it reached the small porch at the front door.

Crystal judged Eddie Ray to be over six feet tall, and in the neighborhood of two hundred pounds. Nondescript brown hair curled over his ears and down his neck, stopping just over his collar. His aquiline nose was slightly off-center. He was not a handsome man, but his expression was encouraging and smiling as he carefully tossed a tennis ball into the tiny hands. He wore a short sleeve knit shirt, jeans and boots.

Mark pulled his truck into the drive behind a reddish brown GMC Sierra. Eddie Ray walked over, Luis trailing after him like a friendly puppy. JT slid out of the truck and said something to Eddie Ray in Spanish, which Crystal did not understand. Was she warning him, Crystal wondered, telling him to be careful, or perhaps not say anything at all? JT introduced Eddie Ray, then took Luis by the hand and walked into the house.

Eddie Ray glowered at Mark, narrowing his eyes and tightening his mouth into a straight, hard line. "Juanita said I oughta talk to you. So talk." He completely ignored Crystal.

She was tempted to laugh at his macho facade. But she remembered the dead woman and her own encounter at the lake. And she could hear her Nana insisting someone was trying to kill her. Eddie Ray didn't look like the man who had shot at her; he was too tall. He might have been the other man, but she didn't think so.

Mark wasted no time. "Would you like to tell us about your activities in East Texas, near Wooden Nickel?"

"Hell, no. I wouldn't like to tell you nothing."

That was a dumb way to start. Crystal decided she could do better. "I was in favor of just sending the police out to pick you up. But JT——Juanita——asked us to talk with you first. So don't give us the stonewall treatment, or we'll call the police now."

For the first time, Eddie Ray looked at Crystal, glowering as if to intimidate her. "I jest tried to scare the old woman, that's all. Ain't police business."

Mark pointed a finger at the tattooed man. "A house was burned down and a woman murdered. That's police business. And you, Mr. Edward R. Dollar, are the prime suspect right now."

Eddie Ray shifted his glare back to Mark. The defiant look vanished. His face paled and his voice quavered. "I didn't know they killed nobody. They didn't tell me that. They said they burnt the house so's she'd have to go somewheres else to live."

Crystal thought Eddie Ray might pass out. His breathing became irregular and his eyes glazed over. Mark put a hand on Eddie Ray's elbow. "Why don't we go inside and sit down, get you a drink of water."

Eddie Ray nodded once and plodded toward the house. If he normally walked like he was stomping on people, as JT had said, the news of the dead woman had certainly changed that. Briefly, Crystal wondered if it was for show, to divert suspicion. If it were, Eddie Ray could get a job as an actor.

The front door opened into a small living room. It was simply furnished, neat and clean. Crystal noticed several children's books on the coffee table and was pleased to see that they looked well used. Mark and Crystal followed the sullen man with the tattooed arms into the adjoining dining room. The Danish-Modern table and chairs continued the style set in the living room. An open door led into the kitchen.

Eddie Ray sank down at a round kitchen table, taking a chair next to JT. She laid her hand lightly on his arm. Mark, not waiting for an invitation, pulled out a chair for Crystal, then sat next to her in the chair directly across from Eddie Ray. Luis was nowhere to be seen.

JT looked up at Crystal. Sadness flooded her eyes, where the tears no longer did. "Can I get you something to drink? Tea? A Dr Pepper?" Everyone at IRS knew that Mark rarely drank anything but Dr Pepper.

Without looking at the woman, Crystal said, "Dr Pepper." She didn't hide her anger.

In a minute, JT placed glasses of ice and soft drink cans in front of Crystal and Mark, a longneck Lone Star in front of Eddie Ray and a glass of ice water on the table at her own place.

JT broke the silence. "I've told Dr. O'Malley and Crystal about the information I gathered and gave to you. But I don't know what you did with it or how it has anything to do with the house burning and a woman being killed. They photographed your truck out there." Her voice had started out strongly. Now, it turned soft and pleading. "Eddie Ray, I know you wouldn't do that. So, please, just tell them anything you know about it."

For a long time, Eddie Ray played with his beer bottle. He made interlocking rings on the tabletop with the bottle's wet bottom, then tilting it over until beer almost spilled out. Finally, he took a long pull on the amber liquid, set the bottle down and looked at Mark. It was all Crystal could do to keep from screaming at him to get on with it.

"I was at the Longneck. That's a bar over in Deep Elum. I'd downed a few, and these guys was talking big and ... . Hell, I just got tired of them acting like they was such big shots." He glanced at JT, then looked back at Mark, completely ignoring Crystal. "So I said I knowed where a hidden treasure was. Well, they all laughed at me. I got kinda mad and said they wouldn't laugh if they knowed it was a ton of gold. They kept on laughing and called me a stupid drunk. So, I went out to my truck and got some of the computer stuff Juanita had brung me."

JT shook her head slowly and looked away. Neither Crystal nor Mark moved a muscle.

"That got their damn attention all right," Eddie Ray continued. "But then somebody said it weren't no good if I didn't know where it was. I said I knowed where it was but I wasn't gonna tell them."

He looked down at the table, and for a minute, Crystal thought that was all he was going to say. Then, without looking up, he started again. "Guess I was trying to play the big shot. Most time, I never got two dollars to rub together. Not for long, anyways. I wanted to shut their face from laughing at me."

Crystal stole a glance at Mark, but his focus never left Eddie Ray.

After a few moments, Eddie Ray continued. "I had another

beer and left. Well, two guys followed me out and grabbed me and banged me up. Said they ought to kick the sh——." He stopped in mid-word and cut his eyes toward JT. "Kick the crap out of me for lying and gettin' people all upset. I told 'em it was true, the computer said the gold was there. They started punching on me again."

He looked at JT, and this time Crystal thought he was trying to make JT understand. "There was two of them, Juanita. I thought they was gonna break me in half." He kept his gaze on JT for several moments, then looked back at Mark. "So, I said I'd bring 'em the location the next night, figuring I won't never go back to that bar no more. And I didn't. But they must 'a followed me home, cause a couple of days later, they showed up here and said if I didn't get 'em that location, they'd snatch the kid."

JT's hands flew to her face and she gasped. Her body jerked. "You never told me that! Oh, Jesus, Mary and Joseph."

"That's when I tried to get you to send him to your mother's."

She began to rock back and forth, as the tears flowed down her cheeks. She crossed herself and said "Oh God. Oh God. Oh God."

"It's okay. It's okay," he whispered.

In spite of her anger, Crystal could not keep from feeling sorry for JT. She could only imagine the pain of hearing that someone was threatening to kidnap your child. And Crystal found it encouraging that this man, working so hard to appear tough, actually showed concern for JT's feelings. *If only he'd worried about Nana.*

Eddie Ray wrapped his arms around JT and spoke softly in her ear. "They won't take Luis. I told 'em where the gold was hid. I even helped 'em search for it. They won't take him. I promise you that. I promise you, nothing will happen to Luis."

JT was crying now. "But what if there isn't any gold? Or I found the wrong lake? They'll come back. They'll try to take Luis." Her entire body shook.

"I'll take care of him, Juanita. You know I will. I won't never let nothing happen to Luis. I love him as much as you do."

For a long time, JT cried and Eddie Ray held her. Finally, she pulled away, fished a tissue out of her pocket and wiped her eyes. "I'd better go check on Luis."

"What happened next?" Mark asked as soon as she was out of

the room. "You said you'd bring the location."

Eddie took another sip from the brown bottle, then frowned at it as if the beer tasted bitter. He set the bottle aside and seemed to be collecting his thoughts.

Crystal and Mark waited.

"I kept pushing on Juanita to find the location. She didn't wanna do it and I was purdy rough on her and threatened to leave. I couldn't tell her about Luis." He looked at Mark, pleading for understanding. "Them guys was serious. What else could I do?"

"You could have told JT. The police. They take kidnapping threats very seriously."

"It would've really upset Juanita."

"Her son was in danger. She deserved to know," Crystal said.

Mark put his hands on the table and leaned forward. "So, JT finally found a lake that she thought had the gold in it. Then what?"

"I told 'em where it was. They made me drive 'em out there and we eyeballed it—found out it was a big damn lake. Not big like Tawakoni, or even White Rock, but damn big to search. And some old lady lived by it. They decided I was the one what had to search the lake for it and that meant I had to scare the old lady off. So I tried a couple of times. But she wouldn't leave."

No, you wouldn't scare Nana off, Crystal thought.

"You told them which lake, but then you had to search for the gold?" Mark asked.

"Yeah. And I had to give 'em half when I found it. But like I said, the old lady wouldn't scare. They was mad as hell. Worked me over again. Then they said they'd take care of it. They'd burn her house and she'd have to go somewheres else. Then I could find the gold. Honest, they didn't say nothing about killing nobody." For the first time since sitting down at the table, Eddie Ray looked at Crystal. "Maybe it was an accident."

Crystal shook her head, her simmering anger again flashing to a boil. Her voice was like a hot poker. "It wasn't an accident. They crushed her skull before the fire burned her."

Eddie Ray swallowed and looked down at the table.

"So, what happened next?" Mark asked.

Eddie Ray let out a long breath. "They called me and said it was all clear, watch out for firemen or anything, but the old woman wouldn't be there. So, I goes back out and looks some more. I don't know how I'm gonna find it."

"What can you tell me about them?"

"Names is Joe and Al. Never heard no last names."

Crystal and Mark waited for more, but there wasn't any. "What did they drive?" Mark asked.

"Don't know. Only saw their car once at night. It's black with fire painted on the hood, you know, like the engine's breathing fire."

"Ford, Pontiac? American, foreign?"

"Couldn't see. It was dark. Pretty sure it was American."

This is like pulling teeth, Crystal thought, impressed with Mark's patience.

"What do they look like?" she asked.

Eddie screwed up his face and shrugged. "Just guys."

Crystal pushed. "One maybe five feet eight or nine, late twenties, dark hair, big nose? The other one almost your height?"

"I guess. Joe's kinda short. You know 'em?"

"Not exactly."

Mark asked, "Did they mention any other names? Did they hang around anybody else?"

Eddie shook his head.

"Just the two?"

"Once they said something 'bout a boss. No name, just 'the boss'."

For a while, they just sat there. The chances were overwhelmingly against any gold in Eula's lake. But just the possibility of a ton of gold—that small, tickly thought—could awaken a powerful greed in people who wanted something for nothing.

Mark leaned over and spoke softly into Crystal's ear. "I don't think sending Luis to JT's mother for a while will put him out of danger. But until we get this straightened up, it's probably a good idea."

"I agree."

"Go talk to JT. Tell her we'll take Eddie Ray to get her car, and she should give serious consideration to taking Luis to her mother's. Or some place that can't be connected to her."

Crystal nodded and went to look for JT.

Chapter 29

AS soon as Crystal was out of the room, Mark leaned over and whispered softly to Eddie Ray. "We'll drop Crystal off at her car and then you can drive JT's car back here——later."

Eddie Ray knitted his eyebrows and tilted his head to the side. "I can take JT to get it."

Mark continued. "No. Because you and I have a little errand to run."

The tattooed man still looked puzzled.

Mark glanced toward the door. "Once we've dropped Crystal off at her car, you and I are going to go see if we can find Joe and Al. But we can't tell JT or Crystal about that. Okay?"

A few minutes later, the three left. Eddie Ray carried a small bundle.

At the parking lot across from the IRS office, they dropped Crystal at her car. They watched her drive off and once her car was out of sight, Mark pulled out and headed toward Deep Elum.

Eddie Ray unrolled the bundle. "This gonna be a little big for you, but it'll look better at The Longneck. Didn't think your feet'd fit none of my boots."

Mark looked at the shirt. He wasn't sure he wanted to blend in too well. It might be better if he were dressed a bit above the regular crowd.

"Won't nobody talk to you dressed like you are."

" Okay. I've got some old ropers behind the seat."

For a while, both men were silent. But Mark's mind explored various aspects of this bizarre situation. What would a ton of gold be worth? He did a few mental calculations and raised his eyebrows. At today's price, over forty million dollars! One could live extremely well off the interest of that and never touch the principal.

Don't get sucked into that kind of thinking, he told himself. It doesn't make any difference what it would be worth. There isn't any gold there. But until Joe and Al and "the boss" realize that, they'll remain a threat.

"What're we gonna do when we find 'em?"

"Try to convince them there is no gold in the lake, or any place around there," Mark explained.

"But the computer says there is."

"Not really. First, it says there are *stories* that say a wagonload of gold was pushed off a cliff into a lake. The computer does not say it is a real, factual occurrence. And second, it does not say it was Eula's lake. That's just what JT came up with."

"But I saw all them stories. They all said the same thing."

"But they were just that: stories."

Eddie pursed his lips and shook his head.

Mark searched his brain. "Okay, Eddie. You've heard about the Loch Ness Monster that's supposed to be in a lake in Scotland? Well, this is sort of like that. A good folk tale."

"But I seen pictures of that monster on TV. It's there, all right." Eddie nodded to reinforce the existence of the monster. "They just ain't found it yet. Like the gold. And you know, I been figuring. That gold'd be worth three or four million dollars. Even havin' to split it, I still got a million bucks."

Mark let that pass. No point making things worse. "Eddie, there is no gold. You've got to believe that so we can convince Joe and Al to back off."

Eddie Ray's forehead wrinkled and his brows furrowed as he puzzled over that. After a minute, he brightened. "Oh, I get it." A smile spread across his face. "We tell 'em that so's they go away. Then we go find it." He chuckled for a moment, then stopped. "Won't work. They're too smart for that. 'Sides, I showed 'em the computer stuff. They know it's there."

Mark waited for a car to pass, then turned left. "Let me do the talking when we get to the part about the gold. Okay? Introduce us, and then just answer any questions I ask you. Nothing more. Okay?"

"What if *they* ask me something?"

"I'll answer."

* * *

By the time they reached The Longneck Bar, the sun had dropped below the horizon and darkness colored the city. Mark drove around the block twice looking for the fire-breathing black car. It was nowhere to be seen.

He turned into a side street and parked. Mark changed into Eddie Ray's shirt, then reached behind the seat, found a pair of mud-caked boots and pulled them on. They walked back to the corner and turned on to Elm Street.

Now, it was Eddie Ray's turn to give advice. "Don't order no Coors and no Heiny beer, either. They ain't gonna have it and it'll make you look like a slummer."

"Slummer? What's that?"

"Some highfalutin' guy getting his kicks by going out and slumming."

"I guess that means no Dr Pepper, either."

Eddie Ray laughed. "Damn straight."

"I'll let you order for me."

Inside, Eddie Ray ordered two Lone Stars and carried them over to an empty pool table. "Know how to play Eight Ball?"

"You can give me some tips."

Mark had played many a game of Eight Ball, but never in a place quite like this. A bar covered most of one wall. The bartender reminded him of those in movies who kept a baseball bat under the counter. Most of the barstools were occupied, the mix of men and women about even. The room was painted, or more likely simply turned, dark brown. In fact, every surface seemed to be either brown or black. A heavy layer of smoke hung in the air and the lights reminded Mark of San Francisco street lamps in a heavy fog.

After a while, his eyes adjusted and Mark began to study the crowd. He felt certain he was the only one not smoking something. Occasionally, the heady, sweet scent of marijuana drifted his way.

Customers filled about half of the tables and booths. Not bad for a Tuesday night, Mark surmised. The men were uniformly dressed in jeans, boots, and knit shirts. The women, on the other hand, presented many different looks. There were skin-tight jeans with midriff tops, culottes and western shirts, dirndl skirts with off-the-shoulder blouses, handkerchief skirts, minis, country gingham dresses, and one young woman wore a granny dress.

The restroom reeked as if it hadn't been cleaned in a month, and Mark vowed they would leave before he needed to visit that filthy place again. Graffiti filled all available space, promising everything from a good time to superior weed to cheap auto body repair.

Every time the door to the street opened, Eddie Ray turned to check out the newcomers. Mark ignored them. Eddie Ray would alert him, and undoubtedly Joe and Al would seek out Eddie Ray.

After six games, Eddie Ray slammed his cue back in the rack. "What the hell was that crap, 'you can give me some tips'? You cleaned my plow six straight games."

Mark grinned. "People act logically, Eddie Ray. I was willing to put up money on these games. Logic tells you that I already knew something about Eight Ball, regardless of what I said."

Eddie Ray grumbled as he fished out his wallet. "Don't know nothing about logic, but I think you conned me."

"Yes, I did. Get to know people before you get into money discussions. And don't brag until you know what the other guy is holding. Your four kings just might lose to four aces."

Two men walked up to the table. Involuntarily, Mark stiffened.

"Finished?" the redheaded one asked.

"Yeah," Eddie Ray said, hardly looking at them. "I've had enough." He held out six dollars to Mark.

"Use that to buy us another round," Mark said. "I'll grab a table. Ask the bartenders if Joe and Al have been in today."

Mark and Eddie Ray lounged at the table, trying to find something to talk about. Eddie Ray wanted to talk about the gold, a topic Mark felt best to avoid in the bar. Finally, Mark said something about The Dallas Cowboys. Eddie Ray became animated and eager to explain why they lost their last game and what their prospects for the rest of the season were.

An hour passed. "You said they usually came in earlier?" asked Mark.

"Yeah. They've always been here by nine or so."

"And the bartender hadn't seen either one today?"

"Said he don't know no Joe or Al." Eddie Ray turned up his bottle for another drink, but it was empty.

"It's 9:30. Let's stick around another half hour."

"Suits me. I hate to go face Juanita." He stood up. "Want another round?"

"No. I'm . . ."

The door opened and two men walked in. They scanned the room and one of them stopped to stare openly at Mark. He took a step in Mark's direction and stopped. Eddie Ray was fumbling with his wallet and hadn't seen them. Finally getting his money out, he turned toward the bar, his gaze taking in the two newcomers. He looked at them and they at him. After a moment, he continued on to the bar. The two men wandered across the room and found an empty pool table.

The whole incident had taken no more than twenty seconds, but Mark felt drained. Rigid as a board, he took a deep breath and tried to relax his muscles. Eddie Ray returned with his beer and slumped down as if nothing had happened.

"Did you recognize those two who just came in?" Mark asked.

Eddie turned to look at them again. "Naw. Never seen 'em before."

"How often did you see Joe and Al here?"

"Like I told you, after that first time, they was here every time I was. Usually, I was here first. Then after awhile, they come in. Like I said." He tipped the bottle up for a long drink.

At ten-fifteen, they left. The drive back to IRS was quiet, Mark trying to decide what to do next, Eddie Ray staring out the window.

Mark stopped beside JT's car. "Eddie Ray, be careful. Joe and Al are criminals. They're dangerous. Try to stay away from them. And make sure JT takes Luis to her mother's—or some place." Eddie Ray got out and trudged over to unlock JT's car. Mark called out to him. "Good luck with JT. Hope I didn't get you in too much trouble keeping you out this late."

Eddie Ray gave a weak smile and got in the car.

Mark believed his story about Joe and Al. Somehow, this big, macho man looked more like a little boy on his way to see the principal than like a criminal.

Chapter 30

CRYSTAL came in, slammed the door and threw her purse across the room at the couch.

Brandi watched with fascination. "Well, I see you had a good day at work."

"Let's fix dinner. I'm starved."

The two women went into the kitchen and began preparing food.

"We had a breakthrough. On Nana's problems." Crystal furiously shredded cheese for quesadillas as she related Eddie Ray's story and the legend of the gold.

Brandi was appalled. "Poor JT. They threatened to kidnap her son."

"She brought it on herself."

"Crystal! You don't mean that. No way she could have known what would happen."

"Well, she started this whole thing that almost got Nana killed. And it isn't over yet." Crystal pursed her lips and closed her eyes for a moment, then looked back at her roommate. "You're right, of course. I do feel sorry for her. I really do. I've never seen such a frightened look as she had when Eddie Ray told her about the kidnap threat. I'm just so upset about Nana. And those hoodlums, Joe and Al, are still out there. I wish we could find them."

"Where'd you say Eddie Ray met them?"

"At some bar. I think he called it Longneck, or something."

"There's a Longneck Bar down in Deep Elum."

Crystal brightened. "That's it. He said it was on Elm Street." She turned the stove on and placed a skillet on it. "You know where that place is?"

"Yeah." Brandi brought tortillas from the refrigerator. "I went there once, oh, a year or more ago."

Unbidden, a thought popped into Crystal's mind: if you want to make bread, you have to get your hands in the dough. "Let's go."

"To The Longneck? Now?"

"Yeah. Let's go see if we can find Joe and Al."

Brandi looked skeptical. "It's a pretty seedy bar. Would you even recognize Joe or Al if they were there?"

"If they're the ones who tried to kill me."

"You understand, I've been there, and I don't mind going back. But it's not a nice place. I doubt you've ever been to a bar like The Longneck."

Without thinking, Crystal touched her sleeve just over the gunshot wound. "I can handle it."

Her roommate looked at the clock. " Okay. It's a little early. Things don't get going down there 'til 10 or 10:30. After we eat, we'll see what you have to wear."

* * *

At 9:55, Brandi yelled. "Have you seen my pliers?"

Crystal came to the door, dressed in blue jeans and a plaid shirt that Brandi judged too nice for The Longneck, but the closest thing she could find in Crystal's wardrobe. A tiny cactus swung from each of Crystal's ears. "I thought you always kept them on your dresser."

"I do and ... and here they are. Well, they were hiding a minute ago." She lay down on the bed and used the pliers to pull up the zipper on her jeans.

"I don't understand why they have to be *that* tight."

Brandi laughed. "That way, guys can't pinch you. Or get your pants off if you pass out."

"Well, I'm not planning to pass out."

"Neither am I. Just a precaution." She giggled. "I once considered just painting myself blue. But I couldn't get the right color."

Crystal just shook her head.

"No. Really, I just like the way they look when they fit really tight. And I'll turn a few heads."

"That beautiful hair will do the trick."

"Mom gave me mousy brown hair. L'oreal gave me this

auburn masterpiece."

"Well, you certainly look good."

"A planned community. You hear about self-made men. I'm a self re-made woman. Dad named me Bertha; can you believe that? So, when I was eighteen, I had it legally changed to Brandi. Considered Kristi. Still not sure if that wouldn't have been better."

"You changed your name?"

"Yeah. Never liked Bertha. Would you? Decided, why should I keep the name of one of Dad's old girlfriends? I didn't like it. And I'm sure Mom didn't either. So, poof, it was gone." She grinned. "Took off twenty pounds, changed the hair, the eyes. I got washed-out blue from Dad. Accuvue gave me these aqua beauties. Decided the nose was fine. Wore braces for two years."

"You just decided to . . ."

"To look the way I wanted to. Oh, and I took a course in make-up. Best money I ever spent. Even the contacts didn't do as much for my eyes as knowing how to put on eye shadow, and eyeliner, and eyebrow pencil. 'Course now, I just have my brows and lashes dyed."

"But I still see you putting on mascara?"

"For body and fullness, gal. Why should only guys have good lashes?" Brandi checked once more in the mirror. "I'll do." She scanned her roommate from head to toe. "And so will you. Let's go wow 'em."

Chapter 31

BRANDI was right. Crystal had never been in a place like this. She thought she had gone to some seedy bars while in college. She was wrong. They weren't even in the same league with The Longneck. It was loud and so smoky you couldn't see across the room. *Must not be any ventilation at all.*

She asked for a Coors, and the waiter roared. "That's a good one. Want a Coors, try the Crescent," he said, referring to an exclusive hotel a few miles away. "Have a Bud Light. You'll never know the difference."

When he came back, he slammed the bottle down so hard beer splashed out and onto Crystal's arm. "Sorry." He reached over and wiped her arm with a beer-soaked rag.

"Get any on your shirt?" he asked, rag ready to wipe down more of the beautiful, black-haired young woman.

"No," Crystal said quickly. "I'm okay."

"Just call for Rick if you need anything. Anything at all." He left, laughing at his own cleverness.

Brandi leaned over the table and still had to yell to be heard above the noise. "See 'em?"

Crystal shook her head no.

They finished two more beers. Crystal went to the ladies room, but could not bring herself to use it. She had never seen a place so filthy. But the trip had given her another opportunity to look over the crowd. She wound through the room one way going and a different way back.

A young man, a big hole in the seat of his jeans, shirt unbuttoned and hanging open to reveal a mass of dark hair, sat on the corner of their table chatting up Brandi. As Crystal sat down, she heard Brandi saying, "... not even if you were as good as you say you

139

are."

On impulse, Crystal blurted out, "Besides, we're waiting for Joe and Al."

The man turned to inspect Crystal. "Joe and Al? Which one of you gets stuck with Joe? Come on, I'm better'n the two of 'em together. I'll take both of you. Besides, Joe and Al ain't coming."

"When I saw Al the other day, he said he'd be here," Crystal said.

"Well he ain't. Big Man's got 'em doing something up in Denton. Didn't say when they was coming back."

Crystal smiled for the first time since sitting down. Denton was north of Dallas, not even in the same direction as Wooden Nickel.

The man saw her smile and misread it. "Hey, I like those little cactuses." He reached over to touch one of Crystal's earrings. She resisted the urge to back away from him. "So, you and me?" He glanced at Brandi. "Or all three of us? What's good for you?"

"Not you," said Brandi. "Just cause Joe and Al ain't coming don't mean we're reduced to taking swamp scum. Buzz off, Buster."

The man looked surprised. "But you and me was——"

"Changed my mind. That's a woman's right."

He left, muttering something about bitches.

"Let's go sit at the bar for a beer and see if we can get anything out of the bartender," Brandi said.

They perched on bar stools and ordered Bud Lights. The bartender was a big man and even so, his hands were too big for his body. He brought the beers over and said to Brandi, "Here's your Bud Light. And I'm your Bud Heavy. You need any help or special 'tention, call on Bud Heavy." He stayed there, grinning at Brandi, his eyes roaming over her.

Crystal spoke up. "Hey, Bud. Have you seen Joe or Al tonight?"

Without taking his eyes off Brandi, he said "No."

"Funny. When I saw Joe the other day, he said he'd meet us here tonight."

Bud turned his head toward Crystal. "You saw Joe? What was he wearing?"

Crystal's pulse rate leaped up and her stomach twisted.

Which one was Joe? She had a fifty-fifty chance. "Fatigues and a cap."

"What'd the cap say?"

Crystal's heart almost stopped. What was written on the cap? Something about a bar. And just when the pause had stretched too long, it popped into her mind. "I'd rather be in a bar."

"Ain't gonna be here tonight. Out of town." He turned his attention back to Brandi.

Brandi gave him a big smile. "You got a phone number for 'em, my Bud Heavy?"

Crystal wondered if Bud had x-ray vision. He seemed to be staring right through Brandi's blouse.

"No," Bud answered. "Tell you what. Give me your number and if I see them, I'll have 'em call you."

"They've already got it," Crystal interjected.

Again, his eyes didn't stray off Brandi. "I know them. Can't keep nothing. Lost it for sure. Give me your number, sweets."

Brandi tilted her head back and hooted. "Not on your life, Bud Heavy. Last time I gave my number to a bartender, I ended up having to change it." She leaned forward and looked into Bud's eyes. "When do you expect them back?"

"Tomorrow."

Brandi dropped some crumpled bills on the bar and got up. "See you then, Bud Heavy." She fluttered her long eyelashes several times, and still looking at the burly man, said to Crystal, "Let's buzz off."

Outside, the two women moved quickly to the car, and once inside, locked the doors and left immediately.

"Wow," Crystal said. "You were right. I've never been to a place like that before. Don't care if I never do again."

"I've been to worse. We got out without being pawed. First dibs on the shower."

"You went to places like that?"

"Yeah. I even went to MicroDate. Once."

"What's MicroDate?"

"You never heard of MicroDate?" Brandi arched her eyebrows and shook her head. "The one I went to had lots of little tables. You sit at one and a guy comes up and you talk for seven minutes."

"Seven minutes?" Crystal asked as she turned right to enter the freeway. "You kept a stopwatch on it?"

"No. They ring a bell, and he leaves and another guy comes, and you talk to him for seven minutes. There must have been a hundred people there. 'Course, you only talk to about a dozen. But that's enough, believe me. It's exhausting."

"What? You pass out your phone number?"

"No. Everybody's got a number. You write down ones you're interested in. Then if any of those have written down your number, the MicroDate people get you together. Think it cost me about thirty bucks."

"You date anybody from there?"

"Nope. I only wrote down one guy's number. I guess he didn't write mine down."

"But MicroDate wasn't like the Longneck, was it?"

"No. It was a nice place. But I went to places like the Longneck. Before I met Tom, I went every place. Met all kinds of scum. Thought that's what men were. Lucky I met Tom. What a sweetheart."

Crystal wondered fleetingly under what circumstances Brandi had met the policeman, but returned to the problem at hand. "Didn't learn too much."

"No, but some. By the way, what were you going to do if Joe and Al *were* there?"

Crystal shrugged. "I don't know. Play it by ear."

"I'll call Tom tomorrow and ask if he ever heard of anybody called Big Man. They may have a file on him. And if they do, we will have learned a lot."

Chapter 32

CRYSTAL tapped on the door, then walked in and sat in one of the chairs in front of Mark's desk. "Find out anything else last night?"

"No. Not really. I tried to call you, but no one was there."

He said it casually enough, but somehow Crystal felt cornered. Did he know she and Brandi had gone to The Longneck last night? What difference did it make, if he did? "We were out."

"So I gathered. What's on your mind?"

"Just wanted to know what you found out last night. JT said you and Eddie Ray went to The Longneck Bar after you left me at my car."

Mark smiled but didn't say anything for a moment. "Well, yes we did. Just as I was dropping him at his car, it occurred to me we might go to the bar and find Joe and Al."

"Did you?" She knew they hadn't found the two thugs, but she wanted to keep her own escapades a secret for now.

"No."

"How long did you stay?"

"Until after ten. No sign of them. And nobody admitted ever having heard of them."

After ten. Crystal struggled to keep her expression neutral. *If Brandi had found her pliers sooner, we might have run into them as they were leaving. That would have been interesting.* She remembered Brandi asking what they were going to do if they found Joe and Al. She hadn't had a ready answer. "What were you going to do if you had found them?"

"I thought I would just tell them that there was no gold—explain to them that it was just folklore, like the old San Saba mine stories."

"My grandmother believes those."

Mark ignored her comment. "They believe the computer said there is a wagonload of gold in Eula's lake. And we tell people all the time that computers don't make mistakes. So they think it's there. But, in fact, the computer didn't say that. That was a human assumption. It simply reported a possibility." Mark tapped his desk with the end of a pencil. "If I could show them the logic of that, I'm sure they'd back off. The question of the police and Bessie's death is another matter. But in the meantime, we don't want them to do anything stupid that might affect Eula. Or Luis."

Crystal stared at him incredulously and decided the man was serious. "Mark, these goons are not logical. If your approach is based on appealing to their logic, you're going to fail. And in this case, failure could be serious. They've already killed one person." She shivered a little, realizing her words applied to Brandi and herself as well. They were foolish to have gone to the Longneck.

"Worth a try. We weren't meeting them in a dark alley. There were lots of people around. Anyway, we didn't find them."

"Promise me you won't do that again," she said, mentally making herself the same promise. "I've got enough to worry about with Nana. I don't want to have to worry about you, too."

"Yes, ma'am." Mark folded his hands like a dutiful schoolboy.

Crystal put up a hand. "Okay. I guess I am sounding like an older sister, or something. It's just that you've been so supportive and helpful through all this. If something happened to you, I'd feel it was my fault."

"Remember that for yourself, too. I'm not the one who's been shot. By the way, how is your arm?"

"How did you know about that?" Her surprise showed in her face as well as her voice. "I meant to ask you that yesterday."

"Bill told me. And no, neither of us has told your grandmother." His demeanor turned more serious. "From what he said, if the guy had been a little better shot, you'd be dead."

"That's a little dramatic."

"Actually, Bill said he was repeating what you told him. Plus, I believe you said if the guy had been a little faster, you might be dead." Mark raised his eyebrows at her, the question he hadn't asked begging an answer.

Crystal squirmed a little in her chair. "Well, I dove under the water and swam away. I didn't try to use logic on them." Her face took on an angelic smile, tinged with a little mischief. "That would be like using garlic on watermelon."

Mark just grinned.

"Mark, I was raised out there and I never heard any folk tales about gold in a lake. Did you?"

"No."

"So, why now?"

Mark leaned back in his chair and stretched his arms over his head. "The power of information retrieval. Remember, JT ferreted those out of the folklore database. It's possible that none of those have been told for fifty or a hundred years. Your grandmother never heard about it. But IR brings out information long forgotten."

"I wish it had stayed forgotten."

"It's like cars. They can do so many good things for us, but occasionally they do bad things. The car is not bad, but it can be used to do bad things. Same thing for a computer."

"I'm sorry JT found the folk tale."

Mark leaned forward on the desk. "Crystal, JT is not to blame here. Remember that. Joe and Al took some information, misinterpreted it, and then broke the law. They ... broke ... the law. They are the criminals, not JT."

* * *

Shortly before noon, JT appeared at Mark's door. He motioned her in and invited her to sit down.

"Dr. O'Malley, please don't fire me. I know I shouldn't have done that. I know I shouldn't have been in the topological database. And I shouldn't have told Eddie Ray about any of our business here. I really like my job here. And I really need it. I promise never to do anything like that again."

Mark appraised the woman sitting before him. Her rich, shiny brown eyes were swollen and red, mascara smeared beneath. She focused on the desktop, unable to look him in the eye. Her voice reflected the desperation he sensed just from her body language. She wore a pretty print dress, but somehow it looked like it had been twisted and stretched. He remembered her reaction when Eddie Ray had revealed the threat to kidnap her son and a wave of sympathy swept over him.

"JT, your job is not in jeopardy. I do not approve of some of the things you did, and when this is all over, we'll talk about that again. But I'm not going to fire you."

"Thank you." The tension that had built up in her snapped and her eyes filled with tears even as she smiled.

"By the way, I would like to see any notes you have on your searches. It sounds like you did a good job. I'm curious as to how you went about it."

"I always keep an audit of what I do. I have notes on all the things I considered in setting up the various searches." She lowered her eyes again. "They're at home. I knew I shouldn't be doing it. I'll bring them in tomorrow."

"Tomorrow will be fine. Now, let's get ready for the presentation to the venture capitalists. And don't worry about your job."

She got up to leave. "I really feel badly about it."

"Bad, not badly," Mark corrected automatically. "You feel bad about it."

JT just nodded and turned to leave.

"However, there is one thing I want you to think about."

JT stopped and turned back. A trace of fear returned to her eyes.

"You might want to let Luis visit your mother, or some other relative, until we get this sorted out," Mark said. "I don't think he's in danger. But you might feel better if he were farther away."

"I always feel best when Luis is with me." Then quickly, she added, "But I will think about it."

Chapter 33

THE regular Wednesday lunch meeting resumed where it had left off two weeks earlier, with Crystal leading the discussion on probabilistic techniques applied to information retrieval. This time, she got through it without any calls from Wooden Nickel.

The technical discussion had concluded and the group was now finishing off the remnants of food. Sally and Phil were talking about the Rangers' win over Seattle last night, which gave the team sole possession of first place in the American League Western division. Mark assured them it wouldn't last. Crystal had just popped a salsa-laden chip into her mouth when the phone rang. It was Bill Glothe.

She picked up the receiver with some trepidation. It turned out there was no emergency. He had called to give Crystal an update on the investigation of the cars IPPI had identified. Arnold was back from vacation. His story checked out and Bill was taking him off the list.

His list now consisted of just one name: Randal Kenderson. But other than his attitude——*and he does have an attitude problem*—Bill couldn't find anything more incriminating than the fact that he owned a puce truck whose license plate fit the partial identification from The Park. Even if they had a perfect match, the sheriff pointed out, it would only prove that Kenderson's truck had been at The Park a week *after* Bessie was killed. Not enough to make a case.

"We'll keep an eye on him, but that's about all we can do. Maybe we need to look a little further than the thirty miles for cars that match what we got. Can you do that? I mean, is that pretty easy and fast? I don't have any good leads to follow right now. I feel like a cowpoke without a horse."

Crystal put her hand over the receiver and spoke softly to Mark. "You haven't told Bill about Eddie Ray?"

Mark shook his head.

"He ought to know." She removed her hand and talked to Glothe. "Actually, we did expand the search on the car and came up with several matches here in Dallas." She looked around the room. Everybody there knew the story. No need to worry about privacy on this matter. "It's sort of a confused and weird story, Bill, but we believe we have a good handle on what happened."

She filled the sheriff in on the details of the folk story, JT's research on the location of the lake, Eddie Ray's involvement, and Joe and Al.

"Unfortunately, the only thing we can tell you about those two is that they drive a car with flames painted on the hood." She described the car as best she could.

"Well, we don't see too many Batmobiles out here. If we do, we'll sure stop 'em. Anything else?"

Crystal looked at Mark. "You want to talk to Bill?"

Mark shook his head.

"I guess that's it for now," she said to Glothe. "I apologize for not calling. We only found this out last night and the morning has been hectic. Sorry."

"No problem."

"Keep an eye on Nana for me."

"Count on it."

As soon as Crystal hung up the phone, Mark asked, "Anything new?"

"Not really. He's checked on all the trucks we gave him. He can eliminate all but Kenderson's."

"I think we know whose truck it was. Eddie Ray's."

"That's what I told him. So, we've got a chance to snuff it out here, before it gets back to Wooden Nickel."

"The big question marks right now are Joe and Al." Mark tilted his head to the side. "Where are they? What are they doing? When will they strike again? And they will; I'm convinced of that."

"Unless we can find them first." Crystal had been feeling better. She and Brandi had found out more in their visit to The Longneck than Mark and Eddie Ray had. She reminded herself that

Mark was helping her; he was not a competitor. Still, it had brightened her spirits. And just now, it gave her another lift to tell Bill Glothe that they had tracked down the truck using her IPPI system, and had stopped Eddie Ray.

But Mark had brought back into focus the real danger. They had not made much progress on the actual bad guys, Joe and Al. And Big Man, whoever he might be. Still, it had been a worthwhile twenty-four hours. She was feeling good.

* * *

Mark decided it was time to put everyone's mind back on the preparations for next Tuesday's visitors. "Now, let's shift gears, folks. We're less than a week away from the big show and tell. I don't need to explain to you how important this is. They pay your salaries, and mine, and next Tuesday is our opportunity to convince them they should continue doing that."

For the next half hour, they reviewed the status of each project. Crystal said her group was catching up. They would be ready. Sally's team had made more progress and expected to stage a dress rehearsal on Friday. Phil, off the hook for a real demo, outlined the information he would present in a brief lecture.

Mark was discouraged. While he understood the numerous distractions—. Instantly, he realized it was degrading to think of the attacks on Eula and the threat to kidnap Luis as distractions. The point was, he could not postpone Tuesday.

I could, he thought. *I could ask them to postpone the trip. Explain to them that extenuating circumstances made it advisable.* He shook his head. Delaying the visit, or just asking for a delay, would only make IRS look bad. No matter how legitimate the reasons, it would weaken their position. Better to just work hard, do the best job possible in the time left, and pray for luck. Hopefully, there would be no more interruptions.

" Okay," Mark kept his voice upbeat. "I think we're all on the right track here. We're going to wow them. I told Crystal and Sally, but I don't think I told you, Phil. The consultant Rooney is bringing is Dr. Lester Krupe. Crystal worked with him at Stanford, so we may catch a small break there. That's not to say we want to ease up any. He's been hired to be critical of our work. We have to make sure it looks good under the microscope."

He studied the group for a moment before continuing. "On Monday—and Crystal doesn't know this yet—Dr. Krupe is giving a talk at UT, Dallas. That will give me a chance to meet him before he shows up at our door."

"I'd like to go hear him," said Sally. "Besides, I've never been to the Texas University campus here."

"Sorry, Sally, but you don't get to see it Monday, either. I want you and Phil to spend that time perfecting things for Tuesday. I'm taking Crystal to provide my introduction to Dr. Krupe."

At the first mention of Dr. Krupe, two small wrinkles appeared between Crystal's eyebrows. Her stomach felt like someone had tied a hemp rope around it and was slowly tightening the rope.

"I want a full dress rehearsal Monday, and keep polishing it until you're completely at ease with it, prepared to handle anything that goes wrong. Then Tuesday, all I ask from you is ..." Mark looked at Sally, then Phil, then Crystal. "... perfection."

* * *

It was nearly six o'clock and Crystal was staring out her window. Business was picking up in the West End. The horse-drawn cabs were lined up and a few had already attracted customers. The sidewalk cafe across the street was filled with people taking advantage of its happy hour. In fact, everybody on the street below seemed happy.

The intercom buzzed, bringing her attention back to the office. She pressed a button. "Yes?"

"Crystal, JT's on line one. She wanted Dr. O'Malley, but he's gone. She sounds ... well, will you take the call?"

"Yes. Thanks, Bobby Don." Crystal picked up the receiver, a slight foreboding hovering above her. "Hi, JT. This is Crystal."

"Oh. I was calling for Dr. O'Malley."

In those few words, Crystal knew something was wrong. "He's not here, JT. Can I help you?"

"I hate to bother you. But Dr. O'Malley spent a lot of time with Eddie Ray last night and ... ." The end of the sentence was lost in half sobs. It was clear to Crystal that JT was struggling to seem calm. Her hand was probably over the mouthpiece of the phone, but the sound of crying was unmistakable.

"JT. Breathe deeply. Try to relax. Take deep breaths. I'll wait.

No need to hurry."

She could hear JT breathing, the sobs subsiding. After a minute, she started again. "I got home a few minutes ago, about the same time as I usually do. Luis and Eddie Ray are gone."

Chapter 34

CRYSTAL could picture JT, eyes red, nervous hands twisting the phone cord. She waited until JT continued. "They're always here when I get home. And if they're not, Eddie Ray leaves a note on the refrigerator telling me where they are and when they'll be back."

Ignoring the contradiction, Crystal asked, "Is Eddie Ray's car there?"

"No. I thought since Dr. O'Malley was with Eddie Ray last night, he might have said something about what he was doing today. Or something ... ." Her voice trailed off.

Several questions popped into Crystal's mind, but she kept them to herself. She remembered her own feelings when Nana was missing. She could only imagine the desperation if it were a child of her own. The threats against Luis made her shiver.

"I'll be over in a few minutes, JT. Try to stay calm. Have something to drink, maybe listen to some soft music. Try not to think about this until I get there. They're probably at the store and forgot to leave a note." She laughed a little, trying to sound casual, but it came out hollow and insipid. "You know how men are."

"Okay."

"And I'll try to locate Mark, also. But please, don't worry. I'm sure they'll show up soon. Probably before I get there."

" Okay."

Crystal pressed the switch hook on the phone and dialed Mark's home number. She stuffed papers into her briefcase as she waited through several rings. Mark's answering machine picked up. Crystal left a message about JT, then tapped the switch hook again and dialed his cell phone. On the third ring, he answered.

"Mark, Crystal. JT just called. Luis is missing. So is Eddie Ray. She's imagining all sorts of things. Anyway, I'm going over.

She actually called for you. Thought Eddie Ray might have said something to you last night."

"No, he didn't." There was a moment's silence. "I'll meet you there."

Crystal snapped her briefcase shut, and got up. She glanced out the window at the busy street below. She was sure no parent down there was worrying about having a child kidnapped.

* * *

Already the traffic was thinning. She took the toll road North for a few miles, exiting at Lovers Lane, then wound through residential streets for a few blocks. Twenty minutes after leaving the office, she was parked in front of JT's house. She pressed the doorbell, and even as she did, she heard a child's voice. She smiled. A wasted trip under these circumstances was a blessing.

"Crystal, Luis is here." JT was smiling, but there was a tinge of concern around her eyes.

Even before they were seated in the living room, the doorbell rang. JT brought Mark into the living room, apologizing all the way.

"Tell us what happened," Crystal asked.

JT sat down and lifted Luis up to sit on her lap. "A few minutes before you got here, Luis called. He was at Rita's house. She lives behind us—on the next street. He came in the back door just as Crystal rang the bell."

"And Eddie Ray?" Mark asked.

"I was just asking Luis when Crystal arrived. Luis, tell us what happened. Why were you over at Mrs. Daughtery's, and where is Eddie Ray?"

Luis wiggled closer to his mother and looked at Mark out of the corner of his nut-brown eyes. Already the young boy had the darkly handsome features common in Mexican men. He pulled his mother's arm around him, but kept his gaze on Mark when he answered. "I was in the kitchen. I just finished a glass of milk and put my glass up." He looked at his mother, waiting for approval. She nodded, and he continued. "Eddie Ray came in and told me to go to Mrs. Daughtery's. *Right now.* And stay there 'til I called and talked to you right here at home." He looked back at his mother.

"Is that all he said?"

"Yes. I asked him why and he pushed me out the door, told

me to just go. *Right now*. And *no questions*." Luis emphasized the last two words.

"And what did you do?" asked Crystal.

"I went."

"Did you look back and see what he did?" Mark asked.

"No sir. Eddie Ray said go and I went. He don't like for me to ask too many questions when he's in a mood."

"He *doesn't*," Mark corrected.

"No, he don't." Luis put his hand over his mouth and giggled. "I get it. He *doesn't* like for me to ask questions." He giggled again and looked at his mother.

Mark continued. "So you didn't see anything else? No other people? No cars?"

Luis shook his head from side to side.

"Did you hear anything unusual? A different car sound or maybe different voices?"

The five-year-old twisted his mouth, as if that helped him think. "No. Oh, Mrs. Daughtery has a different car. A big, new minivan. Green. It's neat. I got to sit in it." He quickly looked at his mother. "But we didn't go anywhere. Me and Willy just sat in it."

"Willy and I."

Luis laughed again.

Crystal leaned forward, getting closer to Luis. "You said Eddie Ray was in a mood. What did you mean by that?"

The little boy looked up at his mother. She nodded an assurance. He looked back at Crystal. "Well, sometimes he gets kind of——ah, I don't know. His eyes get grumbly. And his face wiggles. And he don't——." He cut his eyes toward Mark. "Ah, he *doesn't* want you to talk to him or bother him or ask questions."

"His face wiggles?"

Luis nodded several times.

JT patted her son on the head. "Sometimes, when things aren't going too good, Eddie Ray grinds his teeth and gets a little twitch in his jaw muscle."

Crystal looked back to Luis. "Was he in a mood when you got home from school?"

"No. He was happy when I got home. We played ball for a little bit. I asked for some milk and he said sure. He only got in his mood when he came in and told me to go over to Mrs. Daughtery's and play. Inside. He told me to *play inside.*"

"How do you get to Mrs. Daughtery's house?"

Luis stuck his arm straight out and pointed. JT answered. "She lives just behind us. Luis climbs through a hole in the hedge. Willy is just a year older than Luis and they play together sometimes."

Crystal was still leaning forward, close to Luis, talking very softly. "Does Eddie Ray send you over to play with Willy very often?"

"No. Almost never."

* * *

JT took Luis to his room. When she returned, Crystal and Mark were whispering.

"I gave him a puzzle to put together," JT told them.

"We're just trying to make sense of this, JT," said Crystal.

"There's no sign of a struggle," Mark said. "His truck is gone." He leaned back, but it wasn't a very comfortable chair and no matter which way he sat, it hurt his back.

JT shook her head. "If they came in with a gun, he wouldn't have struggled. And they could have taken his truck."

Crystal tried to sound as sympathetic as she could, while presenting another possibility. "He has gone off before. You said he did just a few weeks ago."

"That was different. We had a fight—an argument. I knew he was going. We weren't fighting this time. And he didn't leave when I was here. He left Luis. And he made him go over to Mrs. Daughtery's." She looked straight into Crystal's eyes. "They took him." Then she looked at Mark. "They took Eddie Ray."

She said it calmly, with no aggression, no disrespect, no challenge. It was the calmness that told Crystal JT had her mind made up. They wouldn't change it.

Mark leaned toward JT. "Could he have gone off drinking? He likes to go to bars."

She was shaking her head before he even finished. "Same thing. He wouldn't leave Luis."

"Did Eddie take any of his things? Shaving gear, clothes?" Crystal asked.

Without saying a word, JT got up and left the room. In less than a minute, she returned. "No. Everything is still here. They didn't give him time to get anything. Maybe they didn't think he'd need anything." Her lower lip began to tremble. "I'm scared, Dr. O'Malley. Can we call the police?"

Mark leaned over and rested his head in his hands for a few moments. When he raised his head, JT was looking at him intently. "It's too soon," he said. "Eddie Ray is a responsible adult who's been missing for, what, an hour, maybe two? Unless we have concrete evidence that he's been kidnapped, they won't do anything for at least twenty-four hours."

JT swallowed dryly. "That will be too late." Her voice, an octave higher than usual, reinforced the panic in her eyes.

Crystal looked at the terrified woman. "I've got a friend in the police department. Let me give him a call and explain what we know—or think we know. See what he says."

"The phone's in here," said JT, heading into the hall.

Crystal's discussion with Tom Hawkins confirmed what Mark had told JT. They couldn't do anything for twenty-four hours. But Tom said he'd spread the word when his shift started at midnight. If they spotted a black car with flames painted on the hood, they'd stop the car and investigate. And they'd keep an eye out for the rust-colored 4x4 Sierra. Crystal told Tom she would phone him with the license plate number in about thirty minutes.

Crystal repeated the information to JT. No tears came, but her eyes revealed her despair. "He's the only one who can identify them. They've got him. They won't let him go."

Chapter 35

OUTSIDE, Crystal and Mark talked for a few minutes before getting in their cars. Mark said he believed Eddie Ray was on the run. His only question was why. Did he run because he was afraid of Joe and Al, or because he was afraid of the police? Was he more involved with the arson and Bessie's death than he admitted?

"I don't know," Crystal said. "Looks like he left awfully fast. If he'd left for any of those reasons, he could have waited and talked to JT first. And surely he would have taken some clothes." She pushed a stray lock of hair back behind her ear. "From what Luis said, it sounds like a spur of the moment thing."

"What little contact I've had with him, I have to agree with JT: he wouldn't have left Luis unless he had no other choice."

* * *

On the way home, Mark stopped at Ninfa's for dinner. Usually, an empanada could coax him out of a poor mood. Tonight, it didn't help at all. Even the peace and quiet of his house didn't lift the gloom. The more he thought about it, the more he felt Crystal's logic was on target. But why now?

It hit him like a charging bull. Somehow, Joe and Al must have seen Mark with Eddie Ray last night, or at least heard about it. Maybe they thought Mark was a policeman. Whatever they thought, they picked Eddie Ray up to get some answers. If he gave them the right answers, they'd probably let him go. If not, well, they'd killed one person already.

* * *

It was after ten when he opened the thick packet of notes JT had given him. One thing became clear immediately: she kept careful records. The detail amazed and pleased him.

She had searched for every mention of gold in the entire

database. The number would have discouraged most people. She eliminated over half by discarding any that talked about trains. Then she limited the stories further, demanding some mention of a wagon. Eventually, she had the list down to thirty-one.

Next, she had the computer analyze each story to determine its major characteristics. The computer produced a list of five that matched closely enough that it concluded they had their roots in the same incident—the same piece of folklore.

One version suggested the gold may have been part of the treasure the notorious gentleman pirate Jean Lafitte took from Spanish ships. A full page of JT's notes indicated she had researched some of the historical accounts of Lafitte. Highlighted in yellow was a sentence about the pirate capturing a sizable shipment of gold. Fearing that the Mexican army would come after it, he sent it to St. Louis for safekeeping. At the end of the account JT had printed in capital letters, "IT NEVER ARRIVED IN ST. LOUIS."

Mark shook his head. It was amazing she had gotten any IRS work done at all. At the end of this section of notes, Mark found a page listing nearly two-dozen characteristics. Beside each one was a number. It took only a few moments for Mark to decipher these. The computer had listed every feature mentioned, then tallied up how many stories referenced each. Lake led the group with six. *Strange.* He thought she had cut the list to only five stories. He checked back. *Only five. Where did the sixth instance come from?*

A small hill or cliff overlooking the lake rated a five. Cliff by itself got two credits. A long and narrow lake received four mentions, while an East/West lake rated a three, as did a lake on high ground, and a lake in the middle of a thick pine forest.

From those, it looked like JT had compiled a list of fifteen attributes.

Mark leaned back and rubbed his neck. She'd done a good job of pinning down the facts. In spite of himself, Mark began to wonder if out there somewhere, deep in a lake in East Texas, probably covered in silt, there just might be a wagonload of gold.

He looked at the clock over his desk. It was nearly 12:30— time for sleep. He walked into the kitchen and poured half a glass of Dr Pepper.

Mark remembered reading that the National Forests of East

Texas covered more than a thousand square miles. The area they called the piney woods must cover ten thousand square miles. A huge area to consider, or search. Eight states had total areas smaller than that.

Of all the lakes in an area that size, how had JT picked out Eula's? Coincidence? Blind luck? Mark believed in luck. If JT had managed to pick Eula's out of only ten lakes, he'd give it to luck—bad luck. But in this case, the odds were just too great.

Mark bypassed his bedroom and walked back to his office. Maybe he'd take just a quick look at how she started eliminating thousands of lakes.

Her notes on selecting a particular lake must have weighed two pounds. The first section wandered around, showing clearly that JT didn't know how to take the minuscule description she had managed to distill from the folk tales and apply it to such a vast number of lakes.

He flipped a page and found a copy of a program she had written. A quick scan brought a grin to his face.

"Very good, JT," he said aloud.

The program eliminated all man-made lakes. One hundred and fifty years ago, Texans weren't managing water. Dams hadn't been built to store water. Flood control meant, don't build too close to the river. Still, it amazed Mark how many lakes were removed from the list.

A second program removed all lakes of more than one hundred acres. From there, JT had let the computer assign probabilities to the remaining lakes, using the attributes winnowed from the folk tales. Several pages of notes brought in other considerations. One caused him to shake his head in wonder. It contained her calculations, based on what appeared to be extensive reading, on how far a heavily laden wagon might travel across East Texas in a day back in the early 1800's.

Where did she get the time to do that reading? The answer turned up on the next page. The computer had searched out a number of articles that discussed the distance wagons covered in a time period. JT had to read only a few pages to gather a lot of information.

The last page contained the locations of six lakes. A red line encircled one. The location was a legal description, but Mark had no doubt it was the same lake he'd seen from the veranda of Eula's house. And where someone had shot Crystal.

Chapter 36

"**YOU** know, this is one of the reasons I moved here." Brandi finished shifting clothes from the washer to a dryer. "A nice, neat, bright laundry, in the same building. And only seventy-five cents a load."

Crystal smiled, but her mind was on other things. She was doing her laundry on autopilot. "Mark wants me to go with him to UT to hear Dr. Krupe give a talk." She had tried to say it casually, but the ripples in her voice betrayed her.

"Take tomatoes. Rotten ones."

"Why are men like that? Dr. Krupe blackballed me because I wouldn't go to bed with him. Phil stole my idea—"

"Hoooold it." Brandi held her hand up. "Phil did *what*?"

"He presented *my* idea for a new project as if *he* had developed it."

"What did Mark say when you told him?" Brandi was all seriousness now.

"I haven't told him."

"Well, come on, gal. This isn't your advisor. This is a coworker. You march in and tell Mark there's a little intelligent thievery going on."

"Intellectual thievery."

"Whatever. The point is, you have to claim what's yours. If I go off and leave my jeans in the dryer, I don't expect to find them there next week."

"Why not?"

Brandi cocked her head to one side and sang, "Finders keepers, losers weepers. Didn't you learn anything as a kid?"

"My idea wasn't lost."

"Sounds like it's lost to you," Brandi said pointedly. "Look, I don't know about computers. I was terrible at math, history, chemistry, and only so-so in English. But I know this. If you want to keep something, you got to hold on to it. I don't lay my purse down in the mall. And if I had an original idea, which is highly unlikely, I'd damn sure protect it."

She paused and when Crystal didn't say anything, Brandi continued. "And all men aren't that way. Is Mark? Tom? Your grandfather? Bobby Don? Anyway, if it isn't worth protecting, it isn't worth having. Don't trash all men because you let a few flakos take advantage of you."

Crystal's eyes opened wide and she glared at her housemate. "*Let* them?"

"Let them. Crystal, you're strong in so many areas. Why are you so willy-nilly about others? Decide what's important to you and go for it. And ask the famous Brandi question: Will they shoot me, or even hit me?"

Without thinking, Crystal reached up and touched the wound on her left arm.

* * *

Deep in her dream, Crystal could hear a bell clanging, but she didn't know what it was. Was it a railroad crossing? Or a fire alarm? She needed to do something. But what? And then it stopped. Suddenly there was a blinding light shining in her eyes, and someone was yelling at her.

"Crystal. Wake up, Crystal. Tom's on the phone. He needs to talk to you."

Slowly, Crystal became conscious and opened her eyes to see Brandi standing in the door. "Pick up the phone. Tom needs to talk to you."

With an effort, Crystal turned over and reached for the telephone beside her bed. "Hello."

"Crystal, this is Tom Hawkins. There's been a fire at Intelligent Retrieval Systems. There's no emergency number posted. So I called you."

His second sentence jarred her to full consciousness. "A fire? Is it bad?"

"The place is still here. Not as bad as it might have been. Can you call the appropriate person, or give me a name?"

"I'll call him."

* * *

Mark felt like he had barely closed his eyes when the phone beside his bed rang. He groped in the dark for the lamp switch, almost knocking over the glass of Dr Pepper that sat on the bedside table. By the fourth ring, he had the light on and his hand on the receiver. At that point, the answering machine picked up. He waited to see who was calling at this hour before deciding whether to take the call or not.

He blinked his eyes and tried to focus on the clock. One minute before three. His groggy mind tried to calculate how long he'd slept, but before he could figure it out, the caller was talking.

"Mark, this is Crystal."

He lifted the receiver. "Crystal," Mark interrupted. The answering machine clicked off. "What's wrong?"

Crystal hesitated a second.

Mark's mind kicked into gear and he didn't wait for a reply. "They found the fire-breathing car."

"No. But they found a fire-breathing office." When Mark did not respond immediately, she added, "Yours."

"What? How do you know?"

"Tom Hawkins, my police detective friend, called. He knows I work there, and apparently we don't have an emergency number posted anywhere."

"How bad?"

"He said not too bad."

"But he called at 3 a.m." Mark paused only a moment. "I'll get there as quickly as I can. Thanks for the call."

* * *

Mark's body drove. His mind raced along other paths, only vaguely aware of the turns and stops the truck was making. He tried to prepare himself. She had said "not too bad." Compared to what? Maybe it hadn't burned to the ground. Maybe only half of the IRS quarters were destroyed. Without willing it or wanting it, his mind jumped to Eula's house. Glothe thought the firemen had done a good job there. Did his offices look like Eula's house, sky showing through all over the place?

No. Mark knew he had installed an excellent fire suppression system. The fire had not destroyed everything. *If* the system worked. They hadn't tested it, at least not very well. When he'd asked about that, the company said you couldn't test that kind of system.

But if there wasn't any damage, why the police? And why call at three in the morning? Probably routine. Probably always call the police. And the owner.

Would his people have a place to work, or computers? How much time would they lose? The venture capitalists were coming in less than a week. Would they have an office to show them? Computers to run demos? The problems in Wooden Nickel had already slowed things, put them behind schedule. They were playing catch-up, struggling to be ready by next Tuesday. Would this bring them to a total standstill?

Crystal said Tom was a friend, so he might call even if there was little or no damage. Tom? That's who she called from JT's, Mark remembered. Could that only have been eight hours ago? If someone had broken in, that might warrant a call. Of course, it could have been an electrical fire. He'd have to post an emergency number. How lucky a policeman at the scene would be Crystal's friend. Even if things were okay, Mark would need to check it over, lock up. She did say it wasn't too bad.

* * *

Twenty-five minutes later, Mark skidded to a stop outside his office in the West End. He had passed three fire engines leaving the area. *Did they always send at_least three units?* He stepped out of his truck, his shoes crunching on small shards of glass that littered the sidewalk. He looked up and saw that three windows on the second story had been blown out. The lights were on and several people were moving about. He jogged to the door and ran up the stairs, taking them two at a time.

He found Crystal and four other people, most likely from the Dallas Police, in the computer room. Mark scanned the area. Suddenly, a wave of nausea swept over him and his whole body sagged. The words "utter disaster" popped into his mind. It looked like an explosion had not only blown out the windows, it had done considerable damage inside.

A large, black, ugly area of charred and melted vinyl flooring dominated the room. A desk was destroyed, a chair, badly burned.

Mark went over and laid a hand on it. The chair had been the very first piece of furniture IRS had owned. A large computer cabinet was lying on its side. The new RAID system leaned against a wall, undoubtedly damaged. Pictures and ceiling tiles littered the floor. Pieces of burned paper were everywhere. The smell of smoke permeated the air. And there was another odor that he could not identify, but brought to mind a fireworks show.

* * *

Crystal and one of the men walked over to Mark.

"Mark, this is Tom Hawkins. He's a detective for the Dallas Police Department. Tom, Dr. Mark O'Malley. He owns IRS."

Tom looked at his watch. "I should give both of you speeding tickets. It's obvious you did not stay within the limit."

"What happened?" Mark asked, in no mood for humor.

"That's what Johnette, Gus and Frank are trying to determine." Tom introduced Mark to Johnette Toofer, an arson investigator, and Gus Penny and Frank DeLira, from the Crime Scene Unit. "Looks like someone tossed a firebomb through the middle window over there. It exploded, blowing out the other windows and starting a rip-roaring fire. The good news is, your fire suppression system worked well. It rang the fire department and put out the fire. Since I don't see any water on the floor, I'm assuming you have an inert gas fire suppression system."

"Yeah. Water and computers don't mix well." Mark looked around the room. "Doesn't look like it worked all that well."

Johnette suppressed a soft laugh.

"You'll have to pardon Officer Toofer, there. Just before you came in, she was commenting on how lucky you were. She thinks the bomb had some sort of acetone accelerant in it, and those are usually pretty tough to put out. A regular sprinkler system wouldn't have helped much. You had a strong explosion in a confined space. Indications are that the fire was immediate and intense. This damage you see probably occurred in ... How fast, Johnette?"

"Under twelve seconds, I'd guess. It's a wonder the explosion didn't damage your fire suppression system. And with the windows blown out, I'm surprised the gas system worked so well. When the fire department got here, there was no fire at all. Just damage." The petite blonde turned back to her work.

"Just what are they looking for? And what is that in her hand?" Crystal asked. The initial shock she had felt was beginning to fade.

"That's an electronic nose, an accelerant detector." Tom looked at Mark. "I'm dry as a bone. Got a soda machine?"

"Yeah."

Mark led the way to the coffee room while Tom explained the basics of the investigation. By the time they returned to the computer room, Tom was just finishing. "When Officers Toofer, Penny and DeLira are finished, they'll be able to tell you what kind of a bomb, how big, where the material came from, how and when it was put together, the experience level of the bomber and whether he was right- or left-handed."

"He always says that," Gus muttered.

"Oh, we can. But only with fifty percent certainty," said Frank.

"About the right or left hand bit," Gus added.

"Actually, sometimes we really can," Frank said. "Tell about right or left handedness."

"What about 'Who'?" Mark asked.

"Forty-two point six percent of the time," Gus replied without looking up from his work.

Tom snorted at that last comment. "Okay, guys. Can the Laurel and Hardy routine and get to work. Johnette's going to make you both look bad." He turned his attention to Mark. "So, how bad is this going to affect you? A couple of those computers look pretty beat up. And I don't know how much smoke was generated. Doesn't seem to be much smoke damage to the walls or ceiling. What about the computers?"

Mark shook his head. "Don't know. The one on its side will probably have some damaged cards. A few days and a thousand bucks and it'll probably be okay. But you never know. We could have intermittent trouble with it for months." He looked at the RAID. "The cabinet leaning against the wall is a large disk system. Could be okay or completely worthless. Just got it a week or two ago. Crystal loaded her data on it this week."

Crystal's mind leaped to her project. *Even without the fire, it was going to be close. Now, the database has to be reloaded——if*

*there's anything to load it on. What's today? Thursday. They're
coming Tuesday.*

"That's a disk system? My God, how much data can it hold?"

"Twenty terabytes," Mark answered. "Fortunately, we
haven't had it long, so it's mostly empty. And if my people are doing
their jobs correctly, the data should be backed up."

"How much is a terabyte?"

"A trillion bytes. That cabinet can hold twenty trillion
characters, letters or numbers. Better yet, think of it as capable of
holding the entire text of every book in the Dallas public library."

"Sounds like a bunch." Tom reached into his pocket and
pulled out a notebook and a pen. "Well, let's get down to business.
Do you know anyone who would have had reason to bomb your
offices?"

"Nobody."

"Just a random kid's prank?" The detective's skepticism
showed in his tone.

"Well ..."

Johnette was shaking her head no.

Tom clicked his ballpoint pen a few times while he studied
the owner. "I'd say you're not over the initial shock yet. Otherwise,
you'd be thinking more clearly. This was not a pop bottle filled with
gasoline and a rag stuck in it. We're talking serious stuff here. This
was an attack on a specific target."

"Maybe they ..."

Johnette and Gus joined in and said in unison with Mark, "...
hit the wrong target."

A touch of color rose in Mark's cheeks as he looked at the
two officers. "You've heard that before, I take it?"

"Any really unhappy customers?" Tom continued.

"No."

"Fired anybody lately, or not so lately?"

"Nobody."

"Disgruntled employees? And don't just give me a quick
'no'. Think about each one before you answer."

Mark shrugged and began to run down the list of employees.
After each one, he said no, then looked to Crystal. In each case, she
shook her head no. "Nobody."

"You didn't check off Crystal," said Tom.

Mark grinned. "Okay. Crystal. No."

"My point is, did you forget anybody else? And this is no time to be lenient. You should be overly critical on—."

Crystal cut in. "Tom, you have to understand. I think it's fair to say everyone likes her job here and we all really get along well." As soon as she said it, she thought of Phil claiming credit for her idea.

"That may just mean you don't know everyone as well as you think you do." Tom scribbled some more in his notebook. "These are almost always tied to an employee in some way or another. Keep that in mind. Let me know if you come up with any possibilities." He looked at Mark. "What's happened around you or Intelligent Retrieval Systems lately that's unusual, out of the ordinary?"

Crystal thought of Dr. Krupe and the venture capitalists.

Mark cast his eyes down. He said nothing.

"Come on, Mark. This wasn't a random act, or a mistake. It was deliberate. And it wasn't a warning, like a brick through a window. From the looks of the bomb, they intended to shut you down. Burn you to the ground. And you're damn lucky they didn't succeed. If we don't catch them, they'll try harder next time."

It wasn't a warning. The words were an echo in Crystal's mind. The same words she'd spoken to Glothe less than a week ago. "Somebody did take a couple of shots at me a few days ago."

Tom's mouth dropped open. "Somebody shot at you? Why's it taken so long for you to tell me that? How many days ago?"

"It was out by Wooden Nickel, the day of Nana's—ah, Bessie's—funeral. That was Friday. I don't think it had anything to do with this. They probably didn't know who I was, and certainly not where I work."

"Crystal, as smart as you are, and Brandi says you're really smart, I know more about this sort of stuff than you do. So just tell me everything and I'll—assign a weight to it—isn't that what you computer types say? I can't believe you work in information retrieval, and won't divulge any."

"They could have been the guys driving the fire-breathing car," Crystal said.

"The one you wanted us to look out for? Here in Dallas? And

you don't think there's any connection? I take back what I said about you being smart. You're a goddamned idiot."

"When they shot me, they—."

"Shot you? A minute ago, it was 'shot *at* you'. You're saying they hit you?"

Crystal waved that aside.

Mark interrupted. "I don't see how they could know about IRS. When Eddie Ray and I went looking for them, we never found them. Eddie Ray was the one who talked to them, not me, not Crystal. They don't know we're connected, and they don't know where we work."

Tom sat down on a slightly charred chair and put his head in his hands. "God save me from the people who have never been around crime, but know all about it." He shook his head, clicked open his pen and looked up, first at Crystal, then at Mark. "Okay. Let's see if I have this straight. Two guys shot you, Crystal. You, Mark, went looking for them. You didn't see them. Your office is firebombed. Oh, and Eddie Ray is missing. Am I leaving anything out?"

"Maybe Al and Joe saw me with Eddie Ray, and figured we were looking for them," Mark said.

"Very good, Dr. O'Malley," Tom said as he wrote more notes. "Now the thugs have names. Go on; tell me you know their last names and who they work for?"

Crystal began hesitantly. "Ah, didn't Brandi ask you about 'Big Man'?" That's who Joe and Al work for."

"No. I haven't talked with her today. It seems like everybody knows a lot about what's going on, but nobody wants to tell the investigating officer."

For a minute, nobody said anything. Finally, Tom snapped his notebook shut. "Why don't we go get me another drink while you two think? In fact, I'll buy for all of us. Then you start at the beginning and tell me everything. Is that a deal, or what? Mostly, I don't want these other officers to hear what naive fools you are."

Crystal, Mark and Tom sat around a table in the coffee room. Crystal and Mark told Tom the folk tale about a lot of gold hidden in a lake and the subsequent attacks on Eula. Periodically, Tom would interrupt to ask a question or just to stop them while he caught up on his notes. Sometimes he just shook his head and let out a sigh or a low whistle.

When the shooting came up, he asked to see the wound. Crystal rolled up her sleeve and peeled back the bandage. That elicited another shake of the head in dismay.

The funeral for Eula, which was really Bessie's, caused Tom to call for a halt while he tried to sort out the legality of the deceptive service. After a moment, he muttered something about it not being his jurisdiction, and told Crystal to resume the bizarre tale.

She had just finished when Officers Toofer, Penny and DeLira came to tell Tom they had finished and were heading back to the station to start the paper work.

"You through with the scene? Can they start cleaning it up, get back to work in there?" Tom asked.

"I'm through," said Toofer. She looked at the other two officers. They both nodded and agreed they were finished.

Mark asked if they had found any real clues to help identify the bombers. Toofer said they had recovered considerable evidence that should shed some light on the situation. Before Mark could decide if she had said anything, she and the other officers left.

For the next half hour, Tom, Crystal and Mark rehashed all the details, Tom pressing hard for more information, Crystal and Mark slowly coming to agree with the policeman's theory.

Tom believed Eddie Ray probably succumbed to the carrot and stick approach. With the gold as the carrot, and Al and Joe holding the stick, Eddie Ray might well have waltzed over to the enemy's side. That would explain why he was missing and how the perps knew about Intelligent Retrieval Systems. Mark suggested that they might have targeted the computer room specifically.

"Possible," said the detective. "Mostly, I think they wanted you out of it, too busy rebuilding to bother them. If they'd hit another room, without the inert gas system, they might have burned this place to the ground." He closed his book. "What I am certain about is, we should call it a night."

Crystal stood up. "Good idea, I'm pooped."

"One last thought," said Mark. "We know about Eddie Ray and Joe and Al. And we know now what they're up to. And if Eddie Ray's in with them, they know that we know. Isn't it logical for them to back off?"

The policeman looked at Mark and sighed in resignation. "There's a place for logic in police work. In fact, it's very important. But if you get hung up expecting the bad guys to act logically, you're going to find yourself in deep trouble."

They walked out to the reception area. Tom visited the rest room while Mark wrote a note to Bobby Don and a brief notice to all the employees. When he finished, he taped the notes to the glass door. They couldn't miss seeing the messages when they arrived in a few hours. He locked the door and the three walked downstairs.

"Tom," Crystal asked as they reached the street. "Is there really any chance your officers might identify the bomber?"

"Sometimes we get lucky. Might find a usable fingerprint on a bomb fragment. Usually, though, we get some help from the victim, like the name of a suspect or two. Gives us a starting place." Tom gave Mark a slap on the shoulder. "Oh, and you owe me. The news noses came sniffing around. We told them it was a small fire in a computer room and they left. No burned bodies, no raging flames. No news. You probably don't even *know* how lucky you are they didn't latch on to it. I mean, a fire-breathing car, a ton of gold, wow! What a story! You'd never get rid of them."

* * *

At 5:30, Mark turned out the light and closed his eyes. He was bone-weary, yet his mind wasn't ready to shut down. It kept turning over the events of the last few days. Nothing made sense, from the first idea of gold being hidden in Eula's lake to the firebombing of IRS. Nothing about it was logical, and logic was Mark's strong suit. He was trying to recall Tom's exact words about criminals and logic when his mind finally decided to rest.

* * *

Suddenly, Mark sat up in bed, his mind completely alert. He glanced at the soft glow of the clock. 5:52. He'd been asleep maybe ten minutes. What had awakened him? For several minutes he didn't move, his ears straining to pick up any unusual sound. Finally he said, "Shannon?"

"Yes, Mark?"

Okay, he reassured himself. *The computer system is working. So, nobody has come down the drive, or else Shannon would have alerted me. And it isn't likely that anybody came through the woods. That's pretty tough in the daytime, even if you know where you're going. At night, impossible. Still ... .*

"Shannon, outside lights on."

In less than a second, the computer began turning on the exterior lights. Within five seconds, more than two acres of land surrounding the house were illuminated. He peered out the window. Nothing moved on this side. *This is ridiculous*, he told himself. *There's nothing out there. Next thing, you'll be looking under the bed.* Even as he berated himself, he went into the den and looked out the window. Nothing. Of course not. What'd he expect?

He made the rounds, pausing at one point to issue another command to Shannon. Finally, at 6:01, he told the computer to turn off the outside lights. Mark climbed into bed for the third time this night.

Once again, his mind refused to quit. Someone could have come down the drive before he got home, he realized. The computer would have announced the person or car, but Mark would not have been there to hear it. Tomorrow, he would program Shannon to store the image, date and time of any arrivals if Mark wasn't there to respond to the message.

Was he being paranoid? Absolutely, he told himself. But it was only a small amount of program code, so why not? Besides, it would be nice to know who had been there when he was away, even if it was just a delivery truck. Like an answering machine for visitors. He drifted off to sleep, mentally writing the necessary instructions for the computer.

Chapter 37

BY 8:15, the entire office was buzzing. Almost everybody had noted the broken windows before they entered the building. Those who did not, saw Mark's note and immediately headed for the computer room to inspect the damage and see how it would affect their work. Mark's message had simply stated there was a fire and made no mention of a bomb, the police or likely motives.

Bobby Don Russell, the computer technician, was the only one working. He had cleared some of the mess and righted the two cabinets. He had disconnected cables going into the RAID, put a call into the service center that he used to repair IRS computers, and was now perched on a charred stool, taking the case off a damaged server so he could study the inside.

Sally, Phil, JT and Pam all shook their heads at the destruction, then wandered back to the coffee room. Phil had gently suggested the rest of the IRS staff get back to work.

"Mark didn't put a time on his note. Wonder when this happened?" asked Sally.

"It must have been pretty late, or he'd already be back in this morning," said Pam.

"It happened at 2:28"

JT said it so softly that Sally wasn't sure what she heard. "What did you say?"

"It happened at 2:28 this morning. I was running a 'search and check' series overnight. The database stopped responding at 2:28:05. The program sent a query every few milliseconds. That's when it stopped getting data back."

"I had one running, too," said Sally. "But I hadn't thought to look at my log."

" Okay. We know when. Anybody got any ideas on what

caused it?" asked Pam.

"I guess it could have been an electrical fire," Sally said and looked over at Phil. He was running his finger around the rim of his cup, a sure sign he had an idea. "What do you think, Phil?"

He continued to stare at his mug. "Hard to say."

"True," said Sally. "But you have some ideas. Share them with us."

Phil was obviously reluctant to talk, but when the three women continued to stare at him, he took a deep breath, let it out slowly and started. "I don't know all the facts, not nearly as many as you. But I've heard enough to suspect this was not vandalism. Crystal's grandmother's house was burned, and somebody died. Mark and Eddie Ray went looking for a couple of thugs. JT, you said Eddie Ray was still missing. I'd say the damage was the result of a firebomb tossed in a window."

"Firebomb?" said Pam, her voice conveying the alarm she felt.

"Good God, Phil," said Sally.

Phil looked at the others. "Anything else we know that might have a bearing on this?"

The four exchanged looks, but no one had anything to offer.

"Has anybody talked to Mark since two-thirty this morning?" Phil asked.

JT and Pam indicated they hadn't. Sally spoke up, a mixture of apprehension and disbelief in her voice. "What are you suggesting?"

"I'm not suggesting anything. But you asked me to share my thoughts. Crystal, Mark and JT are in the middle of this—at least it looks that way from what little information I have. JT is here. I'm just saying that two of the principal players are not here. And Eddie Ray—the *only* link with the bad guys—is nowhere to be found."

Sally took a moment to collect her thoughts. "So you're saying it's tied to Crystal's problems somehow."

"No. I'm saying that's the only connection *I've* come up with. Unless somebody here has made a customer really unhappy."

The corners of Sally's mouth turned down slightly when she thought about the only leads: a puce 4x4 and a fire-breathing car. Were the arson in Wooden Nickel and the fire at IRS really connected?

She stirred more sugar into her coffee. "He wrote the notes after the fire. So I guess he wasn't hurt. You really think it was a firebomb?"

"Looks like it to me. I've seen some before, when I was in the service. And the next question that comes to my mind is, why was Mark here to write the notes?"

JT spoke quickly. "The police called him."

"That's my feeling, too," said Phil. "Could have been the fire department. But, if it was the police, that adds more weight to the bomb theory. And what would start a fire in the middle of the floor? Which is where this fire started. Someone here start smoking?"

No one laughed.

"Where's this leave us for the presentations Tuesday?" Pam asked.

Phil scratched his chin. "Mine is just slides and talk. Doesn't affect mine, unless the slide projector was in the computer room, which is unlikely."

Sally took a sip of coffee. "We weren't ready without this disruption. What do you think, JT? Can we pull it off?"

"If Bobby Don can get us a computer by tomorrow, yes. In fact, we have enough data on my machine to make a demo. But we might have to work this weekend."

Sally was less confident than JT, but it wasn't even her own project that worried her the most. Crystal's project lagged further behind than hers. And all the IPPI data they had loaded was probably lost. Could they postpone the visit?

"Hi, gang. Guess you all know we're going to redecorate the computer room." Crystal tried to sound light and casual, although she did not feel that way.

The questions came in a rush. Crystal answered them as best she could, without divulging Tom's theory that the fire was connected with the assaults on Nana.

Her gaze took in JT. Her lower lip was trembling ever so slightly and it was clear to Crystal that JT was on the verge of tears. "JT, what's the matter?"

"I'm worried about Eddie Ray. It isn't like him not to come home. I mean, when he hasn't in the past, I knew why. He was mad or something. But everything was fine with us. And he left Luis and just didn't come back. And now this. . ." The tears began to flow. "He said they threatened to kidnap Luis if we didn't help them."

Tears gave way to sobs and Crystal put her arms around JT trying to comfort her.

"Is there somewhere you can take Luis where he'll be safe, like your mother's, or a sister or brother?"

JT's arms went around Crystal and she held on as if Crystal might try to escape. She was quiet now with only an occasional shiver running down her body.

Pam offered a few words of encouragement and left. Finally, blowing her nose loudly and wiping her eyes, JT said her mother lived in Fort Worth and had a different name and nobody should find Luis there. She'd take him there tonight.

"Why not pick him up right now? Don't wait; take him immediately. You're going to feel a lot better, and so will Sally and I."

"I couldn't take off right now. I've caused so much trouble and gotten our project behind and now, with the fire and all ... Dr. O'Malley will fire me."

"He won't fire you," Sally said. "Just go take care of Luis."

JT still looked reluctant.

"Look, JT. When Mark's away, who is in charge here?" Crystal asked.

"Phil."

Crystal looked at Phil.

Phil pursed his lips and nodded once sharply. "Mark's gone, so I'm in charge and I'm telling you to go take care of Luis. That's your job today. And we want you to do it right now."

Crystal took over. "Take him to your mother's. You know he'll be safe there. You're not going to get anything done here today, anyway." She saw the worried look on JT's face. "Nothing's going to happen to Luis. But you, and Sally and I will all feel better when you've done this. And Phil. So, get your purse and go."

JT wasn't completely convinced, but she left the coffee room and headed for her office. A few minutes later, she came to the door, thanked Crystal, Sally and Phil, then left.

* * *

A little after nine, the intercom buzzed on Crystal's desk. Pam told her Mark had arrived and gone to the computer room. "Just thought you'd like to know."

When Crystal got there, Bobby Don was giving Mark a status report on the extent of the damage and what he was doing to restore the functionality of each damaged item. But it wasn't Bobby Don's optimistic outlook that got Crystal's attention. It was Mark's appearance. While he did not usually wear a coat or tie at the office, he always looked like he could be in a Neiman Marcus ad. She and Pam were talking about it one day and Pam described Mark's dress as 'casual elegance'. This morning, however, he had neglected the elegant part. He wore faded jeans, a wrinkled knit shirt, and ropers that probably dated back to his rodeo days. He looked freshly shaved, but his eyes gave the impression that he hadn't slept at all.

He and Bobby Don exchanged a few more thoughts on the repairs and then Mark turned to Crystal. "Well, Bobby Don says he'll have your RAID back on-line sometime tomorrow. He hopes. That's the good news. The bad news is that you'll most likely have to load all your data again. Not positive on that yet, but be prepared for it."

"No problem. Can we go to your office and talk?"

Mark looked a bit surprised, but nodded and headed down the hall, Crystal lagging two steps behind. Once inside his office, she closed the door and sat down in front of his desk.

" Okay. What's on your mind?" he asked.

Crystal wasn't certain exactly how to put it, so she opted for bluntness. "Mark, you've got to get out of this. They've firebombed your business. Things are getting too rough."

"Getting rough on me? Four inches to the right and that bullet could have killed you."

"Only one inch to the left and it would have missed me altogether," she countered.

"Don't give me that argument. I carried out research in information value theory and it applies to this case very nicely. The inch to the left may be more likely, but the results don't change too much—from a scratch to no scratch. But results from the other possibility change drastically—from alive to dead."

"Aren't you being a little dramatic?"

"No. Realistic."

Crystal looked at her boss. "I'm in this because Eula is my grandmother, the woman who raised me, who taught me to experience and enjoy the world. She is my only living family. But you ... ."

Mark put up both hands. "Hold it." His demeanor had changed from mildly amused to deadly serious. "This isn't about Eula, as much as I like her. This is about Mark O'Malley. You're right. They firebombed my business. My business is me. That makes me a full-fledged, dues-paying member of this little rodeo. And one of the things I learned early in my rodeo days is that the most dangerous time in a bull ride is when you try to get off."

He paused and placed his hands flat on the desk. "Remember that picture of me your grandmother told you about? The one they captioned 'And the Bull Jumped Over the Moon'? Well, that happened because I turned my back on the bull. I thought someone else was taking care of the bull. I didn't make that mistake again in the arena. And I'm not making it here."

Crystal studied the man in front of her, trying to penetrate the steady stare and read his thoughts. The only thing she saw was a steely determination. Slowly, she grinned. For the first time, Crystal was beginning to see Bull O'Malley.

Chapter 38

"**EULA**, this is Mark O'Malley."

"Hi there, Bull. How's the rodeo business?"

"In the past, I'm afraid. If I got thrown today, I doubt I'd be able to get up."

"I'd bet money, marbles or chalk you would. I don't think you're the kind to stay down long. Now, if you're calling me up for a date, I'm going to have to turn you down. There's this guy that says I can't go out in public. Got to stay hid. Like a rabbit." She laughed. "Or you got something else on your mind?"

Mark had yet to talk with this woman when he didn't smile. "I'd have to say he gave you good advice. However, today, I wanted to ask you about your lake and The Park."

"Well, I'm an authority on both. Let's have your questions."

"This is going to sound a little silly, but I'm trying to correlate your lake and some folk tales about lost gold."

"I certainly consider The Park a gold mine." She laughed. "Crystal told me there was some nonsense about gold in my lake."

"JT, a lady here in my office, has tracked down a lot of information on this folk tale. Much of it does seem to fit your lake. Probably a hundred other lakes, too. But there is one point that doesn't fit." He paused just a second. "All the versions she found specifically say the wagon was pushed off a cliff. Now, on the east side of your lake, there *is* a steep hill. But it could hardly be considered a cliff."

"No, I reckon not."

Mark started to speak, but something in the way she ended the sentence stopped him. He could almost hear her mind tracing something back through time. He waited.

"Not now, anyways." Eula was quiet for a moment, then continued. "But back when I wore pigtails, it was an honest-to-goodness cliff.

"I remember Billy Wayne Simmons stripping off his shirt and then his britches, right down to his under shorts. I was a mite embarrassed. Course, not so much I didn't look. He backed up a few feet, said, 'Told you I'd do it and here I go.' He took a run and jumped off the cliff, screaming like a Banshee. He was holding his nose and his feet was still running even when he was out in the air.

"Well, I was a little scared, seeing as how I was the one what dared him to do it. I ran to the edge just in time to see him hit the water like a fat bullfrog. Seemed like a long time before he came up, and I don't think I breathed the whole time he was under water. But he did come up, coughing and sucking air. And then he was looking up to see if I'd watched and grinning like a kid stomping in a rain puddle."

Eula was silent and Mark could picture her smiling to herself. He remained quiet, not wanting to intrude on her memories. After several seconds, she continued. "You know, I haven't thought about that in sixty years, I reckon. But Billy Wayne told me he saw a wagon wheel down there on the bottom. Said he almost touched it, but run out of air and had to get back to the surface."

Mark felt his pulse quicken. "A wagon wheel?"

"That's what he said. Course, I didn't believe him. Thought he was just trying to impress me." She giggled. "He'd already done that. I don't mean by jumping off the cliff, though *I* never would of done it. But I was impressed when he stripped down to his shorts. That was a sight. I'd never seen a boy in just his under shorts before. Back in them days, you didn't." She paused a beat. "I'd seen lots of wagon wheels."

Once more, Eula retreated into her own thoughts. After a minute, she said, "Billy Wayne went to college and later wrote a book. It told you how to be happy. I always figured if you had to read a book to know how to be happy, you weren't going to be."

"What happened to the cliff?"

"'Bout the time Dan and I got married—no, it was a bit later—a big chunk of it sloughed off. And over the years, it just sort of wore down. It's still a nice hill. But it was an honest-to-goodness cliff back when Billy Wayne stripped off his pants."

* * *

Mark put his hands behind his head and leaned back in his chair. That wasn't exactly what he'd wanted to hear. He was trying to find data that would debunk this silly notion that gold might actually be hidden in Eula's lake. He knew the cliff was a consistent feature in the various versions of the folk tale JT had uncovered. Now, Eula was telling him there used to be a legitimate cliff over her lake. And maybe a wagon wheel on the bottom. Of course, wagon wheels were common back then.

Still, logic dictated that gold in a lake in a populated area for nearly two hundred years would have been discovered. *And if it had been found, you'd think there would have been a mention of it in a newspaper or a history book. Did JT do as good a search trying to disprove its existence? If it hasn't been found, then it's still there. Somewhere.*

Mark mentally shook himself. *If* any gold was dumped into a lake in the first place. There's no hard evidence; just folklore.

He could see how Eddie Ray, or Joe and Al could get obsessed with the idea. Gold had the power to draw you to it, and its shine could blind you to reality.

* * *

"What's your take on Eddie Ray?" Mark was standing in the doorway to Crystal's office.

Crystal turned her head slightly and looked away from Mark. She didn't know where to put Eddie Ray in all this. It should be clear, but it seemed pretty hazy to her. "He's the wild card. When we talked with him, he seemed sincere. But he tried to kill my grandmother— twice. What did he say about that when you guys went to the Longneck?"

Mark dropped into the chair in front of Crystal's desk. "He claimed he had no intention of really hurting her. He wouldn't have hit her with his truck; he just wanted to scare her. Maybe get her to move into town."

"Why would that make her move? That doesn't make sense."

"I agree. But it did to Eddie Ray. He thought she might decide driving out in the country was too dangerous."

"And driving in the city would be safer? What about the brakes? If she hadn't run off the road, she could have gotten hit plunging through the stop sign." Crystal's voice was rising. "And if she didn't get hit, she would have ended up in ten feet of water."

"I'm not taking his side. I'm just telling you what he told me."

"Sorry. Didn't mean to jump down your throat. Go on. What did he say about the brakes?"

"He figured she'd notice she didn't have any brakes while she drove down her own road. Not too steep and she would be going slowly."

"Not Nana. She really zooms down the drive. She scares me on it." Crystal thought about the autopsy report. "And Bessie?"

"He seemed surprised. And genuinely sorry someone was killed. No, that's not right. More than sorry; maybe sad. It's hard to tell with Eddie Ray. He tries to project this image of a real macho tough guy, but I don't think he is." He rubbed his nose. "Anyway, he claimed he didn't know about Bessie, until we told him. Joe and Al said they had burned the house and now the old woman, as they called her, would have to live somewhere else. I don't think any of them even knew her name. They just wanted to search her lake without anybody knowing about it. And if they found the gold, take it for themselves."

Crystal shook her head. "All this because of a folk tale."

"I don't know what to think either. Eddie Ray's gone. Did he run, afraid the police would tie him to the murder? Did he, in fact, commit the murder? I don't think so. Did he go over to Joe and Al? He certainly wanted the gold. Of course, I don't think Joe and Al had any intention of sharing the gold with Eddie Ray. Did he run from Joe and Al, once he knew they didn't mind killing anybody who got in their way?" He sighed and stared into near space. "And on and on."

"Do you think he's connected to the firebomb?"

Mark's head came up sharply to look into Crystal's eyes. "You haven't mentioned a firebomb to anybody else, have you? I don't want to panic everybody."

"No, I didn't. But when I came in this morning, they were all discussing it. Phil said it looked like a firebomb to him. He'd seen them in the army."

"What else did the coffee klatch come up with?" His tone mirrored the look of disgust on his face.

Crystal straightened up in her chair, a glint of fire in her eyes.

"What did you think? They'd come in, find the office had been burned and not talk about it? Of course they did. And with everything else that's been going on, speculation ran amok."

Mark's voice took on a more conciliatory tone. "You're right. Sorry if I sounded harsh. It was a very short night—for both of us. I know that's no excuse. And if I didn't tell you thanks for the call, thanks. I've already asked Pam to get us a sign with an emergency phone number. That way, only one of us loses sleep. Anyway, back to the coffee klatch."

"They decided it probably had something to do with Nana's problems."

"Same as Tom Hawkins."

"Yes."

"Where did you meet Tom?"

"He's a friend of Brandi's; well, she goes with him." Crystal explained. "That arson investigator seemed pretty certain it was a firebomb and all the police there felt strongly it was not random."

"So, we agree Eddie Ray is the link." Mark leaned his head back and closed his eyes for a minute, saying "The link" several times. "And he's on the run."

"I don't think so. I think JT is right; they've kidnapped him."

Mark arched his eyebrows. "You buy that story?"

"Not entirely. I don't know." Crystal rubbed the back of her neck. "I'm confused about Eddie Ray. But I don't think he would have left like he did. I think he would have talked to JT. And he wouldn't have left Luis." She hunched her shoulders. "Look, I don't like the man for what he did to Nana. But in this case, I think he's been forced to leave, whether we call it kidnapping or not."

"My soft-hearted project leader," Mark said with a smile. "Tom was right. You are naive."

"He said *we* were naive, not just me."

"Well, I now believe he ran with the jackals. He wants the gold more than he wants JT."

"Did he say that?" Crystal arched her eyebrows.

"No. But he sounded like that. I'm sure Joe and Al came to see him. I just think he went voluntarily. And if he didn't go *with* Joe and Al, I think he ran *from* them."

"I don't."

Mark pressed his lips together and thought for a moment. "Is JT here?"

"No. I sent her to get Luis and take him away. Some place not easily traceable."

"Expect her back today?"

"I doubt it. I don't know where she's going, maybe Fort Worth. But she had to go get Luis, most likely go home and pack clothes, take him to wherever, probably Fort Worth, and then come back."

"If she comes in, I want to see her. I'll tell Pam. I guess I'd better mention it to Sally, just in case Pam doesn't see her."

* * *

Crystal stopped to check with her people on what progress they were making on the demo. Then she went into her office and closed the door. She knew she should be working on the presentation for the venture capitalists, but she couldn't get her mind off Eddie Ray.

She sat down and placed her forehead on her desk. The more she thought about it, the more she believed Eddie Ray did not go willingly with Joe and Al. She and Mark did agree on one thing: Eddie Ray formed the link between the attacks on Nana and the firebombing of IRS. But he was also the link between these acts and Joe and Al. So, it was through Eddie Ray that the police had their best chance to find Joe and Al. And then maybe Big Man, whoever he was.

Now, Eddie Ray is missing. If you don't want something traced to you, what do you do? You break any links to you. Were there any other links besides Eddie Ray?

Crystal brought up the IRS phone list on her computer and punched JT's number into her phone. She let it ring a dozen times. No answer. Was JT on the way to her mother's house, or in the trunk of the fire-breathing car? Eddie Ray had a foot in both camps. A definite link. JT was the source of information. The thugs would be interested in her as well.

She consulted the telephone directory, picked up the phone and dialed again. After seven rings, she started to hang up just as a sleepy voice answered.

"Guess I woke you up, huh? As long as you're up, can you

check on something for me? This is Crystal."

Tom sighed. "Good grief, Crystal. I haven't been asleep more'n an hour. What do you want?"

"Can you check on any John Doe they might have at the morgue?"

"Yeah. Got anybody in particular in mind?"

Crystal laughed. "You really are still asleep. Eddie Ray Dollar. He's the only link between us and the murder."

"And the firebomb."

"Right, and the firebomb. He's about six two, maybe two hundred pounds, curly light brown hair, blue eyes, and more tattoos than a chief boatswain's mate."

"What do you know about boatswain's mates and their tattoos?"

"Had two dates too many with a guy who served as one. His arms and Eddie Ray's looked a lot alike."

Crystal could hear Tom yawning. "Okay. I'll see what I can find. Call you back when I know something. Maybe an hour."

Crystal hung up the phone. *I will work on the IPPI presentation until he calls. I promise I will work on the IPPI presentation until he calls.* She punched the intercom. "Come give me a status report. And a plan of action. Say, thirty minutes."

* * *

Crystal tried to work, but her mind kept jumping out of IPPI demo plans and into the fires at Eula's and IRS. At one point, she checked the DPS database for cars with flames painted on the hood. There was none listed. She didn't expect to find any. Not the kind of information they captured, but she was grasping at any small straw in sight.

She replayed in her mind everything she could remember of her meeting with Eddie Ray, and everything Mark had said about the visit to the Longneck, trying to sift out any information about Joe and Al. They had a boss, but "Big Man" didn't help her much. She found it disheartening that perhaps her best information came from her own view, through waterlogged eyes, of them shooting at her from the other side of the lake.

She was still thinking about hoodlums when the three members of her group appeared at her door.

Chapter 39

MARK was facing similar problems in his office. He finally finished reviewing a new contract, then walked it over to Phil's office and asked him to check it out, before it went to the lawyers. "They'll tell me if we are protected, etc., but you can tell me if I've promised anything we can't deliver. And make a profit on it."

He wandered back into the computer room to check Bobby Don's progress. He still felt a small catch in his throat when he saw the damage, followed quickly by anger over such senseless waste. The firebomb benefited no one, not even the criminals.

Two men were measuring, with Bobby Don watching and answering an occasional question. One worked on the ceiling; the other on the floor. Two other workers were repairing windows.

"The technician should be here by 1:30 to start on the RAID and the server," Bobby Don told Mark. "Between he and I, we ought to be back on-line tomorrow. Day after, at the latest. I hope." Bobby Don displayed his usual, positive attitude.

"Between him and me."

"Yeah. That's what I meant. Swanners thinks they can replace the ceiling tomorrow. The vinyl depends on what we want. If they have it in stock, ought to go in Monday. I told them we had the big cheese coming Tuesday and we sure could use a floor before then. You want the same stuff that was in here, or something different?"

Mark looked at the floor near the wall. "Same stuff. Or as near as you can get. I'll leave it to your judgment."

"Most of the damaged furniture and stuff will get carted out this afternoon."

Mark looked at his original chair. "See if they can repair this chair."

Bobby Don raised his eyebrows. "Cheaper to toss it and buy a new one. Actually, it looked ready for the dump before the fire."

"See if they can repair it, Bobby Don."

"You got it, Dr. O'Malley."

Mark nodded. Bobby Don did an excellent job and he kept everybody upbeat. Maybe IRS could pay for college for him. He deserved it, Mark decided.

* * *

The phone startled Crystal. She was so absorbed in her IRS work it took a second to identify the annoying sound. Absently she picked up the phone and identified herself.

"They've got a John Doe fits your description. Drunk and drowned in White Rock Lake."

"No ID?"

"None found. Probably came out in the water."

Crystal's mind raced through several scenarios. "They're sure he drowned?"

"Water in the lungs. Alcohol in the blood. He drowned. They know what they're doing."

"That doesn't rule out murder. Could have been tossed in when he was too drunk to swim."

"Thank you for the lesson. They found the body near the shore. He could have walked out. Or crawled. You said he drank a lot. Looks like he got drunk, maybe after a fight with his girlfriend, or maybe after you told him about the murder. Fell in the lake and drowned. Every death is not a murder. There are accidents."

"His truck there?"

"No mention of it. I'll check that out. Got a description?"

Crystal tapped a few keys on her computer and then read the license plate number to Tom.

"Hey, you're faster than my contacts at DPS. Can I call you whenever I need a vehicle ID?"

"Solve this case before it gets worse and you can call anytime. They're sure he drowned in shallow water? Didn't drift up there?"

"No drifting."

"No other bruises, cuts, anything?"

Tom sighed slightly. "One bruise on his forehead. Not

sufficient to cause death, or even to knock him out."

"Check on the truck. If it wasn't there, then how did he get there? It's not like he lived near White Rock."

"It's not my case." He paused a minute. When Crystal said nothing, Tom added, "Okay, I'll check. How 'bout you going down and ID'ing the body?"

Crystal's head jerked back. "What? Ah, shouldn't that be a relative?"

"That'd be best. Got the name of a relative?"

Crystal thought about JT. She couldn't be located right now, and Crystal wasn't aware of any other person who knew Eddie Ray, except Joe and Al with no last names. Maybe she could put an ad in the paper: "Joe and/or Al. Please stop by morgue to make formal ID of man you drowned."

Tom could wait until JT showed up.

In Crystal's mind, a picture of JT materialized, so fragile, so distraught, so terrified for her son, so convinced that Eddie Ray had been kidnapped. Going down to ID a body, even if it weren't Eddie Ray, might push her over the edge.

Mark could do it but he wouldn't want the job anymore than she did. " Okay. Mark or I will go down there right away."

"Good. And thanks; I know it isn't easy. I owe you."

"Hold it. Where do I go?"

* * *

Crystal put the phone down and sat staring at her desk. Until last week, she hadn't seen a dead body since her grandfather died. This would be her second in ten days. A soft tap at her door brought her head up.

"Heard anything?" Mark asked.

"I was just about to call you. JT hasn't checked in, has she?"

Mark shook his head.

"Tom Hawkins just called. Wants me, ah, one of us, to go to the morgue and ID a John Doe that is probably Eddie Ray."

He winced and a small groan escaped his lips. "Poor Eddie Ray." Mark held up a hand. "I know. He got himself into this. But I don't think he was a bad guy. He did something a little dumb, and it may have cost him his life. Pretty expensive mistake."

"Poor JT."

"Yeah. How'd he die?"

"Drowned. They said he was drunk and drowned near the shore in White Rock. They're treating it as an accident, but I'm not convinced. Tom said they found him in just a foot or two of water. You want to go ID the body?"

"Tom didn't call me."

She didn't move or say anything, just looked at her boss.

He sighed. "Okay. Let's go get it over with. Maybe we'll find the venture capitalists there, too."

"Mark! That's not funny." For an instant, though, she pictured Dr. Krupe lying on a white slab.

He picked up Crystal's phone and punched the intercom for Pam. "Hi. I'm going to be out of the office for a while. Contact everybody—*everybody*—and tell them we will have a meeting at nine in the morning. Topic: the Tuesday presentations. Everybody should be there. No excuses." He listened for a moment. "In the conference room." He hung up the phone and turned to Crystal. "Meet you in reception in five minutes."

He left, and Crystal tried JT's phone number again. Still no answer. She punched Pam's number. "Pam? Crystal. I'm going to the –." She stopped. "I'm going to be out of the office with Mark. Will you call JT's house every ten minutes until you get her? If I'm back, pass her to me. Otherwise, give her to Sally. I'll check in when we get back."

Next, she called Sally. They talked for a few minutes. Crystal wondered if she were being melodramatic. Then she remembered Bessie, a completely unthreatening woman in her seventies. And she pictured the computer room at 3:30 this morning. It would be foolish to try to predict what these guys would do next.

"Of course, I don't know, but prudence says she should not stay in that house. Do whatever it takes, but get her out of her house. It's not safe. Have her come over to IRS instantly." She listened for a few seconds. "If it's close to quitting time, have her meet me here. I'll be back and I want to talk to her. But don't let her talk her way out of it. Convince her. I can hear her saying, 'I've caused enough trouble. I'll be okay at home.' Remember, that's what she told us this morning when we wanted her to get Luis out of town."

Chapter 40

THE city morgue occupied a neat, four-story, molded-concrete building behind Parkland Hospital on Harry Hines Boulevard, just a ten-minute drive from the IRS offices. The name on the building said it was the Dallas County Institute of Forensic Science. *Certainly makes it sound more impressive than just a plain morgue*, Crystal thought. She and Mark went in and immediately saw Tom.

"What are you doing here?" She asked.

"Soft-hearted, I guess. Decided it was a bunch to put on you. Hi, Mark. Glad you came along."

They found an assistant whose nametag read "Hamilton" and he and Tom had a brief discussion. Finally, Hamilton shook his head in disgust and led the way downstairs to the basement. He carried probably fifty pounds more than a man his height should, and his slow waddle indicated his feet resented the extra load.

"What was that all about?" Crystal asked.

"Oh, he wanted to do the ID by photo, or video--that's the way they do most of it nowadays. Easier on the family. No health risks. I convinced him we'd just go have a look. The advantage of being a policeman."

"Photo ID sounds okay to me," Crystal said.

Tom just snickered.

They entered a large room, which Crystal guessed must have been thirty feet square. At first glance, she thought the floor was marble, but then decided it was highly polished terrazzo. Florescent lights illuminated the room, but she also noted a light fixture in the center of the ceiling that looked like one from an operating room. Stainless steel sinks lined one entire wall. Surgical tools hung in racks. The room was clean and mostly empty, but still it gave Crystal

190

a chill. In her mind she saw autopsies taking place, and the floor wasn't shiny clean any more.

They proceeded into the next room. Considerably colder, it was filled with gurneys, each covered by a sheet. Hamilton would lift the corner of a sheet, check something, drop the sheet and go to another gurney. Crystal shuddered as she caught a glimpse of a ghostly-white, big toe with a manila tag attached.

On his third try, Hamilton muttered, "There you are," and turned to Crystal and Mark. "Ever done this before?"

"No," Mark said. Crystal just shook her head.

"Well, some people, men as well as women, find it a little hard. So just relax. Breathe deeply. Remember that you came here to see a dead body and you even know who it is. At least, you think you do. So, before I pull the sheet back, I want you to picture the guy. Picture him dead, looking pale, stiff, no clothes on, pretty white. Except for his arms. Think of him that way and then when I pull the sheet back, you won't be spooked. Okay? I've had big, tough guys pass out on me."

"I won't faint," Crystal said.

"You expect it to be your buddy. And you expect him to be dead. So just relax and make sure this is him. Are you ready?"

Crystal and Mark both nodded. Hamilton pulled the sheet back.

It was Eddie Ray Dollar.

Mark stepped over and pulled the sheet down a bit farther. Tattoos told the Eddie Ray Dollar life story. A girl's name, the letters alternating between red and blue, graced one forearm. Crystal noted it was neither Juanita nor Theresa. An eagle, wings spread proudly, soared in full flight. Decorating his left biceps was the outline of a heart with "Mother" engraved inside. This lifeless form had been some woman's son, her pride and joy, a son who had chosen to imprint forever a memorial to the woman who gave him life.

Crystal did not faint. Nor did the pale body repulse her. Instead, she was revolted by the fact that a man had been killed for no good reason. He wasn't protecting his country or family, not trying to save another life. He didn't even die in a crime of passion. He was murdered by a lethal combination of greed and stupidity.

"That the guy? Edward Raymond Dollar?"

Mark shifted his focus from the corpse to Hamilton's round face. "Yes."

Hamilton looked at Crystal and arched his eyebrows in question.

She thought that sounded too formal a name. "Yes. That's Eddie Ray."

Without further comment, the assistant started pulling the sheet up, but Crystal put her hand out and stopped him. She hadn't noticed before. The right shoulder also sported a tattoo, a circle with "JT, ER and Luis" inside it.

Crystal moved her hand and stepped back. Hamilton pulled the sheet back up over the head and turned to leave. "If you'll just come out and sign the Body Identification Form, we'll be through."

Tom was shaking his head. "Can't for the life of me understand why anyone would stick needles in themselves and get tattooed, unless they were drunk."

In an outer office, Crystal took a ballpoint pen, held to a clip board by a piece of string, and filled in Eddie Ray's name. She paused over the next entry. What was her relation to Eddie Ray? A person who had met him once—for an hour? The granddaughter of the woman he tried to kill—or at least scare? Someone angry enough to kill him herself? She filled in "Acquaintance."

She handed the form to Mark. Pausing at the same line Crystal had, he wrote "Friend", signed his name and dated the form.

He handed the board back to Hamilton. "Do you get many—"

"Unidentified bodies? About four hundred a year come in without any ID. We clear up nearly 99% of those."

* * *

At the front entrance, Tom said good-bye and started out the door just as his cell phone rang. "Hawkins." The detective listened, asked a few questions and hung up. "No reports of abandoned trucks, at least none even close to the one you described."

"So, how'd he get to the lake to drown?" Crystal asked.

"Could have left his truck there and somebody stole it. Probably left the keys in it. They weren't in his pockets."

"And since he was a nobody, you don't care?"

"It's not my case, Crystal."

"The bombing of our office is your case. And Eddie Ray is

linked to that."

"So you say."

"Actually," Mark said to Tom, "*you* were the one who connected Eddie Ray to the bombing. Remember? I thought it was a random act."

A picture popped into Crystal's mind, one of a man drowning in a bowl of soup. She'd seen a movie years ago, in which a man got drunk, passed out and fell over with his mouth and nose in the bowl of soup.

"I've ID'd the guy," Crystal said. "So, how about a favor? I know you said they found water in Eddie Ray's lungs. Can you find out if the water came from White Rock?"

Tom grumbled good-naturedly, then turned and headed back into the morgue. "This might take a little time," he said over his shoulder.

"Call and let me know as soon as you find anything."

Outside, it had started to rain. Not a good, cleansing rain. Just a slow drizzle, little more than a mist. *Perfect weather for a visit to the morgue, ID'ing a body*, Crystal thought. She remembered as a child she thought funerals were only held on rainy days. You needed a sad day for a funeral. Today wasn't really a rainy day. But then, it wasn't really a funeral either.

* * *

Crystal took a late lunch, and it was after 2:00 when she walked into the IRS reception area and asked Pam if she had reached JT. When Pam said no, Crystal asked her to continue calling. It was important. She went to her office, closed the door and slumped into her chair. Her head ached, her eyes burned from lack of sleep and her arms and legs felt lethargic. What she wanted was a nap. She closed her eyes. Definitely better.

Sleep had almost claimed her when the telephone jarred her back to full consciousness. She reached over and grabbed it before it could ring a second time. Sally was calling to ask about the John Doe. Crystal filled her in, replaced the phone, and closed her eyes once more.

She had drifted into a restless sleep when the phone, not six inches from her head, clanged. She answered it without opening her eyes.

"Crystal. It's five and I'm leaving. I've been calling JT's number every ten minutes, like you asked. But I haven't reached her. Can you ...?" Pam left the question unfinished.

"Sure. I'll take over. Thanks, Pam. See you tomorrow."

Crystal punched the intercom. "Mark. I think JT is in real danger. They only wanted Luis to get to Eddie Ray. Now that he's dead, they'll go after JT."

"Now that the link is broken, and they've got the information they wanted, it isn't logical that they would come after JT."

Crystal almost screamed. "They're not logical." She brought her voice under control. "They haven't found the gold yet. And JT is the only person who can help them find it. At least, that's probably what they think."

"But there isn't any gold."

"The bad guys don't know that." We're getting off track, she thought. "If I can find JT, I want to get her out of her house and put her up in a hotel. Can IRS pay for that? I doubt she can afford it."

There was a moment of silence. "I guess that could go under employee safety. For how long?"

"Until they catch Joe and Al."

Crystal hung up, then immediately called JT's number. Still no answer.

She punched the intercom. "Carol. How have you all done today?" She listened as Carol outlined their work toward the presentation. "Okay. Bobby Don thinks he'll have the RAID back tonight. I'll zip everything onto flash disks tonight. You be ready to load the DPS database onto the RAID as soon as you walk in the door tomorrow."

Carol asked what they did if the RAID was not ready. "We run it on my machine. I've got eighty gigabytes. If the server isn't working Tuesday, we just carry my machine into the conference room and hook it up. Let's move."

Crystal reached into a drawer, withdrew a flash disk and began backing up all the data from her computer, stopping every few minutes to dial JT's phone number.

Just before seven, Crystal's phone rang. "What are you doing at the office?" Tom asked. "Doesn't that Mark guy ever let you go home? Worse than being a detective."

"Actually, it feels like I haven't done any IRS work the last two weeks. What have you found?"

"Well, I heard from the medical examiner. I hate crow. I've always hated crow. Too tough to chew. But you were right. The water in Edward Raymond Dollar's lungs did not come from White Rock Lake. It was plain, ordinary, algae-free, Dallas municipal tap water."

"So this calls for a new paradigm," said Crystal.

"Right. Just what I was going to say. We're reclassifying Eddie Ray's death as a homicide. I'll be in the loop now. And I'm sorry I sounded disinterested this afternoon. I *did* get only about two hours sleep last night." He paused but Crystal said nothing. "That's an excuse, but you could have said something sympathetic."

"Sorry, Tom. I'm too tired myself to think straight."

"Anyway, if there's a connection between Eddie Ray and that house fire, and I believe there is, we're now talking about two murders."

"Plus the fire-bombing."

"Right. I'll give Mark a call and fill him in. I don't want to sound melodramatic or anything, but watch yourself, gal."

* * *

Half an hour later, still unsuccessful in reaching JT, Crystal headed home. Driving on the freeway, she glanced in the rear-view mirror and tensed all over when she saw a big 4x4 behind her. It was baby blue, and the woman driving it was definitely not Joe or Al.

Getting a little spooked, aren't we? Crystal admonished herself. *Just lighten up a little.*

* * *

At the house, she quickly set her computer to dial JT's phone every three minutes. Brandi was working late tonight, so Crystal fixed herself a grilled cheese and a green salad, sat at the table and pulled out her notes from work. The computer continued to dial JT's number. Crystal would hear nothing until JT, or someone, answered.

Chapter 41

JT left the door open and raced over to grab the ringing phone, but by the time she got there, the caller had hung-up. She berated herself for not being faster. *It could have been Eddie Ray.*

She walked back and closed the front door, picked up the grocery bag and took it into the kitchen. The milk went in the refrigerator, but she put the frozen pizza on the counter. That would serve as dinner.

She jumped when the phone started ringing again. This time, she snatched it up before it finished the second ring, saying hello, a touch of apprehension in her voice.

For a few seconds, there was no sound. Then she heard, "JT. This is Crystal."

"Hello." Her voice quavered.

"Will you do something I ask you to, without questioning me?"

Silence.

"Will you?"

"Something happened to Eddie Ray."

"I'd like to talk with you about Eddie Ray in person, not on the telephone. But I need you to do something—right now. Will you do it?"

Again, silence. "Please, JT. This is very important—for Luis."

"What do you want me to do?"

"I want you to leave immediately. Don't pack. Don't make any phone calls. Don't answer the phone if it rings. Don't stop to eat. Just leave immediately after we hang up. Go to ... go to the Renaissance Hotel, on I-35 at High Line Road. Do you know where it is?"

196

"Yes."

"Go. The company will pay for it, your meals, whatever expenses you have. I'll meet you there."

"Is Eddie Ray ...?" The unfinished question hung in the air, persisting like the sad echo of a foghorn.

"We'll talk about that when I see you at the hotel."

"You said ... for Luis."

"JT, you may be in danger. It's important that Luis keeps his mother. Please leave now."

"Eddie Ray is dead?"

JT noted the hesitation and she knew the answer. Finally, Crystal whispered, "Yes."

JT's hand covered her mouth and still a sob seeped out. All day, that thought had tried to insinuate itself into her mind. But it was only a possibility. Something to nag at her, to worry her. Not reality. When it became too unbearable, it could be dismissed, at least temporarily, with a simple "I don't know that. No one has said that."

Now, it was real.

"You may be in serious danger," Crystal was saying. "Leave right away. Will you do that?"

"Yes."

"I'll meet you at the hotel. Please, hurry."

JT sank to the couch, buried her face in her hands and wept. Eddie Ray brightened her life. No one else had insisted she feel good about herself, demanded she see herself as pretty, forced her to laugh and enjoy life. No one else had ever made her feel loved as a woman. And he had been so good to Luis.

Her head jerked up, and she caught her breath. Crystal had told her to go because Luis needed his mother. She let out a moan. *Eddie Ray, I love you.*

She rushed to her room, pulled a small, soft suitcase from the closet, then crossed the room and opened a drawer. She was reaching in when the phone rang. It wasn't Eddie Ray. It would never be Eddie Ray again. She looked toward the insistent noise coming from the other room. JT sorted through the possibilities. *It isn't Crystal since she told me to leave immediately. It isn't Luis. I told him not to call. I would call him.*

The ringing stopped. She returned to packing. She took

panties, bra, and hose out of the drawer and placed them in the bag. From the bathroom she retrieved her tooth brush and various cosmetic items. She went to the closet and selected a skirt, blouse and shoes.

For a minute she surveyed the room, looking for...she didn't know what. Tears filled her eyes when she saw a picture sitting on the dresser of Eddie Ray and Luis. She picked it up, pressed it to her lips, then placed it in the suitcase. She closed the small bag and took it with her into the living room.

Even though she felt silly, she checked the front yard through the window before opening the door. *Nothing there. Of course not.* She went out, quickly locked the front door, hurried to the car and put her things in the back seat. She got in and started the car. On the front seat was a toy pickup, Luis's favorite toy. Eddie Ray had given it to him.

She had backed up about twenty feet when a black car swung into her drive and stopped behind her. A shiver ran down her back as she saw two male forms behind the windshield and flames painted on the hood.

Chapter 42

JT locked her door and watched in the mirror as they approached, one on either side. Her mind screamed one word—Luis. She moved the shift to drive, cut the wheels sharply to the left, and took her foot off the brake. The tall man on the left was reaching for the door handle as she mashed down on the gas pedal. The tires grabbed the concrete drive and the car shot forward and to the left. She whipped across the grass, missing the Mimosa tree, hopped off the curb and sped down the street. In the mirror, she could see she had knocked down the tall man.

Her eyes refocused on the road just in time to see the car in front of her. She jerked the wheel to the right. It wasn't soon enough. Her car clipped the front bumper of the white Lumina and JT cringed as she heard it crease the full length of her car. As the Lumina scraped along her car, JT could see the frightened look on Miss Bennet's wrinkled face. The old woman's car spun to a stop across the narrow street.

JT didn't slow down. At the corner, she turned left and raced down the short block to Lovers Lane. The afternoon drizzle had left the roads damp and that always seemed to make traffic heavier.

She was shaking all over. *I need to get away from here before they get to the corner and can see which way I go.* Straight ahead was the parking lot for a strip mall. The toll road was only a few blocks to the left. That would be fast. Did she have any change? She imagined herself sitting at the toll booth, searching for money, while the killers pulled up beside her.

A small opening appeared and JT darted across Lovers Lane, turning neither right nor left, but racing straight across the street and into the crowded parking lot of the strip mall. She found an empty space, parked and turned the engine off. She slumped down in the seat, then reached up and adjusted the mirror so she had a view of the intersection, while she remained hidden.

In less than thirty seconds, a car skidded to a stop at the intersection. Flames seemed to dance on the car's hood and JT felt their heat on her cheeks. In the mirror, she could see the two men, but could tell nothing about their appearance. The wheels were turned slightly, ready for a right turn.

The traffic remained sluggish and JT said a fervent prayer for an opening. *The longer they sit there the better chance they might see me.*

Just then, she saw the passenger pointing over toward the parking lot. A small cry escaped her lips. *If they come into the parking lot, I'm trapped.* She tried to visualize the stores in the shopping center. Even though she had shopped here a thousand times, at this precise moment, she couldn't remember a single store. *What if I try to run to a store and it's closed? Or a bunch of people are coming out and I can't get in? They might pull me right off the sidewalk. Would anybody see—or care? What if I do get in? I have to come out sometime. None of these stores stays open all night.*

Her eyes scanned the buildings. The Inwood Theater was just to her right. There, on its marquee was the current offering: *Kidnapped!* Her entire body began to shake uncontrollably. She gripped the steering wheel as tightly as she could, took deep breaths, trying to calm her frayed nerves. Nothing seemed to help.

A drop of sweat trickled down her side, immediately followed by more. She could feel them traversing a path all the way from her armpit to her waist. Without sitting up, she reached for the key and started the motor, then checked the mirror. The driver of the fire-breathing car was pounding on the steering wheel. Suddenly, he cut his wheels left and swung onto Lovers Lane, causing a lime-green convertible to lock its brakes and then get rear-ended by another car. Brakes screeched and horns honked as the cars behind tried to avoid piling into the accident blocking the slick roadway. The low-slung, black sedan with JT's two tormentors raced east on Lovers Lane.

JT waited a full minute, then eased her car out of the lot and turned west on Lovers Lane. She drove as fast as the cars around her, turned left on Inwood Road and headed for I-35. Her attention was divided between the traffic in front of her and what she could see in her mirrors.

Without warning, a black car appeared half a block behind her. It was closing fast. Her heart rate shot up and her breathing accelerated.

Ahead, the signal light turned red and she slammed on her brakes, stopping inches from the car in front of her. The black car was not slowing down. JT braced herself for the crash, her eyes riveted on the rear-view mirror. An instant before it reached her, it whipped into the left turn lane and raced straight across the intersection, narrowly missing two cars, who responded with blaring horns. JT bit her lip. No flames decorated the hood of the reckless car.

Ten minutes later, she turned onto Interstate 35 heading east. After a mile, she exited at Motor Street, took the service road to Wycliff, crossed under the freeway and entered the parking lot of the Renaissance Hotel.

She knew she hadn't been followed; still she sat in her car, motor running, watching cars come and go. Each one that entered the parking lot caused her to catch her breath.

She was just beginning to relax a bit when a dark car turned in and circled around, stopping, moving forward a little, stopping. As it pulled opposite her, the driver looked right at her, then started up with a jerk and zipped around the end of the row and turned into a parking spot immediately behind JT. The whole episode took less than thirty seconds and left JT shaking. Only when the car was parked, did she realize it was a dark blue car with a white top.

Finally, she turned off the engine, took her small bag and entered the hotel. Her legs felt shaky and she had to concentrate to walk in a straight line. The car's air conditioning had been running full blast, but she could feel the sweat running down her cheeks. She stopped to regain some composure before presenting herself at the front desk.

*　*　*

Crystal entered the door just in time to see JT approaching the elevators. *Either I got here faster than I figured, or she took longer than she should have*, Crystal thought. She called to JT. The woman stopped but did not turn around. Crystal called again.

"JT."

This time JT apparently recognized Crystal's voice and turned to see her hurrying across the lobby. Crystal watched JT's energy evaporating, and was afraid she might collapse.

"Here, sit on this chair for a moment." She took the suitcase with one hand and JT's elbow with the other and guided her to a nearby chair.

"You're safe. Luis is safe. Everything's going to be okay."

Even as she said it, Crystal realized how stupid that was. Eddie Ray was dead. It would be a long time before JT thought of things as okay. But right now, she needed to hear someone say things would get better. She would have enough problems getting through the next few days—or months.

Several minutes passed. Quiet conversation drifted toward them from the dimly lit bar across the lobby. In front of them, two well-worn saddles flanked the entrance to the hotel's restaurant. The tranquil scene belied the events of the day. From the bar, a woman laughed, reminding Crystal of a wind chime tinkling in a light breeze. The thought came to her that she had never heard JT laugh.

Slowly JT's breathing returned to normal. Some color came back to her face and the trembling in her hands subsided. Crystal knelt on the floor bringing her face level with JT's. "There's a public telephone over there." She opened her purse and dug out a handful of change and placed it in JT's hand. "Go over and call Luis. Say goodnight to him. Then you'll know he's safe, and you will sleep better."

Without answering, JT got up and walked over to the phone and placed the call. Crystal sat in the chair. *That was easy. Now, what do I say to her about Eddie Ray?*

* * *

Neither woman spoke in the elevator. Only after they were in JT's room with the door closed did JT speak. "You didn't want me to call Luis from my room."

It was a simple statement, but Crystal knew JT was really asking for an explanation, one she had probably already guessed.

"Maybe I was being a little melodramatic, but these people are dangerous. Caution is the best approach right now. Luis is fine?" She knew the answer, based on JT's demeanor when she had returned from the phone, but wanted to reinforce the only good aspect of the day.

"Yes. He and his grandmother baked cookies and he was perfectly happy. He didn't ask about Eddie Ray."

That was *her* way of asking, Crystal knew.

"Eddie Ray is dead. I'm so very sorry to have to say that to you. I could tell how you felt about him. And he made it very apparent he was deeply committed to you. He thought the sun rose and set around you." Crystal thought that sounded a little weak. "That night, when we drove him to pick up your car, he said very clearly his only concern was for you and Luis."

Silent tears covered JT's cheeks. Her whole body drooped as if someone had draped a great lead blanket over her. Her eyes focused on her shoes and she asked without looking up, "How?"

There was no easy way. "He drowned. The police don't know exactly how yet, but they are certain he was murdered. They don't have much to go on. Based on what I've told them, Joe and Al, the crooks who got him into this, are the only suspects at present." That was enough, unless she pressed for details.

"The ones with fire painted on their car."

"Yes."

"They were at my house tonight." She said it as one might say there was a chair in the living room. No emotion, just a fact.

Crystal's emotions raged and she fought to appear calm but her rising voice gave away her anxiety. "At your house? Tonight? After I talked to you?"

"Yes."

With Crystal prodding, JT related the events leading up to her arrival at the hotel. Now it was Crystal's turn to look pale.

She glanced at the small suitcase. "You packed." The instant as she said it, she regretted it. JT had enough problems tonight without Crystal adding to them.

"A few things." Neither her tone nor her look conveyed any feeling of guilt. "I shouldn't have."

Chapter 43

MARK was in his den paying bills when the phone rang. Tom repeated much of the information he had given to Crystal a few minutes earlier.

"We've put out an APB on the car. Crystal thinks she can identify one of them as the guy who shot her. But with Eddie Ray dead, we'll need something else to really nail them. Unless her ID is really strong. And even then, we can't charge them for the death of the woman in the fire. We'll need more. Of course, when you know who, it's easier to collect evidence." There was a brief pause. "That's about it for now. If we pick them up, then we'll go from there. Right now, we don't have much to charge them with, but we'll think of something. Maybe something in their car, or at their house, will tie them to Eddie Ray or the firebomb."

"Crystal thinks JT is in danger," Mark said.

"These guys sound crazy. I wouldn't rule out anything. If I were JT, I'd be worried."

"Hmmmm."

"Two other things," Tom continued.

"Yeah?"

"Call the grandmother . . . the one with the lake. You know her, don't you?"

"Eula Moore? Yes, I know her."

"Call her and tell her to stay out of sight. She's more of a target than JT. I hate to ask Crystal because then I have to emphasize to her how much danger her grandmother is in. I'd call the grandmother myself if she were in my jurisdiction."

"She's supposed to be keeping a low profile now."

"Yeah, you said that. But Wooden Nickel is not Dallas. If she goes to the store, probably half the town will know it."

"I'll call her," Mark said. "She's strong-willed. Don't know how much effect I'll have. Maybe I can get Glothe to call her."

"Give it a try."

"Okay. And number two?"

"You."

"Me?"

"You. They've firebombed your office. I know. You're going to tell me that was to destroy data. I doubt it, but okay. I'll buy that if you'll buy that it was also to send a message. And if they know about IRS, they know about you. Like it or not, you're at risk."

Mark hung up the phone, consulted a slip of paper from his wallet, then dialed Melva's number.

"Eula. How are you?"

"Good as gold. Or is that the wrong thing to say?"

Mark laughed. "Maybe not the best choice right now."

"Why're you calling an old lady instead of a young one?"

"You're pretty young."

"Well, you can go right on flattering me. My mind sees me young. But when I walk up the hill from the lake, I know my mind's eye needs glasses. What's going on?"

Mark told her of Eddie Ray's murder.

"Glad they've moved into your neck of the woods. Maybe some of your police boys can corral them. Old Billy Goat can't." She paused only a second. "Sorry, Mark. I'm just used to picking on Bill. He's right as rain and does his best. And he's a long time friend." She chuckled. "But if I didn't give him a hard time, he'd think I was getting senile."

"Tom Hawkins, the detective who's investigating the bombing of IRS, thinks they may move back to Wooden Nickel at any time. In fact, we both feel you could be in real danger."

"Told you that two weeks ago."

"And you were absolutely right. So now, Hawkins suggests, and I agree, that you should stay out of sight a little longer——until they catch these guys."

"Did that for you before the funeral. Don't aim to hide anymore."

"Just a few days—"

"Too late. Everybody in town knows where to find me. 'Sides,

I'm more of a squirrel than a groundhog. I don't hide well."
"Could you at least be careful?"
"That's why I'm alive today."

Chapter 44

CRYSTAL had been home no more than five minutes when Tom called wanting as much information on Joe and Al as she could provide. Tom and his partner were going to the Longneck to look for the pair of suspects.

She told them what little she could. Tom wanted more.

"That's the best I can do." She listened. "No, Tom, I'm not giving you the run-around. I only saw one of them up close and Eddie Ray gave me a really poor description of them. That's all I know. I'm certain I can pick out the one who shot me and I think I'll recognize the other one. But I can't describe them any better than I have. I can look at mug shots tomorrow, if you'd like. I ought to go with you tonight."

Crystal looked out the window at the new moon while Tom told her what a bad idea that was and recited department policy against a civilian going with them.

The more she thought about it, the more sense it made. She interrupted Tom's litany. "But it's not forbidden and it's not without precedent. The truth of the matter is, if I were a reporter—no connection with any case—I'd probably be allowed to ride in a squad car on a night's patrol. What's going to happen? I'll be between two policemen."

Crystal ran a hand through her hair in frustration as Tom again told her it wasn't a good idea. " Okay. Enough of the arguing. I'm going to the Longneck Bar tonight. I can go with you and your partner, or I can go alone. Your call."

* * *

It was after nine when Crystal, Tom and his partner, Dick Donovan, reached the Deep Elum area. Tom drove past the bar and circled the block, then widened his arc to include the blocks on either side. No sign of the fire-breathing car. Across the street from the Longneck, Tom pulled to the curb in a no parking zone. The three got out, crossed the street and entered the bar.

A strong smell of beer and cigarettes assaulted Crystal. Layers of smoke hung motionless below the dim lights. The Miller Lite neon sign still flickered on and off. It looked and smelled the same as it had two nights earlier.

Crystal and the two policemen weren't five feet inside when the noise level lower noticeably. Crystal felt all eyes focus on them as they crossed to the bar. Tom held up his police ID and addressed the bartender while Dick leaned his back on the bar and watched the rest of the room.

"You work here regularly?"

"Sometimes."

"Most of the time?"

"Yeah."

Bud Heavy kept his eyes on Crystal. *He remembers me.* She turned to study the room, starting with the men standing at the bar. Slowly, she shifted her attention from one man to the next, working her way around the room until she had examined each person.

One man ran his tongue over his lips and grabbed his crotch. Two men turned away, the only ones not staring at Crystal and her two companions. Crystal scrutinized them. She'd only gotten a quick view before they turned their backs to her. One was short and one was tall. In her mind, she reviewed the brief look she had gotten. She inspected their backs. Finally, she decided they were too old. Joe and Al fell in the twenty-five to thirty-five range.

Even with Tom and Dick beside her, she felt uneasy. She turned back to follow Tom's questioning of the bartender.

"You remember one of your patrons, Eddie Ray Dollar?"

"No." Too quick. Clearly, he hadn't given it any thought.

"About six two, brown hair, tattoos all over his arms, always wears jeans and ropers."

"Don't remember anybody like that." The bartender was a large man, probably six-three, two hundred forty pounds. He had both hands on the bar top, his eyes now focused on Tom. He stated his answers in a neutral tone.

"How about Joe and Al?"

"Don't know them either."

Tom smiled at the man. "You don't know anybody named Joe or Al? Surprising."

"Hey, Bud Heavy," Crystal said. "When my friend and I were in here the other night, you said you knew them. Said they were up in Denton that day."

Tom's head jerked toward Crystal, but he said nothing.

The barkeep slowly turned his attention to Crystal. "Don't remember you ever being in here. And I for damn sure didn't tell you nothing about nobody I don't know."

"You said they'd be back the next day." Crystal struggled to keep her voice from quavering. The other night, Bud Heavy had been trying to make a move on Brandi, and he had been non-threatening. Tonight, Crystal found him sinister, dangerous and he seemed even bigger than before. Tonight, he scared her. And she could feel his hate for Tom … and for her.

"Don't know nothing about that. Never seen you before."

"Do you own this dump?" Tom asked.

"No."

"So you don't give a damn if we shut the place down?"

"Not a rat's ass."

"Well, I'll bet Mr. Manachii does. And I'll bet he thinks you should too."

The bartender pressed his lips together. "Ah, now I think on it, I seen a guy in here all tattooed. Don't know his name. Ain't been in the last few nights."

"And they call you Bud Heavy?"

"Just Bud."

"Okay, Bud. Did Eddie Ray talk about knowing where some lost gold was?"

Bud glanced at the men standing at the bar, then back at the detective. He lowered his voice. "Maybe one time. He was sloshed and talked crazy stuff 'bout some gold lost for a hundred years. I was busy. Didn't catch much. Nobody paid him no mind. Like I said, he was drunk."

"Now, Bud, think this out before answering. He was talking to Joe and Al. Do you remember them now?"

For the first time, the barkeep moved his hands. His oversized right hand rubbed his chin and mouth. Crystal could see that Bud was struggling with what to say.

"He was mouthing off to a bunch of guys. Don't know who. And I don't know no Joe or Al. He coulda been talking to some guys named that." He shrugged.

Tom reached into his pocket and pulled out a card and put it under Bud's left hand. "Joe or Al here tonight?"

Without looking, Bud shook his head.

"I didn't think so. If you see them, you call me. I need to ask them a few questions. I *will* find them. And if they tell me you know them, I'm coming back and I'm hauling your ass down to the station."

Now Bud's eyes showed more anger than fear. "Ain't done nothing and you can't haul me downtown."

"Well, maybe you haven't. But I'll take you in while I check that out. And it might take me three or four days to find out whether you have or you haven't." Tom smiled at Bud. "You needn't worry about Mr. Manachii, though. I'll tell him you're helping me a lot, giving me lots of good information."

Tom fixed a cold look on Bud for several seconds, then turned. "Let's get out of this maggot heap."

* * *

In the car, Tom's displeasure showed. "What the hell was that about you and a friend being at the Longneck? What friend?"

Crystal had never experienced Tom's anger before. She tried to sound breezy. "Oh, Brandi and I popped in for a few minutes the other night. See if Al and Joe were there." She looked puzzled. "Didn't she ask you about 'Big Man'? Joe and Al's boss?"

"She did. This where she heard about him?"

"Yes."

"She wouldn't say where she got the name." He shook his head. "Don't *ever* do anything that ... like that again. Aren't you the woman who said one of them tried to kill you? You should know better. So should Brandi."

Her first inclination was to tear into Tom. Who was he to tell her where she could or couldn't go? But before she opened her mouth, she thought of JT. Crystal had just told JT the same thing. You can't go home. You will go to your mother's. She was worried for JT's safety and Tom was worried about her. And Brandi. She decided a better tactic was to change the subject. "Who's Manachii?"

"He owns the Longneck. And it's the nicest place he owns. He's known for the shortness of his temper. I'm sure our friend Bud does *not* want to get Manachii mad at him."

Dick laughed. "I'll say. When he gets mad at someone, he doesn't like to see them again. Of course, *no one* sees them anymore. They just vanish."

"If you knew Manachii owned the place, why'd you ask Bud if he owned it?" Crystal asked.

"See what he'd say. Either way, I get him. If he said he owned it, I'd say Mr. Manachii would be interested to know that."

"So, what'd you find out?"

"Exactly what I expected to find out—nothing. Oh, it would have been nice if you looked over and saw Al and Joe playing pool. But I'd have put five bucks down that we wouldn't see them." Tom watched a black car pass them. "I hate tinted glass. It ought to be illegal." He refocused on the road. "There's a good chance that our friend Bud has already called Joe and Al."

"Do you have the Longneck's phone tapped?" Crystal asked.

Dick chuckled. "Don't I wish."

"Don't we all," Tom said. "We don't have enough to go to a judge and get authorization for a tap. It always works on TV. But I guess all those judges are in California. Sure aren't in Dallas. Judges here usually won't even listen to you."

"Remember that time you caught Judge Roy Bean in the men's room. You got the search warrant." Dick let out a war whoop.

"Yes I did. But the other side of the story is, I ran into the Honorable Judge a few days later and he said if I ever again so much as spoke a single word to him when he had his pants down, I'd—I believe his exact words were— 'cool my buns in jail for a week.' He was not smiling, either."

"Have you *ever* seen him smile?" Dick asked. "I'll bet he frowns while he's having an orgasm." He glanced at Crystal. "Oops. Sorry, Crystal." But he continued laughing.

"Is his name really Judge Roy Bean?" she asked.

"No. His legal name is Roy Pinto. So of course after he became a judge, we all started calling him Judge Roy Bean."

"Not to his face," said Dick. "Then again, Tom was speaking to His Honorable's rear." That started Dick off on another round of laughter.

"It's appropriate. He's got the same, kindly temperament of old Roy Bean. What a sour crab."

* * *

Tom and Dick delivered Crystal back to her apartment. Brandi was working a late shift, so Tom had no chance to grill her about her visit to the Longneck. *Lucky break for Brandi.*

As soon as she kicked off her shoes, she called Mark. "Sorry it's so late, but I just got in and your message said to call whatever the hour."

She filled him in on JT's encounter with Joe and Al and her narrow escape. "She's safe for the time being. Wouldn't hurt if you escorted her to the office tomorrow."

Mark said nothing for several moments. "There's no question she's in danger now. A better plan might be for JT to go directly to her mother's, not come to the office at all. Gives us a day or two to see if we can wrap this up. She said her mother has a different last name and lives somewhere near Fort Worth. So, unless they're more sophisticated than I think they are, they won't trace her there. JT's confident they did not follow her to the hotel?"

"She said she was positive."

"So, if she left from the hotel and went directly to her mother's, she ought to be safe. Call and insist that she do that. Tell her that's her job for a couple of days."

"I'll call her now."

Crystal disconnected just as Brandi came in from work. "Lots of news, but I've got to make a quick call. Grab something to drink and I'll fill you in."

Crystal called JT. "I've just been talking with Mark. He and I have agreed that you should leave the hotel in the morning and go directly to your mother's. Do *not* go by your house and don't come to IRS."

Crystal listened to JT saying she had to work. She had to help prepare for the Tuesday presentations.

"Mark said your job is to call IRS each morning and we'll keep you posted." JT started to protest again and Crystal interrupted.

"JT, Mark said that if anything happened to you because you stayed around to come to work, he would feel responsible. He'd never forgive himself. Sally and I feel the same way. The most important thing you can do is stay safe. And the best way to do that is to go hide out at your mother's. Please promise me that you will not go near your house or IRS. Promise."

There was a slight pause. "I need to make arrangements for Eddie Ray's funeral."

"Isn't there someone else? Some family member?"

"No. No one. I will do it."

Crystal thought for a moment. "JT, we'll make the arrangements. IRS will take care of everything." She hoped she wasn't overstepping her authority. "But you must agree to go to your mother's house for a few days."

"Okay. Luis and I will come for his funeral."

* * *

Crystal had given Brandi all the day's news which led to a thirty minute discussion. Now the two women pursued their own interests, Crystal looking over some IRS papers and Brandi watching the news on television.

"Boy, that would really burn my butt," Brandi blurted.

"What would?"

Brandi muted the TV. "Weren't you paying attention? This last story. Some woman stole another woman's identity. Got all her vital information, date of birth, social security number, mother's maiden name. All that stuff. And then, she used that to drain the woman's bank account, run up huge bills on her credit cards, everything."

Crystal made a sound of disbelief.

"That's not the worst part. They told her, the original woman——the *victim* for God's sake—they told her *she* should change *her* name. Re-establish her credit under a new name. Start over."

"Did she? Did the woman change her name?" Crystal was sitting up straighter now.

"No. She said she would find the thief and if the police couldn't do anything, she would."

"Good for her."

"Know what the police told her? Don't do anything illegal. They told the *victim* that." Brandi's voice was an octave higher. "I think she ought to find the woman and cut her hands off. Can you believe that? They told the victim not to do anything illegal."

Brandi clicked the sound on the TV back on and turned her attention to the next news item. Crystal tuned the news out. *How horrible it would be to have someone steal your identity. Take away ... you. It would change your whole life. I'm with the woman,* Crystal thought. *I'd fight back. I'd go after the person. I wouldn't let them do that to me.*

* * *

Once again, Crystal slept fitfully. She tossed and turned, fell into strange places where she could see herself from afar. Her dreams were troubling, but she didn't know why, couldn't remember what they were, couldn't quite tell if she were dreaming at all.

Then they became frightening. She observed herself, as if she were another person, standing to the side. At one point, her mouth was missing. Later, she watched as she reached up to rub her nose, but her nose was gone. She got dressed and started to put on earrings. But she had no ears. And then she had no eyes. No features at all. She was just a blob. No personality. No identity. She was running, looking back at her pursuer, but there was no one. In her mind, she knew no one was trying to harm her. Physically. But they were erasing her. She was disappearing. Someone had stolen her identity. And she realized she was no longer Crystal.

She woke with a start and instinctively reached up to touch her nose and ears and mouth. She blinked her eyes and looked around the room in the darkness. She could see outlines of things. She shivered and pulled the sheet around her, thinking about the Crystal she had watched in her dream, the Crystal with no features, no identity, not really Crystal at all. And she knew what she had to do.

Chapter 45

CRYSTAL arrived at Intelligent Retrieval Systems just before 8:30. Without even going by her office to drop her purse, she marched straight to Mark's office. Three steps inside, she saw Phil Wilson.

"Oops. Sorry. Didn't know you had somebody with you." She turned to leave.

"Come on in. Phil and I are about finished."

"I'll come back later."

"No, no. Have a seat. It will only be a minute." He turned his attention back to Phil. "That's exactly what I needed from you."

Phil sat casually, legs crossed, hands resting comfortably on the arms of the leather chair. "Well, if everything in that one area really went to hell in a hand-basket, we could lose money. Not likely. But, by tightening that up just a little, add some of those phrases I jotted down, we can eliminate that possibility altogether."

"You're absolutely right. Thanks." Mark looked at Crystal. "You're on."

She had prepared what she would say to Mark, but she hadn't counted on Phil being there. She looked in his direction. He exuded his usual air of confidence and maturity. Older than Crystal by at least twenty years, she had always respected him. At least until last week. What did she say now? She shifted in the chair, not certain where to begin. "The, ah, meeting begins at nine."

Mark raised his eyebrows. "So?"

"Well, this could wait until after the meeting, I guess."

"Come on, Crystal. You came striding in here with a definite purpose. Clearly, you had something on your mind. Let's hear the topic, at least, and decide how much we can cover before nine."

She glanced at Phil. He was watching her, as relaxed as a cat on a sun-drenched porch. Her upper lip began to twitch and she faked a cough and put her hand up to cover her mouth. Both men were staring at her. She had to say something. Her throat seemed to constrict, some part of her not wanting to say anything. She forced herself to speak. "Remember last week? You mentioned a new approach to medical auditing."

"Yes. Phil suggested it. An excellent idea."

"Well." Her voice cracked, like a teenage boy whose voice was changing. She stole a quick look at Phil. He had uncrossed his legs and now his hands were gripping the chair. His discomfort gave Crystal enough strength to continue. "Well, Phil and I had discussed that possibility about two weeks ago."

Phil cleared his throat. "Yes, we did. I believe I mentioned that to you, Mark, when I told you about it."

"I don't recall that, but you might have," Mark said. His voice was perfectly neutral and he looked at Crystal as if to ask where she was going with this.

But Crystal hesitated. *Does this make any difference? I'm not really a confrontational type person. Is it worth a fight, alienating a coworker?*

In her mind, she saw her featureless face from last night's dream. *It does matter! I'm not a rug, to be walked on.* She twisted in her chair and stared at Phil for several seconds. His eyes now focused on his knees and he did not look up.

She turned back to face Mark, and spoke before she could change her mind. "Did he tell you that it was my idea? Yes, we discussed it, but it was my idea." She was shaking and she pressed her elbows tightly against her sides. "I believe Phil will tell you that he brought nothing to the discussion." She inhaled deeply and slowly let the air out, trying to relax. "Isn't that right, Phil?"

Phil didn't look up. "We discussed a number of aspects for such a project."

Crystal's anxiety began giving way to anger. *He's not giving up. Well, neither am I.* When she spoke this time, her voice was low and edged with impatience. "But did you *add anything* to my ideas?"

"We talked about, ah, many things. Ah, I'm sure—"

"Can you name one idea that you offered? One, single idea?" Her face felt hot, but the shaking had stopped and her lip no longer twitched. Her eyes remained focused on Phil and did not waver.

"Well, ah, I don't remember ... ah, probably ... ."

She sat straight, head held high. In her mind, she saw the figure of last night, and the features had returned to her face. Her voice relaxed a little and she said very calmly but very firmly, "Phil, would you tell Mark it was my idea and mine alone? I told you about it and we discussed it, but it was my idea and not yours."

Phil crossed his hands in his lap. He swallowed, then straightened his back. He raised his head and looked directly at Mark. "It appears I gave you the wrong impression. And I apologize to Crystal and to you. It was her idea entirely. I was so enthusiastic about it, I guess I got carried away. I was sorry when you told the group it was my idea, but I didn't have the courage to speak up." He looked back down at his hands.

Crystal debated with herself. He tried to steal her idea and yet he was making it sound like a misunderstanding. *But, I'm getting credit for it*, she reminded herself. *That's what counts. Do I want to alienate Phil for life? Do I want him fired?* Her mind flashed back to Tuesday. *There was a moment when I wanted Mark to fire JT and that would have been a mistake. But this is intellectual piracy.*

Mark broke the silence. "Crystal, I'm sorry I credited your idea to Phil. You can be sure I will set the record straight for the entire group. It's possible I read too much into what Phil told me. Certainly, he was enthusiastic about it. Thank you for clearing up the mistake." He glanced at his watch, then looked back at Crystal. "We've got only five minutes before the general meeting. Phil and I need to finish up. After the meeting, you and I will talk some more."

Crystal nodded and stood up. Her head was high as she walked out of the office, not with a swagger, but with an air of confidence she had lacked for a long time.

Mark began the meeting by stating that he had made a mistake the other day and it was actually Crystal's idea for a new approach to the monitoring of medical costs. He had mistakenly attributed it to Phil.

Next, they reviewed Phil's program for Tuesday. Even though his project was in its initial stages and there was nothing to demonstrate, Crystal had to admit it was a good presentation. Mostly, she was amazed that, in spite of the blow he had received just five minutes earlier, Phil's presence was confident and commanding, showing no signs of the embarrassment in Mark's office.

Sally beamed as she described her plans and showed a small portion of the demo. When she finished, there was general approval, but Mark was silent.

"Any comments from the president?" asked Sally.

"It's a clear demonstration of what the system can do. But I'm thinking that, while you have shown its capabilities, the demo is a little ... ." He cocked his head to one side and stuck his chin forward an inch or two. "Well, the data is a little dull."

The smile faded from Sally's face.

Mark continued. "Last night, no, night before last, I went over JT's notes on her 'extra-curricular' work. Despite the Pandora's box she opened, JT has done some amazing work. Sally, I think you ought to use that to illustrate, not only the folklore project, but the topological project as well. Show how they were tied together. How a seemingly impossible task was made possible using our systems. In fact, not only possible, but done in an astonishingly short amount of time." Mark looked at the group. "It will show off how good these systems are, how they can be tied together, how they can be used in ways we haven't thought about yet. And, it will be fun and interesting. How many times have the venture capitalists seen a search for a ton of gold?"

"Too bad we can't show them the gold," Crystal quipped.

"Right. If we had the ton of gold, we wouldn't care about those guys at all. What do you think of that approach, Sally?"

"I like it. If that doesn't get them interested, nothing will."

Finally, Mark pointed to Crystal.

She hesitated for a moment. "I can, and will, show you what we have planned. Of course, with all the distractions, we're way behind, but we'll be working over the weekend and we'll be ready. But, taking a cue from Mark, maybe we can dovetail with Sally's presentation. What do you think of ... ." She paused and then continued with a flourish in her voice, "The Case of the Puce Truck." Laughter filled the room. "We can show just how that ID went. What do you think?"

"I like it," said Mark. "Of course, we had the additional help of Pam recognizing the address. But, I still think you ought to include it. How's that sound to you, Phil?"

Phil looked startled. His usual confidence appeared to have deserted him. "Ah, well, yes. I think that would make it seem more real. An actual case, regardless of Pam's help, will make for a more solid showing, I would think."

"Okay. We'll include it," Crystal said without looking at Phil. She proceeded to show the rest of their presentation.

When she finished, Mark took over. "For my part, I intend to provide an introduction and a wrap-up. The opening will discuss our accomplishments, much of which the Rooney people will be familiar with. But I want to remind them, nonetheless. At the end, I will outline, briefly, some new projects we have waiting in the wings, including Crystal's medical auditing idea, and the Bowen project. Phil and I have hammered out the contract and it will go to the lawyers this afternoon."

He looked around at the group. "Okay. We know what to do. Monday morning, say ten o'clock, let's have a dress rehearsal. We'll try to go through the whole program. Some of you can play the parts of Rooney people and ask questions. I think we'll video it, in pieces, so each of you can review your own part and see what needs to be fine-tuned. Any questions?"

Sally looked around the room and when no one raised a question, she spoke. "I'd like to remind everyone that Eddie Ray Dollar's funeral is at 2:00 tomorrow at Worthholder Funeral Home. I know most of you didn't know Eddie Ray, but it will mean a lot to JT if you come. She's had a tough time and deserves our support. Try to make it if you can."

"I'll be there," said Mark.

Crystal and several others nodded.

"Anything else?" Mark asked. No one spoke, so Mark continued. "Monday afternoon, Crystal and I will go get our preview of the consultant, at his talk at UT."

Crystal's stomach tightened and her strength ebbed at the thought of seeing Dr. Krupe. Just the mention of his name caused her to feel inadequate. She didn't know what would happen when she met him face to face.

Mark looked around the group, but no one offered anything.

"Okay. Let's get hopping. We want to wow them on Tuesday. Crystal, I need a few minutes of your time. Shall we talk in my office?"

* * *

Mark closed the door to his office and sat on the edge of his desk. "Phil is a real asset to IRS. I think you know that. What he did was ... well, I don't know what he was thinking. I can imagine his enthusiasm and blurting out the idea to me. But there is no excuse for not correcting that, particularly when I credited it to him in the meeting. He apologized to me again, after you left. Said he had never provided a new project for IRS and when I told the group he had this great new idea, well, he just couldn't muster the nerve to stop me. He said he admires you and all the original ideas you come up with." He paused just a second. "Maybe, he's a little jealous."

Mark shrugged. "I'm not defending what he did, Crystal. I'm just telling you what he told me. Which is that he didn't set out to steal your idea. He said he knows he was wrong; has known it for two weeks. But, well ... ."

He walked around his desk and sat down. "He has offered to resign if you or I want him to." He looked at Crystal, but she said nothing. "Phil is a good worker, and personally, I don't want to lose him. He brings a lot to the company, for example, his comments on the Bowen contract this morning. He runs his projects smoothly, deals with his people well. He's not creative, but he's smart, organized, thorough, and has a great eye for details." He paused for several moments. "But it's your call. And I will back you one hundred percent, whichever way you choose."

Crystal looked past Mark and out the window, not really focusing on anything. One part of her said she wanted Phil fired. He stole, or tried to steal, her idea. And yet, how could he have hoped to do that in such a small company, unless he figured she wouldn't say anything? Which she didn't, at least for a week. Was part of the problem her own weakness? No. Just because a person is weak doesn't make it okay to steal from her. The weak need protection more than the strong.

She thought of JT. Only three days ago, she might have fired JT on the spot, if she'd had the power. Looking back on it now, she realized how wrong and very damaging to JT that would have been.

With all the things happening to JT——Eddie Ray's death, the threat of Luis being kidnapped, Joe and Al coming after her—firing her could have pushed her over the edge.

Crystal could understand why JT did what she did. It was harder to rationalize Phil's actions.

Still, the wrong had been straightened out.

"I'm sure that will never happen again," said Mark. "I believe he is truly sorry."

"I'm sure you're right," Crystal answered. She recalled how Mark handled the incident in the general meeting. He had taken the blame, indicating that *he* had misunderstood. Of course, it wasn't Mark's idea that had been stolen. In research, ideas were the most valuable property you had. She thought of Brandi's philosophy: if it isn't worth protecting, it isn't worth having.

"Part of me says he should be fired for intellectual piracy," Crystal admitted. "But part of me says, in this small company, the only way he could have succeeded is if I let him. And he knew that."

The hard line of Mark's mouth softened. "How about this? We've had a trial and I, the judge, find the defendant guilty. In fact, he confessed. What if I put him on probation?"

Crystal nodded several times. "I'm angry with him, though even that is dissipating." The picture of JT, weeping at her kitchen table, edged into Crystal's mind. "Don't fire him."

As she got up to leave, Mark said, "Don't forget our strategy meeting tonight. Rod said he'd be over about eight."

Chapter 46

FOR nearly an hour, Mark, Crystal and Rod had discussed, argued, puzzled and even laughed over the "ton of gold" situation. The laughs were few, generated by various statements made out of frustration. "Maybe the fire-breathing car will burn up with Joe and Al in it." Or "With all that gold, we can put in a first class security system." Or "We leak the story, then sell rights to dive for gold at $1,000 an hour."

Mostly, a feeling of discouragement held center stage. The Dallas police had no hard evidence. Crystal had been shot by some, as yet unknown, thug in Wooden Nickel—maybe Joe or Al; maybe not. Eddie Ray, who never talked to the police and was now dead, claimed that Joe and Al (no last names) believed there was gold in Eula's lake. No real leads had developed on the firebombing.

Bill Glothe agreed that the attempts on Eula's life and the shots at Crystal were related. Tom Hawkins felt certain the firebombing and Eddie Ray's murder were linked, although no evidence confirmed that. Both Glothe and Hawkins saw the probable connection between the Wooden Nickel incidents and the Dallas crimes, Eddie Ray providing the link. But while Eddie Ray's murder was likely a result of gold fever, no concrete evidence established this, and the connection to the firebomb was tenuous at best. Bill and Tom had talked on the telephone, but no strong evidence connected the incidents sufficiently to allow either to allocate any manpower to work with the other.

Mark looked at his two guests. Rod was calm. It wasn't his grandmother who had been attacked. He hadn't been shot or had his business firebombed. Of course, knowing Rod as he did, Mark decided Rod would be relaxed even if it were his office.

Crystal, on the other hand, had much more at stake than even

Mark had. It was her grandmother, the woman who had raised her, her only living relative. And it was clear to Mark that the things happening to JT had shaken Crystal badly.

"What are we going to do?" asked Crystal for the tenth time. "We can't just sit around and wait for them to attack again. They've killed two people already." She slammed her fist on the arm of the chair.

"The police are on the lookout for the car," Mark said. "Tom is trying to get a line on Big Man. Bill Glothe is keeping an eye on Eula. JT is out of harm's way. Like it or not, that's the best that can be done for now."

Her frustration voiced itself in a question she already knew the answer to. "Why can't Bill put an around-the-clock guard on Nana?"

"You know—"

Mark was interrupted by his computer. "Mark, you have a visitor I do not recognize. Here is a picture of the vehicle."

Mark walked over and looked at the computer's monitor. He clenched his teeth and stared at the image. "Damn."

"Who is it?" she asked.

"It's not a great picture. But there are flames dancing on the hood." He felt the same adrenaline rush as when he approached the loading chute at a rodeo. He looked at his two friends. "Let's get out of here." Mark started for the door, retraced his steps and picked up his cell phone.

Crystal detoured enough to look at the picture on the computer's monitor. There on the screen was a picture of the black car with fire painted on it, as if an inferno under the hood was beginning to escape. She shuddered, as the flames caused a chill to race through her.

"We'll go downstairs, Crystal," Mark said taking her hand and guiding her to the stairs. Rod closed the door behind them.

"Can we make a run for it?" she asked.

Mark's mind raced through several options. The fire-breathing car was probably blocking the drive. At best, they'd have to go over flowerbeds and bushes. His Chrysler was too low to the ground to do that very fast. The truck would stand a better chance of getting out quickly. Even at that, Joe and Al might get off several shots at them. And with three of them in the cab, even a wild shot would have a good chance of hitting someone.

"I don't think that's a good idea." He looked around the garage. "Let's get out of here." He headed toward the outside door, stopping just long enough to snatch a lariat off the wall and slip the circle of rope over his shoulder.

"You've got a truck," Rod whispered. "Why don't you have a gun rack mounted in the back window?"

Mark knew Rod hated guns. "Right about now, I wish I did."

He turned off the lights in the garage and eased the door open a crack. The night appeared black as pitch. Mark stepped outside, Crystal right behind him. A thin sliver of moon offered no illumination except to backlight a wispy cloud that floated in an inky sea. Millions of stars crowded the black sky, some winking at one another, others shinning as unwavering beacons. On an ordinary night, Mark would have stopped to marvel at the grandeur. Now, his mind was clouded by flames that brought cold rather than warmth.

Crickets and katydids were chirping away, with the occasional hoot from an owl adding to the late summer symphony. Underneath nature's music, Mark could hear tires slowly crunching gravel.

"They don't have their headlights on, just parking lights. And they're not to the cement drive yet. So they can't see us. Let's just slip out and head for the woods. Crystal, hold my hand. Rod, take her other hand. We don't want to trip over each other. It's about fifty feet straight across the grass."

Without a word, Crystal reached out and found Mark's outstretched hand. They crept across the grass like three kids in a graveyard on Halloween night. They were about halfway to the trees when the car rolled quietly off the gravel and onto the cement drive. Mark turned his head and stared into the darkness. From this point, he should be able to see the car. On cue, the soft amber running lights came into view. He still could not make out the car's form, but the image from the computer monitor glowed brightly in his mind.

When they reached the trees, Mark turned to the right, moving slowly and cautiously. Leaves and twigs covered the ground under the trees. They walked carefully but their footsteps sounded incredibly loud to Mark and he worried that the gunmen might hear them.

Mark stopped and Crystal bumped into him, but no sound was made. He strained to listen for manmade sounds. The car engine was purring. *They're still inside the car, probably with windows rolled up. Good. They can't hear us.* Just as he started to move again, the engine stopped. The three crept forward until Mark judged they were almost straight across from the car.

Mark hadn't formulated a plan, but suddenly, he knew what he would do. What he didn't know was whether it would work.

He pulled the cell phone out of his pocket and punched in some numbers. Pressing the phone to his ear, he listened to a short ring and then his computer answered with a single word: "Yes?" Mark cupped his hand around the phone and whispered into the phone, his lips touching the mouthpiece. "Shannon, this is Mark. Lock all outside doors. Turn the music on, now." Within a few seconds, the sound of classical music drifted from the house. "Louder," Mark said into the phone. The volume increased a little. "Louder," he repeated. "Add outside speakers." Abruptly, the music cascaded over them, drowning out all other sounds.

Mark turned to Crystal. "Stay right here, so we can find you when we come back. We'll be gone only a few minutes. Rod, let's go."

The two friends moved out of the trees, crept across the grass and soon were crouched behind a large pyracantha bush not ten feet from the fire-breathing car. They had been there only a few seconds when they heard a car door open. Then another. Mark put his mouth near Rod's ear. "I'm going to turn on the lights. Cover your eyes. When I call you, grab the rope and pull as hard as you can." Then into the cell phone, he said "All outside lights on."

In an instant, blazing light flooded the area around the house. The sudden change from pitch black to brilliant light overwhelmed the human eye. Mark had shielded his eyes and now peeked between two fingers to look at the car. One man stood on each side of it. The closest one covered his face with one hand trying to block out the light. His other hand held a gun, but it was clear he couldn't see anything at the moment.

"What the hell's going on?" one yelled. The other simply screamed curses at the lights.

Mark studied the position of the nearest man, mentally measuring the distance and angle, then spoke into the phone. "Lights out." Immediately, the area plunged into total darkness. He stood up, swung the rope over his head a few times and let it fly.

Mixed in with the music, Mark heard a metallic thunk. He jerked the rope. It came back to him with no resistance.

"What was that? You hit the car?" yelled one of the men.

"No, didn't hit the god dammed car. Didn't do nothing. See anything?"

"Naw."

By now, Mark had recoiled the rope.

Rod whispered into Mark's ear. "What're you doing?"

"Trying to lasso one of them. I'm going to try again." Into the phone he said, "Lights on."

Again, the bright flood lights turned night into day. The two intruders were obviously confused by the blaring music and erratic changes in light. They were yelling back and forth, and although Mark couldn't hear exactly what they were saying, it seemed to him that neither was paying any attention to the other.

He looked at Rod, who gave him a thumbs up. Into the phone, Mark once more said, "Lights out." Not wasting any time, he immediately stood up, twirled the rope three times over his head and threw the loop out. The instant it reached its length, he pulled. With disappointing ease, it came back.

Rod leaned over and whispered in Mark's ear. "Roping never was your strong suit."

Mark frowned. Unfortunately, it was true. Maybe Eula was right and he failed in the rhythm category. "Just out of practice."

"Got anything else in mind?"

He had played his trump card and hadn't won the trick. Now what? "One more try at this. Then, we hike out through the woods."

"Come on," the man on the far side of the car was yelling. "Let's get it on."

"Can't see nothing."

"Joe, goddamn it, get your ass over here."

Mark commanded the computer to turn the lights on and make the music louder. He resisted the urge to put his hands over his ears.

In the blaze of lights, which seemed to get brighter each time they came back on, he studied the scene, tried to think of it as a rodeo arena. He imagined his stocky target was a raw-boned maverick, dazed by the lights and disconcerting music, just standing there making it easy to rope him.

Joe started to amble toward the front of the car. Mark measured the distance and direction to the enemy, then whispered into the phone, "Lights out. Music louder."

He pictured the target moving as he twirled the rope. Even in the dark, his mind locked on the man as the rope picked up speed. Without consciously thinking about it, he let the hemp glide through his hand. One second, two seconds, and he pulled it back.

This time, it didn't come.

"Rod, now."

He and Rod pulled. The rope came toward them, grudgingly, foot by foot. They could hear the man yelling, although they couldn't recognize his words. Even over the deafening music, though, they could hear the thug's voice getting closer.

Soon, Mark could identify the outline of the man only a few feet away. The rope went around one shoulder and across his chest, trapping one arm to his side. He was desperately trying to free that arm and at the same time grabbing at the grass to slow his movement. He was three feet away when he turned his head and saw Mark. He struggled to turn the hand of his trapped arm.

The first clear view Mark had was of the nose of a pistol swinging around toward him.

Chapter 47

THE sounds of drums and trumpets crashed through the dark void. Somewhere, a man was screaming, but the air was saturated with noise. It was impossible to pick out just one, distinct sound and the orchestra overwhelmed the man's feeble shriek. In a single instant, the explosion of a gunshot mixed with the blaring music, and Mark was hammered to the ground.

The symphony's crescendo peaked, then subsided, still filling the air with the discordant notes of Sibelius. Mark felt like a big Brahma bull had tossed him into the dirt. He looked up to see Rod, silhouetted against the sliver of moon, standing over an inanimate form. Only then did his mind piece together what must have happened. Rod had pushed him down just as the gun fired. And apparently, Rod had knocked the shooter unconscious.

"Let's get this guy into the woods," Rod said.

Mark pulled himself up and he and Rod struggled to drag the inert lump back into the cover of the trees. Crystal met them at the edge and helped them haul the man behind some dense undergrowth. Once there, Rod tied the shooter securely to a tree.

"You need to gag him," Crystal whispered.

Rod tore off one of the captive's sleeves and made a gag.

"Crystal, can you tell if this is one of the guys from The Park?" Mark asked.

"I think so. I think this is the one who shot me."

"Keep an eye on him. He's not going anywhere, but if he makes any noise, hit him over the head with this gun," Mark whispered as he placed the weapon in her hand. "Come on, Rod. Let's see if we can bulldog another maverick."

The two men inched their way back toward the open space. The closer they got, the louder the music was. Near the edge of the trees, Mark stopped and signaled to Rod to shield his eyes. Then, he spoke into the cell phone. "Lights on."

Once again, the clearing was as bright as a day in August. Mark had covered his eyes and now eased his fingers apart, keeping the bright floodlights from shining in his eyes, but allowing himself to scan the yard.

The other gunman was nowhere in sight.

Again, Mark spoke into the cell phone. "Music, softer."

The intensity of the sound lessened some, but was still loud enough to wake those only recently dead. Mixed in with the music, Mark could barely hear the second man's voice. Again, Mark commanded the computer to lower the volume. Now, he could make out some of the words. "Joe, where ... hell ... what ... shoot ... quit screwing ... damn tired ... leave ... ass ... minute."

If we have Joe, that's Al out there yelling. Just then, Mark saw him. He was about to go around the corner of the house. "Rod, get me another lariat from the garage. I'll try to keep track of Al. Meet you back here."

Without a word, Rod slipped off toward the garage. "Unlock garage door. Lights off, music off," Mark commanded. The complete quiet, coming so quickly after the ear-piercing noise, shocked the senses. As darkness crashed over them, a noise erupted from the corner of the house. In spite of the danger, Mark had to grin. Apparently, Al had tripped and fallen in the garden. With the music off, the stream of curses coming from the area of rosebushes echoed across the yard.

Knowing where Al was, Mark sneaked out from behind the pyracantha bush and started across the yard to find a better position from which to track his quarry. He knew his yard well and could move around it without benefit of light.

A gunshot fractured the quiet. Instinctively, Mark dropped to the ground. He lay there, trying to listen over his pounding heart and rapid breathing. His first thought was that Crystal had a gun. But he told her to hit Joe, not shoot him. The gunshot reverberated around the yard, making it impossible to tell exactly where it had originated. Mark believed it had come from the general direction of the rose garden, where Al was. His mind skidded to a halt. *Was it from that direction, or is that just where I want it to come from? Actually, I'd rather it came from some policeman arriving on the scene. No, it came from Al. Was that a deliberate shot at me? An accidental shot, perhaps caused by Al's tangle with the rosebushes?* Mark thought for a moment. *It couldn't have been aimed at Rod; the house is between Al and Rod now. Crystal is too far in the woods to be visible from where Al is, even in daylight. Unless she's moved in closer. Still, it's pitch dark. He couldn't possibly see her. It was either directed at me, or just a warning shot, telling me not to get too close.*

Mark closed his eyes, trying to shut out all sensory perception except his hearing. Al was silent. *Like a rat in a maze, he's learning. Not giving his position away, and now he's got me down on the ground with no cover. I can't turn the lights on to see where he is, because he just might be sitting over there looking my way. If he's quiet, he'll hear me when I move. If I turn the music up, I can't hear him. I'm losing my advantage. And he still has his: the gun.*

For several minutes, both hunters were like two killer submarines lying silent, each waiting for the other to move, to make a noise, to make a mistake. Then a thought popped into Mark's mind. "Shannon. Zone seven on."

Instantly, Mark realized his mistake. "Cancel that. Cancel zone seven." Again, his heart pounded rapidly. *That was stupid. This is no time for mistakes.* He took a deep breath and started slowly. "Zone eight, on."

It took several seconds for the sprinklers to pop up and start spraying water over the garden area. It took only one more second for the yelling and invectives to start. While Al swore, Mark jumped up and ran to the shelter of some forsythia bushes. He had just settled there when he heard the unmistakable sound of a tire being punctured. And then another.

Al undoubtedly heard it also, for another pistol shot rattled the night air. "Somebody mess with my car, somebody gets dead. Joe, where the goddamn hell are you? I'm really getting pissed and when that happens somebody pays." He fired another shot. Glass shattered.

Mark commanded the computer to shut the sprinklers off. Now that he knew Al's location, there was nothing to be gained by having him spray bullets around the yard.

Chapter 48

CRYSTAL heard the shots and a shiver ran through her. She had no doubt these men were capable of murder. She believed one of them had killed Bessie, a seventy-year-old woman who lived on popcorn. They had shown no compunction about shooting a woman sitting peacefully in a rowboat, not threatening anyone. And Crystal remembered one of the men tramping through the underbrush, looking for her, intending to kill her. Even in the darkness, Crystal was certain the man who shot her now sat tied to a tree just a few feet away, his life on the other side of *her* trigger finger.

Now, she could hear Al yelling, although she could not make out what he was saying. She did catch one word: Joe. Was Al calling for help? Had he captured Mark or Rod?

Behind her she heard Joe making noise. She turned and stared into the darkness. The moon provided little light and under the trees, not even that got through. But after so much time in the darkness, her eyes were able to distinguish shapes. She moved closer to her prisoner. With some distaste and apprehension, she put her hand on the gag. He jerked his head, as if he might scare her off with such a ferocious move. The rag was still firmly in Joe's mouth, but he had managed to chew on it some. The sounds were muted and unintelligible. Nonetheless, he was able to make noise.

That's all I need. Have him make enough noise so Al finds us. She moved to the right. He turned his head to follow her. She pointed the gun at his face. "You can see well enough to know I've got a gun and right now it's pointed at your head," she hissed. "Stop the noise or I'm going to shoot you." Even to herself, it didn't sound very convincing.

He tilted his head to one side and then to the other, making several sounds.

Crystal imagined he was smirking. Her mouth fell open. She had the distinct impression he was mocking her. He might even have been laughing, although with the gag, it was impossible to tell. "Are you saying I won't shoot you?" she whispered.

He nodded yes and started making noises again, now louder.

She looked at the gun and then at Joe, her anger rising. "You're right; I won't." She looked at the gun again and lowered it, until it was just level with Joe's left temple. She hit him with the barrel. His head jerked back. Somehow, that startled Crystal. She decided the movement was not so much from the blow, but from surprise that she had actually hit him with the gun.

"I'm not sure how hard to hit you. So you can help me. You keep making noises and I'll hit you a bit harder each time. You stop making noises when I'm hitting hard enough. Okay? Shall we start? You make a noise and I'll hit you harder."

Joe stuck his chin out in a defiant move and made a noise, a little louder than before.

Crystal looked at him. "Okay, if you say so." And she hit him in the temple again, harder than before. "Was that better?" She raised the gun and waited. Even in the darkness, she could see Joe blink his eyes and stare at the shadow that was his jailer. He did not make any more noise.

Her thoughts flashed back to the gunshots. Neither Mark nor Rod had a gun. She was willing to bet Al wasn't shooting at deer or armadillos, which meant he was shooting at her friends—her unarmed friends. She was the only one on her side who had a gun and she was sitting over in the woods like a wallflower at a dance. Rod had tied Joe to a tree. She wasn't really needed here. Maybe she could take the gun to Mark and even the odds a little.

She moved around behind Joe, hoping he wouldn't notice she was gone and start making noise again. Slowly she crept away, one hand in front of her to avoid running into trees. Her other hand held the gun aimed straight ahead, her finger on the trigger. *This is ridiculous. I don't think I could fire this gun even if Al jumped up in front of me.* She stuck the pistol in the back pocket of her jeans. Only a few paces in front of her, she spotted an area not quite as dark as where she was. She had reached the yard.

* * *

Behind the forsythia bushes, Mark listened. Al had stopped yelling. The only sounds now were the cicadas, enjoying the summer evening. The water had heightened the smell of the grass, still warm from the day's hot sun. The moon, a tiny rip in the black curtain of sky, masked the danger.

For a brief moment, Mark was seduced into marveling at the beauty of the night. Then, underneath the nighttime noises, Mark detected another vibration. It took a second to decipher. Then it hit him. Someone was walking on dry grass. The steps were tentative, cautious, one foot placed down, a hesitation, then another, great care being taken not to give away location. Mark turned his head to the right, then the left, trying to pinpoint the intruder. Finally, he was sure. The footsteps were near the car. Al was moving back to guard his car, his escape route. Mark positioned himself carefully on the opposite side of the bushes from the car, then spoke into the phone, "Lights on."

He peeked through the bushes just in time to see someone disappear behind the pyracantha bushes. Mark's heart rose in his chest. It looked like Rod!

"Don't do nothing sudden like or I'm blowing a hole in you." The voice was cold and menacing. "Get up and keep your hands where I see 'em. Got nine millimeters lined up on you. Something happens I don't like, I pop a cap."

Chapter 49

MARK froze. His breathing stopped but his heart raced, hammering savagely on his ribs.

"Get up, asshole. Now!"

With an effort, Mark slowly stood up. He heard Al step closer, then suddenly the blast from the gun swept over Mark. The shock wave bent him over. The sound so enveloped him he couldn't tell if he had been hit.

"That's so's you know I ain't screwing around. Next one'll be right in your skull. Turn around, real slow like."

Mark took an inventory of his body. His ears ached from the concussion of the blast, but he had not been hit. With care, he turned to face Al.

The gunman had taken a few steps back and stood with his feet wide apart. A dark, nine-millimeter pistol pointed directly at Mark's chest. But the man seemed to be looking beyond Mark.

"You. Veeerrry slowly move your ass up by your loser friend here. Don't try nothing stupid or I'll do both yous."

* * *

Crystal had no trouble moving slowly; she felt paralyzed and barely able to budge at all. Like walking through deep water, she inched herself over beside Mark.

"I'll be damned. Joe told me he'd done killed you, that lying sack of shit for brains. Now, can't find him." Al looked at Mark and tilted his head to one side. "You off him?"

"No."

"Then where the hell is he?"

Crystal's body shook and she thought she might start crying at any moment. She stole a glance at Mark. Why does he seem so calm, she wondered, irritated that she was shaking and he didn't appear to be concerned. *Maybe this is no different from riding bulls. They're mean and violent and can kill you. One false move could be fatal. Every second is dangerous. Just like now.* But she hadn't ridden bulls, or done anything hazardous in her whole life. The most dangerous thing she'd ever done was say no to a man who had never heard that word.

An image of Dr. Krupe forced its way into Crystal's mind. He was dumping her research into the trashcan, all the time sneering at her. The mental picture persisted, but then an image of Nana flashed through her brain, then one of Bessie, then Eddie Ray, and her eyes refocused on Al and the large pistol aimed at her and Mark.

And Lester Krupe was not important. His image slowly evaporated.

"I asked you a question." Al aimed his pistol more carefully at Mark's forehead.

"Ah, two of my friends captured Joe and are taking him to the police station, as we speak."

Al let out a howl of laughter. "As we speak. Ain't that a hoot." He turned deadly serious. "You think I oughta worry about fuzz coming, you're dumber'n Joe. You're the one what's got a worry on that. First sign I see of cops, you gets a new hole in your head. And I don't miss."

He turned his attention to Crystal. "That piss ant shot at you. If I shot, you be dead. Now, 'fore I spill your brains on the grass, where's the gold hid?"

Crystal didn't know what to say. Panic gripped her so tightly she could hardly breathe. In her mind she heard Nana saying, *When in doubt, tell the truth.* "Ah, I, ah, don't think, ah, there is any gold."

With horror, Crystal saw the muzzle flash. She felt the shock wave brush her ear. A desperate gasp escaped her lips as she ducked her head and put her hands over her ears.

"That's to straighten out your thinking, bitch. Try again. Where's the gold?"

Crystal realized she had not been shot, but she couldn't stop her knees from shaking. She looked toward Al, but she could only see the gun, still pointed at her, looking three times as big as before. Al had disappeared and only the gun remained. The gun was yelling at her. She tried to think what to say, but her mind wouldn't function.

Her gaze was riveted on the black hole of the muzzle, growing larger and larger, while her mind replayed the flash of fire, leaping out toward her. She willed the shaking to stop, but it continued as she felt herself drawn into the black abyss of the gun. Ideas darted around in her head all mixed together, but nothing came out her mouth.

Mark answered for her. "According to the legends, it was pushed off a cliff and into the lake."

The pistol shifted toward Mark. "Don't con me. Been there. Ain't no cliff."

"Not today. But there was up until about fifty years ago. Apparently, over the years it has sloughed off and it's now just a steep embankment. If we go out there, I could show you where the cliff used to be."

Crystal watched Al think that over. The nose of the pistol lowered a fraction of an inch. His eyes, so close together he looked like a cartoon character, were squeezed half shut as if that helped him think. *Any delay is good*, Crystal thought.

"Seen that hill coming down to the water. That where the cliff was?"

"Yes. But I can show you more accurately when we get there."

Al laughed. "Yous two ain't going nowhere. Big Man told me to find out what you knows and leave you here—dead." Al cackled. "Done the first part. Now I pop yous and boogie." Al raised the gun barrel slightly.

"Wait!"

This time, Crystal could hear fear in Mark's voice and it sent a new chill down her back. The scar on his cheek seemed much redder than she remembered it.

"The gold isn't in the water now," Mark said.

Al squinted and wrinkled his forehead. He narrowed his beady eyes again. "Whatcha mean?" He tilted his head to the side. "You already snatched it?"

"No, we haven't taken it. But when the cliff sloughed off— fell into the lake—it covered up the gold. I've run some simulations on that and I think I know exactly where the gold is right now."

"What's similations?"

Mark corrected people's grammar and diction all the time,

and for an instant, Crystal wondered if he would correct the gunman.

"That's when the computer analyzes all the data and then recreates what happened."

Al looked puzzled. "Cliff falls in the lake again?"

"Not actually. But the computer figures out exactly how it happened and shows us what the results would be."

Al seemed to be studying this new information. Suddenly, the gun hand straightened. "Big Man don't like computers. Says they screws things up, makes it harder for him to do his thing."

Without thinking, Crystal blurted out, "But it was the computer that found the gold in the lake for him." Drops of sweat had formed under her arms and now were beginning to run down her side. She was so tense that breathing seemed to demand a conscious effort.

She was vaguely aware of a slight pressure on her right hip. Then slowly, like a Polaroid picture developing, an image began to materialize in her mind—that of the gun in her back pocket. Could she move a hand around to it without Al noticing? Trying to show no change of expression or body position, she gradually began to drop her right arm. She didn't know how much time they had before Al did ... something terrible. She refused to let her mind form anything more specific on what Al might do. But any sudden movement would surely draw his attention. Quarter inch by quarter inch, she eased her arm down.

Once more, her mind was bringing an idea into focus. This time, it was a question. *What will you do when you get the gun in your hand?*

Her arm stopped moving. Would she shoot him? *Could* she shoot him before he fired first? One side of her brain was saying, if you wait for him to shoot first, you or Mark will be dead. Or both of you. The other side argued that she couldn't just shoot him. *But it's clearly self-defense. It's still killing a person. And doing nothing will kill two people,* the argument in her brain continued.

Crystal wasn't sure whether she could pull the trigger or not, but she knew she needed the gun in her hand by the time she made up her mind. Her arm began to move, slower than bread rising.

Al's eyes refocused on Crystal. "Naw. He said leave you dead. I bring you, he gets down on me. Don't nobody cross Big

Man." He leered at Crystal. "Up to me, I take your ass home. I got beer, a little coke. We get it on." He paused, a lecherous smile forming as he savored the idea. Then, it was gone. "Shit. Big Man said leave you dead."

Crystal was shaking again. "He wouldn't have to know." Tears welled up in her eyes. "I wouldn't tell. He wouldn't find out."

"Damn. Sounds good. Bet you's hot as my pistol." He snickered, then shook his head. "Naw. You ain't that good. Big Man'd shoot my ass off."

Mark's hands had been at his side and he gradually moved them up a little. Al saw the movement. "Get them hands over your head."

Crystal looked at Mark. He seemed to be trying to tell her something, to convey a message with his eyes, but she couldn't make it out. He glanced at the phone in his hand, then back at Crystal. In that instant, she knew what he was going to do. She murmured softly, "I go right."

"What'd you say, bitch?" And to Mark, "I told you, get them hands over your head."

Mark nodded slightly. As he moved his hands up, he looked at Al and said, "Before you shoot our ..." And just a little louder, as the phone passed opposite his mouth, "...lights out ..."

Darkness rushed in from every side, blanketing the area in black. Crystal dove to her right. The roar from the nine-millimeter ravaged the night. There were no more crickets, no more cicadas serenading one another. Only the reverberations of the gun blast.

But even as the black cloak enveloped everything, Crystal thought she saw, out of the corner of her eye, Rod. On his bicycle.

Chapter 50

ANOTHER shot shattered the night. Crystal continued rolling to her right, trying to put as much distance between her and the shots as possible, hoping she wasn't rolling in an arc back to Al. Now she could hear a cacophony of thumps, groans, screams, and other noises she couldn't identify, all coming from the general direction of where Al had been standing. Grunts and curses filled the void after the echoes of the shot died down and she wondered if Mark had attacked Al. The unmistakable thuds of fists hitting bodies mingled with sharp intakes of breath and involuntary groans.

Crystal had rolled maybe thirty feet away and lay listening to the struggle, wondering if she should get up and run. But her eyes had not yet adjusted to the sudden darkness and she could see absolutely nothing. Al was yelling. Breathing was sounding more labored. And mixed in was an occasional metallic clink.

Then, as suddenly as it had become dark, it became quiet. And out of the quiet, a soft voice said, "Mark, can we have lights, please."

The lights revealed a strange scene. Rod was sitting on top of Al, who appeared to be unconscious. Underneath Al's head lay the front wheel of Rod's bicycle. The nine-millimeter pistol rested no more than three inches from Al's outstretched left hand.

Crystal was bewildered. Mark, telephone in hand, sat on the ground about fifty feet to her left.

"What on earth happened?" she asked.

Rod gave his shy laugh. "Seemed like you two were in a bit of a pinch, so I thought I'd help out. And since I can't throw a lariat, I did what I do. I rode my bike. But just as I came around the corner of the house, picking up speed, Mark turned out the lights. I bloody well nearly missed the bugger. But I did graze him enough to knock him down—about the time he fired his second shot. Then it was just a matter of settling him down."

"You rode your bike into him? Into a criminal shooting a nine millimeter pistol?" Crystal was shaking her head in utter amazement.

"Seemed like the thing to do. I was coming pretty fast. Down low over the bars, I didn't figure to make much of a target." Rod laughed. "Of course, since you two were drawing his fire, I guess I didn't have to worry about that."

Mark walked over and extended a hand to help Rod to his feet. "I see you got the rope."

Rod bent over, picked up the pistol and stuck it in his belt as Mark retrieved the rope from the back of the bicycle and began to hog-tie Al.

Rod gripped the butt of the pistol and spread his feet. "What next, trail boss?"

"We call in the cavalry."

"Amen," said Crystal.

The two men dragged Al's body over near the drive and Mark tied him to a tree. He opened the driver-side door of the fire-breathing car, searched a minute, found a newspaper and wadded up a page and stuffed it into Al's mouth. He handed the phone to Crystal. "Try to raise Tom while Rod and I go get Joe Baby."

Crystal could hardly believe her luck. Tom actually answered when the operator rang his line. After he got over his surprise and after being assured that the thugs were under control and nobody was hurt, he got angry. "How could Mark do such a stupid thing? I guess I should expect that of a bull rider. But I thought he'd grown up. He could have gotten all three of you killed."

Only a few minutes earlier, Crystal had been thinking the same thing. Now she found herself defending Mark. "If we had sneaked off and hid in the woods, they would have left. And *you* and the police haven't been able to find them. They probably would have attacked Nana again."

Tom grumbled on a minute more, then asked, "They driving a fire-breathing car?"

"They sure are, and I can tell you in all honesty, I could feel the heat."

"Dick and I will be right out. It's time I met Joe and Al. And I want to see this fire-breathing car."

Mark and Rod were leading Joe, like they might lead a pony. Mark shoved Joe against the car and pulled the gag out of his mouth. Instantly, he began yelling invectives at them.

"Should I try again?" Crystal said to Joe as she pulled the gun out of her back pocket. Immediately, he stopped yelling.

"Wow!" said Mark, looking genuinely impressed. "I should have let you talk to Al. Would have been a lot easier on Rod and me both."

"Joe and I have come to an understanding." She smiled, clearly pleased with herself.

Mark turned back to Joe. "Okay. Now we know you two are working for Big Man. What I want to know is: where is he?"

"I ain't telling you shit-heads nothing."

"Be best if you helped us before the police get here. And we've already called them." He looked at Crystal and she nodded.

"Ain't got nothing on me. You mother——-"

Crystal raised the pistol in her hand. Joe stopped in mid-word and looked at her. She smiled at him. "No more nasty language, Joey, or I'm going to try again."

Joe glared at her, but he continued in a subdued voice. "Turned down the wrong drive, that's all. Ain't no crime. And then you mother--, ah, you guys rope me and drug me all around and tries to strangle me and tie me up. And the bitch threatens to shoot me in the head, and pistol-whips me. I'm one's oughta be calling the fuzz."

Mark stood in front of Joe, nodding his head through the whole speech. He continued nodding for several seconds after Joe stopped. Joe squirmed and turned his eyes away, focusing on his unconscious cohort.

Crystal's mind raced through various schemes like an automatic sequencer trying to break a combination. And like the tumblers in a lock, the pieces finally clicked into place.

"Mark, have you got a portable scanner?" she asked.

"Sure. In the office." He furrowed his brows in question.

"I want to show Joey something I think will change his mind." She slipped the gun back into her pocket and hurried off, stopping by her car to grab a black case from the back seat.

In the office, she opened the case and put her portable

computer on Mark's desk. A quick search found the scanner. She plugged it into her portable, then flipped on the computer.

Her fingers drummed a steady beat on the desk while she waited for the computer to check its memory. "Come on, come on," she whispered as it loaded the operating system from the hard disk into memory. In her mind, she already was writing the instructions she would need to pull this off.

The instant the computer was ready, she began pecking on the keyboard, entering commands, occasionally backspacing over a few mistakes, and proceeding on to more commands. "That ought to do the trick," she said out loud. "Nothing too elaborate." She quickly checked the code she had just written, nodded in satisfaction. "Maybe a quickie test," she whispered.

One minute later she picked up the machine and headed out the door.

Mark was still talking to Joe, but Joe's only response was to shake his head.

Crystal came up to stand directly in front of Joe. "Got something I think you'll be interested in, Joey. My good friend Tom Hawkins—he's a detective with the Dallas Police Department—he and I have been looking for you and your buddy Al because we think you killed Eddie Ray Dollar. And since you've been so thoughtful as to bring your car here, I think we can prove that right now."

"Whatcha talking 'bout? We didn't do no Eddie Ray. Who the hell's him?"

"I think you did. You and Al. The police got some good tire tracks out where you dumped him in the lake. Remember White Rock Lake?"

The short thug had refused to look at Crystal, but at the mention of the lake, he abruptly looked her in the face. "Don't know nothing 'bout White Rock." He took a quick look at Al's inert form.

"Well, we can find out quickly. Let's just match the tread on your tires with what the police have for the murderers' car. Okay? Maybe you didn't, maybe you did. We can remove all doubt, one way or the other, in just a few moments."

Joe's focus jumped from Crystal to Al to Mark, then started around again. Sweat seeped out of the pores in his forehead and ran down his pudgy face. His tongue traced his lips every few seconds.

Crystal opened the micro, then looked at Joe again. "What I'm going to do is this. I'll scan the tread pattern of your tire." Joe looked puzzled. "That's like taking a picture of it with the computer. We'll be able to see it on the computer screen." She paused. "Let's see, it was the right front tire the police gave me. So, I'll scan your right front tire and then compare it with the one the police got at the murder scene. You can watch and decide if they match. Mark, help Joe over so he can watch."

Crystal set the portable computer on the car, pressed a few keys, then held the scanner on the tire tread. "Can you see okay, Joe?"

Sweat dripped to the ground as Joe nodded. Slowly, Crystal moved the scanner along the tread of the tire for several inches. As she did, a picture of the tire's tread materialized on the bottom half of the computer's screen. When the pattern reached from one side to the other, Crystal stopped.

"Okay. This is the pattern from your tire that you just watched me scan into the computer. See the little nick on the tire right here?" She put her finger on it.

Joe nodded.

"And here it is on the computer's picture. See it?"

Again, Joe nodded.

"So, this is a good picture of the tread on your tire," Crystal said.

Joe's attention was riveted on the computer screen.

"Now, let's bring up the tread the police retrieved from the crime scene." Crystal tapped a few keys and a pattern appeared in the top half of the computer's screen. The words "Murderer's Car - Eddie Ray Dollar Case" were written above it in boldface letters.

"The top tread pattern is from the murder scene. The bottom one is from your tire. You watched me scan it. Right?"

Joe made a nervous nod.

"Now, Joe, watch this closely, because this will tell us, and the police, if you killed Eddie Ray. Let's move the top pattern—the murder scene tire track—down and see if it matches the tire tread from your car that you just watched me scan into the computer. If it matches, you and Al murdered Eddie Ray. If it doesn't, then I guess you didn't murder him."

Joe's eyes never left the computer's screen. Slowly, Crystal moved the top pattern down until it overlaid the bottom pattern.

"My God," said Mark.

"No. No," Joe shouted. "We didn't off him. You can't hang it on me."

Rod was leaning over Mark's shoulder looking at the computer. "Look at the nick in the tread here. It's a perfect match. That's incredible."

"We didn't take him out. Big Man done it. He forced us to dump the body. But we didn't kill him." Joe was mewling, his eyes filled with sweat and tears.

"We don't have Big Man." Mark spat the words out, as cold and hard as he could make them. "We have you. And Al. And your car is the one that was there."

"He weren't killed there. He didn't drowned in no lake. Big Man snuffed him at his house. Then made us drag him out and dump him in a lake. Honest, all I done was carry a dead body and throw it in a lake." Joe was almost crying now.

Mark just looked at Joe without moving a muscle. Then slowly, he shook his head.

"I'm telling the truth." Joe was pleading. "The Beard tied Eddie Ray's hands behind his back. Then Big Man stuck his head in a sink. Then he pulled him up and asked him where the gold was. He said he told him everything he knowd 'bout the gold. So Big Man pushes Eddie Ray's face in the water again. When he comes up, he was breathing hard. Big Man wants to know who he brung down to the Longneck. So's he tells Big Man your name and where you work."

Crystal's gasped. Mark didn't react.

Joe swallowed and seemed to be having trouble breathing. "Big Man gets out of shape and slams Eddie's face back in the water. Then brings him up and said he better tell him something else. Eddie Ray's coughing and then he goes, 'You killed the wrong woman.'"

Crystal bit her lip so hard she could taste her own blood. She covered her mouth with her hand.

Joe cut his eyes toward her, then back to Mark. "Big Man was mad. He shoved Eddie's face back in the water and held it there. When he pulled it out, Eddie's choking and gagging. Big Man goes

'Okay, where's the brat?' And he says he ain't saying. And Big Man looks at him real mean like and says, 'You know but you ain't telling?' And Eddie Ray goes 'You ain't getting the kid. No way. No how.'"

Joe looked down at the ground, his breathing labored. "Big Man's going crazy. I ain't never seen him so mad. He yells right into his face, 'You'll tell me.' And he slams his face back in the water and holds it there. Eddie Ray tries to get out, but Big Man's strong and he smashes his face against the bottom of the sink. Just keeps it there. And The Beard holds Eddie Ray's back down."

Joe licked his lips and glanced at Crystal, then looked back at Mark. "After while, Eddie Ray don't struggle no more. Big Man finally yanks his head out and he ain't coughing or nothing. Big Man pulls his head way back and yells at him again. 'Where's the kid? You tell me where that kid is.' But he's dead." Joe looked at Crystal. "I told Big Man it was too long. He shouldn't keep his head in the water that long." His voice became a whimper. "All I done was carry the body away. I never killed nobody."

Mark looked straight into Joe's eyes for thirty seconds without saying a word or even blinking an eyelash. Joe couldn't meet his gaze. When Mark finally spoke, it was almost a whisper, but the tone was menacing. "Joe, here's the way it is. If you don't tell us where Big Man is in the next minute, I'm turning you and this computer over to the police and you're going to find yourself on death row, waiting for them to stick the needle in your arm. There's no other way out for you. You'll just sit there in your cell all by yourself and wait and wait, until they come for you and then strap you down. You can scream, pray, cry, struggle, whatever. It won't make any difference. You'll be tied down on the death table. They'll stick that needle in you. You can watch them. And then you're dead. Think about that."

Joe's body shook and his head was jerking up and down. "Big Man's gone out to Wooden Nickel."

"What?" Crystal screamed. She snatched the gun from her pocket and stuck it against Joe's fat lips, then forced it into his mouth. Mark put his hand on Crystal's arm but she shook it off. "Why did he go there, Joe? Don't give me any crap." Crystal moved her face to within an inch of Joe's. "Why did he go to Wooden

Nickel? What's he planning to do there? Tell me or I pull the trigger?"

Joe was shaking all over and his face was wet with sweat and tears. His eyes opened wide with fear as he watched Crystal.

"On three, I'm pulling the trigger. "One." Mark put his hand on Crystal's arm again. She ignored it. "Two."

Joe made a mewling sound and nodded as much as the gun in his mouth would let him. Crystal pulled the gun out of his mouth.

"Oh, shit. I'm dead either way." He shook and his voice was little more than a child's voice. Now, he refused to look at either Crystal or Mark. "He's gonna find that old woman. Said he'd get the gold if he had to cut off her fingers one at a time. He's gonna kill her." The last sentence came out as a moan. His head was on his chest now, tears streaming down his face.

Mark grabbed a handful of Joe's hair and yanked his head up. "When did he leave Dallas to go out there?"

"I don't know. After we come here."

Mark's tone was much quieter now. "Joe, this is important. Because if he kills that woman and you don't tell us everything you know, I'll guarantee you get tried as an accessory to that murder also. They're going to tie you down and jab that needle in you."

"All I knows is we was ready to bone out and he goes, 'Soon's The Beard gets here, we're gonna go find that bitch and rip it out of her.' Then we split. I swear, that's all I know."

"Who's The Beard?"

"I don't know."

Crystal raised the gun up in front of Joe's eyes.

Joe stammered, "Some taco with a beard down to his waist. He's meaner'n Big Man."

"What's Big Man's name?" Mark asked.

Joe frowned and looked at Mark like he was crazy. "Big Man. That's his name."

"He doesn't have another name, maybe a last name?"

"Never heard him called nothing else. Big Man. That's it."

Mark just looked at him. Crystal still had the gun pointed at Joe's face, no more than six inches from his nose.

"I'm trying to help, man. I'm trying. I'm telling all I knows. Beard keeps a piece in his belt behind his beard." He was crying again. "I'm trying to help. We didn't off Eddie Ray. Only dumped his body." Sweat was dripping off the end of Joe's nose. "I swear."

"What kind of a car does he drive?"

"White Benzo. Dark windows." Al groaned and Joe cut his eyes over for a moment. He looked back at Mark. "The Beard drives a ... a ..." He screwed his face up trying to think. "One of them fancy Jeeps. Black. Never washes it. Got a weenie dog thing on the hood."

Crystal's hand covered her mouth. The blood had drained from her face and she looked on the verge of fainting. But she held the gun steady, aimed right at Joe's face.

Mark turned to Rod and handed him the portable phone. "Tom should be here any minute. If he calls, you know what to tell him. Can you keep these two losers until he gets here?"

"No problem. Crystal's shown me how to deal with them if they give me any trouble." He pulled out Al's nine millimeter.

Mark grabbed Crystal's arm. "I'll drive. We can call Glothe from the car. Sorry to leave you with the garbage, Rod."

Chapter 51

WITHIN minutes they were racing down Interstate 20 in Mark's Chrysler. Crystal had already called Bill Glothe's office. He was off duty but the dispatcher would try to locate him. Wooden Nickel had not moved up to 911 status yet.

Crystal tried Melva's, where her grandmother was staying. No answer. Out of desperation, she tried The Park, not expecting anything. Again, no answer.

Her thoughts turned to earlier years, when she ran free in The Park. She remembered the time her grandmother built her a tree house in a big oak up on the hillside, north of the house. Crystal had thought it was strange. She asked her grandmother why she built it; Crystal hadn't asked for it. Nana smiled and said, "When you get mad or really worried about something, you can go sit in the tree house and work it out. Just you. No old Nana to get in the way of your thoughts. 'Course, I'm here if you need to talk. But sometimes, you just need to be by yourself. This is your place, nobody else's."

Nana had been right. At first, Crystal hadn't thought a private place up in a tree would be all that great. Soon, she realized how wrong she was. Whether she was mad, sad or glad, she found the solitude, peacefulness and beauty of the tree house impossible to resist. It made her feel special to have a place that was hers alone, and it rarely failed to make her feel better.

When she grew older, she would paddle the boat out and float in the middle of the lake to solve her problems. She wished she were there now. But she knew neither the lake nor the tree house would help her tonight.

She stared out the window. Off the interstate she could see pools of light, where farmhouses had security lights. Were they worried about their lives right now? Were their grandmothers in danger of being ... . She refused to allow her mind even to form the word. They passed a service station. Almost too late, she thought to look for a white Mercedes Benz or a "fancy" Jeep. Then, her view was blocked as they passed a bus.

"Wow," she said to Mark. "I've never passed a Greyhound before. How fast are we going?"

"Don't ask. Let's just say we're making miles." Mark smiled at her. "If we get pulled over, you'd better ditch that gun."

Crystal looked down at Joe's pistol in her lap. "Guess I should have left it with Rod." She picked it up to move it onto the seat between her and Mark, but instead she held onto it. She liked its weight. Its power felt good in her hand. With the gun in her hand, she felt she had control over Joe. She hadn't thought about it at the time, but now she did. The gun had given her power. She put it back down in her lap, her hand resting on it. "I'll try Melva's again," she said and dialed the phone. After a while, she hung up. "No luck."

"Maybe good luck. If you can't find her, neither can Big Man or The Beard."

"Unless they already have."

"Come on, Crystal. Don't go there. Joe said they didn't leave until sometime after Joe and Al. Maybe they haven't left yet. We don't know. But even if they left earlier, the chances are pretty good they wouldn't have gotten there and left already. And do they know where Melva lives, or even that Eula is at Melva's? They might be looking around at The Park. It will take some time to ask around town and find out where she's staying. If they can at all." Mark tried to sound as upbeat as possible, but the worried look belied his optimistic statement.

They passed another small town. "My gosh, we really are moving, aren't we?"

"Nobody is passing us. And we haven't passed any Mercedes or Jeeps. Mostly just eighteen-wheelers."

"I keep forgetting to look for them."

"Not to worry; I'm watching." They passed another truck. Mark glanced briefly at Crystal, then refocused on the road. "I didn't know the police had any tire tracks from where they found Eddie Ray's body. Good thing you had a copy of them. I don't think Joe would have told us anything otherwise."

Crystal laughed a small laugh, with little joy in it. "Actually, they don't."

"But ... ." Slowly, a smile crept over his face. "You pulled a little computer magic."

"Just enough."

Crystal drifted into silence again, as more thoughts of her grandmother and granddad filled her mind. Every few minutes, she pressed the re-dial button, but each time the phone provided no relief to her worry.

She tried Glothe's office. The dispatcher said she would give him the message the minute he called in. "Call a deputy. Get someone out there. Her life is in danger. Do you understand that? Her life is in danger."

The dispatcher said she would send a deputy out to check at Melva's.

Crystal called information for Bill's home telephone number, then dialed it. Each ring seemed to get louder and louder. After fifteen rings, Crystal could no longer stand the sound, and hung up.

Chapter 52

EULA and Melva labored up the three steps to Melva's porch, each carrying two bags of groceries. Melva put hers down and searched through her purse looking for keys.

"Why didn't you keep them in your hand when you got out of the car?"

Melva continued to poke in the deep recesses of the bag. "Not the help I need, Eula. If you'd carried three bags, I'd of had a free hand for the keys."

"Why do you lock your house? Any burglar worth his salt could get in quicker'n a frog snatching a fly. Quicker'n you are."

"For the insurance company, why else? Somebody steals something, I can tell 'em it was locked up tighter'n a new boot. Isn't that why we do most things? To please insurance companies?" She pulled out the shy keys triumphantly. "See, I found 'em. I'm not fast, but I'm dependable."

They carried the groceries into the kitchen and began putting them away. Before they were half finished, the doorbell rang. Melva grunted in annoyance, put down a jar of pickles and started out of the kitchen. "Won't hurt my feelings none if you finish without me."

Melva opened the front door to find two men standing on the porch. Her first inclination was to laugh. But she didn't. One man was probably six feet tall and must have weighed three hundred pounds. His clothes looked expensive, but gave the impression the big man had slept in them. The other man was a short, thin Mexican.

"You don't look like you're from Publisher's Clearing House, so I guess you got the wrong address. Who you looking for?"

The two men glanced at one another, not quite comprehending. After a moment, the taller man said, "Are you Eula Moore?"

"Who wants to know?"

"Big Man wants to know," said the Mexican. He put his hand in the center of her chest, pushed her into the living room and followed her in. "Are you Eula Moore?"

The other man came in and closed the door behind him.

"Haven't decided as yet whether to tell you."

"Don't get clever or smart with me, old woman."

Melva smiled at him. "I tried clever and it went right over your head. I certainly won't waste smart on you."

The Mexican grabbed the front of Melva's dress and pulled her in close to him. "Where's the gold?"

Melva looked at the man's hairy face. He smelled like stale smoke, mixed with chili spices. His eyes were mean. "In my teeth, you nitwit. Do I, or this house, look like I got any gold lying around?"

Without turning loose of her dress, the man slapped her across the face with the back of his hand. "I'll knock those teeth out, bitch. And that might be the nicest thing I done to you."

* * *

"Might be the *last* thing you ever done." Eula stood in the doorway to the kitchen, a double-barreled shotgun leveled on the intruders. She had listened to the previous exchange while she found Melva's shotgun and loaded it. Now she stood, feet apart, eyes unwavering, finger on the trigger. "First thing you ought to do is get your grubby paws off my friend."

For several seconds, no one spoke or moved. Eula sized up the two men. The one on the left was probably six feet tall with yellowish gray hair, which was cropped short and started halfway back on his head. His eyes were a dull gray and made Eula think of burned-out light bulbs. She guessed he must have been at least a hundred pounds overweight. But in spite of his nondescript appearance, Eula was certain he was in charge, accustomed to giving orders and getting his way.

The Mexican looked wary, like he spent a lot of time looking over his shoulder. He was maybe five feet seven inches tall, with long, black hair tied in a pony tail. His eyes reminded Eula of a lobo, always looking to get an advantage on you and quite willing to attack when your back was turned. But the most striking thing about him was his beard. Full, thick, black and streaked with gray, it extended down well below his waist. Instinctively, Eula kept her eyes fixed on him. *The fat man's in charge. But the attack will come from the wolf. And without warning.*

From the kitchen came the insistent ring of the telephone. Everyone ignored it.

The taller man grabbed Melva from the Mexican and pulled her over in front of himself. "I'll just hang on to her as long as you got that shotgun pointed at me." He turned Melva around and put a huge, flabby arm around her neck.

Eula's hands were steady, her eyes unwavering. "I know what you are—pond scum. But I don't know who you are. Did I hear something about a big man? Surely ain't one of you two. You both look like small, little boys to me."

The Mexican shifted his weight. The end of Eula's shotgun moved over slightly. He tilted his head toward his partner. "He's Big Man, and it ain't smart to mess with him." His macho tone was accompanied by a defiant look in his black eyes.

Eula cackled. "Big Man. I'd called him Fat Man. Bet he can't tie his own shoes." She glanced down. "I was right. He wears slip-ons." She laughed again. "If he's Big Man, then I guess they call you Baldy, right?"

"If you got up close, you'd call him Skunk," said Melva.

Both Eula and Melva laughed. The Mexican moved his left hand up slightly.

"I got a nervous finger, Skunk," Eula said. "Don't move too much. Maybe I ought to explain something to you city boys. I can tell you're city boys, so don't try to deny it. Country boy'd know by now he was in a bad situation, and be apologizing, trying to back out gracefully. City boys ain't that smart.

"What I got here is a shotgun loaded with double ought shot. Now I'm not gonna try to educate you too much—don't think you're much on learning. But so's you know, at this range, double ought will blow a hole in you the size of a soup bowl. And I can shoot the eye out of a skunk at fifty yards. Wouldn't want to get any closer."

The Mexican sneered. "Shooting people ain't the same as shooting animals."

Eula noted the bravado in his voice and decided it was for

real, reaffirming her feeling that he was dangerous. "I'm of the opinion you two *are* animals. So, don't you worry none. I'll do just fine."

Once again, with great caution, the Mexican moved his left hand up near his belt. Eula watched the slow movement. The image of the wolf came into her mind once more. She could see the wolf moving ever so slowly just before it pounced on its prey.

"Big and Fat Man, you've used up your fool time for the day. So, you just let go of Melva. And Skunk," she nodded the nose of the shotgun in his direction, "keep your hands still."

"Just got an itch on my belly need to scratch." And his hand slid slowly under his beard near his belt.

Chapter 53

CRYSTAL was still listening to the phone ring as Mark turned left on Tumbleweed Road. They were less than five minutes from Melva's house. In frustration, she slammed the portable phone closed, shutting off the irritating ring.

"It's not bad, necessarily, that they don't answer the phone, Crystal. It probably means they're not home and not in danger. We'll be there in two or three minutes." Mark smiled and Crystal knew he was trying to sound upbeat.

She made an effort to return his smile, but the result looked more like a dying patient's attempt to be brave. Her frequent calls during the trip had gotten nothing but a constant, lonely ring. Just as bad was the inability to get Bill Glothe. It was Glothe's day off and the dispatcher thought the sheriff had gone fishing. The dispatcher said she would send a deputy out, but her manner and tone did not give Crystal any confidence.

As if reading her thoughts, Mark said, "The dispatcher did say she'd send somebody out. I'm sure everything will be okay."

Crystal just stared out the window and said nothing.

The trip had been bittersweet. The current situation had raised to the surface of her mind dozens of fond memories of happy days at The Park and of a grandmother who had also been mother, confidant, teacher, and friend. Sweet, wise, witty, sarcastic, insightful, it was her Nana who had taught her the beauty of nature and of silence. Nana had opened Crystal's eyes to the importance of solitude, straight talk and quiet visits with good friends.

But the memories also brought into sharper focus the dangerous situation being played out tonight. She shuddered as she thought of Joe and Al, and knew without a shadow of a doubt that they were capable of killing without compunction, without remorse, without so much as a thought that the action would end a life; that the action, once taken, could not be reversed. Then she imagined how much worse Big Man and The Beard must be. Both Joe and Al seemed genuinely afraid of Big Man. For all their macho attitude, they dared not cross him. And Joe said The Beard was worse. Neither Big Man nor The Beard would appreciation a wonderful Nana, one who could never be replaced.

* * *

The gunshot exploded in the small room, reverberating from wall to wall with nowhere to escape, mingling with screams of pain. Melva flinched and closed her eyes. Blood splattered the wall and within seconds its smell permeated the room. The Mexican sank to the floor, grasping his left shoulder with his right hand, continuing to moan. A .32 automatic lay on the floor a few feet in front of him.

Big Man's eyes popped wide with surprise. "You ... you shot him."

"You're right quick, Fat Man. I told you I shoot skunks real well."

The Mexican looked up at Eula. "I'm bleeding bad. Need some help." He tried to get up.

"Stay right there, Skunk. Only cause I'm soft-hearted I didn't shoot you in the head. Wouldn't a tried your heart. Don't reckon you got one." She nodded her head toward Big Man. "Soon's your buddy Fat Man lets go of Melva, then we'll see about getting you some help. Not before. What's it gonna be, Fat Man?"

Big Man tightened his grip on Melva, desperately trying to shrink his big body behind the tiny woman.

Eula raised her eyebrows. "Sorry, Skunk. Your pal ain't gonna help. And I couldn't care less, 'cept for the mess you're blood's making. Looks like we got ourselves a Mexican standoff."

The wounded man looked up at Big Man, pleading with him to let the old woman go so he could get some help. Big Man ignored him. The Beard tried to raise himself.

"Skunk, listen carefully. The next shot will be right in the face. Look what it done to your shoulder and then think about your face. And you oughta know by now, I *will* shoot."

The Mexican slumped back down on the floor, the moans subdued but constant.

Several minutes passed, while Eula tried to figure how to get Melva away from Big Man. Finally, she moved a little toward them. "Melva, you're a good bit shorter than Fat Man. I believe I could blow the top of his head off and never muss a hair of yours."

Big Man slumped down and pulled Melva up as tall as he could.

"'Course, I guess I could come over and just stick the barrel right in his fat gut and pull the trigger. Sure wouldn't hit you then."

"Yeah," Melva said. "But you might get blood all over my favorite dress."

"You gonna stand here till dinnertime, Fat Man?" Eula asked. "My guess is you'll need to eat a lot sooner than I will."

"I could break this old bitch's neck. How would you like that?"

"I reckon you could. And I wouldn't like it one bit. But you know if you did, I'd blow your little head right off your fat body. How would *you* like *that*?"

Big Man didn't say anything.

"What I thought. So, we'll just wait 'til the sheriff gets here, or you get some sense and give up. Frankly, I don't see any way on God's green earth how you can win."

Quiet settled over the room once more, broken only by the subdued moans from the Mexican.

* * *

Suddenly, Crystal screamed. Ahead was Melva Larson's house. In the soft glow of her porch light, Crystal could see Melva's car parked in the driveway. Sitting directly behind the car was a Jeep Grand Cherokee. Black. Dirty.

"The fact that his car is still here means he hasn't gotten what he wants," Mark said evenly. "Eula is alive, Crystal."

Mark coasted silently in behind the Jeep and turned off the motor. "Let me go check things out."

Crystal shot him a look as if he were crazy, and opened her door. She looked up to see Bill Glothe's car silently ease to a stop next to them. By the time she reached the front of Mark's car, Glothe was beside her.

"Sorry. I was fishing. Dottie sent Slim out, but on his way here, we had a big accident over on 34. Slim had no choice but to stop and deal with it. What's the situation?"

Crystal filled him in on Big Man and The Beard. Bill just nodded. When she finished, he pulled on his jaw, then said, "Stay here. Let me go see if I can resolve this quickly and easily."

* * *

Inside, Eula was trying to figure out some way to get to the phone without letting Big Man out of her sight. If she left the room, the fat man would probably choke Melva, or get the gun, or both, and then she'd have more trouble.

Eula could see Big Man's beady eyes scanning the small room, searching for anything that might help him. The Beard's gun lay on the floor just a few feet away, near one of Melva's overstuffed chairs. "Trying to figure out how to get over and pick up the gun, all the while staying behind a little old ninety-pound woman? Don't think you can do it. Not sure you could bend over far enough to pick it up, anyway."

"Y'all might have a Mexican standoff," Melva said. "But I got to go to the bathroom." Raising her right foot, she brought her heel crashing down on Big Man's instep. He let out a yell. At the same moment, she grasped both her hands together, moved her torso to the left and drove her right elbow into his ample stomach. He gasped as she knocked the wind out of him. Melva grabbed his arm, now loose around her neck, yanked it up and started for the other side of the room.

Eula saw Big Man move toward the gun, but Melva was in the line of fire. Eula couldn't shoot. She stepped to one side, but as Melva came closer, there was still no room for a shot.

* * *

Outside, Crystal, Mark and Bill all jumped as the roar of a gunshot came from the front room of the small house. They ducked behind the car. The front windows of the house continued to rattle.

Crystal gaped at Mark, saw that he had heard the same thing she had: a woman's scream.

Bill drew his revolver, looked at Crystal and Mark, and sighed. "Stay here by the cars." He eased his head up and studied the house. The door was still closed and the window shades drawn. It was quiet.

"Crystal, pull on the lights in the car. Mark, go pick up the radio in my car and call the dispatcher. Just push the call button. Tell her to get somebody out here quick. And I mean right now. We've got a bad situation. And turn on my headlights. Let's get as much light on the house as we can."

Without waiting for a response, he turned and ran to the corner of the house. He peered around the corner, looking toward the rear of the small frame building for a moment, then turned back toward the front door.

Crystal turned on the car lights and crouched behind the right side of the Chrysler, her heart racing, her breathing spasmodic. Was Nana even in the house? Was Melva there—and still alive? Her mind could not ask that question about Nana. Who screamed? And could Bill handle the situation? A feeling of doom spread over her. Unbidden, images flashed in her mind of her Nana, lying on the floor, covered in blood.

She remembered Al's gun on the front seat of the car. She ran around, yanked open the car door and grabbed the gun. She was scared and shaking all over, but a fierce determination wiped out any hesitation. Within seconds, she crouched by the edge of the porch, gun clutched in two trembling hands.

Glothe looked back to see Crystal standing at the porch, a gun in her hands. "Good God, Crystal," he whispered, loud enough for her to hear. She was looking at him but didn't move. "Wait. Don't do anything yet. Give me a chance first."

She nodded slightly.

"This is Sheriff Bill Glothe." His voice was loud, full and carried a strength of authority that surprised Crystal. "Two of my deputies are here with me. Do not put up a fight. Just come on out with your hands high and leave your weapons on the floor inside the house. You got nowhere to go. We ain't gonna shoot you if you come out with your hands high above your head." He paused. "Do it now."

Crystal listened to Bill, sounding tough, and like he had help. She knew there wasn't anybody to help. She and Mark were the two deputies. She looked at the gun in her hands. Again, the debate raged in her mind: could she shoot a person? This time, a firm answer emerged. Self-defense was nothing compared to the defense of her Nana. *I will shoot.*

* * *

Inside, the reverberations from the gunshot were dying down. Melva finally had dodged out of the way and Eula had swung the shotgun around and pulled the trigger. The large pellets hit the pistol, knocking it away from Big Man's grasping hand. The overweight thug let out a high-pitched scream.

Eula's shot hadn't touched him, but it took him a few seconds to realize he wasn't hurt. In those seconds, Eula had broken the shotgun open, dumped the empty shells on the floor and was pulling two shells out of her pocket.

Big Man looked around for the gun. When he didn't see it immediately, he shifted his weight and started to move toward Eula.

Without looking up, she said, "My bet is, you'll be half a second too late—which in this case, will be a lifetime. Remember old Elmer, Melva? He *almost* beat the train across the track."

"Yeah. Never did find all of him."

Eula snapped the gun closed and leveled it at the thug, all in one motion. He stopped in mid-step, close enough to reach out and touch the end of the shotgun. He looked at the gun, measuring the distance. He looked up at Eula, measuring her resolve. Slowly, he backed up a few feet, his hands instinctively going up over his head.

* * *

Crystal could hear Mark talking into Bill's radio, calling again for help. But they needed help *now*, not in fifteen minutes. Was there anything she could do? She stepped up on the porch, the pistol out in front of her, and began easing slowly toward the front door of Melva's house. She had to do something.

Bill waved a hand with its index finger extended up. "Give me one more try."

She nodded once but didn't back up, didn't lower the gun.

He took a deep breath. "I got two deputies here and more on the way. So don't get yourself all shot up for nothing. Put down your weapons and come out with your hands over your head. Do it. Me and my deputies won't shoot if you got your hands up high."

"Bill, I'm willing to bet my old corset you ain't got two deputies with you."

Crystal gasped. That was Nana, sounding as irascible as ever. Her eyes began to fill with tears.

"But if you got the dogcatcher with you, or two pair of handcuffs, I'll give you a skunk and a fat toad."

The door opened and a large man waddled out, hands held high over his head. Right behind him came Eula, prodding him in the back with a double-barreled shotgun. Bill holstered his pistol and took a pair of handcuffs off his belt as he walked over to the huge man.

Big Man lowered his arms and pulled himself up to his full height. "Sheriff, she's got things ass-backward. We came here to ask a few questions and she shoots my, ah, my associate, and just barely misses me. I want to file a formal complaint against this woman. I want her jailed."

"Don't know why I worried about you," Bill said to Eula. None too gently, he pulled Big Man's hands behind his back and snapped the steel bracelets shut. "And I'm willing to bet you don't own a corset."

By now, Crystal had dropped the gun and had her arms around her grandmother. "I was so scared, Nana. When I heard the shot, I ... ." She buried her face in Eula's gray hair and tightened her grip around the old woman's shoulders.

Big Man turned around to face the sheriff. "You got it wrong, here, mister. She's the one what's broke the law, shooting people. When my lawyer gets here, he'll straighten things out and your ass is gonna be in a sling. Tell me what law I've broken. The other bitch opened the door when I knocked, and invited us in. Then this old woman comes in blazing away, like some vigilante. I want her in jail. Now. And I want these cuffs off."

Crystal relaxed her hold on Eula and looked at Bill. "You can charge him with the murder of Eddie Ray Dollar. The Dallas police have a witness in custody right now who saw him kill Eddie Ray."

That seemed to take the spirit out of the fat criminal. His only response was to grumble and repeat his warning to expect his lawyer.

Bill turned his attention to Eula. "You said two."

"Other one's inside," Eula said to Bill, all the while patting her granddaughter on the arm. "You'll need an ambulance. And somebody to clean up Melva's floor. He put a lot of blood down."

"Was that the shot we heard just before I yelled at you?" Bill asked.

"Naw. I shot him earlier. Thought he could sneak a gun out. Mistake on his part. What you heard just a minute ago was me moving a pistol out of Fat Man's reach."

Bill just shook his head.

Melva appeared at the door, a .32 in her hand.

"Melva," Bill said. "Would you call the dispatcher and ask her to send an ambulance out. Tell her *I'm* requesting it. And I'm getting just a little tired of waitin' and gettin' no help."

She nodded and went inside without saying a word.

Another sheriff's department cruiser pulled up and a deputy got out.

"Guess I better see what damage we got inside." Glothe looked over at the deputy. "Slim, take this pile of cow manure and put him in the back of your car, and keep an eye on him." Bill turned back to Eula. "You said you had a fat toad and a skunk. I reckon I've seen the fat toad. Let's go look at your skunk."

Chapter 54

IT was nearly midnight by the time Eula, Melva, Crystal and Mark got back to Melva's house. Crystal had not taken her hand off her grandmother all evening. Now, she collapsed in a chair, swiveling it so she wouldn't see the large blood stain on the floor near the front door.

"Well, I guess it's all over now," said Crystal. "Looks like the Mexican killed Bessie, with Roscoe Bigmine, AKA Big Man, aiding. And Bigmine killed Eddie Ray, with the Mexican aiding."

"Don't forget burning down my house." Eula was still going strong. "Should have heard Sam when I phoned him. Woke him up." Eula giggled. "He was grumbling and I said, 'Sam, we got Bessie's murderer, and the man behind it, and a murder in Dallas. And tomorrow, I'll give you my exclusive story on how I captured them.'"

"*You* captured 'em?" asked Melva. "Don't I get any credit?"

"Sure do. But I've been meaning to ask. Why'd you take so long to stomp old Fat Man's foot?"

"Thought I had on tennis shoes. Then I was really needing to go and trying to think what to do, and I remembered I had on these leather shoes." She stuck her foot up. "They got a good stomping heel. So I let him have it."

Eula looked at Mark. "You've been awfully quiet. Don't like our Friday night shindigs?"

"No, no. The party was—well, it wasn't boring. But my ears are still ringing from our encounter with Al. So I guess I'm a little out of it. However, I do have some news. When I talked to Tom while we were at the police station, he told me that when they searched Al's garage, they found chemicals like those in the firebomb."

Crystal let out a long breath. "Fantastic. That ties up all the loose ends."

"Not quite," Mark said.

Everybody stared at him.

"There's still the matter of the gold."

For a minute nobody spoke.

"Which reminds me," said Eula. "Crystal asked me if I ever heard anything about any buried treasure around these parts, and I said no. Last night I was thinking about Dan. I still do that a lot. And I remembered something he told me way back when we was courtin'.

"He said when he still wore knee-pants, his granddad—Popi is what he called him." She looked at Crystal. "That'd be your great-great granddad. Popi told him about a drifter used to come through Wooden Nickel ever once in a while. Popi thought he was just an old crazy guy. Probably was. But Popi was a young whipper snapper, so who knows how old the drifter was."

Eula stopped to scratch her ear before continuing. "Anyways, Popi said the old man would rave on about living with Indians for ten, twelve years before he managed to escape. Said they kidnapped him, killed his dad and all the men with him. But before the Indians caught 'em, his dad had his men push a wagon into a lake."

When Crystal spoke, her voice was more like a gasp. "What was in the wagon?"

Eula smiled. "The old man said it was loaded with gold. Course everybody laughed. Just some old drunk talking foolishness. Looking for an audience. Maybe somebody'd buy him a drink."

Crystal whispered. "What lake?"

"The old man didn't know. Didn't remember, after all those years. He said he was maybe eight or nine when the Indians captured him. Thought it was somewhere in this part of the state. He poked around a lot. Course, nothing come of it." Eula laughed. "And a few people did buy him lots of drinks, trying to find out more about the treasure. Most folks didn't believe a word he said."

Crystal wouldn't have either—before the events of the last week.

Mark asked, "Did Popi know the drifter's name? Did he tell Crystal's granddad?"

"No. I don't remember... ." Eula stopped and closed her eyes. No one made a sound. Crystal didn't even breathe. After a minute,

Eula opened her eyes and looked at Mark. "Haven't thought about this in more'n fifty years. Three J's." She nodded several times. "Yep, that's what Dan said. Three J's."

"What did that mean?" asked Crystal.

"That's how your granddad remembered. Three J's. The drifter called himself Jimmy Joe something with a J. Jones. Johnson. That's it. Jimmy Joe Johnson."

"Did he ever find anything?" Crystal asked, her face flush with excitement.

"Dan asked his granddad that. Popi said he didn't know. The guy finally quit coming around. Popi thought maybe people quit buying him drinks."

Crystal knew it was silly. But, with her breath coming faster, she asked, "Did he ever search in your lake, here in The Park?"

Eula laughed. "Beats me. That would've been fifty years 'fore I was even thought about."

Chapter 55

MONDAY morning at ten, the dress rehearsal began. Mark had invited all the employees of IRS to attend, as well as three outsiders, two of whom Crystal didn't know. Another woman was setting up video equipment. Mark introduced the four people, explaining that they would provide an audience unfamiliar with the projects.

Mark made his introduction, brief and to the point, not trying to oversell IRS.

Next up was Phil. While his presentation Friday had elicited no suggestions for improvement, he had made some anyway, using specific examples of cost savings possible with this program. The effect was good.

Crystal had suggested to Mark that her project follow Phil's, leaving Sally's buried treasure act for the grand finale. Crystal and her group had worked six hours Sunday to fine-tune the twenty-minute presentation. She felt confident. After a brief introduction on the basic idea of the Identification from Partial Plate Information project, she proposed a hypothetical situation: The Case of the Puce Truck. She went through much the same stages as had happened in reality, even crediting the partial plate information to a computer surveillance system.

Sally's program was completely changed. She started with the folk tale of the missing gold, which immediately got everyone's attention. The two people Crystal didn't know had paid only perfunctory attention to Phil's talk and to hers. Now, they were sitting up and taking notice. Sally showed how the folklore database could be used to research the basic idea, tie together the various versions, check out others, and eventually come up with a consensus.

"Is this a real example?" one of the visitors asked. "Or did you just make it up for interest's sake?"

"Ripped from the pages of today's real life," Sally said with a smile.

"Are you going to tell us more about it?" another visitor asked.

"A bit more," answered Sally and she launched into the use of the topographical database to pinpoint the location of the hidden treasure. Not an eye strayed from her, not a cough was heard, not a chair moved. She pointed out that the researcher had to use some of her own creativity, but it was the database and retrieval software that allowed it to happen. She emphasized that a seemingly impossible task was not only made possible, but was accomplished with a relatively small effort.

Her presentation was a huge success, prompting many questions, including one from the woman running the video equipment: did they find the gold? Sally just smiled, looked coy and said that was one question she could not answer.

With Al, Joe, Big Man and the Beard all behind bars, JT had returned Saturday for Eddie Ray's funeral. Today, she beamed through the entire presentation and Crystal realized it was the first time she'd seen JT smile in a month.

Mark provided the wrap-up. It was brief, tying together the previous work, outlining the new projects waiting in the wings, and hinting at additional work which would improve efficiency. For this presentation, he added, ". . . and make money for all IRS employees." That received a hearty round of applause.

The woman handling the video equipment provided each of the project leaders with a DVD of his or her presentation.

"Excellent," said Mark, after everybody except those actually working on the projects had left. "I think I'll invest in this company." Everyone laughed. "Molly has given each project leader a DVD. Scrutinize it this afternoon, search for anything that might not be clear. By the way, we are expecting William Rooney, himself. He's the president and CEO of Rooney Associates. Bob Ingram and Jack Wyzinski from Rooney should be here, as well as Dr. Lester Krupe, an IR expert from Stanford, who is a consultant to Rooney Associates. And I'm sure I've already told you that Crystal worked with Dr. Krupe while she was at Stanford."

Crystal visibly winced at the mention of her nemesis. But her stomach did not tie itself in knots. And she thought to herself, he won't have a gun aimed at my head, and he won't be threatening Nana.

Mark finished giving instructions and encouragement to the group, then asked to see Crystal for a minute. While the others filed out of the conference room, Mark said, "I've got to go straight from the lecture to the airport to pick up the Rooney people. So, I'll just have to meet you at UT for the lecture. Sorry."

Actually, Crystal was glad. Maybe she'd get sick and not go. "Fine. I'll see you there. Three, right?"

"Yes. But be a little early and perhaps we can catch Dr. Krupe before his talk. I won't have much time afterward. With the traffic and all, I'm going to be pressed. I don't think it's a good idea to keep Rooney cooling his heels at the airport."

* * *

Crystal had seriously considered not showing up for Krupe's talk, but at 3:00, she entered the auditorium where the Learned Lecture Series was being held and slid into a seat near the back. She picked out Mark sitting on the second row. Fortunately, there were no empty seats near him, giving her an excuse for not sitting up front with him.

Students and faculty filled almost every seat in the lecture hall, all eagerly awaiting the speaker. But Krupe was not in evidence. *Of course not*, thought Crystal. *He likes to keep you waiting. More than once, I've seen him be ready to walk to the podium or into a room, but delay so people would have to wait for him.* At first, she believed he just wanted to be "fashionably late." Later she realized it was a show of power.

Unconsciously Crystal slouched down in her seat as Lester Krupe and an attractive brunette walked onto the stage. The woman waited patiently until the crowd noise subsided and then gave a brief, but impressive, introduction to the afternoon's speaker.

With an air of importance, Dr. Lester Krupe stepped to the podium. Even then, he stood there and surveyed the crowd for nearly a minute before he spoke. Veins of silver highlighted his rich, black hair and his six-foot frame appeared as lean as ever. Wide-set, striking green eyes scanned the eager faces in front of him, occasionally stopping for a moment to scrutinize someone. The air of complete confidence that Crystal, at first, had found so attractive in her dissertation advisor, now came across as arrogance. As always, his mouth formed a half smile.

He turned to the right and then to the left, studying those in attendance. She had seen him do that before, presenting his profile to all his audience. He knew it was a striking profile, and everyone, particularly the young women, should get the opportunity to see it.

He hasn't changed a bit since I was one of his "most promising graduate students." She could still hear him saying that to the Dean of the Graduate School, not two months before he basically destroyed her hopes for a Ph.D. *If I were that promising, why did he tell me I wasn't graduate school material?*

Now, he was thanking UT-Dallas for honoring him by inviting him to speak to such an alert and intelligent group.

The lights dimmed slightly as Dr. Krupe clicked up his first slide. Crystal's thoughts had over-shadowed his opening statement, but the slide instantly grabbed her full attention. The topic of his lecture was the very same topic of her research while she was at Stanford, the topic he had trashed when he dismissed her and told her she had no talent for graduate studies.

Crystal sat up in her seat and leaned forward, her every fiber drawn to the screen and the lecturer. What approach would he take? Would he go in the general direction she had been following, or would he branch off to a totally different area? Would he pick up where she had left off and move forward?

Ten minutes passed, then twenty minutes. Krupe projected slide after slide after slide. Crystal stared, transfixed, frozen, not moving a muscle, not blinking an eye.

Dr. Lester Krupe was presenting *exactly* what she had done. Not parallel, not close, not similar. Precisely.

She couldn't believe what she was hearing and seeing. At one point, she gulped for air, as she had been unconsciously holding her breath. Her work, which he deemed so worthless, so beneath his consideration, so unworthy of dissertation material, so below Stanford's standards, now provided the subject of his address at the University of Texas Learned Lecture Series. Not simply the subject, but the essence, the total content.

Considerable time had passed since she was at Stanford. But she had lived and breathed this subject matter. It had consumed her mind twenty-four hours a day, seven days a week. She had dreamed about it. She had thought about it in the shower and during meals. It had been her passion. It had been her life. There was no mistake, no fuzzy memory. This *was her* work.

When he finished, the audience applauded. Crystal stumbled out the door, the tears seeping out of her eyes blurring her vision. And as the tears began to flow in earnest, she whispered to no one, "They're applauding Dr. Krupe ... for my work."

Chapter 56

CRYSTAL arrived at her apartment dry-eyed but in a blue funk. Brandi ordered a pizza and by the time the deliveryman rang the doorbell, she had pried out of Crystal the reason for her dismal mood.

"Old Dr. Poop strikes again," said Brandi, mouth half full of pepperoni and cheese.

"I'm so angry I could spit. But there's nothing I can do."

"What do you mean, there's nothing you can do?"

"He's the great authority, the national figure. What am I? Nothing." Crystal took another bite of pizza.

"Dammit, Crystal, you're not nothing. And except when Dr. Crap gets in the picture, you know how smart you are. Whenever that bastard pokes his nose into your life, you crumble." She fixed her eyes on Crystal and waited until Crystal met her gaze. "He's a lecher and a thief."

"I agree. I'm really mad."

Suddenly, Brandi jumped up and came around to Crystal. "Lie down on the floor." Crystal wrinkled her brow, cocked her head to one side and looked quizzically at her roommate. "Now. Do it, dammit. Just lie down on the floor." She pulled Crystal's arm.

Crystal shook her head in dismay, but laid down on the floor.

Brandi stood over her. "You're really smart and I'm really dumb. But you're a doormat and I'm wiping my feet on you." She put a foot on Crystal's stomach and began moving it back and forth.

"Brandi!"

"If you don't like being a doormat, jump up and knock me against the wall. Right now. Do it!" Brandi commanded. "Otherwise, I'll just keep walking all over you."

Crystal got up and gave Brandi a little push.

"Shove. Hard. Come on. Do it!"

Crystal gave her roommate a mild shove.

"That's mad." Brandi shrugged. "At least a little. You've been playing the part of a doormat with Mr. Crap. It's time you played the angry part. The man's a dirt bag dumped on society. You need to put him in his place."

Crystal looked doubtful.

Brandi put her face about six inches from Crystal's nose. "Do you even care that he drummed you out of graduate school unjustly? Do you?"

"Yes."

"Do you care that he stole your ideas and passed them off as his own?"

"Yes, I do." Her voice strengthened.

"Are you the same person who pushed a loaded gun into Joe's mouth and threatened to pull the trigger?"

"I'm the one."

"Now that was mad. You impressed even me with that. You can play mad." Crystal started to object, but Brandi held up her hand. "I know. I know. Joe was a dimwit and Kreep is smart. Is that it?" Brandi returned to the table and grabbed another piece of pizza.

Crystal picked up her beer and took a sip. "I guess."

"Guess, schmess. This Krook has got you buffaloed. You think he's so smart he must be right. Did he cop your stuff and pass it off as his own?"

Crystal nodded.

"Is that smart? Right here in your hometown, where a smart bozo might suspect that you, being interested in retrieval stuff, might come and hear him. Sounds like what my mother would call a blinking idiot."

"No. It's supreme confidence."

Brandi snorted. "I'd call it supreme arrogance. He probably expected you to be there. He just threw it in your face, knowing you wouldn't challenge him. What an asshole."

Crystal toyed with a slice of pizza, but still hadn't taken a bite.

"So, what's it going to be tomorrow when old Stupe comes to IRS? Doormat? Or angry, avenging, wild woman?"

"Not a doormat," Crystal said. She took a bite of the pizza.

"At least we got you on the right side of the tracks——on your feet."

Unbidden, a picture of Phil taking credit for her idea popped into her mind. He had stolen her idea. *Am I being too harsh,* she wondered? *Are people going to think I cry "wolf" all the time? Am I going to have any credibility at all?* Deep lines creased her forehead. *But I'm not making these up. These are real cases. They happened.*

She let out a long breath. *Maybe I bring these things on myself?* She dismissed that offhand. *How could I bring that on myself?* But after a moment's thought, she answered her own question. *By being a doormat.*

* * *

They were cleaning up when Crystal said, "How am I going to be this avenging wild woman? That's a role I've never played."

"Ha. Ask Joe. I'll bet he can tell you." She laughed. "I still can't believe you shoved a gun in his mouth. That takes moxie. That's an angry, avenging, wild woman."

"Well, I can't very well stick a gun in Dr. Krupe's mouth."

"Don't write that off yet," said Brandi with a grin. "But, here's Brandi's outline. Three steps. First, stand up. No more doormat, no matter what old Drup says."

"Got it. On my feet." Crystal was feeling better already. "Of course, you realize that staying on my feet is what caused him to dump me in the first place."

They both laughed.

"Remember, no matter what Kreep tells you, he thinks your work is really good. What's the old saying? Plagiarism is the sincerest form of flattery."

"Imitation."

"Close enough." Brandi held up two fingers. "Number next is, get some proof. Never hurts to have a smoking gun or an untouched photograph."

"That's tougher."

"You're tough enough. Three. Backup."

"Where am I—."

"Me. I'm coming with you tomorrow." For an instant, Brandi looked worried. "Dr. Mark won't mind, will he?"

"No. He likes you. Of course, Rooney's people will be there. And Mark's a little nervous about them."

"Rooney? That the vulture capitalists?"

"I love it! I have to remember to tell Mark that one. Vulture Capitalists." Crystal's mood was definitely on the upswing. Then, she sobered a bit. "But where am I going to get the smoking gun or photo?"

Brandi shrugged. "That's your problem. But the one semester I actually worked in high school, I took lots of notes. Surely, you've got notes. You didn't throw everything out, did you?"

"No. But I don't know if that will help. He'll just say I copied it from him."

"Doormat or avenging beast?"

Crystal nodded several times. "Ask Joe."

Chapter 57

WHEN Crystal and Brandi stepped into the IRS conference room the next morning, conversation stopped. Crystal wore a conservative navy dress, one-inch heels, a single gold strand around her neck and minimal make-up. A brushed gold disk adorned each ear.

Brandi had chosen a different look. Her auburn hair looked as if there were gold threads woven throughout. Her aqua eyes were so bright they appeared to be backlit. Thick lashes might have been made of velvet and a subtle violet eye shadow matched the color of her dress. A hint of blush and perfectly outlined lips and lip-gloss made it difficult for the men to keep their eyes off her.

Her dress, unlike her style in jeans, was soft and loose. The silk draped itself seductively over her shapely body, stopping just at the knees. Matching three-inch heels accentuated near-perfect legs.

Mark came over to greet them. "Crystal, hello. And Brandi. I didn't know you were stopping by this morning. Where are you off to looking so gorgeous?"

"Good morning, Mark. Actually, I wanted to hear today's presentations. I understand they're really good. You don't mind, do you?"

The smile on Mark's face vanished and several moments passed before he answered. "Well, you probably wouldn't enjoy them. And I'm not sure Mr. Rooney and his associates would feel ... well, it is a confidential meeting. You know any other time I'd love to have—."

"Nonsense." Dr. Lester Krupe laid a hand on Mark's shoulder. "We'd love to have this lovely lady stay." By now, Krupe had moved around Mark and was ogling Brandi.

"Ah, she's not a member of the IRS staff, Lester."

"Then she can stay as my guest." He put a hand on Brandi's shoulder. "Come on over here and let me find you a good seat." He led her over to a chair next to his.

Mark looked at Crystal, disapproval written all over his face.

Crystal turned up her mouth and shrugged. "She wanted to come. Insisted. She's my backup."

Just as Mark started to question that statement, William Rooney called to him. Mark shook his head and went to see the head of the visiting delegation.

Crystal got a cup of coffee and moved over close enough to hear what Brandi and Krupe were saying.

"Where did you get your Ph.D., Brandi?"

"Oh, I didn't actually finish it. So, don't bother to call me Dr. Brewer, Dr. Creep."

"Ah, it's Dr. Krupe." He reached over and took her hand. "I think they're going to start the talks in just a minute. After this is over, why don't you show me some quaint Dallas bar and we can discuss your interest in I.R. over cocktails." He patted her hand and his eyes remained focused on her low-cut dress.

Crystal thought perhaps she should step in, then quickly decided Brandi could take care of herself, even with Dr. Krupe.

"I don't know, Dr. Crap." He dropped her hand and a frown descended over his face. His focus moved to her eyes. After a moment, she fluttered her velvet eyelashes and said, "Selecting the right bar should be the man's job."

His expression turned to confusion, followed by a big grin. "Yes. Great idea. Actually, there's a very nice one in my hotel. And it's Krupe. Dr. Lester Krupe." He refocused on her breasts.

Crystal stood only a few feet away, half-turned so that she could see them out of the corner of her eye, yet not appear to be spying on them. But at this point, she had to turn completely away and bite her lip to keep from laughing aloud. Dr. Krupe had met his match.

"You have such beautiful hair, Lecher. Is it a toupee? You can touch mine if I can touch yours. Deal?"

Again, confusion set in on Krupe. "Lester. It's Lester Krupe. It rhymes with soup."

"Like poop?"

Once more, Krupe dropped her hand and stared at her eyes. At that moment, Mark called for everyone's attention. The presentations were about to start.

Brandi leaned over to Krupe, placed her hand on his and whispered. "See you later, Lecher."

Krupe opened his mouth to respond, but no words came out.

Brandi sashayed over to a chair near the back and slipped into it. Bobby Don, who was there to make certain the projector and computer worked smoothly, occupied the chair beside Brandi and was so captivated by her that he did not hear Mark the first time he asked Bobby Don to close the door.

Mark gave the introduction, much as it has been rehearsed the day before. There were no questions from the guests.

Next, Phil made his presentation. Crystal had noted the improvement from Friday to Monday. And though there still had been no suggestions for changes, Phil had once again refined and polished it. When he finished, he fielded several questions from the three Rooney people.

Crystal envied his easy, confident manner, and she was happy to note that Dr. Krupe did not say a word.

Crystal approached the lectern feeling confident. Phil's talk had gone very well and the comments on it were positive. Her presentation would certainly be more impressive. She greeted the audience and started her opening statement, describing the basics of the Identification from Partial Plate Information, or IPPI, project.

Immediately Dr. Krupe interrupted her. "Crissie. Are you actually working on this project?" His tone was one of disbelief. "Or are you just making the presentation?"

She looked over toward Krupe and there stood Al, his gun aimed directly at her head. She saw the muzzle flash, heard the roar, felt the shock wave pass her ear. He was yelling at her. He wanted an answer.

She blinked and refocused her eyes, and in front of her sat Dr. Krupe asking for an answer. Her mind cleared. She thought of Joe and Al and she realized Dr. Krupe could only hurt her if she allowed it.

Her eyes strayed and she saw Brandi, remembered her saying: plagiarism was the sincerest form of flattery. *My work is good enough for the 'imminent authority' to claim it as his own. He doesn't believe I can lead such a project? He's wrong. I can lead projects and I can stand up to him.*

"Les. You don't mind me calling you Les, do you?"

The consultant looked indignant. "Actually, I do. Call me Dr. Krupe."

"Fine. Call me Crystal. Or Ms. Moore." In the back, she saw Mark wince. "But to answer your question, Dr. Krupe, I conceived the idea, and have been the project leader on it from day one."

Crystal stared at her nemesis, but he made no further comment. After a moment, she proceeded to explain the basic operations of the IPPI project. Next, she clicked up a slide that said, "The Case of the Puce Truck." She explained the problem and the use of IPPI to trace the truck's owner.

She was just starting on the next section when Krupe interrupted her. "What about other information? Like a dented fender. How do you handle that type of data?" Before Crystal could answer, he continued, his manner and tone heavy with ridicule, "Or do you just have to *throw away* good information?"

"As you can probably understand," she said, "adding in information about a dented fender, or any other information of that type, will not change the search criteria, nor its results. That type of information is not available in the database for matching."

Krupe sneered. "So you throw away——."

"No, Dr. Krupe. We do not throw away anything. That information is attached to the entry. When the system identifies possible matches, it supplies the extra information so the police can use it as a further tool in finding the specific vehicle. We do not throw away any data, whether it is absolutely factual or questionable. But we do assign a degree of reliability to each piece."

Her answer did not seem to please Krupe. "What about the position of the characters? Does this system, that you helped on, consider the positions of the data?"

The subtle inference was not lost on Crystal. *I am the one who controlled Joe.* "The system I *designed* takes every possible advantage of any information on position. It even uses information on position that is not 100% certain. The mathematics can get rather involved and I don't want to *confuse* you, but if you would like to study a paper I wrote on it, I'll be happy to give you a copy after these presentations are over."

Krupe made a short laughing sound. "You wouldn't confuse me, Crystal." His demeanor turned caustic. "What about situations near the state border? Can it cross state boundaries?"

"If the adjacent state is using the program, yes."

"And this radius approach. What if the circle crosses the state line? Will it translate properly across borders?"

"Certainly." Krupe started another question, but Crystal ignored him and went right on. "It will handle those types of searches just as if there were no boundary there. Of course, as you can perhaps figure out, if the witness knows which state the license is from, that becomes a moot question."

Krupe was getting more irritated with each answer. "What about searches based on zip codes?"

"Absolutely."

"Area codes?"

"Naturally."

William Rooney broke in. "Lester, I think you've proved that the system will handle anything you can throw at it. Shall we move on?"

Krupe was breathing faster and his face was florid. "Just one more, please, Bill." He turned back to Crystal, contempt in his manner. "I don't suppose it can handle input from non-human sources, can it?"

Crystal looked puzzled for a moment and the beginning of a twisted smile appeared on Krupe's face. She turned her head to look at the graphic displayed on the screen. Nodding, she turned back.

"Dr. Krupe, when you interrupted my presentation, I was just about to put up another slide." She clicked the remote control and an image filled the screen, a picture of the puce truck. "In actuality, this example I presented came from a computer-controlled surveillance camera. This is the actual picture. The computer interpreted the data, picked out the characters—and their positions——and fed them into the IPPI program. To answer your question, the system is already doing that."

Bob Ingram spoke up before Krupe could open his mouth. "Excellent presentation. And an excellent system. I feel certain it will be a huge success. When will it be ready to market?"

Crystal gathered up her papers and looked at Mr. Ingram. "Today."

Sally's presentation followed her dress rehearsal plan exactly. Like the previous day, it caught the interest of the listeners immediately. And as during the rehearsal, the first question was: did they find the gold? Sally smiled her coy smile and said, due to a confidentiality agreement, she was not at liberty to say.

Mark provided the wrap-up and thanked the visitors for their attention and intelligent questions. "Now, we have a lunch being set up in the next room. We're having a sumptuous spread from Sonny Bryan's. For those of you not native to Dallas, you're in for a real treat. We'll show you what barbecue really means. But we're a few minutes ahead of schedule, so please help yourselves to drinks at the table over here." He pointed to a long table filled with a wide variety of drinks, plus ice, glasses, and fruit slices. A woman in a bright pink dress stood smiling behind the table, ready to lend assistance. "This will give Rooney Associates a chance to visit with IRS."

Crystal was parched and ready for a drink. She considered a beer, but decided perhaps a glass of tea might be a better choice right now. She and Sally were quietly congratulating each other. Two feet in front of them, William Rooney and Krupe faced the bar, getting drinks.

"So, what is your overall impression, Lester?" Rooney was shaped like a steamer trunk turned on its end. His head was almost spherical and with his gray hair cropped to a quarter inch, it looked like a melon sitting on the end of the trunk. His eyes were clear, but held no expression. They took in information like a camera, not commenting, simply recording. He had small hands, better suited to writing checks than throwing a football. His voice sounded like rocks rolling in the surf.

Krupe drained the martini just handed to him and held up the glass to the woman in pink. "Another." He turned his attention back to Rooney. "I liked what Wilson had to say about his work. Always good to see the commercial aspects. Sally's work was interesting. A little dramatic, perhaps. Crissie's little project didn't seem very original."

Crystal's whole body stiffened. Within seconds, she could

feel the blood pounding in her temples. She remembered the feeling of power she had with the gun in her hand. She glanced at her briefcase lying on the conference table. Without a word, she handed her glass to Sally and stalked over to the table. She popped open the briefcase, found what she was looking for, and marched toward Krupe.

Chapter 58

KRUPE had emptied his glass again and held it toward the bartender. He turned back to Rooney. "And not very worthwhile. Probably a waste of your money."

Crystal stepped in front of Krupe, her face flushed, nostrils flared, muscles tense.

A quizzical look came over his face. "Yes?"

Her heart hammered in her chest. "Lester."

He arched his eyebrows, but said nothing.

"You didn't like my presentation today?"

"Well, I just thought it wasn't very . . . worthwhile."

Her hands were pressed against her back and she could feel the adrenaline surging through her body. "That's what you said about my work at Stanford."

Krupe blinked several times and forced a smile. "Well, I didn't want to bring that up today."

"But it was good enough for you to present at the University of Texas Learned Lecture Series yesterday." Her voice was husky and she almost spat out the words.

The professor's mouth twitched and he glanced at Rooney. Krupe swallowed, took a deep breath and stretched up as tall as possible and looked down his nose at Crystal. "Certainly I did not present your material at the Lecture Series. It might have been in the same area but it certainly was not your feeble work. Now, if you'll excuse us."

"No, I will not excuse you. And it was definitely my work." She brought her right hand around from behind her back and waved a folder in front of him. "Here is work I produced two years ago. Work you had access to. And it is the same work you presented yesterday."

The twitch at Krupe's mouth started again and he licked his

lips. His face turned noticeably paler and his focus shifted right and left, trying to find something to latch onto.

Crystal was still holding the folder in front of him. "Shall I read some of this to Mr. Rooney?"

"I don't know what you have there, or where you got it, but it is hardly relevant. And you are making a fool of yourself." His voice had risen and his usual control seemed to be faltering.

By now, Mark had come over. "Dr. Krupe may be right, Crystal. This may not be the time or the place for this." He put his hand on her elbow but his eyes were on Rooney. She pulled her arm free.

"I'm in no rush," said Rooney. His voice was so gravelly that Crystal had the urge to clear *her* throat.

Krupe seemed to have recovered somewhat, although the vertical lines between his eyebrows grew deeper. "Okay. I warned you," he said to Crystal. "The work you did at Stanford was poor, sub-par. It was not up to graduate school standards. There. Are you satisfied?"

"No. Not really." Crystal's voice was now calm and she could tell her blood pressure had dropped. "Let me make just two points. What you presented yesterday was exactly what is in this folder, work I did at Stanford, work you undoubtedly have a copy of. Second, let me read you something." She opened the folder, looked at Rooney, then at Mark. She read off the paper, "This is excellent work. Some of the best I've seen here." She closed the folder and looked at Krupe. "Does that sound familiar?"

He did not answer nor did he look at her.

"Those are your words, Dr. Krupe. Written, and dated, in your own, unmistakable handwriting. Addressed to me and written on the paper you presented at UT."

The entire room had grown quiet. All attention was focused on the duel between the consultant and the IRS employee, the professor and his former student. Even the bartender was caught up in the confrontation. Brandi moved over to stand right behind Crystal. Phil watched without moving a muscle, while a tiny smile formed on Sally's face.

Crystal realized she wasn't breathing and tried to start taking in small amounts of air without being noticed. The scene remained motionless. Dr. Krupe closed his eyes without saying a word. The tic at his mouth started once again. Rooney shifted his weight from one foot to the other.

A full minute passed. Crystal was determined not to break the silence. Krupe had to respond to her accusation. He had to respond to his own words written on her paper in his own hand. She could wait. She *would* wait.

In the back of her consciousness, she could hear the muted sounds of lunch being set in the next room, could smell the pungent aroma of barbeque sauce wafting in through the open door. A strange calm descended over her, even as she challenged her former advisor.

Finally, the consultant opened his eyes and looked at her. "I am the scientist here. I am the national figure, the authority, the *consultant*." On the last word, he looked directly at Mark. Krupe's mouth twisted into a sneer as he refocused on Crystal. "You are nobody. I do not have to answer to you. I do not have to answer to someone who couldn't even finish her dissertation. And Mark's judgment has to be questioned if he hires someone of your caliber." He turned to the bartender and said, "Another."

No one else moved, or even breathed, it seemed. The room was a tableau, frozen in an instant by some strange cosmic force.

Rooney broke the silence. "You are the consultant, Lester. My consultant. And you certainly don't have to answer to Ms. Moore."

Krupe looked back at Crystal, a smirk on his face.

"However," Rooney continued. "As my consultant, you have to answer to *me*. And I expect that as a national figure and authority, as you describe yourself, you will have to provide an answer to the scientific community. But, I'd like to hear your answer to Rooney Associates right now."

Crystal didn't feel that Mr. Rooney was taking her side. His words were said without menace or pre-judgment. He simply wanted to resolve this dispute now. That was okay. Confidence was pulsing through her veins.

Krupe rubbed his chin and studied the floor for a minute. Then he tilted his head back slightly and stared down at Crystal. "I didn't want to say this to everybody. I was trying to keep you from suffering too much embarrassment, perhaps ruining your chances in this field for all time. But you wouldn't let it alone." He took a deep breath and looked at Rooney. "I shouldn't have done it, but Crissie—"

"My name is Crystal."

"If that's important." He paused momentarily, then continued, but his voice had lost some of its richness. "Crystal was struggling, couldn't seem to come up with anything original. She was a good kid and I didn't want to see her drop out. She worked hard. She just didn't quite have it when it came to originality."

Crystal thought of Big Man trying to get Nana arrested and of his threats to call his lawyer and create trouble for Glothe. She smiled. It amazed her how much Dr. Krupe sounded like Big Man: all huff and no substance.

"I gave her the idea for this paper. In fact, I almost wrote it for her. When she couldn't finish it, I decided to reclaim my idea and my work. And I presented it at the University of Texas. My real mistake was in feeling sorry for Crissie, ah, Crystal. I should have just said she wasn't graduate school material and let it go. But since she couldn't handle the ideas I gave her, why should I let them go to waste?" He had a forced smile on his face as he looked from Rooney to Mark.

Crystal knew that even a few days ago such comments from Dr. Krupe would have thrown her into deep depression. She would have hung her head and blundered off to cry in a darkened room.

But Dr. Krupe no longer intimidated her. Now, his words slid off her like butter off a hot knife.

"Dr. Krupe, a few minutes ago, I didn't read everything you had written on my paper. I'd like to read the rest of it now. I think Mr. Rooney will find it interesting."

She was speaking softly, confidently. Sally and Phil moved closer. Mark leaned in toward his employee. Brandi was smiling.

Crystal opened the folder again, looked directly into Krupe's eyes for a moment, then back at the paper. She read the words slowly and distinctly, hoping no one would miss the meaning. "This is extremely creative work. I never thought about applying I.R. techniques in this area or in the manner you have. Very creative. Wish ... I'd ... thought ... of ... this ... first." She closed the folder and looked at the consultant. "Again, this is written and dated, two years ago, in your inimitable scrawl."

No one moved. It was so quiet Crystal could hear Krupe breathing. Rooney stuck out his hand. "May I?" he asked Crystal.

She handed the venture capitalist the folder. He opened it, and for several minutes studied the page. Then slowly he flipped through the remaining papers in the folder. Without comment, he handed it back to Crystal.

Pam appeared at the door. "They're ready with lunch." Then, looking at the group, she said, "Oops. Sorry. Didn't mean to interrupt," and she ducked back out.

Rooney's stubby fingers covered his chin and half his mouth. He let out a long breath and turned to his consultant. "Lester, we'll talk about this later."

Brandi stuck her head in between Crystal and Mark. "Sorry, Lecher. I made a mistake when I called you Dr. Crap. It should have been Dr. Crook."

Krupe looked up when she addressed him, then looked back at the floor without opening his mouth.

Once again, Rooney broke the silence that had descended over the group. "Well, Mark, let's go try that wonderful barbecue you've been praising."

He started toward the door, but stopped abruptly and addressed Crystal. "I liked your presentation and I see it as a very successful project." Then, he turned his attention to Brandi. "You have lovely hair. And beautiful eyes." He raised his eyebrows and for a brief moment, his eyes twinkled. "And the ability to capture the essence, succinctly." He chuckled as he strode out the door.

Brandi grabbed Crystal. "You did it. You were a wild woman."

Krupe turned to the bartender and asked for another martini.

Epilogue

AT the soft knock, Mark looked up to see Crystal and Eula standing in the doorway to his office. Nearly six weeks had passed since the terrible encounter with Joe, Al, Big Man and The Beard. And Dr. Lester Krupe.

"Come in, come in. It's not a surprise, since Crystal told me she was bringing you in today. But it is certainly a pleasure." Mark rose and walked over to meet them as he spoke.

"What a silver-tongued man, this Bull O'Malley is," said Eula and she reached up and gave him a hug. "I guess silver is an okay word."

"I'd say so," Crystal said.

"Sit over here. It's more comfortable." Mark motioned them over to the couch and easy chairs that defined the conversation area of his office. "How did today's business go?"

"I'd say fine. Crystal is pickier."

Crystal grinned and raised her shoulders, causing the large swordfish dangling from each ear to swing back and forth. "Like store-bought rolls. Okay, but could have been better, I would think."

"And congratulations," Eula said to Mark. "Crystal tells me you got the next chunk of change from the money people."

"That's right. And Crystal is partly responsible for that."

"And no consultant looking over your shoulder."

"Crystal gets all the credit for that. She showed Rooney their consultant was, uh, not doing a good job for them."

"Or as Brandi puts it," Eula said, "Dr. Crap don't know jack." The wrinkled old woman cackled.

Crystal and Mark both laughed.

Eula narrowed her eyes. "But I got a bone to pick with you two. I met Sally Whatshername out in the hall and she wanted to know what happened. I can't believe everybody here doesn't know everything. That kind of information not spreading like wildfire is rarer than feathers on a skunk. And ain't this an information retrieval place?"

Mark looked at Crystal and raised his eyebrows. Crystal shrugged. "I wasn't sure how much you wanted people to know, Nana."

"I didn't kill anybody," Eula said, a shade of disdain in her voice. "Why should I care if they know everything? Course, I'm not going to force feed them either. But I've always said, if people are hungry, feed 'em."

Mark and Crystal looked at each other, not really knowing what to say.

"That's the trouble with you young people. You think too much. If you work out every last detail before you start, it may be too late. Let's just do it. Crystal, find out who's interested, and order in lunch for that many. I'm buying. I'll fill 'em with food and answers at the same time. Any objections, Bull?"

"Just one," Mark said, looking amused. "The office knows me as Mark."

* * *

Almost the entire office joined the lunch in the conference room. Crystal wasn't certain whether it was to hear Nana's story or for free food.

"I'm thinking you've heard all this," Eula started. "So you ask and I'll try to answer. Much as I know, anyway."

JT spoke very softly. "Was there any gold?"

Eula smiled. "Well, I guess the answer is no." There was a low murmur of disappointment. "And yes."

Everybody laughed, but their curiosity was not satisfied. Sally put her sandwich down and said, "If there is a yes component to the answer, then start by telling us how you found it."

"Fair enough. Bu--ah, Mark's got a friend of his, Josh . . ."

"Kinsolving. He works for Schlumberger," Mark said.

"That's the one. He came out to The Park with a great big blue truck and all sorts of stuff on it. Wonder it didn't break my bridge. Anyway, they loaded some kind of instrument in my boat and took it to the far end of the lake. It had a steel cable tied on it running

288

back to the truck. When they got it to the end of the lake, they pushed it into the water and then pulled it back to the other end using that steel cable. Did that several times and drew a bunch of charts."

Mark broke in. "The tool was an electro—".

"Hold it," Eula said. "You're going to bog down my story. Anybody wants a technical description can ask you after I finish. Let's just say it worked like a big metal detector." She looked at Mark. "I know that ain't exact, but it'll do."

Everybody laughed.

"So we got a back hoe and dug where the charts said to," said Eula, grinning from ear to ear. "Sure enough, about fifteen feet down we hit some wood and then the metal." She stopped, looked at the rapt audience, then picked up her sandwich and took a big bite.

Mark just grinned. Crystal said, "Come on, Nana. You're being mean to my friends. Tell them or I will."

Eula picked up a napkin and dabbed at her lips. "Well, it wasn't gold . . ." There was a collective sigh of disappointment. "Exactly. It was silver. Seems some people back in them days called silver 'Mexican gold'. Somewhere in the retelling, it went from 'Mexican gold' to just plain gold." She shrugged. "Oh well."

Sally spoke up. "Shoot, a ton of silver isn't anything to sneeze at."

"Well, turns out it wasn't a ton either. Probably a thousand pounds and that just got 'xaggerated over time, I suppose. We only found nine hundred, sixty-seven pounds. Guess some of it's still stuck in the mud down there. But I'm not complaining. It'll rebuild my house that got burned."

There was a low buzz of excitement among the group. A buried treasure, even if it wasn't a ton of gold, could still be thrilling.

"None of you asked, but I'm going to tell you anyway. I know some of the stories talked about pirates and all. But since it was on my land, I think I'm entitled to my own theory. And I think it came from the San Saba mines down in the Hill country."

Several eyebrows were raised, but no one said anything.

Eula continued. "The San Saba Apaches was always trading a lot of silver. But no one could ever find out where their mine was. Well, Jim Bowie, you know—the knife man— got to be friends with Chief Xolic there and got initiated into the tribe as Xolic's son.

Afterward, the Chief told Jim where the mine was, even let him get some of the silver for himself. Well, old Bowie got a little greedy and brought in some men to help him dig out more. When the chief died, Tres Manos took over and he ran Bowie out, tried to kill him.

"I think it was some of Bowie's men who had that wagonload of silver. And I think it was the San Saba Apaches who followed them and killed them for stealing the silver. Mostly to protect the secret location of the mine. Nobody's ever found it since.

"That's what I think." Her chin jutted out, daring anybody to contradict her.

No one did.

* * *

It was Wednesday, and the weekly seminar had just concluded. Mark and Crystal were walking to their offices when Mark said, "Shall we have dinner together tonight?"

Crystal stopped, her eyebrows knitted, and looked at her boss. "Is this like a date?"

A boyish grin spread over his face and Crystal thought he might even have blushed just a touch. "Well, ah, I'm not sure. But I'll pick you up and I'm paying."

Crystal looked at the very intelligent, handsome man standing in front of her, looking like a school boy. "I want to know if it's a date."

"Okay, then, yes. I'm asking you out on a date."

She thought of her Nana and her granddad. "I'd love to."

the end

A note from the author.

Thank you for reading *A Ton of Gold*. I hope you enjoyed it. If you did, it would be a great favor to me if you would leave a review (it could be only three or four sentences) on Amazon so others would know what you thought of the book. You can do so by clicking this link: http://amzn.to/1FYeaKq

And here's what *New York Times* Bestselling Author Bobbi Smith had to say about *A Silver Medallion,* the next Crystal Moore suspense --

A Silver Medallion is a gripping, action-packed adventure from talented author James Callan. Crystal Moore is a tough and savvy heroine . . .

Named a winner in the International Readers' Choice competition.

Winner in the ETWG novel contest for suspense/thriller category over entrants from across the U.S. and Europe.

Named Best Mystery of 2016 by the Readers Passion Book Club.

A Silver Medallion, the second title in the Crystal Moore Suspense series, reads like a gold-medal thriller from page one ... Crystal emerges as a compelling heroine with a big heart and bold personality... From BookLife Prize in Fiction

A Silver Medallion ... is the thrilling sequel to A Ton of Gold ... The page-turning suspense kept me up well into the pre-morning! **Alyssa Elmore for Readers' Favorite (On Barnes & Nobel)**

If you would like to read the opening chapter of *A Silver Medallion*, the next Crystal Moore Suspense, it starts on the next page. I think you will enjoy it.

A Silver Medallion

Chapter 1

CRYSTAL Moore drove slowly along the sandy road that curved through the property she had roamed as a child. Her grandparents had christened it "The Park" when they purchased it over fifty years ago. To Crystal, they could have named it Serenity. The tall, stately Southern pines, the oak and hickory trees, the mirror-still lake, the peaceful quiet, all worked to cast a spell of tranquility over her.

Crystal's maroon LeSabre crested the hill. Two hundred feet ahead, her grandmother stood under a maple tree, its autumn foliage creating a golden halo above her grey hair. Eula Moore was staring at the small storage shed about twenty feet behind her cedar-shake house. She aimed a double-barreled shotgun at the door of the building.

Fifty feet from Eula, Crystal switched off the ignition, eased out of the car, and moved forward, careful not to crack a twig or crunch a dried leaf. Now she saw her grandmother's right index finger curled around the trigger. Whatever was going on, she did not want to distract her Nana.

Eula Moore pointed the shotgun at the shed, her wrinkled hands as steady as those of an eye surgeon. "Don't make no sudden moves. I got a nervous trigger finger. I might just blow your head off."

Nothing moved.

"Now, very slowly, come on out in the open, and keep them hands over your head where I can see 'em."

1

Experience told Crystal her grandmother had heard the car, but Eula's attention never left the shed. The elderly woman stooped down, gaze still fixed on the building, picked up a rock with her left hand and made a sweeping, underhanded throw. As the chunk of limestone arched skyward, Eula pulled the ancient shotgun up and once more trained it on the shed.

The rock struck the tin roof with a satisfying bang. No animal came bolting out the door. The noise echoed and died away. The birds stopped their chirping. All was quiet.

Crystal crept up beside her grandmother. "What's in there, Nana?" she whispered.

"Animal. Person. Beats me. But I didn't git to seventy-five being careless."

Eula Moore, five feet two inches tall, ninety-five pounds with short-cropped grey hair, held a strategic position. No one could leave the shed without coming into her gun's sight. And no one could see her without first revealing himself. Eula looked frail, but her voice was strong, her will stronger. "Better come out 'fore I start shootin'."

A slight breeze wiggled the leaves on a towering oak tree shading the area. A squirrel sat motionless. The scene was as peaceful as a painting of a country lane. Except for the shotgun.

A few moments passed. Then a single finger came into view. Gradually, it turned into a whole hand, waving in a small arc. "*Por favor, no dispare.*" The tiny brown hand fluttered again. The voice quavered slightly. "Please. No shoot. No shoot."

Eula didn't lower the gun or take her gaze off the shed. "*Por favor*? Spanish?" Eula said to Crystal. Then to the tiny hand, "*Manos arriba.*"

Now, two hands waved. But no body appeared.

"You need to work on your Spanish, Nana. He may not know what you're saying."

2

Eula snorted. "*Pardon* me. I didn't go to S.M.U. Or Stanford. Maybe you can do better."

Crystal turned toward the shed. "*Salga con las manos arriba.* Come out with your hands up."

A foot materialized in the opening. "Hands up." Then a body began to emerge. "Hands up."

Was it a child? Little more than five feet tall and slender as broomcorn, she could have been a girl of fourteen. Her uncombed hair, nearly reaching her waist, appeared as black and shiny as obsidian. Pink and blue embroidery decorated the rough-woven, white dress hanging from her shoulders and stopping just short of her scratched knees. Well-worn leather sandals revealed feet accustomed to no shoes at all.

The small hands trembled slightly as the young Mexican edged forward, but she held her head high and her back ramrod straight.

Eula waggled the barrel of the shotgun at the girl. "Far enough. Hold it right there. *Alto.*" Eula focused on the girl, but spoke to Crystal. "Okay. So I don't remember my Spanish good enough to find out what I got here. See what you can do. But don't get in my line of fire."

A cloud drifted away, allowing the sun to play fully on the girl's face. This was *not* a child. Those large eyes could not develop such sadness, such pain, in such a short life.

"*¿Como se llama?*" Crystal asked.

The thin young woman maintained her focus on the gun. "Rosa. Rosa Bonita Lopez."

"*¿Habla Ingles?*"

"*Un poco.*"

"*Hablo Español un poco. Vamos probando con Ingles.* Let's try English," said Crystal. The young woman's expression did not change, nor did her attention waiver from the shotgun. "Okay. Your name is Rosa Bonita."

"*Si*. Yes."

"And what were you doing in the shed?"

The Mexican woman's forehead wrinkled and she tilted her head slightly to one side. *Is she puzzled by the English or by what kind of an answer to give?* Crystal tried Spanish again. "*¿Que hacias en el cobertizo?*"

After several seconds, Rosa looked at Crystal. "Food."

"You were looking for food?"

"*Si.*"

"Are you hungry?"

Eula made a small grunt. "Dumb question."

"*Si*. Yes."

"When did you eat last? *¿Cuándo comiste por última vez?*"

"*Ayer en la mañana.*"

"Yesterday morning!" Crystal turned to her grandmother. "She's probably starving. Let's take her in and give her something to eat. Then we can find out why she's here."

Eula didn't move or lower the shotgun but Crystal walked over, smiling, took the young woman's hand and led her into the house.

* * *

Inside Eula's large country kitchen, Crystal gave Rosa a tall glass of orange juice while Eula put the finishing touches on a chicken and rice meal she'd been preparing for her granddaughter's arrival. Rosa drank the juice without stopping and her dark, wary eyes remained focused on the chicken as Eula moved it from pan to serving dish.

"Why haven't you eaten?" Crystal asked.

"*No dinero.*"

"Where do you live?"

"*No casa. No casa.*"

"No home?" Crystal glanced at Eula, then back at the Mexican girl. "*¿Por qué?*"

"I run away."

"From your husband? *¿Esposo?*"

"No." Her sad eyes closed for a moment, then softly, "No."

"Parents? *¿Padres?*"

"No. From *hombre malo.*"

"*¿Quien?* Who is the bad man?"

"*Señor* Blackwood." Rosa scrunched her mouth and eyes as if she had bitten into a piece of spoiled fruit.

"Who is he? What is your relationship to him? A relative? *¿Un familiar?*

The Mexican woman shook her head violently from side to side. "No. *No familiar.* I am ... his ..." She furrowed her brows and cocked her head to one side. "How to say *esclava?*"

Crystal looked down for a moment as she searched her limited Spanish vocabulary for a translation. Finally, she looked up at Rosa. "The only English word I can think of for *esclava* is ... slave."

Rosa's head bobbed up and down. "*Si. Si.* Slave. I am his slave."

Order a copy at: http://amzn.to/28LIdWs

If you would like to read the opening chapter from **Over My Dead Body**, one of my cozy mysteries, it starts on the next page.

Chapter 1

Syd snorted and thrust his chin toward his adversary. "Over my dead body."

The man almost smiled. "If you insist," he said easily.

Seventy-two year old Syd Cranzler squinted against the bright Texas October sun and scrutinized the well-dressed man in front of him. Syd was probably six inches shorter than the man, but Syd's voice had more iron in it. "Was that a threat?"

"No sir, Mr. Cranzler," Duke Heinz said.

Syd didn't like this city slicker, wouldn't have even if he weren't trying to steal Syd's homestead. Even Duke's clothes irritated him. The conservative black pinstriped suit, power-red tie and black wing-tips polished to perfection made the man look like he was posing for a magazine picture in New York City. And what was this "Duke" bit? Did he think he was John Wayne? "Why don't you just mosey on down the road a mile?" He jerked his hand up and pointed. "Lots of land there."

They stood on pine needles under three towering trees. Forty feet behind them was Syd's small, frame house, looking like a giant, square tumbleweed.

Bud Wilcox, Pine Tree's City Manager, pushed his straw hat back a little and took a step forward. "Syd, Pine Tree wants this shopping center *here*, inside the city limits. Think of all the tax revenue we'll get."

"So's you can waste even more'n you do now? It ain't your house and land, Pipsqueak."

Bud reddened at the nickname Syd often used on him, but kept his mouth shut.

A mud-caked '92 Camaro rattled to a stop half off the black-top road. A man got out and started across the yard to where Syd was shaking his finger at Bud.

Duke started to speak, but Syd cut him off. "And don't tell me again it's twice what it's worth. You don't know what it's worth to me. And what's this 'fee simple' bit?" He cocked his head to the side. "You think I'm simple? Take your money and go back to Jersey."

Bud waggled his balding head. "It's a lot of dollars."

"He don't need your money," said the man from the Camaro. "He stole enough from me."

"Stay out of it, W.C.," Syd snapped. But his focus never left Duke. "You keep your money; I'll keep my land."

Duke spread his hands. "Mr. Cranzler, the Supreme Court says eminent domain can be used to obtain land needed for a project in the public interest."

"I know all 'bout the Supreme Court, and how they trampled all over people's property rights. I'd like to see some private company try to take the land *they* live on. They'd change their tune right fast. But that case was decided for a Yankee town. This is Texas. We still believe in property rights down here. And this ain't in the public interest. It's in Lockey Corporation's interest."

Duke smiled as he pulled a folded paper from the inside pocket of his coat. "Here's the court order, and it's signed by a judge right here in Texas." He held the paper out to Syd.

Syd ignored it. "Judge McFatage, right? He'd sign anything for a price."

Bud Wilcox leaned in. "Now, Syd, you shouldn't talk about the Honorable McFatage that way."

"Honorable, my foot. He's for sale. Common knowledge. You know what they say: he's the best judge money can buy. And it looks like Lockey's the buyer."

"Look, Mr. Cranzler," Duke said. "We're going to start dirt work in three weeks. I'd like to have all the paperwork in order by then. You've lost this fight. You might as well recognize that. You can delay signing. But by fighting this, you may end up getting less money and paying a lot of it to lawyers. You can't stop it. This project *will* be built. And it starts in three weeks."

"Three weeks?" Syd pulled on his chin and a sly grin crept onto his leathery face. "I'm bettin' my lawyer'll have my appeal filed before then. And I'm thinkin' I can tie this up for years. You sure Lockey wants to wait that long?" His head bobbed up and down as he continued. "Be a lot faster to go somewheres else." Now he laughed. "Bet they're gonna cut you loose when this don't happen. Can your butt."

Duke's smile faded and his eyes turned hard. "Two months from now, this will all be asphalt."

"Like I said, over my dead body."

Duke put the paper back in his pocket. "Old man, you'll hardly make a bump in the pavement."

Order your copy of **Over My Dead Body** here: http://amzn.to/1c81TFJ

Here are a few of the reviews for *Over My Dead Body*.

I love this book! *Over My Dead Body* had me reading almost non-stop.

— Eileen Obser

Oh my word! I was asked to read and review *Over My Dead Body*, but I had NO idea how entertaining this novel would be – I couldn't put it down until I finished the last page!

— Donna's Bookshelf

If you like a GOOD mystery/detective story, you will LOVE this book. Excellent writing and character development; and expertly builds up the suspense. I couldn't put it down, then didn't want it to end, because it's hard to find such an entertaining book!

— S. Sehon

Over My Dead Body is a well-crafted mystery. It captures the characters and spirit of life in a small Texas town. The mystery to be solved is perfect for the setting - no unbelievable villains, no secret societies - just ordinary crimes hidden in plain sight, where nobody sees it. Father Frank and Georgia are a potent crime-fighting team - lots of fun!

— Adele Weitz

Callan's Father Frank stories are always a treat and this latest is no exception. If you enjoy well drawn characters, a gripping plot and twists to keep you guessing, this is a book you'll want to add to your reading list.

—John R. Lindermuth, Author of *Sooner than Gold*

Father Frank at it again. I love these books. Great character development. Plot is very tricky, with many possible suspects. ... Waiting for the next in the series.

— Fredsuz

Over My Dead Body by James R. Callan had all the components of a great mystery: an intriguing plot, believable and likeable characters and a satisfying conclusion. I highly recommend this Father Frank mystery.

— Patricia Gilgor

This is a can't-stop-reading-and-put-it-down book. The second in his Father Frank mysteries, author James R. Callan has once again penned a winner.

— Piney Woods Books

This is a great book to read when you want to relax and simply enjoy a story. The characters of Father Frank and Georgia Peitz offer some humor along with their sleuthing. The twists kept me guessing, and although I thought I knew early on who-done-it, I was wrong!

— Mary L. Hamilton

Over My Dead Body by James R. Callan had me guessing until the very end. ... You won't want to put it down.

— A Mcgraw

I'm definitely going to read others in the series! When I finished the book I thought, "Glad I read that!"

— Shirley H

About the Author

After a successful career in mathematics and computer science, receiving grants from the National Science Foundation and NASA, and being listed in *Who's Who in Computer Science* and *Two Thousand Notable Americans*, James R. Callan turned to his first love—writing. He wrote a monthly column for a national magazine for two years, and published several non-fiction books. He now concentrates on his favorite genre, mystery/suspense His twelfth book will release in 2017.

Website: www.jamesrcallan.com
Blog: www.jamesrcallan.com/blog
Amazon Author page:: http://amzn.to/1eeykvG